The Battle-Ravens

John-Richard Thompson

Copyright © 2017 John-Richard Thompson
All rights reserved.
ISBN: 978-0692898055

Rascal Press
New York, NY

FOR
MAGGIE CULLEN

*"Fairy tales do not tell children the dragons exist.
Children already know that dragons exist.
Fairy tales tell children the dragons can be killed."*

G.K. Chesterton

Introduction

A Raven in the Snow

John-Richard Thompson

THE BATTLE-RAVENS

A somber, tragic young woman approached her car at the edge of the parking lot and stopped dead at the sight of a raven on a patch of newly-fallen snow; pitch-black, unexpected, as vaguely sinister as a spill of ink on a new page or a splash of old blood on a whitewashed door.

It stared at her without moving, without blinking. As one obsessively attracted to black, the somber, tragic young woman could not help but view this as a portent of something greater than a black bird on white snow. She did not dare move for fear of startling it and so they stood there, raven and woman, both clad in black, both staring, and the wind sighed through the high pines and shook the dusty snow from their boughs.

A portent of something greater than a black raven in the white snow...possibly.

But of what?

Of something to come, of something that had not yet happened, but again – what? The question had lately haunted her. She had turned twenty only days before and, as with all who have ever lived, she longed to catch a glimpse of her older, future self in the hope of seeing change for the better or, in her case, any sort of change at all.

She decided to ask the question aloud, knowing full well the bird could not answer. "Is anything *ever* going to happen to me?"

The raven moved for the first time. It looked shining-eyed up at the trees, back at her, and, no longer interested, it lifted its heavy wings and flew off into the pines.

She had received no answer from the bird she had already begun to think of as The Raven of Destiny – no sign, no omen, no sudden insight or flash of inspiration – and so she got into her black car and drove away.

She did not realize if there had been a way for the raven to answer or if there had been a host of oracles, fortune-tellers, mystics, and shamans in attendance, each one would have looked up from their cards, their amulets, their coagulating entrails and seething embers beneath their cauldrons when she asked the question – "Is anything *ever* going to happen to me?" – and each would have returned an answer she should not have wanted to hear, even if she could:

"Yes."

John-Richard Thompson

1.

Smoke

John-Richard Thompson

1

Eight miles out from the coast of Kerry and the Cliffs of Drumgour, out past the mournful clang of the last buoy where the mists hang thick and deep, the island Skellig Michael rose black and jagged from the sea like the prow of a freighter. Its ragged cliffs and pinnacles tore into the sky, unmoved by the waves thundering in from the west to tear and gnash at its flanks. An ancient stone staircase wound like a scar up its rocky face, in some places so steep the young American Steven Wilcox felt he was climbing an unending ladder.

No one should be here, he thought. *We* shouldn't be here, not at the end of a drizzly winter's day when anyone with any kind of sense is snug at home on the mainland. No one came to Skellig Michael at this time of year, and not in this sort of weather – which was exactly the point, according to Dr. Sweeney. "We want as few as possible to know we're here," he had confided at the start of the climb, "and we want no at all to know *why* we're here."

Every twist and bend brought a new misty vision of churning seas and rock far below, and before long the views became so frightening Steven could continue only by ignoring them. "Don't look down," he whispered while concentrating on each stair, slick with rain, "don't look down, don't look down."

Dr. Sweeney paused above. "Still there?"

"Behind you."

"Glad to hear it," he said in his thick Irish brogue. "Wouldn't do to have you plunging over the side like a fallen angel." Noting the younger man's anxiety, Sweeney clasped him by the arm and looked him straight in the eye. "Now don't you be losing your nerve. I've told you countless times my style of research involves more than poking about in dusty cellars and sifting through ruins with a teaspoon and a toothbrush. We are on a quest for monsters and miracles, Notable Scholar, and such pursuits tend to present unusual challenges."

"Heights," Steven said and tried to smile. "Not so great with heights. But I'm not complaining."

Sweeney gave him a hearty slap on the shoulder. "That's the spirit!"

Higher they went and darker went the sky, with a steady rain falling and cascading down the staircase to scatter into droplets again when pelted by the wind. Seabirds soared through the clouds with skillful tilts and dips of their wings. Steven brushed his long hair away from his rain-streaked glasses and chanced another look down: the hired trawler *Nellie Anne* had disappeared in a mist as thick as the billows above.

Higher they went, and higher still until the two men passed over a grassy ridge and climbed the last of the treacherous staircase to the island's lower, eastern peak. Sweeney stopped to catch his breath. "And there it is," he said, and he aimed his light down a misty pathway onto a wall fashioned of interlocking stones pierced by a low opening. "Come, Notable Scholar. Come and cast your eyes upon a corner of heaven."

Steven bent low and followed him through the opening and he froze in a half crouch, riveted by his first view of the abandoned monastery atop Skellig Michael.

"Incredible, impossible, mad place," Sweeney said in a hushed voice nearly lost in the drifting rain.

A wind-swept, mystical vision in grey it was, with a weathered Celtic cross standing watch over a sunken courtyard. Around this, a collection of domed monastic huts, or *clocháin*, huddled together as if for warmth, all constructed of flat grey rocks fourteen centuries before. Steven thought they looked like stone igloos. Beyond them stood the ruined walls of a chapel dedicated to the Archangel Michael, and beyond that, in the darkening far distance, the serrated peaks of the neighboring bird-sanctuary Little Skellig Island stabbed at the veils of cloud like the black sails of a coffin ship.

"And they actually lived here," Steven said, amazed and appalled.

"They did indeed. Generation upon generation of hardy monks in the darkest of ages, shivering in their homespun robes and marking their days with prayer. No fires for cooking or warmth, for look around? What could they burn? Living on raw seal meat and gull eggs, with only the occasional little *currach* boat to deliver communion bread for Mass. Frightful existence."

The two men crawled into the first and largest cell. The domed roof kept out the rain but, even so, it seemed the cold had seeped through in a deeper way here to tunnel into bone and settle thick within the marrow. "We'll use this one as our headquarters," Sweeney said. His breath clouded the air. He lit a lantern and removed from their backpacks a wrecking bar, hammer, steel chisel and a leather satchel wrapped in layers of heavy plastic.

Steven crouched at the entrance and blew into his cupped hands. "Cold."

"Perishing, 'tis." Sweeney unwrapped the satchel and withdrew a small book, ancient and tattered. "According to this," he said with a snap of his fingers on the cover, "our treasure lies not in one of the five existing *clocháin*, but in the oratory at the far end. No point in lollygagging. Let's get to it, shall we?"

Out they went into the wind and rain again and passed through the huddled structures to a grassy ledge overlooking an ancient burial ground filled with headstones so weathered they looked like rotten teeth. Beyond it stood the oratory, a stone structure with a domed roof like the monk's cells but larger and more rectangular.

Inside, a narrow window opposite the low doorway allowed the cold air in to further chill the cramped, tomblike interior. Dr. Sweeney set the tools down. He scanned the floor from the entrance to the window and back again before opening the small book. "Higher," he said and Steven lifted the lantern. The professor studied the book. He studied the floor. He pointed at the stones and counted silently, lightly jabbing at the air with his forefinger and mouthing the words, "one, two, three." He looked at the book again, tilted it, squatted and touched the granite threshold and a flagstone beside it – "one" – and another – "two" – and his hand came to rest upon a triangular stone, "and…three." He paused with his hand on the stone. Condensed breath swirled into the light.

"You want to do it?" Steven asked.

The professor looked up as if startled. "No," he said. "I think – no…" He held out his trembling hand.

Steven traded the lantern for the wrecking bar. He knelt beside the triangular flagstone and worked the tip of the bar into the packed earth beside it. "Ready?" he whispered.

Sweeney nodded. He moved closer, held the lantern higher. His glasses blazed in the lantern-light.

Steven leaned on the wrecking bar. Dirt and mortar crumbled. He worked it back and forth and pressed down again. This time the mortar gave way and the bar dropped a foot before hitting solid rock again. Dr. Sweeney clutched him by the shoulder. "That's it," he whispered, and his accent seemed to thicken. "God Almighty in heaven above, that *must* be it."

Steven pulled on the bar. The flagstone rose with a deep grinding scrape. Dr. Sweeney leaned forward, his breath tight in his chest, obscuring the younger man with his shadow. "Be you still, be you still, trembling heart," he whispered, and he leaped with a startled cry when something crawled from the hole.

A thin black shape slithered into the light.

"Holy Mother of God," Sweeney whispered. "What *is* that?"

Steven could only shake his head and stare.

Smoke – dust – whatever it was had gathered into serpentine form and squirmed from the hole to the middle of the oratory where it hovered in a black coil an inch or so from the floor.

Steven slid his foot toward it and it pulled back. Impossible, of course; he knew that – *impossible!* – yet this smoky thing gave the illusion of being alive, of reacting to him like a sentient being. Its leading end rose, flattened into a cobra hood of vapor and it hovered before them, watchful, steady. Steven moved his foot again and the smoke stretched and thinned and vanished in a sudden blur through the window.

"What *was* it?" Sweeney asked but Steven still had no answer. Dazed, he glanced at the excavated hole. "Look!"

Dr. Sweeney lifted the lantern. Light spread. It dropped into a darkness of a thousand years and lifted it out to reveal a stack of loose vellum pages with no binding or leather case for protection, the brittle yellow secret of Skellig Michael. He fell to his knees beside the hole. "This is it – this is it." He lifted them one by one. Unlike the pages in The Book of Kells or similar illuminated manuscripts, these appeared to have been hastily written, with no precise calligraphy or elaborate painted knot work; only thin spidery words scrawled in faded black ink.

He carefully set them aside until he came to the last.

Steven moved the lantern closer and Dr. Sweeney stared, barely breathing.

His hand trembled when he lifted the page into the light.

It was a nautical chart.

On the far right, in the east, lay Ireland, clearly recognizable with each bay and inlet drawn with as much detail possible for the time. On the left, far to the west, lay another land, obscure and ill-defined but for one tiny section filled with fine script and an arrow pointing to a small black cross. Those lands had not yet been named, nor could he tell if the cross indicated land that would become the Canadian Maritime provinces, New England, or more southerly regions along the eastern seaboard of North America – but it didn't matter, for it *was* North America.

Sweeney traced a quivering finger down a vertical line at the center of the map and stopped at a word at the bottom. "Look at this."

Steven leaned in close and caught his breath when he saw the signature, written in its Gaelic form – *Breandán* – though he used the more familiar English when he said in a voice filled with awe: "Brendan."

"It's him all right. Our wandering lad. And look at the date below."

"516 A.D."

Sweeney slapped his leg with his free hand and cried, "Oh Brendan, my boy, you are indeed a saint to have not only signed your work, but dated it too!"

This single fragile page was by far the greatest find in the life of the renegade scholar Dr. Raghnall Sweeney. It proved an ancient legend true, and that an Irish monk named Brendan truly did set sail one day and discovered a new land far to the west. In time, he would be canonized as Saint Brendan the Navigator, patron of sailors and whales, and the story of his discovery would slip into a dusky world of medieval mythology and be edged out of reality altogether by Christopher Columbus in 1492.

All that had changed now. Dr. Sweeney held the proof in his hand. Brendan was the first known European to set foot on North America. It was a great achievement made even more so by the fact, the now (thanks to them) undeniable, historical *proof* that he discovered it five hundred years before the Viking explorer Lief Erikson set sail and nearly a thousand years before Columbus was born.

"*Terra Draconis*," Sweeney whispered.

Steven glanced at him, puzzled.

Sweeney pointed to the small black cross in the unknown land and the Latin words inscribed at its base. "*Terra Draconis*," he repeated.

"Dragon Land?"

"A logical name, I suppose, if one were to take these other words to heart." He traced his finger over another phrase scrawled in Latin along the centerline of the map, the imaginary border in the middle of the sea. *Hic sunt Draconis.*

Steven leaned in close and translated: "Here be Dragons."

2

They placed the manuscript inside the satchel and brought it to their headquarters in the first cell. Sweeney set the lantern on the floor. Frigid air sank its fangs into his hands. Rainwater dripped from his straggly red-grey hair into his collar but he took no notice of it: not the cold, the wet and dark, not the shadows of his own breath clouds or the outside wind's moaning dirge.

He unwrapped the manuscript.

"You're not going to read that now, are you?" Steven asked.

"I am." He sat cross-legged upon the cold stone floor with the manuscript before him. "We've some time before that brigand of a Captain abandons us. I don't dare risk those stairs without a quick read-through. A fall, a drop, an errant wave – if something should happen at least I'll have known what we found."

"That wind is picking up," Steven said with a nervous glance at the door. "He said he couldn't come back for us if it turns into a gale."

"Oh yes?" Sweeney asked, unconcerned.

"And he said he'd only give us until midnight."

"Did he now? Well, well..." He leaned over the pages. The manuscript had been composed primarily in Old Gaelic with some sections in Latin and others a combination of the two. It also appeared to have been written in secret and in great haste with the author using whichever language sprang to mind. He could read it with ease but it left Steven in the position of either waiting for the professor to tell him what it said or create his own laborious translation later.

Minutes passed in silence broken only by the light sound of pages turning and rain lashing at the entrance.

Outside the wind sighed along the toppled walls and, outside, the strange twist of smoke prowled the ruins, forgotten by the two men who released it from beneath the flagstones. It slid against remembered doorways and wandered through the *clocháin*, touching stone, slithering along the rain-dark rock, gathering memory and dead feeling from cracked walls. Torchlight flickered in blackened chambers and blood once again dripped from the long dead fingers of a withered hand; and cries, tormented keening cries welled up from a forgotten past to coil within the smoke as it crept through the rain, touching, caressing, remembering...

Inside the cell Sweeney sat bolt upright. He stared at a page, lifted it, held it closer to the light. "Not possible."

"It's real, isn't it?" Steven asked, unsettled.

Sweeney rifled through the pages until he found the nautical chart. He stared at the date beside Brendan's name. "Not possible."

"What's not possible?" Steven asked and Sweeney looked up as if surprised to find someone there. "Oh, right," he said, distracted. "It says – well, it says a good many things one expects in a work such as this. I had hoped Brendan might be the author, but it appears to have been written by a monk, a certain Brother Aodhan of *Sceilig-Mhichíl* – that's the Irish for Skellig Michael – and yes, it is real if by 'real' you mean authentic."

Steven relaxed. At this early stage, they could not rule out a hoax. "So what does it say?"

Sweeney peered with an owlish stare over the top of his black-framed glasses. "You shall persist, shall you?" Steven nodded with a half-smile. "Very well. It's decidedly monkish. Typical of the time, highly imaginative. Brother Aodhan tells of a clan warrior named Donal who also happened to be blood brother to our monk Brendan. And there's a witch of sorts. A hag, a crone, a druid priestess, possibly a banshee. Cannot say at this point. And there's a..." Dr. Sweeney averted his eyes.

"There's a what?"

"Let that lie for now. It is not what caught my eye a moment ago. Listen to this." He scanned the page. "Ah, here...and do forgive the rough translation." As usual when reading aloud, he dropped his glasses so close to the tip of his nose that Steven marveled they didn't drop off. *'And in that gold, surrounded by vapor and steeped in shadow, was found the Beast-Child, and it awaiting to come forth in fire, to be suckled by lightning, the last of its kind, the devil-spawn of Lochru, as yet unborn.'* Quite chilled me to the bone, that."

"Why?"

Sweeney lifted his glasses onto his forehead. "Can it be possible you do not recognize the name Lochru?" Steven thought for a moment but had no answer. "Oh now, really. This is elemental. First year Celtic Studies."

Steven shook his head. "No. Sorry, no."

"For the love'a God," Sweeney returned with genuine dismay. "He was a sorcerer in the service of High King Lóegaire! And not some common, run-of-the-mill sorcerer, no – the *Arch-Druid* Lochru, slain by Saint Patrick himself at the court of Tara." Steven shrugged his shoulders and Sweeney, exasperated, pointed to the map. "The date on this manuscript is...?"

Steven sighed. "516 A.D."

"Correct." He pulled his glasses down again and stuffed his pipe with a pinch of loose tobacco pulled from a leather pouch. "You will recall that Patrick arrived upon the Hill of Tara in the year 432. There the High King's sorcerer Lochru accused the young saint-to-be of a host of crimes and blasphemies, after which ensued a spiritual battle for the soul of the Irish people. Lochru cast a series of incantations and levitated high into the air. Most impressive. But St. Pat, clever lad, fell to his knees in prayer and Lochru's levitation spell burst, whereupon the sorcerer plummeted and smashed his brains out upon the stones. Thus came the beginning of the end for the druids and thus came Christianity to the land of my birth. Any questions?"

"No." Steven glanced at his watch. "No questions."

"Not even one concerning how it is that Lochru shows up again in these pages?" Dr. Sweeney lit his pipe and continued speaking through puffs of smoke. "Or why he is credited with fathering a Beast-Child, which is, I must say, a prodigious accomplishment for one whose skull was cracked open and crushed by Patrick nearly a hundred years before?"

"Oh, right. So he was."

"So he was indeed. Now sit you there in silence and remorse whilst I finish this." A ball of smoke rolled from his mouth and struck the wall before spreading through the cramped chamber.

Steven couldn't stand it: the waiting, the smoke, the anticipation, and he sighed again, loudly.

"Right then," Sweeney said with an equally impatient sigh. "Let us start at the beginning, if you insist."

"No, no, it's all right," Steven said and Sweeney countered with a "no, no," of his own. "I cannot concentrate with all the sighing and moaning like Deidre of the Sorrows." He sifted through the pages to the first. "He begins it like so…and again, the translation. Rough." Sweeney tilted his head back while bringing the page closer to the light. "*'I am Aodhan of Sceilig-Mhichíl, a sinner and imperfect in many things.'* As are we all, Brother Aodhan, as are we all," he murmured with an air of mock tragedy. *'Who shall believe me when I proclaim that I do not wish to write these words but am compelled to do so by a power I do not understand?'* A power I do not understand," he repeated. "Now what do you suppose that might be?"

Steven shrugged and said he didn't know. Sweeney did the same.

"*I struggle to stop my hand from writing, but this I cannot do. Nor can I escape the low whispers that urge me ever onward. Smoke hovers still over the holy island, and within my mind, and will not scatter. In darkest night it pours into my ink and finds its way onto these pages. My hand is not my own. Evil things do haunt the blackened air and I fear I cannot drive the poison from my mind until I set down all I have seen. We, the brethren of Sceilig-Mhichíl, have been forewarned by our Abbot that no word of what has passed is to leave our holy isle. This order shall*

I obey. These pages shall be secreted away upon this great rock, there to remain hidden forever or perchance destroyed by the searching hand of time. To me it matters not. Once my tale is set down upon these pages, I shall be set free. Therefore be amazed, you great and small who fear God and who come upon these words by ways I know not. Read here my tale, and contemplate."

"Why would he have to hide it?" Steven asked.

"Ah, that is where we come to the heart of the tale." – a puff on his pipe, a plume of smoke – "This is what I'd read before you interrupted with your howling and wailing. There were three monks."

"Brendan?"

"One of them, yes. The eldest was our author here, Brother Aodhan. The second was our lad Brendan. I shall guess he was in his early twenties. The third was the youngest of all, a chap named Gillain about fourteen years old. They sailed from Skellig Michael to the mainland in one of their little currachs. Don't know if you've ever seen one, a little boat with hides stretched over a wooden frame and a single mast with a sail. They sailed to the mainland where, according to this, there had been a village called…called…" He squinted at a page. "…called *Baile na Sceilge*, now long gone though there remains a little bit of a village called Ballinskelligs, must be built upon the ruins of the old. And in the old one, in *Baile na Sceilge*, there had been a great deal of kidnapping going on for a number of years. Abductions."

"Who was abducted?"

"Young girls. Maidens. Damsels, presumably in distress. No one knew what had happened to them. No one knew their fate. The village elders called for help from the local chieftain. That's where Donal comes in, the knight I mentioned earlier. Brendan's brother. His true brother. Imagine him if you will, tall, with golden hair, a crimson mantle over his armor, and dark blue Celtic knots and spirals tattooed on his arm and half his face as a mark of allegiance to his clan-chieftain. Donal was sent to guard the village against the unknown attacker who'd been thieving away with the unfortunate damsels. On that woeful day…"

"Why woeful?"

"I shall come to that presently." – another puff – "On that day of woe, Brendan met his brother in the lanes of *Baile na Sceilge*, but not in a happy way. When Donal appeared, he did so covered in something…blood, I presume. Probably his own. And soot."

"Ashes?"

"Ashes, yes. Soot. Smoke. Covered from head to toe."

"From what?"

"Ah yes, well…" Sweeney sniffed and turned a page. "From…"

"From *what?*"

Dr. Sweeney cleared his throat. "You know these medieval folk," he said with a dismissive wave. "Simply brimming with fanciful notions. It appears to have been a sort of beastie thing. Fire. Smoke."

"You mean a dragon?"

"No, no – a dragon? No, certainly not, perish the thought. But something very *like* a dragon, I should imagine. Brother Aodhan never calls it by name, other than to call it the Beast or the Evil One, a name usually reserved for the Devil himself. Whatever it was, it destroyed the village entirely. Death. Destruction. Burnings all around. Vividly told, I must say. Flesh melting and falling off the bone. Blistering skin. Houses ablaze and filled with the despairing cries of those trapped inside. The three monks and the knight escaped. They leaped into their currach and off they went, but the Evil One followed." Sweeney licked his forefinger and used it to lift a page from the one below. "Listen to this marvelous…well, listen. *'A black shape appeared within the churning sea. Steam puffed into the sky like the spout of a whale and we beheld a monstrous eye, staring.'* Do you know what a gannet looks like?" Steven cocked his head, puzzled. "One of those seabirds spiraling around us today," Sweeney explained. "The large one, with the wicked-looking bill. It drops into the sea like a dive bomber. They have pale blue eyes, the gannets do. Brother Aodhan says this thing in the water had the same, an eye as blue as a gannet's eye, but so pale it was nearly white, and with a long sliver of a pupil, the same as a goat's eye. Most unnerving. It dropped below the waves again without attacking them, and off it went. They saw its trailing bubbles heading straight for Skellig Michael."

"And that's all?"

"Oh no, there's more, much more. The monks and the knight feared they could not handle this catastrophe on their own, and so they sailed to ask for help from the one I spoke of. The druid witch named Moll. She lived on that first island we passed today, the bird island Little Skellig, known then as *Sceilig Bheag*. A withered old crone she was, wearing a threadbare robe streaked with bird shit and carrying a snow-white gull upon her shoulder. She lived alone in a little hovel, the usual thing…jars of mysterious ingredients at hand, a cauldron bubbling upon the fire."

"For poisonous brews," Steven said with a smirk.

Sweeney ignored the remark. "There's quite a lot of back and forth between the monks and the crone, a bit tedious, with them pleading and she wanting nothing to do with it. A bit of theology in there too, with each side stating their case until they decided there was a higher purpose before them, and one to be confronted only by putting aside their differences and working together. In the end she relented for she knew what they were up against. The monks were clueless. The knight too. Moll, alone, realized their true peril. She also knew they stood a chance – a small one, but a chance nonetheless. She concocted a brew made of various herbs and bark and leaves, and yes, possibly poisonous. She smeared the filthy stuff over the knight Donal's armor and shield, and then came the incantation."

He drew his glasses down to the end of his nose. "This is Moll now. This is what she said:

'From the battle raven, Badb Catha, her sacred herb inspires bravery.
Even this shalt thou wear, for by its charm shall courage cleave to thee.
Wild marjoram then, and with it sage, envenomed bite shall they assuage.
Thyme, this too, for invigoration,
And sweet rosemary to bind this incantation,
Infuse them all, in thickness brew, a plant far greater than the rest.
Anoint thy shield with Dragonroot, and by its charm, be valor blessed.'

"When finished, she placed her hand upon the knight's breastplate and said, 'Something there is that lies within,' and she told him he must be on his guard against it"

"What does that mean?" Steven asked.

"Donal's very question. Moll told him that he must certainly fight the Beast without, but even more, and even greater, he must fight the Beast within." Sweeney paused, gazing at the manuscript. "The Beast within," he said again. "Which could be anything. Self-doubt. Jealousy. Negativity. Fear. Unquenchable anger. I suppose we all have a Beast within of one sort or another, do we not? And how, Notable Scholar, how do you suppose Donal was supposed to fight this Evil One?"

Steven shook his head with dismay. "No idea."

"A sword made by the *Tuatha Dé Danann*. A mystical sword made of silver, called *An Claiomh Gealach*."

"The Sword of the Moon."

"Very good, yes. The Sword of the Moon. Moll commanded the knight to take the sword into battle and warned them that when it was all over, they were not to use fire. She did not say why. She only warned them against using it. Strenuously. That's as far as I got before your Concerto of the Sighs. Let us continue, shall we?"

Steven's head dropped until his chin nearly touched his chest.

"Well?" Sweeney asked.

"Mystical swords. Witches. Druids."

"*Arch*-Druid. Or sorcerer, whichever you prefer."

"I don't prefer either one," Steven said. "And I certainly don't prefer a Beastie Devil thing."

Sweeney, with a steady over-the-glasses stare, asked what could have provoked such an outburst.

"That," Steven said and pointed to the pages. "All these months searching and almost killing ourselves climbing this island. For what? No one's going to believe Brendan's map is real if they hear all this other Evil One bullshit." The professor studied his assistant with a calculated blend of disappointment and amusement. Steven changed his tone. "You don't believe…I mean, seriously–you don't *seriously* believe there was a…no," he said with a short laugh and ran his fingers through his hair. "No, of course you don't." He looked at the entrance where lingering twilight had given way to certain night. "This place has me creeped out."

Sweeney puffed on his pipe. "There are stranger things in heaven and earth than are dreamt of in all of our philosophies, Notable Scholar."

"I need some air," Steven muttered and he crouched low at the doorway. Dr. Sweeney did not look at him when he said, "Be not so single-minded in your Brendan quest. We search for truth in whatever guise it takes and in whichever direction it leads. If this manuscript does not contain the truth we hoped for, so be it."

"Are you so willing to accept failure?"

"Failure!" The professor lifted one of the vellum pages. "This single page is older than the Book of Kells, older than the Lindisfarne Gospels, older even than the Cathach of St. Columba. If the words inscribed upon it are nothing but instructions on how to build a monastic shithouse, it is still the oldest extant manuscript ever found in Ireland and one of incalculable historical value." He lowered the page and resumed his study, but not before adding: "And failure, notable scholar, is born only of a mind closed to possibility."

Steven bristled but did not challenge him. He pulled his hood up and left the cell.

The smoke saw him.

It drifted along the top of a broken wall until it reached its end where it paused…rain passed through it to patter on the stones…and then it started down.

3

In the first cell, dim lamplight illuminated the words Dr. Sweeney continued to translate and read for the first time since Brother Aodhan inscribed them in secret over a thousand years before:

We departed from the hag's dismal hovel and sailed from the bird island, whereupon a smoky odor met our nostrils and to our vision came a fiery shudder upon the clouds. Our brethren lay under siege, and we sped upon our way to the holy isle. Up the staircase we did go, where fire whipped around the clocháin as if the very air atop Sceilig-Mhichíl had been set ablaze. I cannot fully recount all that took place for I had only scattered visions of sight and sound, confused and bound in a frenzied ring of heat and ash and flame.

Sparking bits of flame spiraled like bats made of fire. All around swirled a maelstrom of confusion and death. Shrieks and roars. Firebats swooping low with a dreadful hiss. And then came Donal striding into the inferno with the silver weapon held aloft. Smoke fell and choked my sight and in the midst of all came a roar so immense that I fell deafened to the ground. Death rained in flame. It streaked down as shooting stars to burst upon the rocks and I lay upon the scorched earth and prayed a desperate prayer and awaited the final blast that would take my life.

But it did not happen.

The roar dimmed and fell silent. Gentle night, its moon and blessed stars appeared through the smoke.

Upon the rocks lay the Evil One with *An Claiomh Gealach*, the Sword of the Moon, thrust to its silvery hilt in its eye. Beside it lay the crushed body of Donal, pierced through by venomous sting. His charmed breastplate lay torn and punctured upon his chest.

Smoke darkened my sight once more, but a wind rose and in the clearing pall I saw Brendan striding toward the fallen knight. In his hand he held the weapon pulled from the eye of the Evil One as from a bloody scabbard. "The devil is slain!" he cried, and t'was then he saw his brother's mortal wound. He fell to his knees and held Donal close and the dying knight touched the ragged hole in his breastplate and this he did say, "The fault is my own, Brendan. Forgive me."

"There is no fault, dear brother," said Brendan, confused to hear him speak of such a thing. "It is done. It is over."

The fallen knight writhed upon the ground for the venom did pain and weaken him limb by limb. "The witch will tell all," said he, and these being his last earthly words. Blood foamed at his lips, and Brendan with breaking heart did perform the sacrament of Final Anointing and thus with his sins remitted, the valiant knight did close his eyes and his soul was borne to our heavenly Father; and all were sorely grieved.

There came then a rumble from deep within the slain creature. We feared it lived still and fled to safe refuge, but the strong clear voice of Brendan called us back. "Be not afraid," said he. "We must see this through to the end. The Evil One is slain, but its heart lives still."

Mist rose as thick as the smoke and when it dissipated a sight both pitiful and unforeseen met our eyes. The Devil Beast was gone and in its place lay a thin frail man, ancient and weak, shivering in his nakedness, with a bloody gouge where once his right eye had been. Our Abbot strode out upon the killing field and the aged wretch held out his hands in supplication.

"Do not approach him," Brendan said and he set the tip of the sword against the man's bony chest.

"Release him, Brendan," cried the Abbot in his frail cracking voice. "Can you not see he is but a helpless sinner?"

"Sinner he may be, but far from helpless."

The Abbot commanded one of our brethren to bring forth a robe to cover the naked wretch, and again, Brendan did warn against approaching him. "This is not a man," said he. "This is not a being of this earth."

I heard Brendan's words, but the poor soul appeared so desolate that the warning sounded foolish and ill-placed. Blood flowed from his shattered eye and he whimpered piteously. T'was then I saw a deep scar running along the back of his nearly hairless head. Brendan pressed The Sword of the Moon closer to the man's bony chest. "He is a sorcerer of great power. He is the poisoned heart of the Beast."

The old man's pitiful manner changed at once and I shuddered to see his countenance transform into one of venomous hatred. His remaining eye was so pale blue that it gave his entire eye the appearance of being pure white, and it was then that I saw with a shock of horror the same narrow goat-eye pupil I had seen when the demon-beast peered at our boat from the sea. "Pathetic creatures," said he in a ghastly hollow voice. "Oh, how brave and noble thou art. You, Abbot, cowering in your clochán, trembling as a mouse. Brave warrior of a false god!" He threw back his head with a cackle of demented laughter.

Blood flew from his gouged eye and spattered on the rocks. The Abbot gasped in his rage and ordered us to take the contemptible man away.

"Aye!" cried the shameful wretch. "Shackle me, wrap me in chains, destroy me if you dare! Purify me, if the false god so commands."

"It shall not happen," Brendan said. "For one so foul there can be no purification, no redemption."

The vile man snarled. "And what say you, Abbot? What penalty is to be paid? Or shall legions of demons come to my aid and lead me from peril?" He threw his head back with another maniacal laugh.

"Abomination!" cried our gentle Abbot, his face reddened with unaccustomed anger and humiliation before the prisoner. "Put that thing in chains." he commanded, and with that, the monks fell upon him.

4

While Dr. Sweeney moved on to read of the imprisonment of the sorcerer in the *clochán*, Steven passed beyond the oratory to a low wall at the edge of a precipice where he tilted his flashlight into a void of darkness. Raindrops passed through the light and disappeared as if into the depths of a monstrous well.

A large boulder stood beside him with a deep circular hole the diameter of a dinner plate cut into the middle of its flat top. He reached into the hole and felt its smooth sides, obviously man-made. *Wonder what that was for?*

He turned his flashlight off and listened to the wind and the raindrops pattering on his hood. The end had come. They found it. And now it was all threatened. The professor had a point about the importance of the manuscript regardless of what it contained, but to lose the chance of proving Brendan's voyage was painful to consider.

This latest adventure began many years before while Sweeney was following his passion of rooting about in the cellars and catacombs of the monasteries and churches of Europe and came across a fragile piece of parchment that contained an offhand reference to an Irish monk's voyage into the western sea. By the time Steven joined him, he had already found three more clues. Then came endless days pouring over dusty pages in damp cellars with spiders scurrying in the shadows and whole nights spent in discussion and speculation, all leading nowhere until they stumbled across the small tattered book in a medieval library in Rothenberg, Germany and the reference to the third flagstone in the oratory cell.

Now the search was over, and now its success was threatened by Brother Aodhan's imagination. *We could get rid of the manuscript and present the map alone.* But Sweeney was right: no matter what it contained, the manuscript was a priceless relic and to destroy it would be sacrilegious. *But we don't have to tell the world either. The map will be enough.* If he could convince his mentor to agree, they might stand a chance. No druids, no witches, no mystical swords: only the map.

He looked at his watch. 9:45. Plenty of time, but what about the weather? Wind rushed over the summit with a high wavering sigh and drizzling sheets of rain.

Glancing back at the ruin, he saw the glow of Sweeney's lantern illuminating the entrance to the first *clochán*. He wondered how far he had gotten in the manuscript and was about to turn away when something passed before the distant glow.

He turned on his flashlight again, leaned forward, squinted, and…something, a thin trail of mist or – "Oh my God."

He trained his light on the smoke now curling toward him like a snake and his blood went cold when he realized it was moving *into* the wind.

It crept up the stairs. At the top it lifted, cobra-like, as it had in the oratory. It appeared to study him for a moment before it dropped low upon the grass and slithered toward him.

Steven backed against the oratory.

The smoke veered to the flat rock with the hole in the center where it lifted over the edge like a wave in slow motion and spread until it covered the top with a thin layer of smoky mist.

"Dr. Sweeney," Steven called, and again, louder. "Dr. Sweeney!" He wasn't afraid – not really, there was nothing to be afraid of, but still…the way the smoke hovered and clung to the flat surface: even when the wind gusted, it swirled but did not drift beyond the confines of the rock.

Steven approached it. He hesitated…reached out…a tendril of smoke did the same, stretching, reaching for him, and – *bam!* A hammer slammed down in his mind, crushing him with the first light touch of smoke upon his hand.

The flashlight clattered on the rocks.

Darkness engulfed him but dispersed in a sudden glow of torchlight and he fell into a vision of a time long past wherein he saw and heard *a scream lingering in echoes and a young monk upon the floor of the clochán, lifeless eyes gaping wide, entrails steaming and drooping. A frail wizened man in a tattered robe on the floor beside him, his wrists bound in knotted cord, his lips and teeth bright with arterial blood. Torchlight approaching, monks crying out in terror and shock: "Gillain! Gillain! He has murdered young Gillain!" they call in a language Steven has never heard but nonetheless understands. And the old man in a frenzy, with the strength of five, snapping his teeth like a mad thing when the men approach. Chaos! Hysteria! More desperate monks fall upon him. More cry out with wounds and bites. They drag him from the cell, struggling and cursing, with one eye black with dried blood and the other sharp, bright, pale blue, goat-pupilled, and filled with maniacal hatred.*

They have no way to control him. No way to bring an end to the madness. "Over the ledge!" cries one, and they drag him to the lip of the cliff. Over he goes, but like a demented ape, he snags one of the ledges and here he is again, clambering up the cliff. He scrabbles up over the edge and crouches upon the rocks, glaring at the terror-stricken holy men, and he leaps and sinks his teeth into the forearm of one of his captors

They pile onto him again, screaming their terror, their confusion, their utter helplessness. Behind them, a young man with long black hair and gray eyes lifts a glittering sword. "It must be done this way."

The Abbot nods, unsure, ill-equipped to handle this catastrophe. "He must submit to the penalty of heaven," he mumbles in a quivering voice.

"Heaven holds no threat for me," the sorcerer wails and he spits like a venomous serpent. Rancid spittle lands upon the cheek of the Abbot. In an instant, the holy Abbot's eyes transform to nearly solid white. It lasts only as long as a lightning flash before his own eyes return, and within them deep confusion. "No, no," he says, "no, not the sword." He strides up close to the old man. "Blasphemer!" he cries and strikes the sorcerer-demon across the face. To the monks he says, "Gather driftwood," and they gape at him, frightened to see such anger in one so gentle. "Break up one of the currachs. Bring here the struts and mast."

The grey-eyed monk with the sword approaches the Abbot. "You must not do this," he insists. "We have never done such a thing upon this island. He is filled with deceit and cunning. He ties your judgment in knots and leads you into fatal error."

"Silence!" the Abbot thunders, but the young monk pleads with the older man. "Moll's warning was clear. We must not use fire."

"Silence, Brendan!"

"You must not do this, Abba, I beg of you – do not do it!"

"Take him away," the older man commands and three others fall upon the rebellious monk. His brilliant sword clatters upon the rocks. "You must not," he cries in desperation and they drag him away, struggling. "You must not use fire!"

And the rock, the hole in the rock, the end of a wooden mast torn from a currach jammed into the hole in the rock.

The small man lifted onto it.

His robe stripped away.

Hands bound behind his back with chains. Legs bound to the post. Driftwood and broken keel struts stacked at his feet, piled around him, and torches thrown. "No!" *Brendan cries from beyond the wall and* —

"No!" cried Steven, unable to escape the appalling vision.

Fire lifts.

The small man, calm and unmoved, looks down at the fire crackling higher, burning his legs, his hands, crawling higher, his skin blistering and blackening. "Thus it is done," *he says, and after this comes a wail of demonic laughter. The monks before him quail at the sight of his single staring eye now shimmering red with reflected firelight, and the consuming fire flares, his face blisters and cracks*, and Steven, weak with horror, brought the vision to an end when he dropped into a lifeless faint.

He woke upon the rocks, lying on his back, facing the rain.

His flashlight had rolled into the courtyard and broke.

Trembling, he tried to stand. "Dr. Sweeney!" he called, rising to his knees. *Where is he? Didn't he hear me?* "Help me!"

Smoke hovered on the rock as before.

Steven staggered to his feet. The rock pulsed with fiery light as if a blazing heart throbbed deep inside, and the smoke turned pale and rose into a shape, a figure, a robed phantom standing upon the rock of its doom. It spoke and Steven clutched his head. He tried to push the sound away but he couldn't for it was *in* his mind. He heard it clearly, he saw the heart of fire within the rock, saw the withered hand reach out. "*You are...*" the voice said with a deadly serpent's hiss and the hand reached out with fingers of charred bone grasping, stretching toward him, "*...mine!*" and Steven screamed as it closed around his mind.

5

"Dear, oh dear," Dr. Sweeney muttered. "Burned him, did you? Dear, oh dear, oh dear."

The manuscript contained a string of fanciful lies, not least of which was an execution so out of keeping with everything known of the gentle brothers of Skellig Michael...but still, Brother Aodhan's words were so genuine, so earnest, so disturbing.

Wind clamored at the entrance and whipped a demon's tail of rain across the stones. He thought he heard Steven call his name and was startled to hear what he first took to be the sound of a scream, but the wind howled so fast upon it that Dr. Sweeney shook his head, certain he had imagined it.

He thought about calling Steven in, but decided against it. He would only fidget and ask questions. Better to finish reading the manuscript in its entirety and relate it back to him all at once.

He turned his attention back to Brother Aodhan's tale.

And so it was that Brendan and I did return to the Bird Island of the crone Moll. We carried with us in the currach Donal's torn body shrouded in a sail for later burial upon the mainland, and again we did climb to the secret lair where she did sit in shadows with her savage eyes glistening with wrath. "You used fire," she said for she somehow already knew.

"I tried to warn them," said Brendan and she did turn upon him in a blistering fury: "It matters not if you tried – you *failed*! The Arch-Druid deceived and led you into folly."

"Who was he?" Brendan asked.

"Not was. Is. He *is*, far greater now than ever before. Death is but a pause in this long life. Your fires have given him the air, the smoke, and a spreading presence unknown to him in times past. I dared not say his name before but the time for faint-heartedness has passed us by."

"You called him the Arch-Druid."

"So I did. For that is who he was and who he is and shall remain. The man you burned, nay, the shadow you *thought* was burned is not a man at all. He is the Arch-Druid, and his name is Lochru."

My face went pale and my hands began to quiver. "But Patrick conquered him in battle," said I. "Lochru perished upon the Hill of Tara."

The crone said again, "Death is but a pause within a long life. Once a truth-seeker of great renown, a healer he was, and one who conversed with and understood the creatures of woodland and field and the lower things that lurk in dark holes and under stones. But not the sky, no. The birds were left to others." Here Moll ran her gnarled fingers over the snow-white back of her gull. "As with many others, man and immortal alike, greed slipped as a blade into his heart. Greed for riches, aye, but more destructive came a greed for mastery over all that live."

I spoke then of the scar upon the back of his head.

"The mark of battle with the holy wanderer Patrick," said she.

"Thus came his first death. His spirit drifted then, earthbound, for no form of heaven would have him. It hid in the secret lairs of the forest and searched for one to exploit as a vessel, to give him form and substance, and it being the Beast now slain. He used it well. He inhabited it. He became one with its blood, its mind, its venom, bone and sinew. But now this vessel is broken. And now, through your fire, has the Arch-Druid been released to find another, stronger vessel." She jabbed at the fire with her staff and the sparks did race to the air. "There are mysteries and secrets, and answers I must have. Bear the fallen knight Donal hither to my dwelling."

This we did. We carried his torn body up the high cliffs and she bade us lay him down upon the stones. Moll touched the armor where had entered the fatal tooth. "Venom, deep and powerful. No man could withstand such a sting." She thrust her hand through the ripped breastplate as if grasping for the heart of Donal. Something snapped. "All becomes clear," she did say in a croaking whisper. She withdrew her hand and to our great wonderment, she held up a golden chain, now broken, with a blood-red gemstone set within it.

Brendan stared. "How came my brother by such a treasure?"

"You are brave and true of heart, young grey-eyed brother, but you must now bear a truth that shall come more painful than a viper's bite."

"Tell me."

"I must, for only truth bound to action can save us now. The Beast and Lochru were as one, the vessel and the vile contents within. So I have said. But this Beast was not the greatest of its race, nor the most powerful, nor the most wicked. Such creatures are of ancient lineage, older than the mountains, some as old as the sea. For many long years did Lochru lie within his Beast and keep to his hidden lair, greedy and ravenous. In this time, he contented himself with sly maiden-raids upon the surrounding villages, for t'was he who did steal the lost maids of *Baile na Sceilge*. Night hid him, and shadows, and so it seemed he would remain for the ages. But alas, he was awakened to further action. His thirst for revenge was great. His instinct for retrieval was greater."

"What has this to do with my brother?"

"A great hoard of gold there is, gathered year by year and age by age. This chain once lay amongst the crowns and chalices. Donal found the lair and Donal did remove it from the treasure mound. I know not how he found the place for its entrance is known to few. Neither do I know how he took such a thing and survived, for above all things, the

Beast guarded well its treasure and knew and coveted every particle of gold even to the smallest fragment." The witch gazed upon the dead man stretched out upon the stones. "But Donal did take and for a time did survive."

"And that is why it came," said Brendan. "That is why it destroyed the village."

"Aye, and why it came to *Sceilig-Mhichíl*. It followed your brother."

"It overtook us in the currach," said I. "Why did it not kill us when it had the chance?"

"For fear of losing its gold at the bottom of the sea. I have said this Beast was not the most powerful of its kind. Thus it swam to the island to lie in wait for Donal. It cared nothing for the holy isle, nor any upon it. It cared only for its stolen gold and would do all in its power to retrieve it."

Brendan's brow darkened and he gazed upon his slain brother. "To be the cause of so much death, I would not have believed it of him."

"Few among us could withstand the lure of the creature's gold, or more, the fiendish arts of Lochru. Judge not harshly the soul of a mortal man with mortal flaws. Donal resides now in the Hall of Knights, at peace and at rest. Turn from this now, and prepare yourself, for grave peril lies ahead, and days of darkness."

"But surely it has ended," said I. "I saw the Beast slain by the silver sword plunged into its eye. I saw the sorcerer consumed by flame. What have we now to fear?"

With no further word, she did bend low before the cauldron. She grabbed a fistful of flaming embers in her bare hand and held them upon her outstretched palm. She blew upon them and her fingers glowed when the coals brightened into flame. "Fire holds little danger for us." She tossed the coals back into the hearth and held up her palm, unburned. "For us, fire is a sacred tool. Lochru had no fear of it. Indeed, he desired it. It was his only means of escape. He could do nothing without it, go nowhere without it. Had he been bound in ice and floated to the far regions of the frozen north he would remain forever thus, harmless and weak. But you have fulfilled his greatest desire. He could not burn without *wanting* to burn. And so, fire came to him. And so, fire released him."

"Released him how? His soul? Can such a creature have a soul?"

"His spirit, aye. Warped and twisted into evil form, but aye.

And now he shall come again, first in spirit, and second in bodily form."

"It is certain?" I asked.

She stared at the coals: "It is probable."

Brendan asked what could be done.

"One thing only," said she in a voice filled with ruin. "Within the cave well-hidden below the Cliffs of Drumgour lies the wealth of Lochru, his gold marvelously wrought, hoarded and piled with the bones of untold numbers of maidens. Virgins of youth and purity they were, but fair maidens cannot last. Held without food or drink they withered unto death beneath the pitiless eyes of their keeper. It was the creature's miserly lust for gold and untouched maidens and all things it can only hoard and cannot use that formed the heart of its great evil. Yet in this cave lies evil greater still."

Fear crept into Brendan's voice: "Can there be one greater than the one now slain?"

"Far greater," said Moll, "and far more dire. For there, amidst the gold and bones lies the offspring of evil, the Beast-Child, as yet unborn. Donal's golden chain must be returned to the place, and then…" Here she did study Brendan, but gentle now, with no trace of scorn. "I wonder if all I shall ask is within your ability."

"What must be done, shall be done," said the young monk.

"So I believe. And yet to you must fall the greater trial."

"Tell me."

"This Unborn Beast-Child must be taken from the secret cave, and by its removal, be rendered powerless. But listen well. If one solitary, fragment of gold is separated from the Beast-Child; even but the merest particle, the curse of Lochru shall come upon us all." She held up Donal's golden chain. "Put it with the rest. It has done its worst and caused great harm, and must be returned to its rightful place."

"But if we take the Unborn from the cave, will it not be separated from the gold? How can this be done?"

Moll retreated into the hovel and did return with a chart. This she did unroll and spread upon the rocks. "They must be taken together," said she, and with crooked finger traced a path across the western sea to a line drawn through the center of the chart. "This marks the edge of the known world." She scraped her finger beyond the line to the void at the far edge. "And here, far to the west, lies a vast wilderness unknown to all but a chosen few. There the Unborn must be brought with its attendant gold."

"But if we remove the gold from the cave," Brendan started and Moll held up her hand. "Bring it together, all of it," said she, "the gold and the Unborn. The bones of the lost virgins may rest as they are. They ceased to be of interest once the life had left them. But the gold must never be separated from the Unborn."

"Bring them where?" Brendan asked.

"You must bring them both to the far land, the Dragon Land, and there leave them guarded by a cross fashioned from the sword *An Claiomh Gaelach*." She noted my surprise that such as she would speak of the cross, and she did say, "Aye, so I have said, for it has much power in worlds beyond your own." She pointed then to the dead knight. "And your brother's pierced, envenomed armor, bring that too and leave it. But mark me well. For even there, in distant lands, if one bit of gold, no matter how small, is removed from whence it lies, so shall the Beast-Child be born."

"Where shall we put it?"

"Find a secure and hidden cave in the Dragon Land. Go thou naked into it and sweep the floor before thee to barest rock. Chance not the merest fragment attaching itself to thy garments upon leaving."

"And if it does?" Brendan asked.

"Then all is lost," said she, and in a voice of despair said, "As it may already be." Here she did take up her staff and lifted her seagull onto her shoulder. "Follow me."

This we did along a path nearly enclosed within a vast cleft in the rocks that did block the moonlight.

"Fire is once again the key," she said, "though it is a key to a lock that must never be opened. The Beast-Child can only be born of fire, and if such a thing comes to pass, the very heart of Lochru shall rise from his own ashes and conjoin within a new creature ten times and ten times again more powerful and terrible than any before. It shall be the sole descendant of the oldest devils. All their power shall be gathered unto it. It shall become the very thing that Lochru has sought since first he was corrupted; the true vessel he has waited for and the path to supremacy over all that lives."

"Is there nothing we can do?" Brendan asked.

"Only this one thing. Your journey to the Dragon Land will be long, and one filled with danger and hardship. Cold will be upon you, and darkest night, but you must not fend them off with fire. Carry no torch in the darkness. Light no fire for warmth or cooking. Hear this: fire will not be fire as you know it. Fire will be as a living thing, with thought and guile and cunning. Fire will stop at nothing in its effort to midwife this abomination."

We broke from the shadows into the moonlight at the edge of a high cliff where a multitude of sea birds did wheel in tangled circles before us, seemingly aglow with pale moonlight upon their wings.

"And if fire does find it?" Brendan asked in a defeated voice. "Is there no hope?"

Moll gazed at the spiraling birds. She studied their patterns of flight. "The Three are the final hope," she said at last.

"How do you know this?" asked Brendan.

She did not take her eyes from the birds. "I have been told."

Brendan looked at them, wheeling and circling, but saw nothing. "What are the Three?" he asked. "Are they knights?"

"Only one. Only their leader. And in this lies grave danger, for this leader will face trials unlooked for and unexpected." A clutch of gulls broke from the main flock to soar in frenzied coils of flight. "These Three, but especially the one who is separate, the leader, the Knight of…" She hesitated. "I see a white bird but cannot divine its meaning."

We looked out upon the countless white birds circling around us and the druid crone did acknowledge our bewilderment. "'Tis none of these," said she. "The white bird I see is like no other, as this knight is like no other. This knight does not join and cannot join. This knight is one who suffers a deep and bitter desolation of the soul."

She drew closer to the edge of the cliff and stared at the patterns of flight. "A column of wood is shown to me now. This shall guide them. And there is snowfire."

"Snowfire," I repeated, for I had never heard of such a thing.

"A coming together, when all things seen and unseen align, one against the other in great battles of ice and flame. And there is Donal's armor, anointed once more, and once more the silver sword *An Claiomh Gealach*, but only – hear me! – *only* if the Knight of the White Bird can overcome the desolation within and become valor blessed. If so, and if the last of the older world's demons is thus destroyed, so too shall come the final destruction of Lochru and his passing for all time. That is all," she said and backed away from the cliff as one who is suddenly taken ill. The birds dispersed until nothing remained in the black air but empty moonlight and the roar of the waves far below.

"A column of wood," Brendan said. "This I do not understand."

"That is all."

"But how shall I find a place to leave the gold in the far lands? And how long will it take to get there?"

"That is all."

And so it was.

Great was my fear on that day when noble Brendan set sail with his band of fellow mariners, all blessed, all true. I desired to join them but my age was too great and my limbs too weak to endure such a journey. For me, it remained only to write down in secret such things as have passed, to what ends I do not know. But oh, how my heart did ache on that day to see them go. And to see the small craft weighed down with gold and the mystic Sword of the Moon fashioned into a cross, and to know that in its midst there lay the hellspawn of Lochru; and to know not whence they journeyed, even to the end of the earth.

I end now this part of my tale and gather it with the others, and turn to a new time, a better time. For there came a day filled with warmth and sun, when gathering bird eggs on the great cliffs, I beheld a sight that will never die.

It was a sail, and it came from the west.

Thus I turn to new pages and tell of Brendan's adventure and his tales of the unknown land and the wonders he saw and terrors he faced, and what became of the Unborn and its attendant gold, of where in darkness it lies and where it must remain, hidden from fire until the final day of the world.

"Now you're talking, lad," Sweeney whispered to the page. "Tell me where you've been and what you saw there."

He no sooner turned the page and read the first word when Steven entered the *clochán* behind him. "Admirable timing, Notable Scholar. I am about to read of Brendan's voyage."

A shadow fell across the manuscript. Sweeney looked up.

Steven's eyes – his hand, a rock – *down!*

Sweeney gasped, the stone connected with a blinding flash, the floor rose up, swirling, black, falling, and that was it – nothing more.

John-Richard Thompson

II.

Fire

John-Richard Thompson

1

Days later and a vast ocean away, Steven Wilcox balanced a flashlight atop a cemetery headstone. Snow swept down to pummel and batter him. He dropped to his knees, lifted a tire iron, and *crack!* – down it came upon a pile of stones at the foot of a low hill. Ice chips flew. He slammed it down again.

A rock moved. He brushed the broken ice away. Several deep grooves had been cut into the stone, but so long ago their edges had nearly disappeared. "Ogham," he whispered, and his pulse quickened.

He wedged the tire iron beneath the stone and pulled. The rock tilted and broke free with a hollow thump to reveal a hole like the mouth of a stone well. Wind and snow funneled into it with a great whistling sigh.

He grabbed the flashlight and the voice came again, pulled him in, forced him to look. *"Closer,"* it hissed and his own feeble inner voice resisted, urged him to run across the field, into the woods, it didn't matter where – *just run!* – but the fire ring crackled and the charred hand reached from the flames to clamp around his throat and draw him in *"closer…"*

He turned his light into the void. Its beam fell upon a floor of rough granite, four feet below the entrance. He tilted his hand, the beam lifted, and, "my *God*," he whispered when it surged back to him a thousand times over in shimmering waves of gold.

He clicked off the light and collapsed against the rocks.

Far more than he expected, far, far more; yet he had to have it – *all* of it. He had to find a way to follow both voices, the one that led him to the secret cave and his own voice, nearly gone, subsumed by the diseased whisper of the robed figure in the flames. He stared with wild, feverish eyes past the headstones into the driving blizzard. *"Destroy it!"* his mind screamed from somewhere deep within his ravaged brain.

He crawled to a three-foot high silver cross lying half-buried in the snow. "Can't, can't destroy it, can't…" He dragged the cross to the hole and dropped it at the entrance. "Go thou naked into the cave," he said through clenched teeth and struggled to remember the ancient warning he had translated from the vellum pages. "Sweep the floor before thee to barest rock and chance the...no, chance *not* the merest fragment attaching itself to thy garment." The darker, stronger voice intruded: "*Yours,*" it hissed and he banged his clenched fists against his temples as if that might drive the poison from his mind.

"Go thou naked," he said again and he pulled off his gloves and scarf and dropped them into the snow. He took off his coat. "Sweep the floor before thee to barest rock." He slipped out of his boots and pulled off his sweater, his flannel shirt. "Go thou naked, sweep the floor." His undershirt went next, sticking with sweat in spite of the cold, then his trousers, underwear, socks, and the icy air tore across the field like a pack of winter wolves to slaver and bite. Blood abandoned his limbs and raced to his heart, leaving his flesh as pale as cold marble He picked up his coat and fumbled through the pockets until he found a whiskbroom. After a last look at his clothes lying flat and empty around him, he squeezed through the entrance and dropped to the stone floor.

Entombed winter closed him in its fist. His body rebelled with tortuous shivers that made the flashlight clatter when he set it on the lip of the entrance and pulled the cross inside.

The ancient hoard lay in a mound far larger than he imagined: golden chalices inlaid with rubies; golden shields, helmets, armbands; medallions edged with diamonds and set with fiery gemstones; gold coins overflowing from jeweled coffers; tangles of necklaces, bracelets, and torcs lying amongst sacrificial bowls, plates, and perfume-pots; all embossed or engraved with Celtic knots and spirals, all gold, all glistening. Two chain-mail gauntlets and a breastplate pierced with a ragged hole in its center lay at the edge of the mound, rusted into near disintegration, yet even these took on a burnished glow in the dim light and those few places untouched by decay sparkled like stars.

"*Closer...*"

He stepped forward, staring at the gold. His breath came heavy; his pulse quickened; but then he saw *it* and his thundering heart turned to ice.

A wooden chest two feet long and one foot high lay half-buried in the coins like an ancient wreck exposed by the shifting sand. Bound in rusted chains and bands of iron, it was the only object in the mound that did not reflect the light but seemed to swallow it whole.

"*Closer...*"

He dropped to a shivering crouch and swept the floor below the entrance with the whiskbroom. "Chance not the merest fragment." Frigid rock seared his shins. His teeth chattered. He moved forward, sweeping stone, sweeping dust, sweeping every fragment of gold from his path.

He lifted a gem-encrusted dagger and dropped it with a cry when a ghostly face floated up before his own, gaunt and bloodless. He cried out again when he realized it was his own reflection peering back from the surface of a shield. "No, no," he whispered, "no, no, no." He knew he had frightened the priest at the church that afternoon and now he saw why. He traced a bony finger over the sunken cheeks of the apparition in the shield. The priest had offered to help but what help could anyone give, then or now? What amount of kindness could extinguish the fire in his mind or stop the disintegration? His appearance, his actions, his mind and soul, the very essence of the haunted stranger was fast corroding into something no longer recognizable as the sane, rational, scholar of only a few days before.

With an anguished cry, he knocked the shield away and scattered the reflection.

"Chance not the merest fragment attaching itself to thy garment," he whispered and he climbed onto the cold metal and swept back and forth, straw scratching gold, back and forth.

He reached the chest. Its chains had frozen into the coins. He shoved it with the heel of his hand and it gave way with a deep rattle. He stuck the whiskbroom between his teeth and used the chains to carry the chest down the mound to the entrance. After scanning it with the flashlight to ensure no gold had attached itself to the old wood or rusting bands, he pushed the cross aside, slid the chest outside, and with a last look at the gold – *his* gold – he scrambled out of the cave.

He dressed as fast as possible with shaking hands so numb he could not feel the cloth, the buttons, the zippers. He stuck the whiskbroom in his coat pocket and stamped his feet to get the blood moving, though it seemed that nothing would ever warm him again.

But it was done! He pulled the protective cross from the cave and tossed it into the snow. He would return in daylight to replace the rocks over the entrance. Nothing would happen to the treasure before then. Snow would drift over the hole and the cross and cover his tracks.

He cowered when the poisoned voice came again, but distant now, and hollow, like a voice at the end of a lightless tunnel. *"Gather it close,"* it called, *"for it is done,"* and with the sudden, unexpected relief of a fever breaking, it set him free. The charred hand released its grip. The icy voice faded. Its words *"it is..."* trailed off, *"...done,"* and drifted into silence. The churning of his mind dimmed and smoothed and his own thoughts returned whole and complete for the first time since he touched the smoke atop Skellig Michael.

The wind dropped with a sigh, as if it too had been riled up and guided by the voice, now gone.

Snow fell, but lighter than before: he saw the windows of a farmhouse emerge at the far edge of the field, and further, a string of lights illuminating the vertical stripe of a ski slope on a nearby mountain. All the world seemed to stop and take a cool deep breath and he realized in that unexpected moment of serenity that he hadn't eaten in days. The thing had seized him and despoiled and starved and plundered him for its own ends. He scooped up a handful of snow and wolfed it down. He started on a second but stopped in mid-bite at a rumble like the deep, irritable growl of a waking beast.

A dog barked near the farmhouse. The sound carried over the field and reached him as a second, louder rumble passed through the sky. Clouds shuddered with light deep inside.

He swallowed and took another bite, but stopped again and stared straight ahead at a sphere of light in the snow, drifting toward him at eye level. It approached the headstones and passed between them. He'd heard of ball lightning but had never seen it. He didn't know anyone else who had ever seen it. *Is this ball lightning?* It wavered and quivered but made not a sound as it floated toward him.

Another thought stopped him dead: he looked from the chest to the clouds and back again. Fear gripped him. "No, I was promised," he whispered, and with a burst of fury, he cried out to the flashing skies. "You *promised* me!"

The silent illuminated ball passed him by and hovered over the chest. There it exploded with a sound like a rifle shot and burst into a thousand tiny pieces of fire. The shock wave sent Steven down onto his back, stunned. A sickening odor of sulfur washed over him. He rose to his knees and crawled to the chest to scatter the droplets of fire into the snow.

A sharp blade of lightning gutted the clouds. Its trailing thunder quivered into a resounding clap so loud he felt it between his shoulder blades. "Only the gold," he said in a clamped, panicked whisper, "not the chest, only the gold!"

He pushed the chest onto its side and scanned it again with the flashlight and the ancient manuscript's warning tore through his mind, *'If one fragment, no matter how small, is taken from the cave, then shall the Beast-Child rise again, born of fire.'* But the written words warned against removing the gold from the cave, only the gold. They said nothing of the chest itself. The envenomed voice said the same: "*Remove the Child from the treasure cave, but the golden plunder, that must you leave behind, all of it, even unto the last fragment. In doing so, all shall be yours."*

That was what it told him, that was what he heard, that was what he did.

Deceived!

Great swaths of light shimmered in the sky. Electrical charges crackled in a dance of raw power and with them came the true warning and counsel of the manuscript, thundering down through the ages. *'Fire shall be as air and breathe unto it life.'* Words set down in smoke passed before his eyes, stark and black against the remembered page. *'Fire will become as a living thing, with thought and guile and cunning. Fire will stop at nothing to midwife this abomination.'*

A tangled coil of charges passed over the trees on the far side of the field. They lit the snowy boughs in a sear of white and hung for a moment like a monstrous falcon sizing up its prey before slamming down in some distant field or wood. A moment later, they gathered into a single crackling bolt and raced back into the sky.

'Fire shall have a will of its own to search and seek, and by doing so, shall find.'

He clawed at the chest and turned it over again, searching every inch for a hidden piece of gold, a fragment overlooked, something previously unseen. "Nothing," he said in a frantic whisper. "Nothing here, no gold, nothing, nothing."

He froze, paralyzed by a dagger of thought.

Moving like a man in a trance, he nestled the flashlight under his arm and pulled the whiskbroom from his coat pocket.

He held his left hand under it. With his right, he separated the straw, one strand at a time, and he froze again with his gaze nailed to a single, tiny, delicate link of golden chain that had dropped soundless into his palm.

2

A somber, tragic young woman recently turned twenty-one stood at the back door of the Chinese restaurant and squinted at the lighting in the falling snow. "Strange," she said. If lightning could talk, it might have said the same about her. Her squint, with its near collision of her thickly-mascaraed eyelashes, had turned her eyes into bold slashes as black as Van Gogh crows, vivid against her abnormally pale skin. Her long straight black hair blew over her face and she closed the door and stood in the middle of the squalid kitchen, waiting for Uncle Lung to hand her a jug of soy sauce. He made no effort to do so but she refused to ask him again so she stood there, tapping her black fingernails on the counter until the dining room doors banged open and her co-worker, Pearl, stormed into the kitchen like a gunfighter entering a saloon. "Come on, Raeven," she snapped. "Think I want to spend the night in this hell-hole?"

The somber woman shrugged her shoulders and nodded toward Uncle Lung.

"Hey, Collapsed," Pearl hollered. "Where's that rice juice?" Tall and angular with a shock of red hair and nearly twenty years older than Raeven, she had long ago lost all fear of the cantankerous chef.

"Loody-hee!" he yelled in return. Uncle Lung had been in the United States for over forty years yet his English remained limited mostly to "garbage-y" (meaning "garbage", or "bad"), what sounded like "loody-hee" used to mean "look here", and the entire score of the musical *Annie*.

"*You* loody-hee," Pearl snapped. "I asked for it a half hour ago." With that, she swung on her heels and banged through the doors again. The wiry old man scowled and handed Raeven a filthy plastic jug with a wad of aluminum foil jammed into the top as a stopper. The greasy handle slipped from her hand, the jug fell, the foil stopper shot out and soy sauce gulped into a puddle on the floor.

Uncle Lung responded with a fusillade of howling Cantonese. "Couldn't agree more," Raeven said. She shook her hair down to its accustomed place over her face and backed out of the kitchen into the lounge where Pearl sat at the bar with an unlit cigarette dangling from her lips. An empty glass on the bar in front of her held the remains of a Mai-Tai with its ice cubes melting in the shade of a tiny umbrella.

"The man is mad," Raeven said as she passed.

"An effing lunatic, always was, always will be, world without end, amen."

"Still snowing," Raeven said. "Lightning too. Really strange."

The blizzard had swept across the Canadian border to assault northern New England with a vast mantle of snow, five inches by three o'clock, eight inches by nightfall, and well over a foot and a half when the clocks struck ten.

Not a single customer had been in all night. The manager, Uncle Lung's twenty-two year old nephew Joe Li, had already decided to close early, though he had not yet told Raeven or Pearl. Instead, he mentioned that it might be a good idea to spend an hour or so refilling the soy sauce containers. Raeven thought otherwise but left the response to Pearl, who did not disappoint. "You think I hauled my shapely butt all the way up here in a blizzard to pour rice juice? No way. Get Asthma to do it." As with the soy sauce, Pearl never called Uncle Lung by his real name but drew from a long-collected list of words associated with *lung* whenever referring to him. "Hey, Collapsed!" she now yelled. "Get out here and help out with the rice juice." She looked at her watch. "Oh, eff that," she said. "Time to call it a night. Sparky called a few minutes ago. Said he just plowed the Coachlight Road and we should head home before it fills up again."

"Maybe..." Joe hesitated, glanced toward the kitchen and pushed his glasses up to the bridge of his nose with his habitual quick, salute-like gesture. "Maybe we could close early."

Pearl lit her cigarette and puffed out a gorgeous plume at the *No Smoking* sign. "You're kidding, right?"

"The snow," he countered, suddenly unsure of his decision.

"Oh, my God, Raeven, go over to that calendar, mark today's date in red." The photo above February portrayed a colorful dragon parading through a fire-crackered street in San Francisco's Chinatown. "We'll get it framed, call it 'The Night we Closed Early for Once in our Miserable Freaking Lives'."

"Hey, Joey," Raeven said and the bartender looked up from the bar sink. "Happy New Year."

Pearl squinted at the calendar. "Oh, that's right! Tomorrow's your New Year. I forgot all about it."

"It's Chinese New Year, not mine," Joe said, saluting his glasses up his nose. "Mine is the first of January."

"Which year is it?" Raeven asked, still gazing at the picture. "Year of the what?"

"I'm not sure. Maybe the Year of the Cock."

"Oh, whoop-dee-doo!" Pearl cried and burst into raucous laughter.

Joe's face flushed and he stammered, "I mean the Rooster."

"I *knew* this was gonna be my year! Well, well, well. Year of the Cock."

"Rooster," Joe said, trying to force a wedge of dignity into the conversation. "Year of the Rooster. And I'm not sure, it could be the Year of the Horse or Dragon. Could be anything, for all I know."

"Hey Emphysema!" Pearl hollered while wrapping a scarf around her neck. "Happy New Year!" The kitchen door creaked open to reveal the Uncle Lung's tight-lipped frown that guarded his gold-capped front teeth from view. "Gonna do something to celebrate?" she asked. "Something new and different? Like get all drunk and naked and stuff and par-taaaaay?" He scowled and retreated and she leaned back on her barstool with a ringing peal of laughter that slipped into a graveled smoker's cough. "I crack myself up," she said, coughing and laughing at the same time. "Year of the Cock, my kind'a year."

Raeven lifted her long black coat from the back of a chair. "Assuming it is the Rooster, is that a year of good luck?"

Joe grabbed Pearl's empty glass and tipped it. The ice cubes clattered into the sink. "No."

3

The newly-plowed Coachlight Road already had two fresh inches of snow by the time Pearl's car rounded a corner and, "Whoa, whoa, whoa," she said and tapped the brakes to keep from sliding over the ice. Fire roared inside a car parked at the side of the road. It lapped against the roof and curled against the rear windshield like a wild thing frantic to escape. It had not yet broken through to the outside air, though black smoke slipped through a crack in the driver's side window.

"What should we do?" Raeven asked. They were on an isolated stretch with no lights and nothing in sight but pines and snow banks glistening with reflected firelight.

"Call Sparky. Use mine. I got him on speed dial."

The signal did not have far to go, only two miles to where the town snowplow grumbled along the narrow roads like a great flashing monster rooting in the snow. Its driver, Sparky Grant, answered: "Hey what's up, Pearls before Swine?" he said after seeing her name come up on the display.

"This isn't Pearl," Raeven said and Sparky winced. "It's Raeven. I have Pearl's phone. There's a fire." He heard Pearl's voice in the background, "Let me have it," and then into the phone, loud and clear. "Hey Sparkles, I'm up on the Coachlight Road near the Grey's farm. There's a car on fire, like a big one."

"Big car?"

"Big fire."

Thirty-two, unmarried, blond, tall and lean as a whip, Sparky Grant was the only policeman in the town of Burne Notch, New Hampshire, population 1,062. He was also Chief of the Volunteer Fire Department and the man responsible for keeping the roads clear of snow. "I just plowed up there," he said. "I saw the car too. Think I did anyway. Massachusetts plates. I was going to check on it later. It's on fire?"

"Yeah, inside, flames and stuff – whoa, there's a big one just came through the side window."

"Don't go near it. The gas tank could blow if it hasn't already."

"I'm going to drive past it." When Sparky protested, Pearl said, "I'll go fast. It'll take us all night to get home if we have to go the back way." She put the car in gear and Raeven slumped in her seat as they passed. Beside her, fire roared through the burning car's cracked window and snapped at the air. "We're past," Pearl said into the phone.

"I'll be up as soon as I can," the policeman returned. "You don't see anybody nearby, right?" When she told him no, he said: "OK, let her burn. The blizzard might put it out anyway."

Two minutes after passing the car, they came upon its owner walking alongside the road, disheveled, with long filthy hair and a scraggly beard. He tried to climb the snow bank when they approached but it was too steep and he slid down again. "Well, now *there's* a fine specimen," Pearl said, grimacing as she slowed down.

"Don't stop," Raeven said but Pearl ignored her and told her to roll down her window.

Raeven did. "You all right?" she asked. The man stepped closer. Her eyes widened with alarm when she saw his bloodless pallor and eyes behind his cracked glasses burning with the frenzied look of a cornered animal.

"Ask him if he needs a lift," Pearl said.

Raeven couldn't do it: she found the idea appalling, but he saved her the trouble by mumbling, "I'm fine, not going far."

"Lean back, Raev." When she did, she noted the wooden chest bound in chains, held under his arm, tight against his side. Pearl leaned over her and smiled. Her front teeth were smeared with lipstick. "You got a red car?"

"Yes…something happened."

"I'll say. Hope you got insur–" Pearl glanced at the outside mirror between Raeven and the stranger. "Whoa, look at that." The stranger turned. Raeven spun around in her seat. Pearl adjusted the rear-view mirror. Far behind them, the burning car appeared around a bend in the road, engulfed in flames and slowly rolling toward them as if left in neutral on a low incline. Smoke billowed from its flaming tires and its garish light shuddered on the snow covered pines – all strangely beautiful, which made it all the more sinister. "You ought'a get in before that thing gets here," Pearl said to the stranger. "Come on, it's cold. I'll find Sparky for you. He's the town cop."

The dome light snapped on. She reached up, puzzled, but it went out before she touched it. A dull hum rose over the sound of the engine.

"I don't need a lift," Steven said, and though he struggled to remain calm, his voice crackled with anxiety. The headlights began to flicker. The dome light went off and on again. He turned and walked away.

Pearl followed. The engine purred. Tires crunched on the ice.

Steven stopped again. "I'm *fine*," he said, irritated. A smell of burning rubber drifted on the air. Behind them, the flaming car nudged up against a snow bank and stopped until the snow melted beneath the fire and released it and on it came again, slow and steady.

The hum grew louder. Steven looked up and saw the power lines alongside the road swaying back and forth in the wind. The headlights flashed again. The hum deepened. A jet of sparks hissed from a transformer at the top of a pole. "I don't need a lift," he said without lowering his eyes from the humming lines.

"Okay, okay," Pearl said but made no effort to drive away. "But I really think you should…" Another jet shot up, this one higher, brighter, more urgent. "What's going on up there?" she asked, leaning over the steering wheel.

Steven looked from the power line to the burning car and back again. He had to do something, he had to get away from them, had to get *them* away from him. Without warning, he leaned into the window. The chest banged against the door, the chains clattered, and he clamped his hand around Raeven's throat.

She fought back and shoved his hand away. He reached for her again. "Go!" she cried and Steven pulled back when Pearl jammed the shift into first gear and stepped on the gas. The tires spun, the car careened off the far snow bank, and off they went, fishtailing down the road. Once out of sight of the stranger and the burning car, Pearl slowed again and stopped. "What the *hell*? Are you okay?"

"I'm fine," Raeven said though she wasn't. Her heart had not yet stopped racing. She looked in the side-view mirror but saw only firelight above the treetops. "Did you see that thing he had under his arm? That wooden chest thing? Gave me the creeps."

"*That* gave you the creeps? Not the creepy guy who tried to strangle you or the creepy burning car? The creepy *chest* gave you the creeps?"

"Yeah – but he did too, and the car…everything did."

"I'm calling Sparky again," Pearl said and reached for her phone.

4

The following afternoon, Raeven sat at a desk in her room above the funeral parlor where she stared through her veil of limp hair at a blank sheet of lined paper while her iPod shot the sounds of Siouxie and the Banshees singing *Painted Bird* deep into her brain. A word from the song jumped out at her: "Absurd," she said and said it again: "Absurd." She lifted the pen. "Perfect."

Writing her own epitaph, though not a daily habit, was nonetheless a satisfying one. She wrote no name, no date of birth, no date of death, only two words in block letters:

IT'S ABSURD

"Perfect," she said again, and it was. Death could be no more absurd than this…whatever she was doing.

How to get by in life? Raeven could not answer that puzzling question. No matter the occasion, no matter who she was with, or where, she felt lost, misunderstood, and judged; a profoundly lonely stranger in a world that should have been familiar but never was. She often daydreamed about avoiding life's crazy absurdities by doing away with herself but could never quite bring herself to do it. Oh, yes, if a tree fell on her one night while crossing the parking lot, that would be fine. Sometimes she lay in bed and thought if the ceiling suddenly opened up and a guillotine blade dropped, that would be fine too. But do it herself? No. Suicide required more courage than she possessed at that point in her life. And besides, she didn't really want to die. What she really wanted was to *Cease to Exist*, to evaporate into some new realm of no thought, no feeling, and no pain. Soothing oblivion.

She had turned twenty the previous winter on a day in January filled with sickening smells from the kerosene heater and obnoxious banter from the men at the lunch counter. She began the day with a sense of desperation, of hatred of the men, of walls closing in, and by late afternoon was so coiled with frustration she feared she might explode. Her imagined life played out in her mind in an endless loop of horror. Years working in the diner with the same dull, hopeless people. Never finding a soul mate or even a casual friend. Warmth and joy of laughter were never to be hers. People she had known all her life would continue to stare at her, continue to whisper whenever she passed. The town she was born in would be the town she would die in. And then it happened. She looked at the counter, at a plate holding the tooth-mangled remains of a sandwich. Her tip glistened in the florescent light. A dime.

"I must escape," she whispered.

Two minutes later, she quit. It was a mistake to work there in the first place. She couldn't work around people. She needed to find a job more suited to her talents and interests, something involving isolation and maybe dead people. Night security at a morgue. That would do. In truth, she felt she shouldn't have to work at all. Work didn't suit her. She hated sunlight, hated pleasant weather, mirrors, talk of any kind, telephones, and most of all, she hated people.

"Not escape this, not escape here," she whispered that day on the way to her car. "Escape *everything*."

That was when she stopped dead at the sight of a raven in the snow.

Later that night she packed all her black clothes, boots, eyeliners, Tarot cards, her collection of crystals, iPod, and a used laptop into her seventeen-year-old black car for the move sixty-three miles north. "I'll call when I get there," she said to her mother, though she suspected she never would. "It's better this way. I won't bother you anymore with my clothes and piercings, my music."

"I suppose you know best," her mother said with a chilly edge of sarcasm. She stood at the side of the driveway with her arms folded tight across her chest. "You'll be back."

"Maybe. Maybe not. But I have to go."

"Why there? Why up north?"

Raeven shrugged her shoulders with an expression of genuine bewilderment. "I have a feeling that – I don't know what it is, but here…" She touched her chest with her fingertips. "I have to go."

Her mother nodded, though she clearly did not understand. They hugged quickly, stiffly, like two boards briefly stacked together, and as her daughter drove away, Mrs. O'Connor whispered, "Bye Cindy," and turned without a second look and went back inside her mobile home.

Raeven had told the truth when she said she did not understand why she felt compelled to go north. A serious life-changing move would have taken her south to Boston or further to New York City. But north? Up north she would find only towns smaller than her own, with even more suspicious, uncomprehending stares, and less opportunity.

Even so, it was the bravest thing she had ever done. It was the *only* brave thing she had ever done, the only true risk she had ever taken, yet she felt she had no choice. Desperation had pushed her toward the mountains and into the anonymous new world of Burne Notch.

No one knew her there. No one there had ever heard of Cindy O'Connor (a name she would never again utter aloud if she could possibly avoid it.) No one there knew anything about the Trailer of Pain, as she would have referred to her family home when talking to a friend, if she'd ever had a friend. Up north, she could become the person she truly was and live with the name she had chosen for herself after seeing the Raven of Destiny in the snow.

She would tell no one her real name. She would tell no one of her past. As her new self, her *true* self, as Raven – no, *Raeven*, even better – she would embrace her otherness, her isolation and her gloom. She would no longer hope to belong and fit in. She would no longer try. She would inhabit the fringes and the shadowy places where she felt most at home and when the time came – *if* the time came, she would finally summon the courage to do what she needed to do in order to Cease to Exist.

She found her job at the Golden Panda restaurant on her third day in Burne Notch. She had stopped in for a container of white rice and saw the surprising sight of the tall, non-Asian Pearl Morgan racing around the dining room, clearly in need of assistance. On her way out she saw a help wanted sign near the front door.

She didn't want to work in a restaurant, but two things became clear very quickly: she needed money and restaurant work was the only job available and the only work she was qualified to do.

She returned the next day for an interview wearing all black, platform boots, a leather skirt, and a silver stud through her left eyebrow. Pearl took one look at her and said, "Who died?" When Raeven responded with only an unsmiling stare, Pearl knew Joe would never hire her. On her application, she claimed to have no last name. Joe said she had to have a last name. How could he cut her a check otherwise? "You can pay me in cash," she said but he persisted. This was unexpected. She hadn't thought of a last name. "All right, my last name is Raeven, also with an *e* after the *a*," she said without thinking about it."

"I thought your first name was Raeven with an *e* after the *a*."

"It is. They're both Raeven, both spelled the same way."

Joe wrote it out: *Raeven Raeven*.

In the line marked address, she wrote: *Marcotte's Funeral Parlor, above viewing chapel*, and for previous employment, she wrote only one word: *Bat*.

"Joke," she said without a smile when Joe looked up from the form.

"Are you from around here?" he asked, fascinated.

"I am now."

"From where?"

"Somewhere else."

He surprised Pearl by offering her the job then and there. He didn't even flinch when she said she would prefer not to wear a uniform, though she might consider a black apron if he insisted.

Her black hair hung limp and mournful over most of her face and hung below her shoulders. Her wardrobe, invariably black, ranged from floor length Victorian dresses to leather bustiers and corsets barely seen beneath flowing black robes and featured a bewildering array of accessories: fingerless leather gloves, tarnished silver chains and buckles, fishnet stockings, hats and veils, black faux-fur coats, combat boots, black ostrich plumes; all dependent upon the day and mood. Thick black mascara raccooned her eyes. Her fingernails too – black. She sometimes wore black lipstick, but never glossy: it looked more like soot than lipstick, as though an obscure initiation rite had required her to kiss the inside of a chimney. Occasionally she wore actual soot as eyeshadow, and even tried it as rouge, though she gave it up when she saw it marred the effect of her ghoulish, drowning-victim pallor. Though rarely seen, she wore a small bit of red in the form of a heart stabbed and dripping blood tattooed on the back of her right shoulder (another tattoo, the word *doom*, had been inked in home-made tiny black letters on the inside of her left wrist). Last, she wore a touch of gold in the form of a class ring from a school she never heard of, bought at a flea market for its black onyx stone.

She turned up the volume on the iPod and sang along. A few seconds later she stopped, turned her head, and sniffed. Something...she looked over her shoulder. Burning oil. She removed her earphones. A smoke detector's shrill call came from somewhere downstairs, muffled and distant, maybe from the main house. *Seriously? Another fire?*

She opened the front door of her studio apartment on the second floor of Marcotte's Funeral Parlor. Smoke hovered in the stairwell. "Mr. Marcotte?"

A calm voice wafted up the stairs. "No need to be alarmed."

"What's going on?"

"Nothing serious I'm sure." Her landlord appeared in the smoke at the foot of the stairs like an underfed demon. "I've called the Fire Department. You may wish to evacuate to be on the safe side. I, myself, was on the way out the door when you called."

She threw on her coat and slipped her feet into her boots and, within seconds, a wail of sirens shuddered through the walls. "Evacuate," she muttered and scanned the room; bed, clothing, books...*what should I take?* The siren wailed, louder, closer. She couldn't think. The window flashed with red when a fire truck rumbled into the driveway.

She ran to the bed and grabbed a small stuffed monkey and ran down the stairs. Yellowish brown smoke coiled around the lights. Every breath felt like a coat of dirty oil brushed upon her lungs. She ran past the funeral chapel where a body lay in an open casket against the far wall, surrounded by swirling smoke, and she exited through the front door at the same moment the siren's wail choked off and several pick-ups and cars roared up behind the ancient fire truck. Norris Marcotte stood in the driveway in his trench coat and Burberry scarf looking as much like an embalmed cadaver as was possible while still alive. His wife Beth, as obese as he was emaciated, stood to his right. Behind them stood their son Raleigh, part-time hearse driver and, in winter, part-time worker on the town snow-plow with Sparky. His friend and coworker on the snowplow, Chip Dubec, stood nearby, tall and muscular with black hair and bright blue eyes, as handsome as Raleigh was hideous, yet the same in personality and temperament – two identically odious peas in the same pod, as far as Raeven was concerned.

She approached Mr. Marcotte, still wiping the smoke from her eyes. "Were you planning to tell me?"

Raleigh laughed through his nose. Raeven glared at him. The elder Marcottes were ghoulish (which appealed to her), but Raleigh made her skin crawl. He rarely spoke. He stared and grinned, and his grin was so threatening and sexual it made her cheeks burn. She turned away, only to be confronted by Chip Dubee's haughty sneer. She shook her head and turned from them all with a shudder.

Volunteer firemen rushed about the funeral parlor in search of a fire. One enthusiastic young man broke a window with his axe. Several minutes later Sparky Grant approached the Marcottes and said: "Minor stuff, no problem."

"Did you put it out?" Beth Marcotte asked.

"Well, no. Just turned the furnace off. She was smoking up

some. How did it happen?"

"I was with a client," Norris said with a shrug. "We were in the display room when suddenly – smoke. Possible fire. Went to the office. Called you. Have no idea beyond that."

Sparky lifted the front of his fire helmet. "It'll be all right now, but you'll have that smell around for a while." He released the helmet, thinking it would fall forward, but instead it tilted back, carried by its own weight, and clattered on the driveway. He picked it up with an awkward laugh and turned to Raeven. "So Pearl told me you two ran across a guy up on the Coachlight Road, the one whose car caught fire. She said he tried to do something to you."

Raeven heard Raleigh snuffle through his nose behind her. "No, he didn't," she said. "I think he was lost."

"He's lost all right," Sparky said and turned to Raleigh and Chip. "We saw his car when we were plowing, right?" The young men nodded but didn't say a word. "I don't know what could'a happened, I can't quite figure it out. He's still around. Howie called me from the hardware store and said he was there not two hours ago. And he was at the church yesterday before this all happened. Told Father Toomey his name was Steven Wilcox." Norris Marcotte uttered a gasp of surprise. When Sparky asked if he knew him, the mortician shook his head and said he didn't, not at all, suddenly remembered something he forgot to do, nothing important, nothing at all.

"Anyway," Sparky continued, turning back to Raeven after a lingering gaze at the red-faced mortician, "anyway, that might not be his real name. Who knows? I found out that car was reported stolen from Logan Airport and I think he might be involved in a burglary at the church. Howie thought so too, said the guy was acting awful strange. You know that great big propane tank in the back? Howie said the thing toppled over on its own and almost fell on that guy, nearly broke through the floor…but I guess that wasn't anyone's fault, just weird, that's all. So if you happen to see him…" He turned to include the Marcottes in the conversation. "If you see him, call the station. My sister Judy will call me and I'll handle it from there."

Norris returned a stiff smile.

"Very strange guy," Sparky said and Raeven agreed. He looked at her hand and smiled. "Nice monkey."

She stared at him, confused, and then her breath stopped. She looked down. Her fingers were closed around a small brown monkey with a tan face. Joe Li had given it to her after winning it at the carnival the previous October. "Oh," she whispered and her heart skipped a beat when she realized it was the only thing she rescued from the fire.

After the last of the firemen left and Norris closed the chapel door, his wife turned to him and said, "What in heaven's name was all that about?" Norris put his forefinger to his lips and led her into the display room where twenty-two polished caskets reclined along the sides of the long showroom, each one horizontal upon its own stand and glistening beneath its own subdued pin spot. Her eyes widened when he reached into his pocket and fished out a tightly rolled wad of fifty and twenty-dollar bills. "Nearly seven thousand dollars," he said. "Tax-free, assuming we don't declare it, which, of course, we won't."

"Where did you get it?"

"The man Sparky is looking for, Steven Wilcox," Norris said. "Uh-huh, the very same," he said in answer to Beth's raised eyebrows. "The client I was with when the smoke appeared. As Sparky said, he was indeed quite strange. Scruffy. Nervous." Norris pointed to a plain casket in the shadows at the far end of the display room, made of cheap plywood with a thin veneer of varnished pine and lined with powder blue cloth. A dark blue pine tree had been silk screened on the interior of the lid. "He bought that casket," he said. "Lot 26."

"Who died?"

"He never got around to telling me. I expect he'll call later. I tried to interest him in one of the more expensive models. I explained that Lot 26 was used mostly as a cremation casket, but he insisted. Not only that, he insisted on that particular casket – that very one. If it was only to be used for show, he didn't want it. I agreed, of course. We can easily get another from the supplier for the showroom. He asked for a vault too. I arranged for a burial plot at St. Bernadette's Cemetery, but he came back to the vault and asked if we had something stronger than the standard six inch width of concrete. I told him about the twelve inch. In all these years, I have yet to use one, but he latched onto the idea, even after I pressed him to spend his money on a more upscale casket. Like this one," Norris said, stroking the wood of a richly-polished mahogany coffin he called Pallbearer's Choice.

"Is there a point to this?" Beth asked and wrinkled her nose at the ceiling. "That smoky smell is awful, I wonder what we can do about it."

"No real point, no," Norris said, "though the items he bought came to considerably less than seven thousand dollars, which was the only point I needed. And then came the smoke. At the first whiff he turned on his heels and fled."

"He must have a fear of fire," Beth said, uninterested, still gazing at the ceiling.

Norris agreed. "From the look in his eyes, I'd say an *extreme* fear of fire."

5

"I can't…" Steven's voice choked, his eyes were blinded by tears.

The line crackled with static and shocked silence. "Let me call you back," Dr. Sweeney said in his musical Irish accent.

"No, it's too late, it's too…" Grief welled up and overflowed, shattering his words. He leaned his forehead against the cold metal of the pay phone. "It's too late."

Dr. Sweeney responded, careful and slow: "You found it."

"It's all true."

"Oh, come now, Steven. And wouldn't you be looking at me askance were I to dare suggest such a thing?"

"It's *true*," Steven shouted and in a hoarse whisper said, "Every word of the manuscript. True."

Silence, and then a quiet, "My God."

"The gold, the chest…the thing inside…"

"Don't do anything Steven, don't – "

"It's too late." Steven held the receiver to his ear, pressing as hard as he could to stop the tremble in his hand. "I know what I have to do."

"You *don't* know. And I say this now as strenuously as I can: you must not use fire. You must not even think of using fire."

"It's too late," Steven said and his tears trickled into his beard.

"Has fire…?" Sweeney began, but stopped as if afraid to finish the question.

"It's too late to stop it. Fire is everywhere, it's coming from everywhere, it's too late."

Steven shuddered at the memory of the cigarette lighter popping out after he set the chest down on the front seat of the rented car. He brushed it onto the floor and it lit something on fire under the seat, paper or the carpet – he couldn't tell. He opened the door and set the chest down on the road and slid it away from the car. A second later, something silver flashed and the cigarette lighter tumbled onto the road. The hair on the back of his neck rose at the sight of it lurching over the ice toward the chest, struggling to reach it, glowing brighter and leaving a trail of melted ice behind. He leaped out and crushed it with the heel of his boot, and the fire spread inside the car, forcing him to abandon it.

"Too late," he said again.

"It's not," Sweeney returned. "You must wait for me. Do you still have the manuscript? It may help us."

Steven could no longer speak. He tried, but his voice lay trapped in his throat. He pulled the receiver from his ear. Words came through, but smaller now, fading, "...you *must* wait for me," and cut off with the drop of the receiver into its cradle.

He had heard enough. He hadn't killed him. That was all he needed to know.

The unexpected pay phone at the closed-up motel stood as a small comforting jewel set into the night, the only visible light. Steven discovered the small cottages on his first night in town, before he started looking for the silver cross. He broke the lock on the back door of the one furthest from the road and always approached it on foot through the woods to prevent any suspicious tracks leading from the road. When he had the car, he parked it at a distance.

Each cottage contained two single beds, a table and a small woodstove that he hadn't dared use for fear of someone seeing the smoke, and later, for fear of the prowling fires.

He had left the chest unguarded and buried in the snow near the back door while he went to the hardware store and funeral home and he nearly collapsed with relief when he returned and found it still interred beneath its burial mound.

The cottage windows and back door had been boarded up the previous October and night and day had become one inside, as dark and cold as a tomb. He had sprawled upon the bed fully clothed with his mind tormented by dreams of fire and snakes, and now, nearly twenty-four hours after finding the cave, he lay there again, drenched in sweat in spite of the cold, staring at the circular ripples of lights made by his flashlight on the wooden ceiling.

How *could* this have happened? How could a life so full of promise and expectation have taken such a despairing turn?

Such questions were useless now. He knew that but asked them all the same. They were a way to pass the dark hours and didn't matter. It was too late for anything that truly mattered.

He knew what he had to do.

It was the only way out.

A terrible inevitability began to form around it, as though it had been part of his plan all along, even when his thoughts revolved solely around the search for the gold. First there was the money used to buy the casket, the vault and an obscure plot in the local cemetery. How had he thought to bring so much with him? He didn't remember withdrawing it, didn't know where it came from. And then came the trip from Boston, the car, the revolver now lying on the table beside him – he remembered none of it. He had no memory of renting a car (*did I rent it?*) or where he got the gun. How could he remember? He was a different person then, operating with another's mind, one filled with fire that led him to the place where the gold lay hidden for over a thousand years.

Inevitability.

And then there was the old man, Mr. Parenteau, found outside his house, his heart failed "possibly due to electrocution by lightning." That's what the mortician told him when he asked about the body in the chapel. "He had burn marks, and putting two and two together, we assume he was struck by that strange lightning."

But the lightning couldn't have killed him on purpose. Steven remembered the ball lightning and, after, how the charges wove together and hovered above the forest like a falcon before slamming down somewhere beyond his sight. *It's not connected. It can't be. I'm the target – why would it go for someone else and not me?* Then again, why not? So many strange unconnected things coming together…

Everything falling into place.

He moved to the table where the stolen manuscript lay beside his own translation written on a yellow legal pad, and the items he had purchased at the hardware store: rubber gloves, hacksaw, fire extinguisher; and in the center of all, the curse, the hateful thing, the cause of all ruination: the wooden chest.

He began his work. The hacksaw blade glimmered in the flashlight's glow and spit flecks of rust onto the table and floor. He cut through the two chains that bound the chest. They dropped to the floor with a dull clatter. A thin iron band remained, so deteriorated he could pull it apart with his fingers, and he would…but not then. He had one thing left to do.

He carried the chest outside, set it in the snow, and returned to the table where he gathered the ancient pages. He carried them to the cold wood stove and slid the circular iron stove lid to the side.

He checked the door again to be sure it was closed and returned to the stove.

He lit a match and held it to the edge of Brendan's nautical chart.

A small flame crawled up the side.

It had to be done. No one could know. No one could search for it a second time, or worse, find it.

The page began to curl. Smoldering black spread over the new world, *Terra Draconis,* and into the sea. Fire followed to the centerline and moved past it to the ancient Irish coastline, blackening and burning as surely as any Viking raid. Tears rose to his eyes. In spite of all, he was still a scholar and believed with all his heart that he was committing a crime against civilization. His life's goals and all he stood for went up in flames as thoroughly as the fragile page, but he had no choice. It had to be done.

A second page followed, and four more, and the stove roared when he dropped the remaining pages inside – all but one. He then pulled his translation out in handfuls from the legal pad and these too he consigned to the flames.

He held the last remaining page of the original manuscript over the stove but pulled it back and crumpled it into a ball. "Not this," he whispered and stuffed it into his pocket.

The ceiling shuddered with a wide circular glow of orange light that narrowed and disappeared like a full lunar eclipse when he slid the round iron lid back into place. The stovepipe clicked as it carried heat and smoke straight up through the roof. He held the fire extinguisher on his lap and stared with every muscle tense and every thought concentrated on the stove. If it moved, if it so much as quivered, he sat coiled to spring from the chair and run from the cabin.

Nothing happened. The muffled roar of the fire faded. He moved the chair closer.

Almost over. No one would know. No one could possibly know. He lifted the lid and looked inside. Fragile black skeletons of pages broke into smoldering pieces. One drifted up, carried out of the stove on an updraft of heat. Its edges glowed but quickly died and the ash fell. A second, larger piece floated up. Steven waved it from his face and looked inside again. Ashes drifted up the stovepipe.

He sat back, filled with crushing sadness. All over now. Failure had risen like an unexpected inferno to consume his life, his plans and goals, all of them gone, never to come again.

A sudden glow upon the wall behind the stove caught his eye. He stared at it, barely able to summon enough curiosity to wonder what it might be. He looked over his shoulder. The thin ashy residue of the burned page floated in the air. Its edges still glowed, but instead of fading, the glow spread.

He reached up to touch it but snapped his hand back, startled, when it puffed into flame. It shot across the room, swooping down when it reached the wall, and up and back again, streaking through the air like a bat with a trail of smoke marking every twist and turn. It flew to the door and veered away to spiral through the cottage before racing to the boarded windows and back to the door again.

It was trying to get outside, Steven realized. Trying to get to the chest!

He looked for something to hit it, a broom or blanket, but another thought stopped him cold. *The stovepipe…the rising ashes…*

He ran to the door and threw it open. Thousands of fire-bats streaked through the air. Some hissed and disintegrated when they landed on the snow, Others spiraled in wild gyrations that lit the nearby forest in wavering shades of orange. Most had gathered upon the chest where they writhed and jostled like mindless spermatozoa mobbing an egg cell to be the first to break through. The one inside the cabin tore past him and seared his cheek in its rush to escape.

He grabbed the fire extinguisher and ran to the squirming flames while shielding his face with his arm. "Get away!" he screamed and the fire-bats rose in a solid, blazing mass. He pulled the trigger on the extinguisher. A white cloud exploded. Those he hit disappeared but there were too many and they swarmed around him, burning him with their wings. He reeled away and looked up at the roof where the manuscript's ashes poured from the stovepipe like real bats from a cavern. Lifting into the air, each particle burst into flame and swooped down to join the surrounding frenzy.

Steven lifted the chest and staggered through the snow but the fire-bats followed to torment him with a sound of a thousand torches waved in the air. He held the extinguisher high as he ran, trailing a cloud of white behind. He passed between two cottages. Wind rushed down the road and sent the bats tumbling and he ran with the soot-blackened chest in his arms. More struggled to reach him, but the wind blew too strong and sent them hissing into the snow or higher into the air where they fizzled and spiraled with their fires dying and their wings crumbling and drifting into ash.

6

"If I hear that effing song one more time…"

"Leave him alone, Pearl." Joe Li was also sick of the endless loop of songs from *Annie* but put up with it as long as it made his Uncle happy. The night after the blizzard had been slow due to the poor conditions of the roads. The last customer left a little after nine and Pearl and Raeven now sat at the bar while Joe wiped it down with a rag. In the kitchen, Uncle Lung sang along with his CD player about the sun coming out tomorrow in a cracked, piercing, off-key voice that only occasionally ventured somewhere close to the actual tune.

"Collapsed!" Pearl bellowed. "Enough with the howling like a tom-cat, Jesus God, that's so annoying I could kill myself."

The CD player stopped. The door swung open. Uncle Lung leaned into the dining room and shouted, "Garbage-y!"

"Garbage-y yourself, you old grump." Uncle Lung withdrew into the kitchen, but not before sending a withering frown her way. "And don't screech anymore!" she called after him.

Pearl had worked at the Golden Panda since the day it opened and was as much a fixture as the cheap plastic lanterns, red tassels, and posters of the Great Wall of China tacked to the unassuming paneling. She wore black eyeliner that met at the outside corner of each eye and trailed off at the temple in an attempt to recreate the epicanthic folds of Asian eyes, "for atmosphere," she explained whenever anyone asked (though how she imagined her light green eyes and red hair might add to the Chinese atmosphere remained a mystery). "Atmosphere" was also the excuse she gave for the ancient red satin jacket she wore night after night. It originally had a golden bird embroidered on the back, but was so old and worn the design had devolved into in a mass of hanging gold threads.

Joe dropped the rag in the sink and leaned against the ice bin. Something was wrong with Raeven. The two women had their traditional after-work drinks in front of them, a Mai-Tai for Pearl and a pewter goblet of pomegranate-flavored tea for Raeven; but unlike most nights, she took no part in the conversation.

She sat beside Pearl with her eyes lowered and hair dangling and said nothing unless spoken to, and even then, gave only morose, one-word answers. It reminded Joe of the days when she first started working at the Panda and he assumed she was preoccupied with the fire at the funeral parlor. She told him she had already put most of her clothes in the trunk of her car to prevent the smell of smoke from permeating the fabric (though she did not tell him she had rescued the carnival monkey he had given her before all other things, before clothes or books or music; she did not mention the monkey at all).

Raeven wasn't beautiful. That was undeniable. (According to

most of the regular male customers at the bar, Pearl was not only nearly twice Raeven's age but was about twenty times more attractive too.) Joe thought the strange young woman was beautiful...well, maybe not *beautiful* beautiful, but interesting. She certainly wasn't as hideous as some of those customers whispered across the bar. Chip Dubee referred to her as "the corpse" or sometimes "the dead dog." She was interesting, unique, with an icy demeanor that gave not the slightest trace of encouragement to a potential suitor, and – most alluring of all (for him) – she seemed wholly unaware of it. Even better, she seemed wholly unconcerned. She didn't care.

Romantic Goth. That was the category he placed her in after finding the term online. Even now he couldn't help but think of her as the only truly interesting and unique person in Burne Notch...the way she placed her hands on the bar, with each one covered in lace so old and delicate he was amazed they hadn't ripped. Even that was interesting. It wasn't beautiful but it was romantic. It was interesting. It was unique. It was cool.

"Did you lose anything in the fire?" he asked.

She stared at her goblet. Her hair hung flat and lifeless over her face. "No."

"Good thing you got out, huh?"

"Go on, Raev, answer him," Pearl said with a smirk. "Say, 'nah, I wish I burned alive.'"

Joe smiled. "Yeah, stupid question." Not knowing what else to do, he asked if anyone wanted a refill. "I better not," Pearl said. "I gotta get home and check on the birds."

"Oh, to heck with your birds, have another."

Pearl reluctantly agreed – "but gimme one of Raeven's horrible pomegranate tea concoctions this time." Pearl had an enormous collection of exotic birds and worried about leaving them alone whenever she worked a double shift. "How about you, Raev? Another?"

"No." She stood and put on her long black coat.

Pearl shrugged and gave Joe a wide-eyed 'who knows?' glance. "You're going to stay in your place with that smoky smell?"

"Yes."

"Suit yourself. Want me to pick you up tomorrow night?"

"That's fine. Or I'll drive. Doesn't matter."

Joe followed Raeven to the front door to unlock it. As he turned the key, she stood in the darkened foyer behind him with her black coat and black hair melding into the shadows. "Would you..." he started to ask, but hesitated. He wanted to cheer her up but wasn't sure this was the best time or way to do it. He pushed his glasses up. "Would you like to go out sometime? You know, nothing too…you know, maybe a movie or something?"

She didn't answer. He unlocked the door and opened it. Light from the Golden Panda sign in the parking lot spread over his shoes. The silence was awful, like a weight dropped on his shoulders. He stood in the foyer, paralyzed, with blood rushing to his face, waiting for her to say something. "Would you?" he asked again.

"No."

7

Steven arrived at the funeral home with hands raw from the long walk with the chest and his beard frozen over with residue of breath. The imposing white building with the manicured hedges and yew trees sat back from the road, solemn and dark but for a front window flickering with light from a television inside. He slipped along the side of the house behind the yews to avoid the light from a nearby street lamp and came to the door of the funeral chapel.

Locked.

He stepped back and saw the window broken by the volunteer fireman earlier that day, now covered with a square of heavy canvas. He slipped his hand beneath it and felt open air. He loosened the canvas at the bottom, pulled it away from the pane, and lowered the wooden chest to the floor inside.

A car approached. He froze, blending into the shadows, and watched it pass. Closer, the street lamp spilled its glow upon the icy driveway and filled it with a million flecks of light that mirrored the sky overhead, glittering with stars. And it was cold, so cold. He took a deep breath: frigid air filled his nostrils and threatened to freeze his gathered tears. "Go," he whispered. "Go."

He pushed the canvas aside, turned his back to the house, and laid his hands on the windowpane to hoist himself up.

He did not see the thin dagger of glass still embedded in the lower sash. He dropped. It tore through his jeans and slid into the back of his leg like a knife into a sheath. He gasped and reeled from the shock, desperate to scream but stifling it in his throat. He gripped the sides of the window and moved his leg forward. The glass broke off with a snap.

He swiveled around and dropped to the floor inside and reached for the glass. It lay deep in the muscle with less than an inch protruding. He tried to grab it. His fingers slipped in blood. He tried again but then – "No," he whispered. "Keep it. Feel it."

He carried the chest down the hall, dragging his leg, jolting with pain with every step. A hot tickle of blood rolled down the back of his knee and over his calf. The caskets in the display room lay as before, now lit by wide rays of muted light cast by the street lamp seeping through the windows. Down the center row he went, passing through light and shadow, lurching toward the casket called Lot 26 reclining at the far end with its lid open. In the darkness, its blue satin took on a dark gray hue and the silk-screened pine tree, black.

He set the chest on the floor and stuck his hand in his front pocket and into his coat. "Damn!" he whispered, realizing he had forgotten to bring a jackknife – but there it was again.

Inevitability.

Everything falling into place.

He spat on his fingers and washed the end of the broken glass clean of blood before grasping it tight between his thumb and forefinger. He pulled. The glass dagger moved. His fingers slipped and he whimpered. He grabbed the side of the casket and reached for the bloody shard once more. *Now!*

The glass eased from the muscle with a gush of following blood. "Oh God, oh my God," he whispered and pulled it from his leg. He clenched his jaw and closed his eyes, fighting down the pain. Seconds passed. A full minute. He opened his eyes again and wiped the bloody glass on his jeans and lifted the pillow in the casket. With a single quick stab, he opened a wound in the satin lining beneath.

And now the wooden chest. He jammed his fingers beneath the rusted final seal.

It snapped apart. Flecks of rust fell on the carpet.

Unused for centuries, the leather hinges crackled. The lid whined open and there it was, nestled in the rotted remains of what may have been a homespun monk's robe: shimmering, black, glossy as a serpent's eye, and vast within its confines, as if the darkest places of the earth, the undiscovered tombs, hidden bat-ridden caverns and depths of the lightless sea had concentrated every varying shade of midnight black into this one glistening shell.

He lifted it out of the chest and set it over the tear in the lining. The satin ripped at the edges. He pushed it down, forced it through, the torn sides closed, and the egg was gone.

He replaced the pillow. No one would ever see it again. It

would be interred in the casket and the thick concrete vault and buried under six feet of earth, protected from all fire, all flame, all warmth of any kind, hidden away for eternity. "No," he whispered with a sudden flare of panic. "Not like this." He picked up the empty chest and backed away from the coffin. "Not like this!"

He followed the spotted trail of his own blood between the rows of coffins, down the hall and past the chapel to the broken window where he clawed his way outside and fell beside the yew trees.

Blood seeped from his leg. He clapped his hand over the back of his thigh and jammed his fingers through his torn jeans into the wound. Pain exploded and filled him with raw sensation. Blood coated his fingers, slick and hot: he wiped them over his face, over his beard. He drove his hands into the snow and lifted a crunching handful to his face. So cold, everything so cold, so *alive*! Blood, snow, cold, night and stars, always there, never really seen, never really felt. "Beautiful," he whispered, "Beautiful…"

A car pulled into the driveway. He flattened himself against the clapboards with a startled gasp. Headlights swept across the garage and yews. The car stopped. The lights snapped off. A young woman climbed out.

"Beautiful…"

Raeven did not notice him. He was a shadow, the same as all the other shadows. When he moved, she thought he was a yew tree swaying in the wind. But then he stepped into the glow of the streetlight; the man from the Coachlight Road, the car thief who tried to strangle her. He looked like a ghoul, thin and wild-eyed, with blood smeared over his face and saturating his jeans.

"Beautiful," he whispered and she fell back against her car, terrified. "I won't hurt you," he said and approached with halting steps. "I don't want to be alone, not for this." He stood before her with one bloody hand outstretched and the other in his coat pocket. "Please don't run. I can't do it. Not like this. I can't do it alone. I don't *want* to be alone. I need someone with me. Let me look at you. Please."

"Don't…" Raeven whispered.

"The night, you are the night," he whispered – that's what she thought he said, but before she could respond or even begin to wonder what he meant by it, he stepped up close and took his hand from his coat pocket.

He jammed it into hers.

"What are you…?" she started, but before she could finish, he took his hand from her pocket and clapped it on her shoulder. Raeven was so frightened she felt hollow, as if she'd been emptied of all but her thundering heart. He looked into her eyes. She was startled to see his were filled with tears.

"Beautiful," he whispered again and leaned closer. His lips touched hers. She closed her eyes and held her breath, terrified to move, but his kiss was gentle, no more than a touch of cold lips upon hers, and he pulled back.

He smiled a small, mournful smile and lifted his hand. Raeven saw a glint of steel. She opened her mouth to cry out, but had no time. He twisted the barrel and pulled the trigger. A flash, a crack, his head jerked – a fan of misty red spattered over the white house and he dropped at her feet and stared up at her with deadening eyes while his blood pumped thick and steaming into the snow.

8

Beth Marcotte was incensed. Blood on the house, blood staining the carpets in the hall and showroom, blood smeared upon the wall below the window. "How are we *ever* going to clean this up in time?" Norris tried to calm her: "These things happen," but it didn't help. After the ambulance attendants carried Steven's body the few steps into the mortuary (after first arguing whether or not to bring him to the hospital), Norris tried to calm his wife again. "At least it's over."

But it wasn't. "Oh, no," Beth cried from inside the chapel. She had gone in to turn out the lights and now pointed at the body Raeven had seen when rushing from the fire earlier that day. "Look at Mr. Parenteau."

The old man who died in the lightning storm lay in peaceful repose in his casket with his face and suit dotted with black oil. Long streaks of grime cut across the silk-screened pine tree inside the opened lid.

Norris looked up. The oil had dripped from a heating duct hanging directly over the casket. "Oh my, that must have come from the furnace." A drop fell and landed on Mr. Parenteau's powdered cheek with a muffled splat.

"What are we going to do?" Beth asked. "The wake is tomorrow morning. The casket is ruined."

"I can redo his face easily enough. And I suppose we can get the jacket dry cleaned before the service begins. But the casket…that oil has seeped into the lining."

"You'll have to replace it."

"I can't," Norris said.

"We have no choice. Get one from the cellar."

"I can't, Beth. It's Lot 26. This is the last one we had. It will take days to get another."

"What about the one in the display room?"

"Oh, no, we can't." He reminded her of the deal he had made with Steven, how he promised to use that exact same casket. "Poor fellow. He requested that coffin specifically, and all along he was buying it for himself. Rather poignant, isn't it?"

"Not as poignant as the Parenteaus seeing that filthy lining," Beth snapped. "Use the display. It's the same model. No one will know the difference." She pointed at Mr. Parenteau's damaged coffin. "We'll use this one for Wilcox and insist on a closed casket ceremony. I don't know why you decided on having a service anyway. If there *are* any mourners, we'll tell them it's closed because he was disfigured by the gunshot. That way no one will see the oil, no one will know the difference."

"I suppose..."

"All right then," she returned. "Let's clean up Mr. Parenteau and switch the caskets. No one will ever know." Norris stared at the corpse and did not turn away until Beth turned out the lights and asked if he would need Raleigh to drive the hearse.

"Hmm?" he asked, still pondering the ethics of the casket switch.

"The hearse. Is Mr. Parenteau going to be buried in St. Bernadette's?"

"No," Norris said.

"Where then?"

"Nowhere," Norris replied. "He's going to be cremated."

9

The casket slid on the rollers.

The iron door slammed.

Gas jets hissed.

Fire lifted. Shellac blistered.

Brass handles heated and began to glow.

Wood caught fire with a puff. Varnish melted and fell in molten drops. Inside, the lining caught fire, the suit coat and trousers puffed into flame. Hair crackled and skin blistered. Rosary beads melted.

The satin beneath the blazing pillow burned away and fire

touched it, fire embraced it, hot fire caressed the black secret so long embedded in gold and darkness, and it quivered and glowed.

Fire-bats lifted from the flames. Confined and frantic, they swarmed over it, wriggling as before, like spermatozoa at an egg.

This time one broke through.

A crack formed and the remaining fire-bats drew together into a single jet of flame that poured into the black shell like a fevered lover to expand it and fill it with life. Licks of fire surged in and out, the crack widened, the egg fractured and broke apart, and with a final triumphant rush of fire, something wicked was born.

10

Far, far to the west, on the other side of the earth, an old, old woman shuffled to a table carrying a steaming pot of oolong tea. The fire she had built to ward off the cold had done its work and her small, nearly bare house bore no further trace of the chill she felt earlier in the day. Her joints were stiff and sore, but she was used to it and often woke with pain.

She poured the tea and breathed in the fragrant steam. It wouldn't be long now. Another year or two, maybe even this winter. She would sleep and pain would pass forever.

Jin Feng was eighty-seven that year. She had no fear of death. Those occasional twinges of uncertainty she'd had as a young woman now seemed no different than anything else from that time; distant and golden, a dream of the past. She had nothing left but the gentle slip from life. It was a journey she hoped would not take place in her sleep. She wanted to be awake and quiet and aware. Her granddaughter did not understand, and that was as it should be. She had much to learn before she reached the time of understanding.

She lifted the cup to her lips, but suddenly froze.

Her hands began to tremble. She dropped the cup. Tea spattered over the table and Jin Feng sat back in her chair and stared straight ahead at nothing.

Not long after, a young woman stepped into the tiny house and stopped at the door, startled by the silence. Grandmother did not often speak and was not one for making noise around the house, but this was more than the silence of an old woman sleeping. It was the silence of emptiness, of no one there.

She looked at the table. A teacup lay on its side. Tea leaves lay spread in a fan over the bare wood.

She pushed her hood back and released her long black hair.

She called but no one answered. She opened the front door and called outside, but again heard no answer. Wind rustled in the pines. Several large black birds sat on a barren branch, silent, staring. Maybe crows, but much larger than crows. She looked down at the snow. Her own tracks blended with a smaller set, hers coming in, the others going out, accompanied by the indentations made by a cane.

She closed the door and leaned against it. Grandmother rarely went out these days, not on her own, and especially not on such a cold day. And then another thought...the floorboards creaked when she crossed to the hearth and knelt beside it. She lifted a brick and peered into a hidden chamber.

The golden box was gone.

11

Far to the east, high atop a jagged windswept island, a large flat stone quivered in the moonlight. Something deep inside began to throb. Tiny fissures crackled over its sides and through them came a red glow beating with the steady *thump, thump, thump* of a pulse newly revived. A crack formed at its base and jolted up the side. Flecks of stone fell away. The crack raced toward a hole in the center that once held a mast long since burned to ash, and the rock shook as though the earth itself trembled and Skellig Michael had finally been conquered and began to break apart.

Rainwater inside the hole came to a boil. The fissure widened. Startled gulls and gannets shrieked from their perches and took to the air to wheel and call in the moonlight, and a resounding crack echoed through the ruined monastery when the rock split in two.

One of the larger seabirds, a gannet with white feathers and pale blue eyes, spiraled down, attracted by the throbbing glow deep within the broken stone. It settled down clumsily and, after cocking its head and staring for a moment, it leaned forward to snap at the rock. A flare of fiery light darted out with the same triumphant rush of flame that had pierced the shell across the western sea. The gannet shrieked and slammed against the side of the oratory in a tangled heap of smoke and singed feathers.

The light in the rock dimmed and with a slowly ebbing *thump...thump.....thump...*it went out.

The gannet lay on the ground beside it, motionless.

Others circled above and filled the night with their cries. One by one the birds landed on the ruins and settled in the crags and broken walls and the wind hummed a dreary song above the broken rock, already cooled and dead as the gannet.

But the gannet was not dead.

It moved....

It paused into stillness..

It moved again.

With a sudden gasp, it rolled onto its side and onto its feet and lifted its wings, outstretched and black with rising smoke, and it climbed upon the shattered rock. The moon hung low over the horizon and the gannet, now blind in one eye, hissed and stared with the other, pale as mist with a slit pupil; and it spread its blackened wings and stared at the moon, and beyond the moon and over the sea, staring deep into the west.

III.

Gold

John-Richard Thompson

1

Norris Marcotte finished lunch in his office and now stood with his hand on the doorknob, reluctant to enter the mortuary prep-room where Steven Wilcox lay waxed, embalmed and rigor-mortised upon a steel table. This unaccustomed feeling of dread began soon after the Parenteau cremation the night before, with lights dimming and wavering, shadows seen from the corner of his eye, and an imagined sound of claws scrabbling across the linoleum floor, as if a rat had scurried under a workbench.

He opened the door and it swung inward, silent on its hinges. Fluorescent lights above the embalming table hummed and flickered.

The mortician looked around the room: hydraulic body lift, cremation urns, embalming machine, jugs of formaldehyde, cosmetics cabinet, drainage chemicals; nothing out of place until his eyes settled on Steven Wilcox. He stared, perplexed.

The body lay upon the steel table, clad in one of the Salvation Army suits Norris provided to his indigent clients. His mouth gaped wide open with the wax on his lips jagged and torn as if they had been pried apart. A trail of thick grey liquid trickled from the corner of his mouth. Norris touched it…sticky, like mucus. "Oh, that can't be," he whispered and he gingerly sniffed his finger. It had the same peculiar odor he'd lately noticed, but much stronger, a smell of rotting vegetation, wet leaves, a faint trace of sulfur.

He wiped his finger on the inside of Steven's jacket and used the heel of his hand to push on the dead man's chin. Steven's mouth closed with a click, but opened again when he released his grip, slowly, like a clam. He was about to retrieve a clamp and a jar of wax from the cupboard when he noticed something else. Leaning closer, he touched the cadaver's beard and parted the wiry hair with his fingers.

"What in the world…?"

Long thin scratches had gouged the skin from chin to lips.

2

Friday night in the Golden Panda, with every table full. No one could have reasonably expected Uncle Lung to handle every order alone but he refused to work with anyone else. On busy nights the strategy gave the sordid kitchen the look of an insane asylum with one inmate on the loose, running to and fro, shouting and throwing woks. *Bang!* The kitchen doors swung open and slammed against the walls. Customers from all sides added to the din with requests for food ordered long ago; and drinks, more drinks; and, over all, Pearl's booming voice: "I'll garbag-y *you* if you don't give me that moo goo!"

On this night the chaos was particularly acute. Raeven could barely function. She wanted to, she insisted on it, but also insisted on wearing a long black Victorian mourning dress, black lace gloves, a black veil, and her traditional black combat boots. This, along with the occasional mournful, distracted sigh, proved too much for her customers to bear. "Hey!" one snapped at Pearl. "You mind telling Dracula's wife or whatever she is we been waiting a half-hour for our drinks?"

"I'm on it," Pearl said, and escorted her into the kitchen. "Gotta get a grip, ok? You shouldn't have come to work tonight."

"I know," Raeven said with a despondent sigh. "I didn't want to be alone. I can't stop thinking about my poor…"

Her words trailed off and Pearl studied her with a scowling half-squint. "Please don't tell me you were going to say 'my poor Steven', okay? Because if you do, I might ask how some weirdo who tried to rape you on the Coachlight Road—"

"He didn't try to rape me. He tried to strangle me."

"Oh well then, terribly sorry, my mistake. So I might ask how some weirdo who tried to *strangle* you can be your poor anything."

"He could have been mine," Raeven said, weakening.

"Yeah, and he could have been your poor random serial killer for all you know. You're so morbid, Raeven. You admit it, so it's not like I'm not coming up with anything new. The only reason you're going nuts over that guy is because he's dead. Deceased. It's why you encouraged Skeleton Marcotte with this memorial idea, just so you can be all morbid and shit, as if anyone will show up. Listen – head on home. You shouldn't have come tonight. Don't worry, I can handle it…and if I can't, too bad, they'll get over it."

Raeven took her advice and drove home by way of the Coachlight Road, now fully cleared of snow and sparkling with ice. She focused on the road and the play of headlights over the snow banks until she came to the spot where Pearl had come upon Steven's burning car, and farther, to the place where they first saw Steven himself. She slowed and stopped and sat for a moment, staring down the long stretch of empty road before snapping off the headlights.

She turned off the engine and rolled down the window. An icy gust blew her hair back and lifted the veil, now pinned to a feathered hat. She swept it back from her face and opened the door and stepped shivering into darkness.

A glimmer of starlight on the bordering snow banks defined the otherwise darkened Coachlight Road. She felt the bracing chill in her nostrils and fell into the rhythm of her breath and thoughts of Steven and the pointless, gorgeous absurdity of his death until a shiver roused her from this reverie. She was about to climb back inside when she happened to glance up in time to see a shooting star pass overhead.

It streaked across the night sky with a silent radiance far more brilliant than any meteor she had ever seen. It no sooner burned out when another shot across the canvas of stars and dark, and, within seconds, the sky above Burne Notch was striated by glittering bands of light. Swathes of luminous green shimmered among them in mystical, undulating waves. This was the *aurora borealis,* the Northern Lights. Raeven had never seen them before and she leaned against her car, entranced by the display, oblivious to the cold, hesitant to breathe for fear it might cause the lights in the sky to dim and die.

Behind her came a low rustle of boughs. She heard it and turned, but saw nothing.

She looked up again. The Northern Lights brightened, the meteors continued to fall, and together they cast their pulsing glow into the woods and over her car and the frozen road. Again, she sensed a shuffling in the branches beyond the snow bank but saw only darkness and surrounding trees.

"Is someone there?" she called. Her voice sounded small and intrusive.

The sound came again.

Whatever it was, it was coming toward her.

Her hand wandered over the car door in search of the handle. Meteors fell, the sky glowed green, but the faint illuminations only increased her sense of menace when they exposed something hunched in front of the car.

She found the handle and opened the door. The interior dome light spread through the windshield, another shooting star fell, and she stared, bewildered.

A single evergreen no taller than an average Christmas tree stood in the road in front of the car.

Must have been there before. But no, I sat here and looked down the road before I turned the lights off.

A rush of wind exhaled through the woods. She leaned inside the car and snapped on the headlights. The tree stood on the icy road, motionless, with its pale roots spread around the base of its trunk like tentacles.

Beyond it, about twenty feet away, another pine tree stood in the middle of the road. A star fell and joined the headlights to illuminate a third one on the snow bank further along, leaning with its roots spread over the gathered chunks of plowed snow as if frozen in the act of climbing down to join the others.

Someone must have put them there. The thought frightened her and she quickly glanced at the forest before slipping into the car and locking all the doors. *Maybe they fell off a logging truck. I didn't notice them before, that's all.*

They stood without a single bough moving in the wind, yet she could not shake the feeling they remained motionless by choice, tense and watchful, like spiders poised to snag an unsuspecting fly. She started the car and drove around the first tree. When she passed the second, she drove so close that its branches scraped along the passenger door.

She drove a few yards beyond it and stopped while looking in the rear view mirror. The brake lights cast their red glow over the trees, now three of them, motionless in the road behind. *But I only passed two.*

She looked in the side mirror. The one on the snow bank was no longer there.

3

The lights in the sky did not show themselves to Raeven alone. Elizabeth Grey, owner of the field beside Steven's hidden treasure cave, saw them while standing at her front door. Her husband Jerrod had asked her join him in the dairy barn to see if she could help explain why the cows appeared so nervous of late. She studied their skittish behavior and pronounced them all to be 'foolish', thereby (in her mind) solving the mystery beyond all doubt.

"Foolish or not, there's something wrong with them," Jerrod said. "They've been like this since last night."

"Well, I don't know," she said, no longer interested, and trudged back to the house. A somber, dour New Englander, Elizabeth Grey had not yet gotten over her irritation at Jerrod for taking in that dog that belonged to their deceased neighbor, Mr. Parenteau. Tred. What kind of name was that for a dog? When she reached the door, she glanced up and snorted as if disapproving of the sky for making such a spectacle of itself. "Come on, mutt," she sputtered and went inside, no longer interested in the foolish ways of stars and cows.

On the ski slope, Maurice Garand and his teenage son Tim saw the lights while on their nightly routine of riding on the chairlift to check on the lift house before shutting down for the night. Tim saw them first. "What are they?" he called to his father in the chair before him.

"Northern Lights," Maurice yelled over the clanking cables.

The sight enchanted Tim Garand, but his father thought about the lightning of a couple of nights before and wondered if there might be a connection: if so, he didn't want to be caught in the open, not with electricity in the sky. "Timmy," he called over his shoulder. "We're not going to take the lift down tonight."

"Why not?"

Before his father could answer, his chair slid into the lift house entrance. Beside it, empty chairs clattered out through an exit door after rounding a large turret. Tim pushed at the safety bar, trying to open it early so he could jump out as soon as his chair slid inside. As usual, the bar jammed. He hit it with his fist, it clicked open, and his chair swung into the lift house. "Why don't you want to take the lift down?" he asked and leaped off with a single practiced bound. The chair clanged and spun around the turret for its return trip back down the mountain.

"Just don't," Maurice said. "We'll take the toboggan down tonight."

A visitor in the neighboring town saw them too and stared at the shooting stars through the window of his motel room. Unlike those in Burne Notch, he had a distant, more enlarged view and saw the meteors falling within the *aurora borealis* in a pattern, streaking in from different directions and converging above a single point upon the dark mountain. Impossible, but still…he leaned closer to the window and whispered, "What the devil is down there?"

4

"He tried to molest you," Pearl hissed from her seat beside Raeven in the grim, claustrophobic chapel at Marcotte's Funeral Parlor. Beige drapes covered all four walls from floor to ceiling save for the main double entrance doors and a single door in the rear, close to where Steven's closed casket lay upon its stand. Raeven and Pearl sat in the front row of folding chairs. Nearly fifteen others, curiosity seekers mostly, sat whispering in little groups behind them. "Why are you doing this?" Pearl asked. "You didn't even know the guy."

"You don't understand."

"Understand what?"

Raeven shifted her gaze from the long stemmed white rose in her hand to the identical one she had placed on Steven's closed casket. "It's absurd," she said with a dreary sigh. "Nothing matters."

"Oh, please," Pearl said so loudly that Norris Marcotte, standing as straight and still as a crease in the drapes, cleared his throat in disapproval. "This is nuts, Raeven," she said, dismissing him with a wave. "If nothing matters, there's no point in acting all black widow over it because, y'know, nothing matters."

Raeven lifted her lace veil. "Even nothingness deserves respect."

Pearl returned her steady gaze until she broke the spell with a snap of well-chewed Doublemint gum. "Yeah, whatever." She looked around the room and out into the hall. "Hope Skeleton puts out some doughnuts." Raeven lowered her veil and sighed. Pearl snapped her gum. "Christ, I wish I could smoke."

Several more guests filed into the chapel, among them Joe Li wearing a black suit with a crisp white shirt and subdued gray and blue tie.

"Hmmm, Joey in that suit, what a hunkaroon," Pearl said. When Raeven glanced at her with deepening annoyance, she countered with, "What? You know I like 'em young and juicy." She looked at Joe again, held up her hand so it looked like a claw and, leaning close to Raeven, whispered: "Grrrr said the cougar-in-training."

Raeven ignored her but did turn for a quick, disinterested glance at the young man in the back of the room.

Twenty-two years old, handsome in an intellectual bookish way (though, without his glasses, his strong features and jaw line made for a look more athletic than intellectual), Joe Li could hardly have been more different than his cantankerous uncle.

He was born forty miles south of Raeven's hometown and spoke Cantonese as badly as Uncle Lung spoke English. He had never been to China, was too 'American' to live up to his family's rigid expectations, too rebellious to follow his grandfather's strict orders, but not rebellious enough to follow his own heart. His was a half life, made worse by his cramped, narrow existence in Burne Notch, his "exile" as he called it…and then came the day interesting, unique, almost-beautiful Raeven applied for a job. He focused on her now, all in black, staring at the casket, utterly oblivious to his presence in the back row.

The organist played a solemn dirge on a small Hammond organ. Norris hummed along but stopped when Father Toomey entered through the smaller side door of the chapel. The priest glared at the mortician, obviously annoyed to have been called from his evening cocktails without prior notice. He strolled unsteadily to a small wooden lectern to the right of the casket. He was a large, ruddy-faced man, bald but for a monkish rim of hair too dark to be natural and with so much recently gained weight that his belt looked like it had been pulled too tight around a black sausage. He removed a few pages of notes from his inside jacket pocket, unfolded them, set them on the lectern, and flattened their creases with the heel of his right hand while putting on his glasses with his left.

"Good evening," he said and Norris signaled for the organist to end the hymn. "Good evening," the priest repeated, but stopped again when Sparky Grant entered the chapel, fireman's helmet in hand. He nodded toward the casket. "There," he whispered to a man entering behind. Father Toomey had never seen him before. No one had, and they gaped at the stranger walking toward the casket like a man in a trance.

His eyes glistened with gathered tears behind his black-framed glasses. Long red hair streaked with gray hung wild and tangled down to his shoulders but for a patch shaved above his right temple to accommodate a gauze bandage. He wore a brown tweed jacket over a burnt-orange sweater, torn and faded jeans, and ancient red high-top sneakers with laces nearly the same orange color as his sweater. He held a long black overcoat and sky-blue woolen scarf draped over his arm.

Pearl turned in her seat and beckoned to Norris Marcotte. He bent down to listen. "Whatcha do, hire a clown?" The mortician scowled.

Father Toomey leaned over the lectern. "Excuse me," he said and pulled back, overcome by dizziness. He grabbed the lectern, smiled, and shook his head: "And so…so yes. We are about to begin."

"I am a friend," the stranger said without taking his eyes from the casket. Raeven looked up. She studied him as he took a seat off to the side, his coat balled up on his lap and his eyes still focused in a trance-like way upon the casket.

"So, yes," Father Toomey continued. "As I said, or, as I was about to say..." He lifted a page from the lectern, turned it over, and scanned the one beneath. Pearl snapped her gum. The priest murmured, "As I was saying...as I...yes..."

Beth Marcotte entered the chapel. Her husband turned to her with a smile and she startled him when a strangled cry gurgled in her throat. Norris followed his wife's horrified gaze: "Oh *no*, sir, no, you mustn't!" he cried, shocked by the sight of the stranger lifting the lid of Steven's casket. He flew across the room. "It's closed, sir, a *closed* casket service!"

Too late. The lid settled against the back wall and revealed to all the pungent oil stains. Father Toomey gazed at the ruined lining and then at the Marcottes, his eyes narrowing.

"Well!" Norris exclaimed, "Would you just, ever...what on earth?"

The stranger stood before the casket with his head bowed, staring at the face of his former assistant, so lifeless, so secret, and his heart nearly broke. *Look at you, dear boy. You truly did find it. I know that now for certain. There can be no other reason for this, the senselessness of it all, the utter ruin.* Raeven lifted her veil and was about to join him at the casket when the stranger startled them all by turning to face the mourners: "I am Raghnall Sweeney, friend of the deceased," he said with an Irish accent.

"Raghnall?" Pearl whispered, leaning close to Raeven. "That's a name?"

"Did he tell you anything?" the stranger continued. "Any of you? Did he give you anything: papers, a map, anything at all?"

Several people looked at Raeven. Sweeney noticed and approached her. "Did he say something to you?"

"No. Nothing."

"Tell me," he said, staring into her eyes.

"He did say something..." She hesitated and glanced around, uneasy.

He took her by the hands. "Tell me. It's rather important."

She leaned forward. "He said I was..." She hesitated, lowered her face to hide behind her hair. "Beautiful," she whispered as low as possible, but the scene had so entranced the other mourners that the word had no competition and was heard by all.

"Yeah, sure," Raleigh Marcotte murmured from the back of the room and Pearl spun around in her chair: "Shut up, grease-ape."

"That's all?" Sweeney asked without taking his eyes from Raeven. "Nothing else?"

"No."

"You're certain?"

Raeven shook her head, and then, a memory: "Oh..."

Sweeney crouched before her. He tightened his grip on her hands.

"I forgot about it," she continued. "He said something about the night – I can't quite remember, something about me and the night."

Sweeney sat back on his heels. "He said..."

"I'm not completely..." She faltered, unsure of herself. "It didn't make any sense."

"Was it...?" Dr. Sweeney paused. He did not want to ask the question, did not want to hear the answer. He looked down and caressed the back of her hands with his thumbs. He felt her stiffen, sensed she was about to pull away from him, and he looked up again: "Did he say you were the night?"

Hearing it aloud solidified her memory. "Yes. That was it. What did he mean?"

Sweeney went pale, as if all the blood had drained from his face. "Are you certain?" He let go of her hands. "He said that you – specifically *you* are...?"

"The night, yes. I didn't understand what he meant."

Sweeney wiped his mouth with the back of his hand. Raeven saw his fingers tremble.

"What did he mean?" she asked again and her chest tightened with a sense that something had gone terribly wrong and that it somehow involved her. Dr. Sweeney saw his fear reflected in her expression and fought to regain control. The last thing he needed was to frighten her this early. "Probably nothing." He stood and smiled to reassure her, and addressed the others. "Anyone else? Anything at all odd or unusual?" Hands went up, throats cleared, chairs squeaked: Father Toomey told him of the theft of the silver cross, "after he came to see me at the church," he said with a nod at the casket. Pearl spoke of what she called "the attempted molestation". Sparky recounted the strange happenings along the Coachlight Road; and Raeven – having already told all she knew – stood and approached the coffin to study the face of Steven Wilcox for the first and only time.

Though he lay waxed and powdery with his eyelids and lips sealed shut, she felt she could sense the essence of the man: delicate, studious, with a small nose and thin light brown eyebrows. In spite of his intention to have a closed-casket service, Norris could not resist working on such a challenging gunshot wound. He had skillfully concealed the most obvious damage and left Steven's glasses on as a final touch. The cracked lens and black electrical tape around the hinge were so sad, so pathetically human, and provoked in her a genuine sense of pity. "Poor man," Raeven whispered and her morbid self-absorption dropped away. She had never seen his eyes in daylight and did not know if they were blue or green or brown, but even with his eyes closed, he looked remarkably lifelike in spite of the mortician's cosmetics, as if he was breathing and his lips quivering. She leaned over the casket for a closer look. No. It was the light.

She touched his forehead. Her black lace gloves prevented the clammy chill of his skin from penetrating through to hers. The illusion of life was maintained, and now, aware that the others were watching and how disturbing and macabre it would be, she bent down for a final kiss for all eternity. She saw her reflection in his glasses, saw her face approaching and the black veil lifting. Her lips touched his and she froze.

They *were* moving.

She felt them tremble beneath her own and then came a sudden cracking sensation followed by a jolt of pain. She leaped with a cry but could not pull back. She was hooked on something. It had cut into her upper lip and held it firmly against the dead man's mouth.

She tried to scream but couldn't. She wedged her fingers between her mouth and Steven's. She felt the wax over his lips split.

Panic surged. She pulled back again. This time she broke free. Her hand shot to her mouth. Blood poured over her lace glove and her thoughts collapsed into pure, mindless horror at the sight of a small withered claw reaching from the dead man's mouth, as black and leathery as a parrot's foot, with three thin fingers in the front and one at the back, each tipped with a shimmering black talon.

She spun away from the casket. Those who saw her struggle now gasped at the sight of blood streaming down her chin. Father Toomey also saw the grasping claw and recoiled from the lectern, too shocked to speak.

"What happened?" Pearl cried and rushed to her side. "Raeven, what happened?"

"In there," she stammered and pointed at the casket. "Something in there!"

"Close the lid!" Sweeney yelled to Norris Marcotte. "Close it!"

Norris, stupefied with confusion, couldn't move, couldn't think. Sweeney ran to the casket and reached for the lid. As he did, Steven's mouth cracked open as though giving in to an unexpected yawn and something darted out so quickly that Sweeney saw only a dark blur before slamming the lid down. "How do I lock this?" he asked. "Does it lock?"

Norris continued to stare with bulging eyes and mouth agape.

"Come, come, man!" Sweeney said. "Help me with this thing. And you, Constable." He pointed at Sparky. "Escort these people out of here – now!"

Most did not have to be told. They began to rush to the door the moment Norris approached the casket to snap the locks into place (a thing he dearly wished he'd done before the service began).

"Someone get a towel!" Pearl cried.

Dr. Sweeney rapped the top of the casket with his knuckles. "Do not open this." After acknowledging Norris' stricken 'certainly not' expression, he called to the priest. "Have you any spirits, Father? Whiskey, vodka?"

Father Toomey, too unnerved to worry about appearances, withdrew a small flask from his jacket pocket. To his dismay, Sweeney unscrewed the top, pulled Raeven's hand from her mouth and dowsed her bloody lip with scotch. She cried out and tried to cover her mouth again but Sweeney grabbed her by the arm and lifted her from her seat. "Where's the loo?" he called to Norris.

"Rest room, it's in the hall."

"Quickly!" he said to Raeven. "And please – everyone leave this room at once."

With a firm grip, he escorted her to the bathroom where he pulled her hand away and lifted her upper lip. "Take a swig," he whispered and handed her the flask. "Don't swallow." Raeven winced at the sting. "Slosh it around and spit it out." She did. The scotch had turned bright red. "Now another bit for the outside." Raeven braced herself and he poured the last of the spirits over her outer lip. After the stinging sensation passed, Raeven opened her eyes and nearly screamed at her reflection in the mirror. A single deep gash led from her right nostril down to her lip.

Pearl appeared behind her with a large white towel. "Cover it with this."

Joe Li stood beside her. "Is she all right?"

"She'll be fine," Dr. Sweeney said in an attempt to sound reassuring. "I apologize for the distressing scene, but there's always a danger of infection with this sort of thing. Come, my dear, back inside where you can sit down."

By the time they returned, all but Sparky, Father Toomey and the Marcottes had been persuaded to leave the chapel, though a few of the more curious lingered in the hall. Beth closed the double doors and muffled their voices while Sweeney helped Raeven to a chair. Pearl and Joe sat behind her. Father Toomey, still at the lectern, fumbled with his papers. "A lizard," he muttered without looking at them. "I saw its claw, it was a lizard."

"Maybe an iguana," Beth Marcotte ventured.

"Oh, come on, guys," Sparky said. "That doesn't seem likely. An iguana? My nephew had one and I can't imagine that lazy thing bothering to climb into a coffin. And he sure as heck wouldn't have climbed into someone's mouth."

"This guy knows what it is," Pearl said with a nod toward Sweeney

"I do have an explanation," he said. "I do. But right now, it's very difficult for me to..." He peered over his glasses, first at Pearl, then at Raeven and Sparky, and when he spoke, his voice drifted into a whisper. "I suppose the best thing to do in this...in these peculiar circumstances, is to simply have out with it." He paused and looked down at the floor and tried again: "I believe it may have been a..."

"A what?" Sparky asked, impatiently.

Pearl echoed him: "A what?"

Dr. Sweeney studied their faces, so intent, so full of questions. The events of the past few minutes were no doubt the strangest that any had experienced in their lifetimes. To lead them further along such a path would stretch their capacity to accept and believe beyond its breaking point. Indeed, it had nearly done so with his and he was more prepared than most to accept the strange, the other-worldly, and the unexplained. *How can I tell them what I suspect? No, it's too soon for that.* "I believe it was a lizard, as the good Father here surmised," he said with a short laugh. "In point of fact, a draco lizard, from the Latin *draco*, which–as you know, Your Grace–translates as serpent."

"Oh, yes," Father Toomey said, distracted and eyeing the flask at Raeven's feet. "Draco translates as serpent."

Exchanged glances followed, and eyes narrowed with doubt. Pearl, displaying the latter, asked: "So where did it come from?"

"Distant regions," Sweeney said with a jovial smile. "It's quite harmless"–a quick glance at Raeven's lip–"usually. Steven was my assistant. We were studying the draco. I'm sure this specimen got loose from the lab."

"What lab?" Pearl asked and looked around at the others. "We have a lizard lab around here?"

"Steven brought it with him," Sweeney explained. "It was cornered and frightened and got a little frisky, that's all. And now, my dear," he said to Raeven, "we had better whisk you off to hospital. That nasty cut requires medical–"

A loud thump from behind stopped him. His eyes widened behind his glasses. Another thump came, louder than the first. This time the casket moved.

Sparky stepped up beside him. "What's *in* there?" he whispered.

Sweeney did not take his eyes from the polished wood. "Get them out of here," he returned. "Quickly. And then come back."

Another thump. The coffin rocked on its stand.

"Okay, everyone out of here," Sparky said, backing away, and he shepherded them out of the chapel. Pearl was the last to go, but stopped at the door. "Hey Sparkles. Be careful and stuff." Sparky answered with a half-hearted smile. He closed the door behind her and lingered, reluctant to return.

Sweeney stood beside the coffin, staring at its lustrous surface. "Have you any sort of weapon?" he asked without turning away.

"Gun." Sparky released the safety strap and pulled his revolver from his holster to check the chamber. "Is it really that dangerous?"

Sweeney nodded. "It is." He leaped, startled by another thump, this time followed by the sound of fabric tearing and a bang so loud it sounded like someone had hit the inside of the casket with a hammer.

"Holy shit," Sparky whispered. "What *is* that thing?"

The casket jolted with another sharp blow. Sweeney held up his hand. "Listen." Sparky moved up close enough to hear a muffled rasp from the back of the casket, like a rat gnawing the edge of a board. He looked at the professor and swallowed hard. "It's chewing its way out."

"Dear God," Sweeney whispered. The two men backed toward the center of the chapel, Sparky with his revolver drawn and the professor with his eyes glued to the coffin. The gnawing grew louder. Wood splintered.

The chapel door cracked open behind them and Raleigh Marcotte leaned inside. "You guys figure out what it is?"

"Close that door!" Sparky yelled and Raleigh jumped, startled by a screech of wood and another loud crack. The casket lurched and toppled off its stand. When it hit the floor, it rolled over to reveal a gaping hole with the wood splintered outward.

"Where is it?" Sparky asked. "Is it still inside?" And again, to Raleigh. "I told you to shut that door!"

Raleigh stepped inside and closed the door behind. He focused on the fallen casket, the same as Sparky and Dr. Sweeney, but his vantage point gave him a broader view of the chapel and he saw something crouched in the corner to the left of the casket, small and black and glistening. "Guys," he whispered, craning his neck. "It's there."

Sparky saw a blur dart under the drapes. He tapped the professor on the shoulder. "Over there."

A small bulge climbed behind the drapes and stopped halfway up the wall. "Want me to shoot it?" Sparky asked.

"I'm not sure it will have an effect."

"A *bullet?*" Sweeny nodded. "Well, okay," Sparky said, "but I think we need to find out." He aimed his revolver and fired. A loud hiss and squeal came from behind the drapes and the bulge dropped to the floor. Voices called from the hall. Someone knocked on the chapel door. "You all right in there?" Pearl asked.

"Raleigh, watch that door," Sparky said. "Make sure no one opens it." He called out. "Don't worry, we're fine. I had to shoot it," and then – "Don't!" His shout stopped Dr. Sweeney in the act of reaching for the lower hem of the drape. "Don't," he said again and rushed through a row of folding chairs to join him. "It might not be dead." He got down on his hands and knees. "Step back." He leaned down with his ear nearly touching the floor and lifted the fabric. Several rows of black scales glistened like the back of a water moccasin.

"Don't touch it," Sweeney whispered and Sparky looked up with a wry smile that dropped in shocked horror when a claw shot out and caught him by the right leg, its talons slicing into the cuff of his jeans.

Sweeney came to his side in a flash, brandishing a brass candlestick like a club. He brought it down upon the bulge in the fabric. The candlestick veered off and clanged against the wall and the claw tore through Sparky's cuff and disappeared.

"Look!" Raleigh shouted. The drapes ballooned outward when the thing sped up the side of the wall and tore through a ceiling tile. Sweeney, Sparky and Raleigh followed the sound with their eyes as it scuttled across the top of the chapel ceiling.

A moment later a scream came from the hall. The door opened and Pearl cried, "It's out here!"

Sparky raced past her. "Where? Who saw it?"

"It went that way," Raeven said and pointed down the hall at the same moment Beth Marcotte appeared at the display room door, shaken. "Whatever it is, it's strong." She led them past the chapel door and pointed to the canvas over the window Steven crawled through the night he killed himself. "Can a draco do that?" She lifted the canvas, now torn at the bottom as though slashed by a razor.

"And how about this?" Raleigh asked. He held up a flattened piece of metal. Sparky took it from him and turned it over in his palm.

"What is it?" Sweeney asked, and the policeman looked up. The fine lines around his eyes deepened when he tried to smile and smoothed again when he found he could not. "My bullet."

5

The admitting nurse looked at Raeven's lip and asked how it happened. Before Joe or Pearl could answer, Sweeney spoke for the first time since they left the funeral home. "A shattered bottle. Top broke off as she was drinking, frightful thing altogether. She'll need sutures, tetanus shot as well." He asked if he and Raeven could wait in a private examination room and nodded toward a nearby waiting area. "You two wait for us in there," he said to Joe and Pearl. "I'll keep close watch on her."

"Hey, we can watch her," Pearl said. "We're her friends."

"Indeed, you are, but I am a doctor."

"Oh," she said, her anger deflating. "You didn't tell us that."

In the examination room, he closed the door and leaned against it while Raeven sat on the table. "Are you really a doctor?" she asked from behind her bloody cloth.

"Ph.D. Archeology and Celtic Studies."

"Well, you took care of me like a real doctor. That scotch stung."

"A bit crude, I know, but I was worried about…"

"Not germs, right?"

Sweeney shook his head.

"What then?" she asked.

"Venom."

Raeven studied a poster that displayed ways to prevent choking, all the while aware of the professor's steady gaze. She took a deep breath and turned to him. "It felt like an electrical shock when it grabbed me. I still don't feel anything. My lip is numb."

"You'll undoubtedly feel it later." With an obvious effort to lighten the gloomy direction of his thoughts, he winked and added, "Imagine, a thing like that harming such a…such a…such an interesting face. Should'a told the wretched thing to bugger off."

"I'll remember next time." She pointed to his head. "A draco grab you too?"

Sweeney reached up and touched the bandage. "A crack on the noggin back home, nothing serious." His smile faded into an expression Raeven thought looked like fear – not heart-pumping fear, but a slow, expanding pool of dread that compelled him to sink into a chair in the corner. "I need to know certain things, though my questions are, perhaps, unanswerable." He took a deep breath and straightened in the chair. "But what's done is done."

"What's done?" she asked and realized at once she was afraid to hear his answer. "What questions did you want to ask?"

"Are you a strong person?"

"I hope I am. I like to think I am."

He thought for a moment and bit his lower lip. "Something has happened. When I tell you this – as impossible and mad as it may sound, I want you to believe me. Indeed, you above all others *must* believe me. I need you with me on this because we haven't much time."

The door opened and an elderly doctor entered the room. "Hi there," he said in a cheerful, hearty voice. "Now what's the problem?"

Raeven reluctantly took her eyes from the professor and lowered the cloth. The doctor whistled. "Well, well, how did you do that?"

"Broken bottle," she said after another quick glance at the professor. "Will I have a scar?" Before the doctor could answer, she said: "I don't mind if I do."

"I don't think so; maybe a little one." The doctor pulled on a pair of rubber gloves and gently touched her mouth. "Extraordinary." He lifted her upper lip. "Three deep lacerations on the inside of your lip and a very nasty one on the outside. Are you sure it was a bottle?"

"What else could it be?" Sweeney asked.

"I have no idea. I've never seen anything quite like it. I'll give you a couple of injections to numb the pain and put in some sutures." The doctor gave her a shot of Novocain and said, "Lie down there and don't move, I'll be right back." As soon as he left the room, Raeven turned to the professor. "It wasn't a lizard, was it."

Sweeney stepped up beside her and looked down into her anxious eyes. "No."

6

Drowsy with painkillers and feeling drained from the events of the night, Raeven returned to her studio apartment above the funeral chapel with her upper lip covered by a thick pad of white gauze.

She took another Percocet and a sip of water from the bottle on the bedside table and turned off the light. A gust of wind rattled her windowpane. She pulled her blankets up close and fell into fitful sleep filled with dreamy musings of Steven, of trees and shooting stars, that so filled her thoughts that their boundaries faded and the blood exploding from Steven's head became as bright as a meteor and his hand reaching out became a tree with each finger a root as hairless as a rat's tail as he reached into her pocket – *did he reach into my pocket?* – and blackness then, swirling, as deeper forms overtook thought and sleep came, deep and restful and calm.

It was not to last.

Downstairs in the main house, Raleigh Marcotte lay sprawled upon the sofa in the living room of the main house, eating walnuts and watching some show about aliens building the Egyptian pyramids. He had learned to crack the nuts by squeezing two in his fist at once. The shells tended to scatter all over the place but that didn't matter. His mother would pick them up later.

The television screen began to flicker. Static crackled. He changed the channel. Same thing. He turned it back again and, without looking, reached into the bag for another walnut and squeezed it against one already in his hand. A small piece of shell dropped and skittered across the floor. He glanced down to see where it went. A black shadow slipped beneath the coffee table.

He knew at once what it was.

With a sharp intake of breath and a muttered curse too soft to hear, he lifted his bare feet and pulled his knees up to his chest. He had never heard of a draco until that day. The weird Irish guy said they weren't dangerous but he saw what it had done to Raeven. *What should I do?* He pulled a walnut from the bag and dropped it. It hit the hardwood floor with a crack.

The shadow darted toward the television. Raleigh sat up, tense, and dropped his head back against the sofa cushion with relief when he saw the walnut roll against the television stand. He leaned over and looked beneath the coffee table. Nothing there.

Something clattered in the kitchen.

He pushed the mute button on the remote control. "Dad?"

Silence, but for the *tick, tick, tick* of the grandfather clock in the hall. He craned his neck and peered into the dim kitchen where a long, thin shadow swung back and forth upon the wall. "Dad?" He lifted a large conch shell souvenir from a side table and held it poised like a weapon before stepping into the kitchen.

He snapped on the light, and…calm, calm again, calm…nothing there but a thick pungent smell of something rotten, old wet leaves, a rotten egg. Maybe a mouse had died behind the stove. He lowered the shell. Several refrigerator magnets lay on the floor. *They must have made the clattering sound.* He picked one up and stuck it back on the refrigerator door, but it wouldn't hold so set it on the counter. He looked at the wall and saw the movement came from outside, from a tree branch waving outside the window above the sink. His fear drained away as quickly as it had come, even as the overhead light began to flicker and dim. "Oh, who knows," he muttered before he snapped it off and returned to the living room where he flung himself back down on the couch and turned off the mute button.

Static again, but clearing. He reached for a walnut. A low hiss came, close beside him. He turned and there it was, staring at him, black and glistening, the size of a rat, crouched on the back of the sofa.

Raleigh gasped and slammed back against the sofa arm with such force it cracked and nearly tore off. The thing scuttled toward him, eyes shining and claws tearing into the cushions. He threw his arms up, hands outstretched, and it sprang. He opened his mouth to scream but he couldn't, his scream was choked off – it was *in his mouth!*

It tore into him. Pain and terror collided and ripped a howl from his soul, but he couldn't scream, he couldn't breathe, he couldn't pull it from his mouth. His throat constricted but the thing squirmed in further, blocking air passages, clawing through blood, tearing into his esophagus. *Air, I need air, I can't breathe!* He tore at his throat and writhed in panic – *air, air, I need air!* He squirmed off the sofa, crackled over broken walnut shells, and banged his fist on the cushions, on the floor, banging in wild bug-eyed panic, unable to breathe, strangling, suffocating until a thick darkness swirled in on him and he fell.

The television's glow flickered over a long thin tail slipping into his bloody mouth like the last of a black snake disappearing into a hole.

He remained there for several minutes, motionless, his pulse stopped and his brain still, and then the television static faded, the picture and sound cleared, the music played, and Raleigh Marcotte opened his eyes.

7

His phone woke him from fitful, confusing dreams. "Hello?"
"Joe, it's Pearl."
"What time is it?"
"Late. She's at my house. She wants to see you."
"Who wants to see me?"
"Raeven."

He arrived a little after three in the morning. He had never been to Pearl's home before. From the outside it looked like every other mobile home in the Amethyst Pines trailer park except for a front door enclosed by a wooden vestibule hung with two heavy canvas curtains slit down the center. "These for the birds?" he asked when he arrived.

"Yeah, don't want anyone getting out," she explained. "Hurry, don't let in the cold." She pulled back the canvas and he stood at the threshold, astonished.

Over the years, the trailer had been transformed into a tweeting, chirping, squawking wonderland of finches, canaries, parakeets, doves, pigeons, two African Grey parrots, a cockatoo, several quail and a large white turkey named Earl. Cages stood on stands, hung from brackets, and sat on the television and side tables, all with an open door policy that allowed their occupants to come and go as they pleased. On the wall above a sofa hung a framed poster of Suzanne Pleshette in *The Birds*, sprawled before a front porch with her eyes gouged out,.

Pearl lifted the turkey and cradled him in her arms. "She's in the kitchen," she said softly, and then cooed to the turkey. "Earl, this is Joe. Joe – Earl."

Joe cleared his throat. "Hey Earl," he said with an awkward wave. "So what's going on?"

"More weird shit," Pearl said and led him to the kitchen where a pale, red-eyed Raeven sat in her black night-gown and stared at the table top, her lip still covered with the bandage. Her long winter coat lay draped over the back of her chair.

Joe said her name. She looked up with an expression of sudden, unexpected relief and rose to meet him, but stopped half-way up – she sat back down again and her expression changed from relief to its usual unsmiling, icy expression in an instant, as though an iron portcullis gate had come crashing down inside.

"What happened?" he asked, still at the kitchen door.

"Raleigh Marcotte was in my room," she said. "Something

happened to him."

"I'll say," Pearl observed while patting down Earl's feathers. "Tell him what you told me."

Joe sat down across the table from her and, without looking at him, she pulled her robe closer. "After you guys took me home from the hospital I went right to bed. I took another painkiller and that helped me sleep until my lip started throbbing again. I sort of half-woke up and I thought I heard a sound, like someone walking on tip-toe, trying not to make the floorboards squeak. I couldn't tell if it was real or still part of a dream, and then I thought maybe it was the pills making me imagine things. But then I heard a step. I was *sure* I heard a step. I turned on the lamp but…nothing. I thought maybe it came from the bathroom. Just to be sure, I got out of bed and shut the bathroom door tight. I heard the latch close. But the front door – I didn't think to check it so I climbed back into bed and went back to sleep. And I felt…" She closed her eyes, repulsed by the memory.

"What?" Joe asked.

"Like…I don't know, like sort of pressure. On my knuckle. Pressure. Hot and wet. I realized my arm was hanging over the side of the bed, but I was too lazy to move it – but then more pressure, and something sliding."

"Sliding?" Joe asked, confused.

"That's what it felt like. So I rolled over and pulled my arm up and I laid like that for – I don't know how long, until I sort of woke up again and I felt my right hand with my left, felt my ring finger, and…" She shuddered again. "And it *was* wet." She closed her eyes and collected herself. "And then I saw the bathroom door open."

"After you closed it and heard the latch click?" Joe asked.

The teakettle began to scream. Pearl set Earl on the floor and rushed to take the kettle off the burner. "Right, okay," she said, "so Raleigh was in your room. And you think he…?" She nodded at Raeven's hand and scrunched her face up in disgust.

"He had already done it by then." Raeven pulled her black flannel bathrobe tight around her neck and told them Raleigh had been under her bed. She was sure her finger had been in his mouth. She held up her hand. The gold class ring with the onyx was gone. "He took it off with his teeth."

"Why would he do that?" Joe Li asked, perplexed. "Why would anyone do that?"

Raeven shook her head. "But I don't even know if it was Raleigh. I mean, it *was* Raleigh, but there was something wrong with him, something…I can't explain it, like he was a version of him."

Pearl groaned. "Oh, great, a second Raleigh, let the world rejoice. Those Percocet are kind of strong."

"You don't believe me."

"It's not that, sweetie." Tea water hissed as she poured it over the tea bags. "Actually, yeah, it *is* that. Those painkillers can do weird things. Made me see green monkeys once. Turned out to be nurses."

"I don't know," Raeven said with a weary sigh. "But even if I imagined he was under my bed, this next this part *was* real, I know it was. All I could think about was washing my hands, so I went into the bathroom and turned on the light, and…"

"And?"

"And there he was. Behind me. I saw his reflection in the mirror, sitting in the bathtub and all sweaty and shaking like he had the flu. His lips and chin were smeared with dried blood, but the worst thing…his eyes were completely black. No whites at all. He reached out and asked me to help him, and that's when I saw…" She shuddered again and closed her eyes at the memory.

Joe leaned forward and reached for her hand. "Saw what?"

Raeven pulled her hand away. "My ring," she said. "On his tongue. I heard it click against his teeth when he asked me to help him."

Pearl squinted with revulsion. "The more you tell, the worse it gets."

"What did you do?" Joe asked.

"I ran. I heard him climb out of the bathtub behind me, I heard the shower curtain swish to the side. I grabbed my coat and he came out of the bathroom, crawling on the floor. I opened the door and looked back and saw him squirming and reaching up for me, asking me to help him, but I couldn't." She writhed in her chair as if covered with ants. "I couldn't! I ran down the stairs, I didn't even put on my boots, and got in my car and…"

"And here you are," Pearl said.

"And here I am."

"Maybe it was a dream," Joe suggested, and Raeven sent him a withering glance.

"That's what I said," Pearl added. She lifted the string of her tea bag and bobbed it up and down in the hot water. "Or hallucination. Those pain killers make you see all kinds of weird crap. Like I said – green monkeys."

Raeven held up her hand again. "So where's my ring?"

Joe laid his own hands on the table, palms down. "I only said it might be a dream because I dreamt of Raleigh too." Pearl stopped dunking her tea bag. It hung above her cup, twirling on its string, dribbling a stream of hot water. "Tonight, before you called," he continued. "I can't remember much, but it was Raleigh. And like you said, something had happened to him. His eyes were like you described them too. Black, like lizard eyes. No whites." He stared at the table and concentrated. "And a blue cage of some kind, I have no idea what it was. And a Chinese character. I don't know what that meant either. I couldn't read it. It was on a box. A metal box, yellow, maybe gold."

"What's that got to do with Raleigh?" Pearl asked.

He looked up and saluted his glasses up his nose. "He's afraid of it."

Pearl and Raeven stared, waiting for more. "Yes?" Pearl ventured. "And?"

"And that's all. He's afraid of it."

A small finch flew over the table, startling them. Pearl lifted both hands: "Okay, boys and girls, let's be cool about this, okay? It's three-freakin'-thirty in the morning and suddenly we got a blue cage and a gold box that Raleigh's afraid of. Why can't we stick with him taking your ring off with his mouth, which is just so disgusting I can't stand it." Another finch flew by. Several more roused from their roosts, increasingly restless. "What's the matter with you guys?" she asked, eyeing first her birds and then her friends. "Come on, everybody, you're giving me the creeps."

Raeven sat back and her shoulders relaxed. "Maybe you're right, Pearl. Maybe it was the painkiller." Her face was drawn and even paler than usual. Her drooping black hair and the white bandage heightened the effect. Seen as a reflection in the dark window, her hair faded into the outside darkness, leaving only the pallid reflection of her face on the glass.

Beyond it, a much darker form lurched across the snow into Pearl's back yard.

His clothes were torn and black with soot and smoke. Dark stains covered his hands and fingernails, now curved, thick and sharp. He approached the mobile home, crouching low, and stepped up close to a set of propane tanks below the kitchen window. The skin on the backs of his hands undulated and rippled with alternating dark gray scales and human skin, each vying to take its place at the other's expense, and his tongue darted out, long, black, and thin, with two separate prongs at the end that quivered in the frozen air before slipping back into his mouth, now caked with dried blood.

He watched them from the darkness, especially the one in the black robe. He stared at her with lifeless eyes and his reptilian tongue snaked out again to taste the air, to taste for the scent of *her*. No one inside could see him. The birds could not see him, but they sensed something. Pearl took her cue from them. "Dream or not, something's going on," she said, her face betraying her alarm.

The birds huddled on the cabinets and fluttered with anxiety.

Something bumped against the wall outside.

Raeven tensed again and clutched the side of the table. "What was that?"

They strained to listen past the rustling feathers and the hum of the wall clock and heard a small metallic *ping*, a tap on a propane tank.

"Something's outside," Pearl said with a glance at Joe and she jumped with a startled cry at the sound of a sudden, piercing howl. Birds roused throughout the trailer, screeching and chirping and squawking, but they could not drown out the sound. "Siren," Pearl said with her hand over her heart. She rushed to the window and cupped her hands against the glass at the same time as the thing outside flattened against the aluminum siding. "Oh wow, look at that."

Joe and Raeven joined her at the window. Low clouds fumed and shuddered with orange light from a distant conflagration below. Moments later, the phone on the wall rang. When Pearl answered, Raeven heard her say, "Yes, she's here…oh, man, okay. Yeah, sure, I'll tell her." Pearl hung up the phone. "That was Sparky," she said to Raeven. "Another fire at the Marcottes. It's your apartment."

8

The firemen had everything under control a little before sunrise on what would turn out to be a dismal morning, cold and drizzly and pungent with smoke. As soon as Sparky gave the go-ahead, the firemen ranged through the charred remains of the funeral home and found Norris and Beth Marcotte in their unburned bedroom, still in bed. It became clear at once that the fire had been set on purpose to cover a crime. Beth's left arm had been torn from its socket. Her neck had been snapped and her throat slashed with such violence that the back of her head rested against her spine. Norris had no head at all. Sparky later found it in the refrigerator downstairs, whole and unharmed by the fire, jammed inside the crisper drawer alongside a bunch of green seedless grapes.

Shocking news such as this could not be contained. One of the volunteer firefighters let the news slip and within an hour the entire town knew the gruesome details of the murders.

Attention once again centered on Raeven, as it had after Steven's suicide. She sat sullen and withdrawn in Pearl's living room while questioned by the state police, fire marshal, and reporters from the *Portsmouth Herald* and *Concord Monitor* (both of whom would highlight the bird-infested trailer in their articles). She was tired beyond endurance and gave answers so lethargic and obscure that she left the interviewers with more questions than they came in with. Eventually, Pearl put a stop to it. She threw the reporters out and asked Sparky to deal with the inspectors and other officials while she led Raeven down a narrow hall to the bedroom at the far end of the trailer. She pulled down the shades while Raeven collapsed on the bed, fully clothed. When Pearl reached for the light switch to turn it off, she happened to glance at the nightstand beside the bed. Her old rotary landline telephone was gone. Everything else was there: lamp, ashtray dotted with cigarette butts, hand cream, but no phone.

She snapped off the light, puzzled, and closed the door. She bypassed the living room and went into the kitchen. A moment later she poked her head through the door and beckoned to Sparky.

"Anything wrong?" one of the state troopers asked.

"No, no, nothing important. I want him to help me make some coffee."

"Coffee!" Sparky said, mortified, as he followed her into the kitchen. "You don't need me to help you to –"

"Shh. Quiet. I wanted to get you alone. Look." She pointed to the floor where the avocado green wall phone she had used the night before lay battered and broken with its insides strewn about the kitchen. "The one in the bedroom too. Gone."

"What happened?" Sparky asked.

"I was hoping you could tell me."

"How would I know?"

"I don't know, Spark." She tried not to raise her voice but fear filtered through in spite of her attempted calm. "But that..." She pointed at the wall. "I don't know what that is either." Sparky set his hat on the table and leaned in close. Deep long marks trailed down to the place where the phone had been, as though it had been raked off the wall with a single swipe of a claw.

9

Dr. Sweeney finished off the last of his scotch with a flourish, set his glass down and leaped from his chair to warm his hands at the fireplace. The sudden movement startled Father Toomey, who was sedentary and overweight and not much given to unexpected activity. "Still cold?" he asked and Sweeney said, "Only my hands." He held his palms to the fire and stared at the flames, transfixed. "Dreadful thing," he murmured. "Makes me wonder if Prometheus didn't deserve his fate, the thief." At that, a log popped and whined like a spirit wailing in despair from somewhere deep inside the wood. "May I smoke, Your Grace? It's a pipe. Drives some people daft, I know."

Father Toomey reached for the Dewars. "We all have our vices. And I'm not 'Your Grace', I'm not an archbishop, heaven knows."

"We refer to bishops in Ireland as Your Grace as well."

"I'm not a bishop either."

"Ah well," Sweeney said with a shrug. "Bishop, archbishop, parish priest. I elevate you to 'Your Grace' regardless. Most call me Professor, or Doctor Sweeney, or simply Sweeney with no formal title at all. It matters not to me."

"Care for another?" the priest asked, holding up the bottle.

"Thank you, no. That first one warmed me up quite nicely."

Father Toomey poured one for himself while Dr. Sweeney lit his pipe and they sat before the fire, each in a comfortable old armchair with a small table between. The late afternoon sun had retired for the night behind a bank of slate-gray clouds. The fire crackled, ice tinkled in the priest's glass, a layer of pipe smoke floated into the deepening shadows, and Sweeney spoke once more to the bright coals: "T'is a dreadful, lovely thing."

Father Toomey concurred. "Poor Norris and Beth. Personally, I couldn't bear them, but still…" A small black cat sidled up to the professor and leaped into his lap. The priest lifted his hand, but Sweeney stopped him: "Quite all right. What's his name?"

"Her. Soot."

He scratched the cat under the chin and she began to purr and rub the side of her face against his hand. A log popped and sparks chased each other up the flue. Father Toomey cleared his throat. "I don't know what to say about all of this."

"You needn't say a thing. I need your help, but you don't have to say a word at all, nor believe a thing I tell you."

"I don't mind talking about it, but believing it? That's another thing entirely. But still, I saw that thing at the wake last night. I saw what came out of that young man's mouth. I hope I'll never see anything like it again. And now comes this tragedy, the Marcottes."

"It will get worse."

The priest sank into his chair. "I know." His double-chin dropped over his clerical collar like a soufflé overtopping its mold. "I don't know *how* I know, but I do. Ever since I met that young man and told him about the silver cross, this town has been hit time and again with tragedy. Even so, I cannot ascribe such things to the supernatural."

"No?"

"I was trained in psychology at the seminary and like to think of myself as having an open mind. However…"

"However some things are simply beyond the pale, eh?" Sweeney stroked the black cat and puffed on his pipe. "Do you believe in evil?"

"No," the priest said without thinking. He raised his hand: "Let me clarify. I used to believe in an irredeemable, take-no-prisoners kind of evil that, in some ways, propelled me into this." He stuck his chin out and touched his collar. "I fancied myself a warrior, a follower of the Archangel Michael, eager to fight the unseen devils of the world."

"What changed?"

"Oh, well…" He dropped his hand from his collar and patted his stomach. "About sixty pounds and nearly forty years. You grow older and learn that we are all imperfect creatures. Friends let us down, relationships end, families fight, a beloved child is caught selling drugs, and all this among people who are genuinely good for the part. Never once, in all that time, have I ever run across anyone or anything that could conceivably be termed 'demonic'. Over time I came to realize that the great battles between pure goodness and black-hearted evil do not exist and never did. A great disappointment, really, to discover that the world and all within it are merely a mediocre, rather uninspiring blend of the two." Father Toomey took a quick sip of scotch. "Perhaps," he said into the glass, but thought better of it. "No." Ice clacked against his nose and upper lip. He lowered the glass and smiled. "And you? Do you believe in evil?"

"Oh, yes indeed," Sweeney said with a slow nod, still gazing at the fire. "I must, for I have seen many things in this world."

"Catholic?"

"I give the same answer. I must be, for I have seen many things."

"Odd to find a scholar and a believer."

"And you can well imagine it has caused me no end of trouble."

"I used to be that too," the priest said.

"A scholar?"

"A believer."

"Ah," Sweeney said, and gazed at the fire.

"I don't mind talking about it. The truth is, if I were a younger man, I would leave the priesthood tomorrow. But now…" He shrugged his shoulders. "It's a job. Benefits. A place to live. I go through the motions of Mass every day, mostly for a bevy of elderly women – my housekeeper, Elizabeth Grey, primary among them, the old battle-axe. As long as I don't slur my words and show up for funeral services and the occasional wedding, all is right with the world. As for actually believing any of it? No. Not a word of it. It all went out with my fanciful views of evil. Baby with the bathwater. Pure good and pure evil? Pure nonsense." He looked at Dr. Sweeney and smiled. "I haven't had a conversation like this in years. A small town like this has little fodder for a restless mind."

"All right then. Let's give it some. Top off your whisky and pour me one too, if you will. I've a lot of questions and I'll need your insight and assistance. First, though, I should like to have that policeman join us."

"Sparky Grant?" the priest asked, surprised by the request.

"If it's not too much trouble. We may need his help."

10

On the way to the parish house, the policeman unknowingly passed over an unwatched and untended culvert made of corrugated steel lying three feet deep beneath the main road where it was installed to prevent runoff from snow and rain from flooding the town. A trail of ice a half inch thick lay along the bottom of the corrugated metal tube and, in the center, lay a pile of broken telephones and what was left of Raleigh Marcotte writhing in frozen torture.

His spine twisted and racked in groaning contortions. He tried to cry out, but his whip-like tongue curled in his mouth and jammed his words. His clothes hung around him in ribbons that fell away in pieces and his flesh, blue with cold and frostbite, now rippled and tore into patches of scalloped gray scales, and he whimpered and reared back with his face distorted in a silent scream when his leg muscles tore away from the bone.

11

"I was going to call you," Sparky said. He sat straight and still in a straight-backed chair beside Father Toomey, unable to hide his discomfort. "But with all the problems with the phones, and plus I forgot to charge my cell. Had to use my car charger."

"Phones?" Sweeney asked, pausing in the act of relighting his pipe.

"Pearl's landline phones were broken, both of them."

Sweeney lit the pipe and waved the match out. "Odd," he said and a puff of blue-grey smoke enveloped him. "So. Let's begin, shall we? I called you to join us because I fear you have been caught in the web. This will be difficult…" He gazed at the fire and then at the policeman. "Come, come, there must be a more comfortable chair for the Constable." Father Toomey, surprised at his lack of hospitality, said, "Oh, of course! Over there, Sparky. Drag that big chair up to the fire."

"Right then," Sweeney began and he set his pipe down in the ashtray while Sparky dragged a third easy chair closer to the fire and sat in it with a nod and half-smile. "I should like to tell you an *immram*."

"What's an *immram*?" Sparky asked.

"An Irish navigational tale, the most famous of which is the Latin text *Naviatio Sancti Brendani Abbatis*, popularly known as The Voyage of Saint Brendan." He leaned toward the fire, with his palms pressed together and his hands pressed between his knees. "My specialty, gentlemen, is archeology, with a strong focus on the Celtic Christianity that flourished in the early medieval period, in the fifth and sixth centuries, primarily in Ireland and the west coast of Scotland. They were isolated from Rome, you see, and they formed their own practices and rituals, some stolen quite cheerfully from the Celtic pagans. They had their own saints as well: St. Bridget of Kildare, St. Columcille, and the great Patrick himself. Among these was Brendan of Clonfert, also known as St. Brendan the Navigator. About a year or so ago, I found mention of Brendan's voyage in an obscure text, which led me to another, and another, and finally to the vaults of a medieval library in Rothenberg, Germany where I found a small book – an actual book, not a scroll – which contained a map of a stone floor."

With that, Dr. Sweeney told his tale of all that happened upon Skellig Michael only one short week before, from the hiring of the off-season *Nellie Anne*, to the discovery of the manuscript and the disturbing tale contained therein. He dared not look at them through much of it.

If he had, he would have seen two polite men doing all they could to appear respectful and hide their doubt – their *extreme* doubt, as each acknowledged to the other with an occasional glance or raised eyebrow.

"So I shall not aver," he said in conclusion, "I shall not suggest in any meaningful way, that the tale told by the monk Brother Aodhan had or continues to have any basis in truth or fact. I cannot do that. Not at this stage, and not to such obviously intelligent men. But the *sense* of it, the underlying truth of evil..." He hesitated, glanced at the priest, then bunched his right hand into a fist and firmly pounded his knee for emphasis when he said, "Something happened to Steven that night." He shrugged. "But what? He was a graduate student, a perfectly ordinary, highly rational young man. And yet, the last image I have of him is back upon the summit of Skellig Michael, standing over me with a rock in his hand." He pointed to the bandage on his head. "Something possessed him to steal the manuscript and to murder the boat owner who took us out there in cold blood, for so he did. Yes, Constable, murder," he said in response to Sparky's widening gaze. "I discovered his body lying face down in the shallows. And then to – I can hardly believe it happened, even now; but to take his own life." Sweeney tapped his forefinger on his knee once for each word when he said, "That. Was. Not. Steven." The fire crackled. The layer of smoke hovered. Ice shifted in the empty glass of scotch. "And as for this....*thing* that has appeared among us."

"It's not a draco," Sparky ventured, furrowing his brow. He withdrew a piece of paper from his back pocket and unfolded it. "Meant to show you this earlier, found it online." He read aloud from the paper. "'The Draco is a genus of gliding lizard from Southeast Asia. The draco is an arboreal insectivore.' That means it lives in trees and eats bugs. 'The ribs and their connecting membrane can be extended to create a wing.'" He folded the paper and returned it to his pocket. "That doesn't sound like something that can flatten bullets."

"No," Sweeney said.

"So what is it?"

"I'm not entirely certain," Sweeney said carefully. "It cannot be easy for any of us to accept such..." His words trailed off.

"So did you go to the police?" Sparky asked.

"Police?" Sweeney returned, confused by the question. "Oh, you mean about the Captain? No. He was lost at sea, according to the local papers. But don't you be going and alerting any authorities about it, not yet anyway. I shall clear the matter as soon as I help clear the one facing us now...though how, exactly, I shall do that remains a bit unclear at the moment."

"How did you get off that island?"

"Marine radio at an automated lighthouse on the far side of Skellig Michael. Someone came for me the following morning, by which time Steven was long gone. God only knows what he did with the boat. Sank her, I suppose. As for me, much of the story ended when he hit me with that rock. I know nothing of Brendan's actual voyage, though I'm certain he and his band of holy brothers ended up here – right here in this very town, centuries before it became a town. Nor do I know how Steven ended up here. Those are things I do not know, but let me tell you some of the things I *do* know. I know that I traced Steven here through trickery of the international call system. I also know that since I've been here, in little over twenty-four hours, I have seen a meteor shower and light show in the sky unlike any I have seen before. I saw it from my motel room in the neighboring town. I have also seen a creature apparently unknown to modern zoology emerge, first from the deceased mouth of an honored student, and then from a solid wooden casket, and remain unscathed by a bullet. A conflagration of biblical proportions has occurred at the very place where we saw the unidentified creature. There have been two brutal murders in the same place and my arrival seems to have coincided with a rash of phone violence."

Sparky sat up. "Phones?"

"I meant to mention it earlier, when you told us of your friend's wall phone. I didn't even know people still had wall phones."

"Cell service is awful around here. Wi-Fi too. The mountains. I can't get mine to work half the time. That's why we don't get rid of the old landlines."

"I planned to check into a new motel this morning but the owner told me all the phones in the vacant rooms had been ripped apart. Heaven alone knows why, but it was enough to convince me not to stay there. I thought I might stay here in one of your spare rooms, Your Grace, if it is at all convenient." Without waiting for an answer, he said, "Now then. Let's begin with the silver cross."

"The one made from the sword?" Sparky asked. "That's what the witch Moll said to Brendan, right? Fashion the sword into a cross? I mean, in your story she told him that."

"That's right. And how did Steven know it was here?"

"I told him," Father Toomey said. "He asked me."

"Yes, yes, but *how* did he know it was here?" Father Toomey glanced at Sparky, who shrugged his shoulders in reply. "Something obviously guided him to it," Dr. Sweeney continued. "Yet why come to you, Father? Why didn't he simply break in and steal it?"

"He said he was writing his doctoral dissertation. A history of the Catholic Church in Northern New England. I didn't believe him, but he was so earnest, and I felt obligated to open the records to him."

"Ahh!" Sweeney said luxuriously and settled down in his chair. "And there is the answer. The records."

"You know...births, deaths, that sort of thing. They're in the basement under the church vestry."

"*Terra Draconis.*"

"Beg pardon?"

"Those were the only words written on the western side of the nautical chart. *Terra Draconis.* Dragon Land. Nothing about a town called Burne Notch, located at such and such a latitude, and in those days, they hadn't the first clue about how to determine longitude. If Steven followed only the chart he would still be wandering about like a lost soul and we would not be in the sorry state we're in. Something guided him to the cross and, presumably, to the cave."

"Who?" Father Toomey asked and he quickly turned away, his expression darkening at the possible answer.

Sparky spoke for them all. "It could be that thing you mentioned before. The mind incarnate, the mind or spirit of that sorcerer guy."

Sweeney caught his gaze with one equally as steady and he smiled, grateful to find a potential ally yet nonetheless troubled to hear his deepest fears uttered aloud. "The mind of Lochru," he agreed. "We shall find that out soon enough." He set his snifter down, moved the cat to the side of the cushion, and stabbed his pipe into his mouth. "So!" he said and clapped his hands together as he leaped from his chair. "To the catacombs!"

"Now?" Father Toomey asked, appalled by the idea. He didn't want to leave the fire, didn't want to leave the snifter of brandy he had poured as a follow-up to the scotch.

"Yes, now," Sweeney said. "The cross is gone, but the records are there. We may at least find out where the cross came from, which may in turn lead us to the hidden cave. Come. I expect you shall join us, Constable. We need to find out how the cross found its way here. We need to find out who gave it to the church."

12

A gray sea under a gray sky, and a small white fishing boat called the *Alison* bobbed on the dark gray waves. Two fishermen, Connor McGuire and Jimmy Dolan, smoked and joked while the boat pulled away from the windward shadow of Skellig Michael. It had been a good catch.

A gannet stared from the cliffs with its single pale eye. Its charred feathers spread and it lifted from the rocks. Thin trails of smoke spiraled beneath its wings and out it flew, out over the sea and down from the cliffs, circling, focusing on the white boat below.

It pulled in its wings and dropped. Connor and Jimmy never looked up, never saw it. They thought of nothing but securing their nets until Jimmy saw the shadow. "Jaysus...!" was all he got out before the enormous bird slammed into him.

Its beak cracked through his ribs. Blood spouted. The bird's body fell limp and Jimmy's arms dropped, his fingers uncurled. "You all right, lad?" Connor cried. Jimmy reached up, his eyes wide with fear, or panic – Connor couldn't tell which but he stepped back when his friend's expression suddenly shifted. One eye dimmed and mortified into blackened scar tissue while the other brightened into palest blue at the same time its pupil lengthened into a long black slit.

The bird hung limp and dead from his chest and Jimmy stood, surging with new life, new energy and power. He grabbed a winch handle and lifted it high.

"What is it, Jimmy? What happened, what are you – " The handle came down with a hollow crack and Connor collapsed like a rag doll. Jimmy lifted him and pushed him over the side without checking to see if he was alive or dead, and Connor McGuire sank near the windward side of Skellig Michael and was lost at sea.

Jimmy Dolan turned the wheel. The bow swung away from the jagged island, away from the mainland, and with a puff of black smoke from its engine, the *Alison* headed westward into open sea.

13

Mary Dodd, forty-five years old and recently divorced with two kids in high school and a nagging problem with her knees, was 'bored out of her gourd' – untrue, but that's what she told her friend Deb over the phone. Mary was the late cashier at Cumberland Farms, the only convenience store within thirty miles open after ten o'clock. With the fire and murders of the night before and a fugitive on the loose, it had been an exciting evening, but nerve-wracking too. Everyone who came into the store gave her a new tidbit of information or warned her to keep an eye out for the presumed murderer Raleigh Marcotte, but Burne Notch being what it was, the traffic and talk died down after nightfall and by eleven o'clock Mary had to resort to phone gossip to keep her fears at bay.

The store was bright, open and airy, and the only building in town with a front wall made entirely of partitioned glass. From the street, a passing motorist could easily have seen her through the windows, all alone, bent over the counter amidst the brightly lit rows of Doritos and Tabletalk Pies and cases of Coors Lite and Moxie. Light streamed through the windows into the small parking lot, unchallenged by any others but those above the gas pumps and, further, a small pinpoint of light above the rarely-used pay phone at the side of the road.

This last caught Mary's eye just after eleven. "Wait...just a second," she said to Deb. A man stood at the pay phone. The tiny light above him cast an aura of light surrounding a body of shadow. She saw no car. She hadn't seen any headlights, hadn't seen him walking on the road. "Someone's out at the phone."

"Can you tell who it is?"

Mary laid the receiver on the counter and squinted through the wide glass windows. Something was wrong, but she couldn't say what. The man stood upright but still appeared bent somehow, as if suffering from extreme curvature of the spine.

"Who is it?" Deb's voice sounded tinny and small in the receiver. Mary reached for it but paused when the man in the booth lifted his arm and tore off the front of the phone. It clattered to the ground and he leaned in close to paw the insides.

That's when she saw the tail.

When her found her breath again, it came out heavy and shuddering. She lifted the receiver. "Call Sparky," she said, going weak in the knees.

"Are you all right?"

"Just call him." She dropped the receiver into the cradle and grabbed the edge of the counter to keep from falling to the floor. *Tail, it was a tail, I know I saw a tail.* She slid one hand over the counter, lifted the receiver again and tucked it under her chin. She looked at a posted set of numbers taped to the register and began to dial. As she did, she glanced at the booth outside.

It was empty.

The receiver swung below the battered phone, suspended by its cord, swinging back and forth like the still warm body of a hanged criminal.

And then came something at the window, standing outside, perfectly still, staring at her.

14

Dr. Sweeney believed the damp moldering cardboard boxes stacked against the granite foundation walls held secrets of vital interest. "It's here, I *know* the answer is here."

"But really, most of this is not important," Father Toomey said. "First Communion records. Old church bulletins."

"It's more than that." The professor ran his hand over the rotting top of a cardboard box. "It always is. Look for the oldest and most decayed boxes. We'll start with those."

"But I'm not even sure Steven came down here," the priest mumbled in dismay.

Dr. Sweeney ignored him. "Constable Grant, you take that section over there. Look for anything old and strange."

"It's all old and strange," Sparky returned.

"I mean *particularly* old and strange. And you, your Grace, tell me once again what my poor Notable Scholar said to you."

Sweeney and Sparky poured over the boxes, opening each and fingering the files within while Father Toomey watched from the wooden staircase beneath a single bare light bulb, the only light in the cellar. Papers crunched. Their brittle edges broke beneath their fingers. Births. Deaths. Marriages. Dr. Sweeney was faster and far more confident than Sparky, though the policeman kept up as best he could, searching for a clue he still did not understand about a silver cross. Simple, and yet something began to nag at him even as he searched, a developing thought…

"Speak!" Sweeney shouted and pulled another box from the shelf. He dropped it on a long low table and jammed his fingers into the files. "He just showed up," Father Toomey began, slurring his words. He held his snifter between his palms. "Starts asking me about the silver cross on the wall behind the altar, who gave it, who found it, things like that. I admit I found it odd. Why would someone assume a cross was found, rather than bought or donated?"

"Why indeed?" Sweeney said with a satisfied grin.

"I told him I didn't know who found it, because I didn't. I still don't. I never gave it any thought at all. It was a cross. Nothing special. Wasn't even a crucifix, just a plain cross like the ones in Protestant churches. But even if it was unique or valuable, I still don't see what good it does us to look through all this when we know he didn't look himself."

"We don't know that," Sweeney said. The priest's drunken whines were beginning to grate on him.

"The cross was on the wall!" Father Toomey said a little too loudly. "Why would someone conduct research to find a thing that's hanging right in front of his eyes? I'm not even sure he ever came down here at all."

"I think you're right."

"Then why are we here?"

"Because we don't know where the cross is now," Sweeney said as if explaining something for the third time to a five year old. "Because we don't know where the cross originally came from. We don't know anything except this: we need to find it or this town is going to burn. Understand?" Father Toomey stared with his mouth hanging open. He blinked twice, sat back against the stairs and folded his hands over his lap. "Good," Sweeney said. "Now, we've got to look through every one of these boxes until –"

The phone in the vestry upstairs interrupted him. "Forget it," Father Toomey said but the shrill insistent spikes of sound would not let up. He moaned and maneuvered his bulk around for a listless climb up the stairs.

As soon as he left, Dr. Sweeney pressed in and clutched Sparky by the forearm. "He doesn't believe a word I've said. I know you have doubts as well, but I suspect you have an open heart, along with an open mind. I shall need to rely on you before long."

"Sure," Sparky said. "Sure, I don't mind."

"Not now, you don't."

The cellar door opened and Father Toomey's voice boomed down the stairs: "It's your sister, Sparky."

"Why didn't she call–" He reached into his coat pocket, looking for his cell phone. "Must'a left it in the car." He checked another pocket. "What did she want?" he called up the stairs, and returned to his pockets, patting his coat and the front of his jeans.

"Something about Cumberland Farms. A call about a broken phone."

Sparky looked up, caught the professor's eye.

"Let's go," Sweeney said.

15

Sparky pulled up to the front of the store and Sweeney gripped the front of the dashboard. "Sweet Jesus…"

Father Toomey leaned forward in the back seat.

Jagged sections of plate glass clung to the frame beside the front door and littered the pavement. Inside, the fluorescent lights flickered wildly over a scene of wreckage. Cases of beer upended. A display of Pringles Chips scattered over the floor. Exploded bottles of Sprite and Coca-Cola.

"I'll go look," Sparky said.

"I'll go with you." Sweeney turned to the priest in the back seat, now staring at the broken window with his lips moving soundlessly. "You stay here, Your Grace. We'll check it out. Do you have your firearm with you, Constable?"

"Yup."

"Right then," Sweeney said, looking into the store. "Let's get to it. Quietly now."

The two men opened their car doors and got out without closing them. The lights inside the store flickered with a hornet-like hum. The coolers at the far end blinked on and off, the same with the Marlboro sign above the counter. Dr. Sweeney stepped up to the shattered window frame to climb through but Sparky stopped him and pointed at the door. He opened it without a sound and they slipped inside.

Four aisles led from the front to the coolers in the back, each separated by a row of shelves and display cases. Broken bottles, coffee cans, spilled laundry detergent and pretzels littered the two center aisles, but they saw no sign of Mary Dodd. Sparky tapped Sweeney on the shoulder. He nodded toward the far right aisle and indicated he would check out the one on the left.

Sweeney swallowed hard and stepped over a pile of newspapers sprawled over the floor, all emblazoned with headlines about the murders at the funeral home. He approached the right aisle, hesitated, peered around the corner. Nothing.

He turned and saw Sparky freeze in the act of taking a step. The two men locked eyes at the same moment.

Sparky pointed to his ear and then to the left aisle. Dr. Sweeney craned his neck and listened. Above the humming lights he heard a low, thick, slurping sound.

He retraced his steps over the newspapers and passed the center aisles to join Sparky, now holding his revolver with both hands. Together they moved around a stack of Michelob Lite and stopped dead in their tracks.

Mary Dodd lay at the far end of the aisle, face up in a pool of blood. A man-thing, naked and reptilian, crouched over her, partly covered in gray scales, partly human, a vile corrupted version of Raleigh Marcotte smeared and dripping with gore.

It looked up at the two men with an expression of brutal indifference. "My God," Sweeney whispered. It hissed at them. A cloud of fetid breath poured down the aisle.

They began to back away.

It rose from a crouch.

A leathery foot slapped the floor. It hissed again, its black eyes now focused upon them with an unwavering gaze.

"Run!" the professor cried. Sparky did not bother to shoot. He turned and fled: a split-second later he saw his own reflection running toward one of the unbroken plate glass windows with Raleigh behind him on all fours, scrambling down the aisle with his thick serrated tail swinging back and forth, slamming into the racks.

The two men leaped through the broken window.

"Behind you!" Father Toomey yelled from the car. A second plate glass window exploded beside them. They ran to the car, leaped inside, and pulled the doors shut. Shattered glass rained over the hood and Raleigh stood before them in the headlight's glare.

Sparky started the engine. He fumbled with the stick shift.

"Go." Father Toomey cried. "*Go!*"

Raleigh slammed a scaly forearm down on the hood. Broken glass leaped as though on a trampoline. Talons screeched into the metal. He climbed onto the hood toward the windshield. His face was still human, still Raleigh, but his eyes stared black and ruthless. His reptilian tongue flicked in and out.

The headlights suddenly died, leaving only the frantic lights in the store to illuminate the approaching horror, now pressing its face against the windshield.

A pitiful drawn-out cry rose from a lizard hiss into an anguished howl, a human cry, the wail of a tormented soul racked to its depths. The three men recoiled when Raleigh's face pulled back from the windshield and began to transform before their eyes. A jagged cut appeared at the top of his forehead.

"Dear *God!*" Sweeney cried when the cut ripped downward.

Raleigh's forehead, nose and mouth split like a mask pulled apart at the seams and his scream shifted into a vibrant, shattering roar when a new, dark-gray face tore through and elongated into a full-toothed reptilian snout.

Two shimmering black horns ripped through his scalp and swept back like ebony daggers. He – *It* – slipped off the hood of the car and stood on its hind legs, silhouetted against the flickering lights. It jammed its claws into its still-human chest and with a gush of blood, tore away the pectoral muscles to reveal a smooth underbelly of dark gray. It lifted its talons, clawing at the air and roaring to the skies, and the sound shuddered through the car and vibrated in the glass, the roof, the seats.

The creature sent them a final, contemptuous glance and ran past them, upright on its hind legs. It crossed the parking lot with long bounding strides, passed the gas pumps and mangled pay phone, and disappeared in the woods across the road.

The headlights snapped back on.

The lights in the store stopped flickering.

"Fantastic," Sweeney whispered. "Utterly fantastic."

Father Toomey sat in the back of the car with his head against the seat, staring straight ahead, unable to accept or fully comprehend what he had seen.

Sparky was the complete opposite, frantic and agitated, unable to sit still behind the wheel. "We've got to do something," he stammered. "We've got to tell somebody!" He didn't know what to do, didn't know who to call, had never come up against anything remotely like the situation he now faced. "We've got to *do* something!"

"The first thing we must do is to keep our wits about us."

"But that *thing*!" the policeman said on the verge of tears.

Dr. Sweeney grabbed him by the wrist. "You are the only person with authority in this town. It won't do to have you flying off in a panic. Isn't that so, Father?"

Father Toomey stared at the roof, unable to respond. Sparky looked from Dr. Sweeney to the priest and back again, and managed to calm down – barely. "What should I do?" he asked in a quivering voice. "Tell me what to do and I'll do it."

Dr. Sweeney tightened his grip on Sparky's wrist. "First of all, no one will believe us. Understand that."

"But I've got to tell the state police."

"They won't believe you, no more than you would have believed me earlier had I told you exactly what I suspected and now know to be true."

"But I *saw* it!"

"So did we all. But it doesn't matter. No one will believe us. Even so, you must call for an evacuation. Tomorrow morning. This entire town must be emptied out as soon as possible."

"How?"

"By whatever means at your disposal. Second, and perhaps more urgent, I must find that girl Raeven."

"*Who?*" Sparky asked, aghast. Finding Raeven surely ranked low in importance in such a crisis.

"I'm certain she knows more than she is letting on. She was the last to see Steven alive and I know he would not have left this world without telling us something more."

Sparky swallowed hard and wiped his mouth with the back of his trembling hand. "She's at the restaurant."

"We'll go there now. But we must not falter in our search for the cross. That is where you come in, Father. We'll take you back to the church. You must continue to search through those records until you find something. Enough of this dreadful place," he said to Sparky. "Let's go."

"But what about Mary? We can't leave her there like that."

"She's beyond our help now," Sweeney said. "We'll attend to her later, but for now, drive on. I must speak to Raeven."

16

The priest sat in the back without moving or saying a word until Sparky pulled up to the front of the church. Dr. Sweeney swiveled around in the front seat. "Brace up, Your Grace," he said. "We need you now."

"Yes, yes," the priest said as he climbed out of the car, old and heavy and tired. "I'll do what I can."

"We'll be at the Panda," Sparky said. "Call us if you find anything."

"Yes," Father Toomey said and closed the car door.

He watched them drive off and trudged through the snow into the darkened church where he turned on every light in the vestry, the church itself, and from the top of the stairs, the single glaring bulb in the moldering cellar. Before going down, he unlocked a desk drawer and withdrew a bottle of scotch, thankfully nearly full. His hands shook so violently he could barely lift it to his lips. He took a swallow and winced as the burning liquid poured down his throat. "God help us," he whispered.

He could not get the image out of his mind; that last contemptuous glance of undiluted evil. He had no hesitation with the word this time. *Evil.* It was something out of that mythological place of fire and brimstone he once believed in so fervently but had long ago receded before the more mundane terrors of ordinary worldly existence. That one shattering glance had brought those long-neglected beliefs thundering back. Whatever that thing was, lizard, reptile, denizen of this earthly realm or not, it was wholly demonic. Everything he once imagined pouring from the infernal pits of Hell paled in comparison.

He shivered again, this time from the cold. He pulled up the collar of his heavy coat and descended the stairs still holding the bottle. The garish light spread as far as it could into the corners.

Where to start?

He shook his head to clear his mind and nearly fell from the resulting dizziness. He lifted one of the boxes, poured its contents onto the long low table, spread them out and ran his fingers over them, searching for something; a date, a mention of a gift to the church. He followed the pattern over and over again, emptying boxes, scanning the contents – births, deaths, priest's records – and dumping everything back into the boxes again.

He looked inside one and immediately started to put it back on the shelf. It was filled with his own papers; old photographs and school records from St. John's Seminary. *Wait…is it still in there?* He pawed through the papers to the bottom and felt around until he found a small velvet-covered box. He opened it to reveal a silver crucifix and chain, a gift from his mother on the day he was ordained and put away several years later. *Why?* He couldn't remember. He draped the chain over his head, tucked the crucifix under his collar and patted it, comforted to feel it cold against his chest – comforted, but not protected. It had no power. He believed that. He *knew* that. It was a token, a charm, no more and no less powerful than a lucky rabbit's foot keychain.

He poured through box after box, emptying and refilling them with nothing standing out and nothing to confirm the reality of the vision seen in the store until – he almost missed it – a brown packet tied up with frayed string at the bottom of a box containing some of the oldest records. He carefully unwrapped the parcel and exposed several folded sheets of fragile paper. He marveled at the fine penmanship with its grand flourishes and straight lines, and when he scanned the first page, his heart beat faster when he came to the bottom and read: *"found in the Stonehenge field, a most marvelous silver object of intricate design..."*

He ran his finger down the next page, searching for a word, a clue, anything that would indicate its whereabouts now. A word jumped out. "My God," he whispered. He held the paper up to the light and he jumped, startled, when the light went out.

Power outage. Maybe a tree gone down? A line snapped somewhere. Too much ice?

He stood motionless in the dark and listened, but heard no sound at all – no wind, no mice scuttling in the walls, nothing but thick silence.

He scraped his foot over the floor and felt his way to the stairs. The brittle document crinkled in his fingers. He banged his knee against the side of the table. "Damn," he whispered. He carefully folded the document back into the packet and slid it into his inside jacket pocket.

Using one hand to feel his way, he climbed the stairs but stopped at a single sharp bang from somewhere above.

He didn't know whether to continue up the stairs and say something or go back down and wait in silence.

The light snapped on again, but fitfully, like a fluorescent bulb that won't quite go on.

He grabbed the bottle, determined to leave the cellar as quickly as possible and make the call to the Golden Panda. Before he did, he felt his jacket pocket, felt the crunch of the document tucked inside. His role was over. He found what Sweeney had asked him to find. There was nothing more he could do or, more truthfully, wanted to do.

The cellar light wavered. He took another hefty swallow from the bottle and climbed the stairs, one slow step at a time. Once in the vestry, he saw the desk lamp wavering too, as if it couldn't decide whether to stay on or off. He glanced through the window. The lights in the parish house and the streetlights out front flashed. Those inside the church flickered too, but in a more random manner. He took another quick gulp of scotch and reached for the phone.

It wasn't there.

"What the devil...?" He froze at the sound of a footstep inside the church. It *was* a footstep, he sure of it, though it sounded more like a watery slap.

He moved from his desk. "Now don't go imagining things," he whispered. Light spread in undulating waves throughout the mostly dark church. He stepped up to the door. His foot touched something. He looked down and saw his old rotary phone lying in a tangled heap of cords and circuitry on the floor.

Panic began to rise. *That thing…it can't be here, it can't!* He closed his eyes and clenched his jaw in an attempt to force it down. He reached through his shirt and clasped his silver crucifix and stepped through the vestry door into the church where he began to breathe freely again. "Oh, for heaven's sake," he said, relieved to see the front door swinging in the wind. He released his lucky token and walked along the side toward the front of the church, shaking his head – *but wait.* He stopped. *Didn't I close that? I'm sure I did. I'm sure I locked it too.*

A shadow moved in the center aisle. He glanced over his shoulder and there it was, crouched behind the altar with the golden chalice and plate held close to its scaled breast, motionless, staring.

Father Toomey fell against the wall. It stepped around the side of the altar and dropped the gold. The chalice landed with a single clang but the plate rolled into the center aisle where it ran up against a wooden pew and dropped into a spiraling clatter, faster, louder, spinning down until it hit the floor with a single, sharp, metallic clap.

IV.

Silver

John-Richard Thompson

1

Only two cars, Joe's and Pearl's, remained in the Golden Panda parking lot by the time Sparky drove up the long steep driveway in the squad car. Still shaken, he told the professor the front door would already be locked for the night and led him around to the back. Uncle Lung howled when they dashed through the kitchen into the lounge where Pearl and Raeven sat a banquette folding napkins while Joe cleaned up the bar.

"You won't believe it!" Sparky cried.

Pearl leaped to her feet, startled. "Believe what?"

"Raleigh Marcotte, he's…I don't know what. Something awful!"

"Well – yeah."

"I told you he changed," Raeven said, woozy from the effects of Percocet and an unfortunate decision to mix it with a glass of wine. Dr. Sweeney sat down beside her. "How did you know that?"

"I saw him in my bedroom," she said, slurring her words.

"He killed Mary Dodd," Sparky said. Pearl's mouth dropped open. Raeven stopped swaying. Joe stopped wiping the bar. "Probably killed his parents too."

"Mary?" Pearl whispered and sank down on a bar stool. "He killed Mary?"

Dr. Sweeney peered at her over his glasses. "Come," he said, nodding to a large circular table near the fireplace. "The time has come for you to hear what we are up against."

Pearl and Sparky exchanged anxious glances and joined Raeven after she staggered the three steps from the banquette to a chair. Joe set a bowl of fortune cookies in the middle of the table before sitting down beside her.

"First – and I say this as much certainty as I can muster – first of all it is clear that something dreadful has come among us." Dr. Sweeney once again related the tale of Skellig Michael as he had for Sparky and Father Toomey in the parish house. At one point in the story, Uncle Lung banged a pot in the kitchen and Pearl jumped. At another, Raeven's head drooped to the side. Dr. Sweeney tapped her on the shoulder. "Try to stay awake," he said, and she sat up again, swaying in her chair. "This may have something to do with you."

"Me?" she asked, trying to focus.

"Her?" Pearl asked, pointing at Raeven with her thumb.

Sweeney nodded. He could not hide his concern as he gazed at the girl in black, exhausted and medicated, her skin pale and blotchy and lip hidden by gauze. He could be wrong and dearly hoped he was. With a shrug, he broke a fortune cookie in half and quickly read the fortune inside. "And so," he said, continuing his tale. "The witch Moll led the warrior Donal to her cauldron whereupon she pulled forth a handful of the foul-smelling, putrid contents and smeared it over the knight's armor and shield."

"What was it?" Pearl asked. "I mean, what kind of plants?"

"Haven't a clue. But that reminds me, Constable…my book of herbals is among the others I brought to Father Toomey's. Do not let me forget it when we return to see how he is managing. Now. Of equal importance – or rather of much greater importance – is the sword. Do you know of the *Tuatha Dé Danann?*"

"More weird Irish shit, I suppose," Pearl said.

"They were the Good People, the beautiful ones, the children of the goddess Danu, the kings and queens and heroes of the Otherworld. Sometimes called faeries."

Pearl rolled her eyes. "Like I said, weird Irish shit."

"Which is why I hate the word faeries," Sweeney said. "It makes it difficult to take them seriously and the *Tuatha Dé Danann* must, at all times, be taken seriously. We shall call them the *fae*, as that is a good deal easier to stomach They were known for having Four Treasures, and these being The Spear of Lugh, The Cauldron of Dagda, The Stone of Fal, and last, *An Claiomh Solais*, the Sword of Light, from which no foe escapes once it is drawn from its scabbard."

"Is that supposed to be the sword we're looking for?" Sparky asked.

"I dearly wish it was, but no. After Moll had brewed her protective potion and smeared it on the knight Donal's armor, she withdrew into her hovel and returned with a bundle tied up in sealskin. As she untied the cords, she spoke of something I honestly have never heard of in all my years of studying the Celtic mythologies. According to the witch Moll, the Sword of Light was not the only mystical sword made by the *fae*. They created two additional blades to help protect the north, south and east. The Sword of Light was made of gold to represent the sun; the second made of some green substance representing the sea; and the third of bronze to protect the earth. All three were imbued with warrior power, fierce, hot and thrusting. Moll tells us the *Tuatha Dé Danann* grew fearful of this concentration of masculine power. They could not tolerate such unnatural imbalance and so they forged a fourth sword. Made of silver. Darker than the others, yet lighter. She was intuitive. She was fatal. And she was called *An*

Claiomh Gealach. The Sword of the Moon."

A siren wailed in the distance and Sparky sat up in his chair with his hands curling into fists. "Ambulance," he said. "Someone found Mary Dodd." When he rose from his seat, the table shifted and upset the bowl of fortune cookies. "I shouldn't have left her there like that. Someone must have the called the Freemonde police because I wasn't around, and my cell phone, where *is* that damned...? I should have been there."

"But you weren't and with good reason," Sweeney said. "This is far more important." He nodded at Sparky's chair. With a muttered, "Oh man," the policeman sat down and stared at the table but did not focus on the conversation until the professor spoke of Moll's reading of the gull flight patterns and her prophesy of the Three, the column of wood and the Knight of the White Bird. "I have no idea what such things might mean," he said, "but I hope to heaven they shall guide us out of this predicament."

"What predicament?" Pearl asked. "I still don't get it."

"Remember the words of Moll," Sweeney said. "Lochru shall return, first in spirit, then in bodily form." His listeners stared at him, though Sparky continued to gaze at the table. Sweeney brought his forefingers up to rest upon his chin. "And so he's come again."

"Who has come again?" Joe asked. "The sorcerer?"

"Lochru, yes."

"A *sorcerer*?" Joe asked as if giving Sweeney a chance to come up with a better, more sensible word.

"Wait a second," Raeven said, shaking her head to clear away her confusion. "Are you saying you actually believe all that?"

"Of course not," Pearl said, jabbing her with her elbow. "He's only telling us what he found on that Michael Island place."

"I am telling you what I found *and* what I believe." He raised his hand to stop the protest. "The mind of Lochru is, or was, already here. If you had known Steven as I did, you would know that some form of calamitous psychological disturbance had befallen him. The mind of another led him here to unleash this thing upon us. If I am correct – and dear God, I hope I am not; but if I am, I expect the bodily incarnation of the sorcerer is on its way here now."

"How?" Joe asked.

"As a parasite, the same as before, only this time inhabiting a physical body much more fully than when confined to the mind alone."

Sparky looked up from the table and cleared his throat. "So what..." he began, hoarsely, and cleared his throat again. "So what do we do now?"

Sweeney turned to him. "We find him and we kill him."

"You mean, just...kill him?" Sparky asked. "Like that?"

"Like that, yes. With the silver sword. It is the only way. There is no reasoning with one such as this."

"But what if you're wrong? What if he's not a sorcerer, which is crazy to think he would be anyway. What if he's just a guy? A bad guy, but just a guy. We can't kill him. We can't *do* that."

"We can for we have no choice. And we must be firm in our purpose. Resolute. Evil takes root and draws power from indecision. Let us pray Father Toomey has had some luck."

No one said a word. Uncle Lung banged another pot. A faucet dripped behind the bar. Joe got up to close it. "Do not give in," he said and everyone looked at him.

"To what?" Sparky asked.

"What?" Joe asked in return. He bent low behind the bar to close the faucet.

"You just said, 'Do not give in.'"

"No, I didn't."

"Yeah, you did," Pearl said and broke open a fortune cookie. "Why do I still eat these things?" She broke off a piece with her teeth before looking at her fortune.

YOU HAVE GOOD BUSINESS SENSE

"Yeah, right, which is why I still work in this dump." She popped another piece into her mouth while Sparky and Joe continued their 'do not give in" debate.

"Why would I say that?" Joe asked, defensive, and saluted up his glasses.

"Okay, okay, so you didn't say it. Let's drop it."

Pearl picked up two more cookies and handed one to Raeven. She broke it open and stared at the fortune, puzzled.

RIDIRE

She shrugged her shoulders and dropped the fortune on the table. Sweeney noticed. "What did it say?"

"Nothing. Misprint."

"Open another," he said and handed her a cookie. She broke it open, read the fortune, and through the beginnings of a yawn, raised her eyebrows in surprise: "How did you do that?" She finished the yawn, "oh, *excuse* me," and showed the fortune to Pearl, who nodded, impressed, as though he had performed a magic trick.

"Do what?" Sweeney asked, bewildered. "I didn't do a thing."

"You had to," Raeven said, but he shook his head and asked what it said. Raeven looked up from the fortune and locked eyes with Joe. "Do not give in."

He came out from behind the bar. She handed it to him.

DO NOT GIVE IN

"It's a trick," Joe began, but a second, distant siren drilled through the walls, interrupting him.

"Oh, man – *again?*" Sparky said and dropped his head onto his arms. "That's the siren at the firehouse." Before Sweeney could protest, he stood and grabbed his coat. "I have to go."

Sweeney sighed and scratched his nose and tapped on the table with his fingers. He swept Raeven's two fortunes into his hand and dropped them into his inside jacket pocket. "Very well," he said, "I've about finished anyway. I'll go with you. We'll meet again tomorrow, all of us, along with Father Toomey. I expect there shall be a public meeting of some kind in the morning. Where would you conduct such an affair?" Sparky mentioned the town hall and Sweeney suggested they meet there at nine-thirty the following morning. "And we'll return here after," he said. "Fireplace. Food available. Places to hide. This shall be our headquarters." He bid them all a good night and after a firm "Keep your spirits up," followed Sparky through the kitchen doors.

"What do you think he meant by that?" Joe asked.

"He wants us to be cheerful," Pearl said. "Like that's possible with all this weirdo shit going on."

"No, I meant what he said earlier. Do you think we'll need them?"

"Need what?"

"Places to hide."

2

Minutes later, Pearl and Joe helped Raeven from the restaurant into the front seat of Pearl's beat up old car. She could walk on her own, but was so drowsy they feared she might fall on the ice.

"What's that?" Joe asked and pointed over the hood of the car. Pearl squinted beyond the glare of the Golden Panda sign into the forest but saw only endless darkness fronted by a few snowy boughs. "No, up there," he said and pointed higher, lifting her gaze above the trees where a mass of cobalt blue light had fused into a soundless web of voltage that hung above a section of the dark mountain. It looked as if the walls of a gully had been spliced together by a net of electricity, silent in the distance, but leaving little doubt of its power and ferocity.

"Is *that* why the fire alarm went off?" Pearl asked. "Who's going to put that out?"

"Maybe one of the power lines behind the ski slope fell. Maybe those are live wires."

"Maybe," Pearl said, but something in her heart told her *no*. She circled around the car to the driver's side. "I'm gonna take Raeven back to my place now. You and Emphysema all right here alone?"

"Sure, we're fine." Joe looked at Raeven through the window, unconscious and illuminated by the dome light, with her head back against the seat. The tape on her bandage had come loose on one side. Joe gazed at her until Pearl closed her door and the light went off.

He stood in the parking lot and watched the car descend along the steep driveway, with the red taillights glowing until they disappeared over a low rise; and it was quiet then, a deep winter silence with no chirping of insects, no wind, and no light but for the sign at edge of the parking lot and those in the high distance.

He could not know it then – no one could for it happened in places far removed from human eyes; but further up, beyond the blue fires, the mountain had begun to shift. Small cracks and fissures opened where once stood solid rock. Rough spikes of stone tore through the ground. The chairlift stretched above the ski slopes. Its cables tightened between the tower supports while the supports themselves whined and twisted…but all in small degrees, difficult to notice. Beyond the illuminated slopes the deeper forest swarmed with movement. Boughs waved and bent with pine trees contorting into misshapen images of their former selves. Roots twisted up from beneath the earth like pale sightless eels searching for prey. They squirmed over the snow and through the thickets, and those few rabbits and other creatures unlucky enough to pass into those parts of the forest did not come out again. Owls long used to certain trees now found them transformed and lethal.

Beyond the ski slopes, in the more secret areas, something far more dangerous than the trees lurched into existence. Power, raw and undiluted, sprang from nowhere by way of the same unknowable forces that brought the trees to vivid life. It clung to the earth and rocks as lichen will, and there built upon itself, surging and throbbing and casting out new tendrils of blue fire, and these stray charges twined around each other and joined with others to form tangled lines of glimmering light; mostly blue, but with faint traces of purple and red where they gained the most strength.

Burne Notch, though no one realized it, was being sewn up.

3

Another fire, this time at the church. The fire truck and a few members of his firefighting team were already on the scene when Sparky arrived. Some never showed at all. Dr. Sweeney held back at the car, mesmerized by fire's glow behind the stained glass windows. "Has anyone seen Father Toomey?" he shouted and stepped around a tangle of fire hoses.

"The cellar, he might still be down there," Sparky said and he ordered his crew to focus on the back of the church and the vestry. Sweeney tapped the policeman on the arm and pointed at the parish house where the front door lay in splinters. "Looks like it broke through there."

"It?" Sparky asked, and then, with widening eyes: "You mean that *thing* did this?" When Sweeney nodded, he said, "oh wow," and headed toward the parish house. "Be careful," the professor called but Sparky had already rushed inside and now stood gazing in dismay at the wreckage of a room that had been so warm and inviting only a few hours before. Furniture on its side. Sofa torn to ribbons. Another landline phone broken and scattered over the floor. Dr. Sweeney came in behind. He picked up a lamp and tried to turn it on but the bulb had shattered.

"Father Toomey?" Sparky called but heard no answer. "Maybe he's still in the cellar," he said, now in a hopeful tone, and rushed back through the ravaged front door.

Dr. Sweeney scanned the overturned chairs and slashes on the walls. The books he had brought to the parish house lay scattered throughout. He stacked those he could find on the only chair that remained upright. He reached under the shade of an unbroken lamp and pulled the cord. "Soot?" he called and a cry sounded in the kitchen.

He worked his way across the ransacked room to the kitchen where a small dark shape huddled in the shadows beside the refrigerator. When he flicked on the light switch, an overhead fluorescent bulb sputtered into a dull blue-white glow. "There now, puss, nothing to be frightened–"

He stopped short. The cat huddled in a corner, its eyes wide with lingering terror. In the middle of the white tile floor, four characters had been hastily drawn in red ink: *t, G, r,* and what appeared to be the beginning of an *e* that ended in a frantic wavering line across the kitchen floor, as though the writer had been dragged away while holding the pen. A red marker at the end of the line lay uncovered in a wide smear of red – *of red blood, not red ink*, Sweeney realized with dismay. "T. G. R. E.," he whispered, and said them together as a word, pronouncing it first as *tee-gree*, and then as "tigre…le tigre."

Sparky called from behind: "They got into the cellar but he's not there. Maybe he–" He, too, stopped in mid-sentence and stared at the kitchen floor, the ink, the blood.

"Does the French word *le tigre* mean anything to you?" Sweeney asked. "Or *tiger*?"

Sparky shook his head, puzzled. "What is it?"

"Father Toomey's last confession, I fear."

4

Cell phones barely worked in Burne Notch at any time, but now, with so much crackling interference, most gave up trying to use them. At the same time, landline phones lay in ruins all through town. No one knew why they were attacked or disappeared, or that the insides of many of the remaining rotary phones in town lay piled in a cave at the edge of a windswept pasture. Unable to escape the surrounding rock walls, electricity crackled through the charred air to illuminate a hoard of gold medallions, shields, crowns, coins, broken phones and circuitry, Mary Dodd's blood-stained necklace, Raeven's class ring, the chalice and plate from the Sacred Heart Church.

An odor of seared ozone filled the treasure cave. Father Toomey smelled it when he struggled into consciousness beneath a sheltering web of electrical charges.

His back had been torn to ribbons. He could feel his flesh sticking to the stone floor in a mass of coagulating blood mingling with shredded fabric. He connected the pain with the last remembered images of himself running with tortured breath from the church to the parish house, the door smashing open behind, the linoleum kitchen floor and the rending claw tearing down his back as he tried to write a final desperate message. He had blacked out and remained in blessed oblivion until he opened his eyes and smelled the charred rot and felt the electrical shocks and the pain scrabbling over his back. "My God," he said with a groan and the sound of his voice caused something to rouse and slither over the floor.

Black and slick, it poked through the blinding electrical cocoon and moved up the priest's body, touching him with light, deft strokes. At its end, he saw a glossy black stinger curved like a scimitar. Father Toomey whimpered when it slipped around the back of his head and pulled it up, forcing him to look.

He followed the length of what he now realized was a tail until his gaze settled upon *it*, the creature, sitting on its haunches against the wall with its front claws gently clacking like wooden wind chimes.

Its nostrils flared when it released the priest and drew back its tail. Father Toomey tried to lower his head and close his eyes but found he could not. Reflections of gold burned upon the surface of its eyes and filled it with hellish energy, as if they were the source of its power. Its hypnotic stare imparted a sensation of extracting the priest's mind from his body, disembodying it and pulling it into places it did not want to go – *Don't give in to it…do not give in!* The desperate words tumbled through his mind at the moment Joe Li said the same puzzling words at the Golden Panda,

The creature leaned forward with a violent hiss and the priest screamed when a claw ripped through the blue cocoon. It pierced him through the leg muscles and hauled him upside-down into the air. His silver cross and chain slipped out of his collar and clattered through the webbing to the floor and there he hung, suspended like a side of beef swinging from a meat hook. The net of electricity closed around him, the creature released its grip and, to his shock, he remained suspended in the air, floating like a fetus inside the web of crackling blue light. Blood flowed from his mangled leg and he had all he could do not to scream again: but he didn't – *Do not give in!* – and he suppressed his cry of pain until the creature squeezed out of the cave with a gurgling hiss and returned to the night for more.

5

Pearl slipped a Patsy Cline CD into the player and turned down the volume to avoid waking Raeven in the seat beside her. She cranked up the heater and began to sing along, softly.

They approached Jerrod and Elizabeth Grey's dairy farm. The lights in the barn flickered as if something was interfering with the power supply. Pearl noticed but didn't give it much thought. She continued to sing as they passed the farm and approached the place beside the pasture where they had first come upon Steven's burning car. *How many nights ago?* She ran through the intervening events that seemed to have distorted time; fires, suicides, violent deaths; and her thoughts wandered further to Dr. Sweeney's creepy tale of witches and monks when her car jolted.

She looked at the fuel gauge. Three quarters full. "What the hell?" The engine skipped again. She pressed her foot on the gas but that seemed to make it worse. The generator light came on. "Oh, no." The dashboard lights dimmed, the CD player clicked off, and the headlights fluttered into dull yellow and lower into black. "Come on, come on, come on," she said, encouraging it, but it didn't help.

The car stalled and rolled to a crunching stop. Pearl sighed and tapped her fingernails on the steering wheel. "Raev," she whispered and shook her by the shoulder. "You awake?"

No reply, not even a moan.

Pearl sat back and stared at the pitch-black darkness beyond the windshield, wondering what to do. *Piece'a shit car.* She felt the seat beside her, searching for her cell phone. She found it and pressed a button but nothing happened. She tried another. Same thing. "Piece'a shit phone." She thought about walking to the dairy farm and using theirs, but decided to wait a few minutes and try to start the car again. She rummaged around on the dashboard until she found her cigarettes and stuck one in her mouth.

She turned the ignition.

Nothing: no sound, no turn of the engine.

She rolled her window down. Cold air slipped inside, chased there by the wind hissing in the trees. Thick snow clouds overwhelmed whatever fitful moonlight tried to break through and even when her eyes grew accustomed to the darkness she could not see a thing.

She looked at the rear view mirror, but in such total darkness she wasn't sure she was looking at it at all. She swiveled and looked out the rear windshield. Nothing. She assumed a bend in the road hid the flickering lights at the farm behind. She did not realize they had gone out too.

She rolled the window back up and drummed her fingers on the steering wheel again, waiting for the cigarette lighter to pop out. A moment later she realized it was as dead as the rest of car. She felt around the seat with unlit cigarette bobbing up and down between her lips and carried on a conversation with her undiscovered purse. "Come on pocky-booky, where are you?"

She thought she heard something outside, a crunch on the ice…she paused, listening, but heard nothing more. She resumed the search for the purse, but stopped again.

There *was* something there. It was in front of the car.

She didn't see it. She didn't hear it. She sensed it the way a wall can be sensed while walking through a familiar but dark room.

"Raeven." She had to struggle to get the sound out. She tapped her leg. Raeven shifted in the seat. The squeaking sound sent Pearl's heart into her throat. "Come on now, calm down," she whispered and the frightened quiver in her voice startled her.

She rolled the window down again, only a crack, and leaned toward it. She wanted to ask if somebody was there but couldn't get her voice to work. Instead, she concentrated on listening. Another hiss of wind passed through the high treetops beside the road and, closer, she heard a light clacking of bare branches like wooden wind chimes.

Something nudged the front of the car.

"Wake up," Pearl whispered, this time shaking Raeven by the arm. "Wake up."

She moaned and pulled her arm away. "What's the matter?" she asked, groggy and slurring her words.

"Something's out there."

"Where are we?" Raeven sat up and looked around, but in the complete darkness it seemed she had not yet opened her eyes.

Another nudge. This time the car slid backward a full twelve inches. "What was that?" Raeven asked.

"Something's outside," Pearl whispered, her hands now gripping the steering wheel and her eyes glued to windshield. "In front," she said and her heart nearly burst at the sound of a door opening.

Cold air rushed in, the seat squeaked, and Raeven got out of the car.

Pearl heard her boots crunch on the snow, but before she could reach for her, before she could react in any way, Raeven put one hand on her hip, threw her head back and called in a loud voice: "Oh, bugger off!"

A moment of deep silence, and – s*lam!* Something crashed down on the front hood.

Pearl screamed. Raeven clambered back into the car, brought to her senses as if someone had dashed cold water on her face. A sound of tearing metal rent the air. "What *is* that?" she cried, seemingly shocked to discover she had been outside. They both screamed when a second, far more violent blow struck the front end of the car. It bounced on its springs, a roar trembled through the steel and glass, followed by a lurch that made their heads snap back – another screech of tearing metal – something cracked against Pearl's window, and then came a tremor of heavy footsteps passing her door and pounding down the road away from the car.

A moment passed with only their quivering breath to mar the silence before the car suddenly filled with light – headlights, dashboard, dome lights; everything snapping on at once, and Patsy Cline once more taking up where she had left off.

Pearl stared over the steering wheel with her hands trembling and her breath coming fast. The front hood had been torn off at the hinges. It lay on the snow bank, illuminated by the headlights, nearly folded in half with a wide dent in the middle and a set of long jagged lines cut into the metal. Her side window had been shattered into a spider web of cracks. "I can't believe you did that," she whispered.

Raeven did not look at her. She gazed, bewildered, through the windshield at the battered hood. Her bandage had fallen to reveal a dark line of stitches above her lip. "But what did I do?"

6

The *Alison* bobbed on the raucous North Atlantic, her fuel gone and engine still. On board, the one-eyed man, once a fisherman named Jimmy Dolan, stared into the northeast at a tiny light in the distance. It vanished with every sickening slide into the troughs, but with each rise upon the cresting waves he saw it again, the lights of a freighter growing larger and brighter.

A voice crackled in the radio below. "Do you read me? Is there anyone aboard? This is *Isolde*, do you read me?" The man's pale eye glittered with inner fire as he opened the seacocks. Water poured into the bilge and the radio crackled: "Are you in need of assistance?"

The man lifted the receiver and told them yes, he needed assistance, his boat was taking on water. The *Alison* listed. Seawater poured over the gunwale and hissed around his legs. Waves pounded the hull, tilting it further; and he calmly stared at the hulk of the freighter approaching with its running lights growing larger and brighter until it blazed on the night sea like a floating city and lowered the ladders for rescue.

7

Dr. Sweeney worked by candlelight at a table in Sparky Grant's living room.

The policeman lay on the sofa behind him, fast asleep, still wearing his boots and smoky clothes. He hadn't meant to fall asleep but he couldn't help it. Within five minutes of sitting down he was on his back, breathing deep and steady with Father Toomey's cat lying curled in the crook of his arm.

The professor turned Sparky's unplugged old rotary phone upside down on the table and began to pry it apart. He unscrewed a small plate, detached a set of wires, broke off a tiny weld and stared into the mangled phone at a small circuit board. "Ahh, so *this* is what you are after." He moved the candle closer. Its light spread over the circuit board and shimmered on a set of connectors, each one coated with a thin film of gold.

8

Inside the Golden Panda, the coals in the fireplace had nearly burned to ash. Joe gave the bar a final wipe when he noticed the lights in the kitchen begin to flicker. "Uncle?" he called, and saluted his glasses up twice while waiting for an answer.

The kitchen door squealed open. "Light," the old chef said, silhouetted by the shuddering glow from behind.

"You finished cleaning?" Joe asked and Lung answered with a wide gold-toothed smile and a hearty nod.

"What's wrong with the lights?"

"No good. Garbagy."

Joe brought the condiments to the cooler. "You done in here?"

"Garbagy," Uncle Lung repeated, this time with some justification for he pointed to three bulging trash bags. Joe returned to the bar and Uncle Lung tossed all three bags out the back door. He picked up two, one in each hand, and carried them to the garbage cans inside the chicken wire cage built to keep out raccoons.

Light flickered on the icy parking lot. He peered around the corner of the cage and saw the Golden Panda sign ebbing and brightening, the same as the lights in the kitchen and, now, the small light above the back door. He scowled and brought the remaining bag to the cage.

The kitchen door opened. Flickering light spilled over the ice. Joe leaned into the cold. "We got any more light bulbs?" Uncle Lung shrugged. He bolted the lock on the cage and headed toward the kitchen. "I'll get some tomorrow," Joe said. He shut the door and Uncle Lung froze, his mind struggling to take in what appeared before him, revealed by the closing door.

It sat on its haunches and cocked its head, staring. Its talons clacked with a sound like leafless winter branches.

Suddenly – "Where's the fuse box?" – Joe's voice in the kitchen intruded upon the shocked silence and the old man wailed.

"Uncle!" Joe yelled. He opened the door. The massive head jerked to the side and slammed against it with such force that it threw him across the kitchen where he struck a shelf and fell to the floor.

Outside, the thing moved. Its clawed foot crunched on the ice. Uncle Lung held his hands up and screamed and the light above the door flashed upon his teeth and the thing stared, covetous, greedy, and like a viper with a mouse – it struck.

Lung's scream cut off when the teeth closed around him, tore his mouth from his face; and with a single jerk, flung the unwanted remainder of his body so high and far it made a slow, crackling tumble through the branches...got hung up on one of the lower, thicker ones...then slid off and dropped lifeless into the snow.

9

If Sparky Grant had any worries about gathering the remaining citizenry of Burne Notch together for a meeting, he needn't have bothered. They showed up in full-throated force the following morning to shout questions about missing and broken telephones, mysterious fires, and most frantic of all, the terrible deaths. He spoke from the stage in the town hall and did his best to provide answers and explanations, but since so many of his own questions had gone unanswered, he struggled to come up with something that sounded even halfway plausible. He hoped to get some guidance from Dr. Sweeney, but the professor sat huddled in a folding chair in the front row, scribbling in his notebook.

"This thing is bad," Sparky said to the crowd. "A special team from the state police is on its way and I won't be surprised if the National Guard is brought in. If so, they'll evacuate the entire area, so you might as well leave now. Today. We've all got to get out of town until it's..." He hesitated. "Until it's killed."

Dr. Sweeney looked up from his notebook.

"Until *what* is killed?" someone yelled and Sparky pleaded with the professor to take the stage.

Sweeney took up the challenge. He bounded up the stairs with his long hair in disarray and glasses askew and he clasped his hands behind his back and waited for the calls and murmurs to die down. "I am Dr. Raghnall Sweeney, Archeologist," he said in calm, practiced tones, "and I echo the assertions made by your constabulary. You must evacuate this town as soon as possible for there is, amongst you now, a predator." The crowd erupted and Sweeney held up his hands until they settled down again. "You asked for an answer and this is it: you now face two incontrovertible facts. First, a thing has come among you that kills without fear of any weapon you may possess. Second, your only chance of avoiding it is to leave town, and to do so before it is too late."

A woman stood and yelled "Too late for what?" and Sweeney turned his steady gaze upon her. "For being hunted down and slaughtered without hesitation or remorse." She blanched and sat again without further comment. "To those who elect to stay – and I have no doubt there are some foolish enough to risk it – I ask only this. Do not wear gold of any kind. Necklaces, rings, chains, wedding bands, earrings: take them off and hide them well."

"What are you talking about?" a man asked. "Who is doing this, a person?"

"No."

"An animal? What kind of animal gives a damn about gold? That doesn't make any sense."

"No, it doesn't. But the fact remains: it is very much attracted to gold. It hoards gold and…" He stopped, distracted by a thought. "It hoards gold and other things," he continued, his voice softer now, as though this new thought overwhelmed all others.

"You all right?" Sparky whispered.

He nodded and said to the crowd, "I advise you all, in the strongest terms, to remove yourselves from town as soon as possible."

The uproar resumed, with business owners like Maurice Garand from the ski lodge most vocal in their protest. "I shall not argue further, nor shall I plead," Dr. Sweeney said with his hands once again clasped behind his back. "We have done our part. You must now decide which you prefer to lose, a few days of business or your lives. As Constable Grant stated, should you choose to stay and manage to survive, the state police and the military will force an evacuation whether you like or not. At the same time, they will be powerless against this thing, which is why he and I shall remain behind after you have gone."

Sparky stepped toward him, his face expressing his alarm.

"Remain!" he whispered, but the professor ignored him. "I say this to you now," he warned the crowd. "This thing cannot be killed in any conventional manner. You may arm yourselves, you may bring in the army, you may use artillery, but I assure you, there is only one way to destroy it." He scanned the now silent audience, searching for a sign of Raeven and Pearl. "Only one way," he repeated. "By only one person, with a weapon as yet unfound." He cleared his throat and adjusted his glasses. "The chances are not good."

When the townspeople began to murmur amongst themselves, Sparky leaned in close and whispered, "What do you mean, we're staying?"

"I'll explain later."

"I'm not staying!"

Sweeney continued to scan the assembled crowd. "Where's Raeven? Why isn't she here? And Pearl?" A tone of nervousness crept into his voice. "Did you call them?"

"With what? You broke my phone and the cell service – only static now. I can't get through to anyone."

"We told them about this meeting last night, didn't we?"

"Yeah, just before we left them at the…" Sparky swallowed hard and drew the back of his hand across his mouth. The two men looked at each other and Sparky suggested they check Pearl's trailer on the way to the restaurant. Sweeney nodded and handed him the notebook. "See if any of it means anything to you."

"Go, everyone," Sparky called before following the professor off the stage. "Do as we tell you – go!" The two men pushed through the crowd, with Sweeney leading the way and Sparky behind him, reading over the first column of entries in the notebook.

T_grea
T_greb
T_grec
T_gred

10

"Raeven get up," Pearl said, shaking her by the shoulder.

"What is it? What happened?" It took her a moment to remember she was in Pearl's bedroom and that the Marcotte fire had destroyed her own bed. Dull sunlight seeped through the red curtains. "Is it morning already?"

"We overslept," Pearl said and shook her again.

"Turn on the light," Raeven said and pulled the quilt up close to her chin. "Why is it so cold?"

"Come into the living room," Pearl said and Raeven, irritated, pushed her hand away and turned on the light. "Why do we have to—" She sat back against the headboard, shocked into silence.

"Don't look, just come out," Pearl whispered, stepping back to the door.

A network of parsnip-colored roots tinted pink by the red curtains had worked through the window frames and the roof to give the bedroom the look of a cavern beneath a forest, with tree roots dangling from the ceiling and clinging to the walls. They had wrapped around framed photos of Pearl's mother and grandmother and covered much of the floor and the lower parts of the bed in a tangle of pallid tentacles. One had twined around a bedpost.

Pearl held out a heavy blue robe. Raeven needed no further encouragement. She sprang from the bed wearing a black t-shirt and gym shorts and donned the robe while following Pearl down the narrow hall to the living room where she collapsed on the sofa. "What *are* those things?"

As if in answer, the front door opened and Sweeney and Sparky barreled into the trailer, startling both women and all the birds.

"God almighty, birds too!" Sweeney cried and when Sparky explained they belonged to Pearl, he took in the flock with a quick glance: "*All* of them?"

"The bedroom," Pearl said, ignoring the question.

Sparky nodded. "Outside too."

Pearl pushed aside the canvas curtains and stepped onto her small wooden veranda. A thicket of pine trees had gathered at the back of the trailer like an impenetrable wilderness sprung up overnight. "What are they?" she asked when she came back inside, but with only a shrug from Sparky and no answer at all from Sweeney, all three turned to Raeven.

She rocked back and forth on the sofa and held the collar of the robe up close to her chin. Her stitches looked like black ants crawling from her lip to her nose.

"She's a little shaky," Pearl said. "We saw the thing last night on the Coachlight Road. It could have killed us, but Raeven stopped it." Sweeney's eyes widened behind his glasses. "Yeah," Pearl said as if she still couldn't believe it herself. "She told it to bugger off and that's what it did. Wrecked my car before going, but off it went. And by the way, it's a whole lot bigger than Raleigh Marcotte."

"I don't know why they keep doing this," Raeven said in answer to a question no one had asked. A groan of shifting metal from the bedroom underscored her words. Sparky pulled out his revolver, looked at it, and put it back in his holster with a look that said 'lot of good that'll do,' before heading down the hall toward the bedroom.

The professor approached Raeven. "You know about those trees."

She shook her head.

"You said 'they keep doing this.' What are they?" She looked up at him but didn't answer. He dragged a chair across the floor and sat in front of her. "You're going to tell me eventually, so you might as well do it now." Raeven's gaze darkened in response and he dropped his head and closed his eyes to collect himself. "We are dealing with something none of us truly understands," he said, trying to control his voice. "If you have an answer or a possible key to an answer, please do not leave us in the dark. I assure you, no one will think you mad or hallucinating, least of all me."

Raeven brushed a feather from her lap. She opened her mouth to say something but Sparky reappeared in the hallway, his face ashen. "We better go. They've broken through the walls."

"What about my birds?" Pearl asked.

"I put a chair up against the bedroom door. Hopefully that will hold them back, but we've got to get out of here, we can't stay. Last night we told Joe we'd all meet at the Panda."

"Wasn't he at the town meeting?" Pearl asked. The two men exchanged quick glances before Sparky said, "No."

11

Snow fell again as they drove to the restaurant, with Sweeney and Sparky in the squad car and the two women following in Raeven's beat-up black Toyota. Along the way, they saw evidence of people packing up and moving out and lines of vehicles moving north or south to the borders of Burne Notch with their windshield wipers pushing away the fluffy snowflakes. Sparky was concerned about the state police: his sister Judy, the town's dispatcher, had contacted them and he felt he should meet them when they arrived so he could explain the situation, though the thought of trying to explain something so crazy and unexplainable made his stomach flutter.

He voiced his concerns and Dr. Sweeney said, "In the great, grand scheme of this whole affair, the state police shall prove altogether useless." Without taking his eyes from the snowflakes dashing toward the windshield, he added: "It is all up to Raeven now."

Sparky nearly drove off the road. "Did you say *Raeven?*"

"I did, alas. And did you look over that list?"

Sparky tapped his coat pocket and nodded, still shaken by his pronouncement.

"Tiger, le tigre, tee-gree," the Professor said. "None make a bit of sense. There had to be more to it. Father Toomey meant for us to find it; it had to have been something he thought we would understand. I have a hope that an added letter or two at the end of the word will give us a clue."

When they arrived at the Golden Panda, Sparky tried the front door but it was locked. "It can't be," Pearl said and looked at her watch. Joe never missed a day of work, never missed opening on time.

Raeven's hair lifted in a breathy gust of wind and caught in her mouth. She pulled it away and said, "Where do you think he is?"

"It's okay," Pearl said, though a hint of apprehension slipped into her voice. "Maybe Asthma's here, maybe the kitchen door is open."

Raeven led the way with Pearl and Sparky close behind and Sweeney in the rear carrying several books in his arms. They passed the wire cage and nearly collided with Raeven when she came to an abrupt halt at the corner, staring down.

An enormous circular bloodstain had soaked into the ice from the cage to the kitchen door.

"Joe…" she whispered. She ran around the bloody ice to the door still ajar. Inside, the kitchen looked no different than the night before until she noticed the broken shelf and drops of blood on the floor. She ran through the swinging doors and called his name into the dark, windowless dining room. "Joe…?"

"He's all right," Sparky said coming in behind her. He snapped on all the lights. "He got away."

"How do you know?"

"His car is gone."

Raeven sat down as though her knees had suddenly weakened.

"But something happened," Pearl said, her brow lined with anxiety and her fingers fluttering nervously when she brought her hand to her lips. "Something awful."

Dr. Sweeney entered through the swinging doors and set the large bowl of fortune cookies in the center of the same large round table they had used the night before. "I've put a pot of water on to boil," he said. "Only Chinese tea around here, I suppose, but it'll have to do. Come, all of you. Sit down. Constable, you continue to peruse that list I gave you, see if anything strikes you."

Raeven sat in the chair across from Sweeney, as far from him as possible. "The Seat Perilous," he said with a wry smile.

"What's that mean?"

"We're at a round table, are we not? Were I King Arthur, which I most decidedly am not, you have chosen the seat opposite his, known as the Seat Perilous and reserved for the one knight who alone can retrieve the Holy Grail. All others perish who sit there."

Raeven shifted from the Seat Perilous to the one beside it. She pushed her hair back from her face and touched her stitches.

"Still painful?" Sweeney asked. "Are you taking the antibiotics?"

"Burned in my apartment. Painkillers too, except the ones I took last night."

"Pity. So…the trees."

"So I saw them on the Coachlight Road near the place where that thing attacked the car last night." She related the story of the trees in the road and the illusion, real or not, that they had crept up on her – a strange tale to be sure, and even stranger (but for Dr. Sweeney more meaningful) when she mentioned the Northern Lights and shooting stars. "I don't think I would have seen them otherwise."

He leaned back in his chair. "I saw the stars too. The night I first arrived, from the windows of my motel room. I saw them drawn to a particular spot like iron filings drawn to a magnet. I wondered then, 'what's down there?' Now I know." He reached across the table for her hand but could not reach it. "They were sent for you."

Pearl glanced at Sparky, who looked up from the notebook.

Raeven snorted and dropped her hands from the table into her lap. "That's ridiculous, how can that be?"

Sweeney slapped his hand down on the table, startling them all. The fortune cookies leaped in the bowl. Sparky and Pearl sat up. Raeven pulled back in her chair.

He took his glasses off and covered his face with his hands, as though bone-weary with deep thought. He dragged his fingers down his cheeks, which pulled his lower lids down to reveal his bloodshot eyes. "I don't know how it can be. I don't know how *anything* can be. I don't what the trees are. I don't know what the stars meant, though I have theories. It is all theory at this point, all conjecture. But that is all we have." He stared at Raeven and reached into his inside jacket pocket. "I have hinted at it," he said, rummaging around for something. "I have skirted the issue, all the while hoping you would make the connection yourself. But obviously you cannot, or will not, so I shall make a direct assault upon the point. Last night you opened a fortune."

"Do not give in," Raeven said.

"Not that one." He dropped two crumpled fortunes on the table. "This one, the one you said was a misprint." He flattened the two narrow strips of paper on the table and slid one to Pearl, who read it and shrugged and handed it to Raeven, who read the single word.

RIDIRE

"What does it mean?" she asked, perplexed.

"It is the Irish form of the word used by Steven. The word he called you."

"Night?"

"Yes, though you assumed he meant *night* spelled with an N. He didn't, and this word is not a misprint. Ridire is a Gaelic word for *knight* with a K. Steven told you that you – yes, you, of all people, *you* are the Knight. With a K." Raeven started to speak but he stopped her by lifting his forefinger with a flourish. "I do not care for the idea either. Indeed, there are a thousand people any of us would have chosen over you, but it is not up to me or any one of us to choose such things, more's the pity."

Raeven turned her head to the side and leveled him with a careful, defensive gaze. "Chosen for what?"

As if struck by a sudden loss of nerve, Sweeney shrugged his shoulders up high, and said, "We are all of us chosen, all of us, chosen for something, though we cannot always know what that something might be; whether high-born king or low-born–"

"Chosen for *what*?" Sharp – pointed – insistent.

"Chosen for…" He paused and took his glasses off again and looked her straight in the eye. "You *may* have been chosen as the one foretold within the flight of Moll's gannets and gulls. The Knight of the White Bird."

"Oh, please," Raeven said with a scornful laugh echoed by a snort from Pearl, who said, "Yeah, right," and turned to Sparky, hoping for a better explanation. "I mean really," Pearl said, "this is kind of – you know, Raeven a knight? Kind of crazy, don't you think, Sparkles?"

"He would be a fool if he did not," Sweeney said. "But crazy or not, I have considered every logical, rational possibility, and one by one, they have fallen by the wayside and I am left with this alone."

A voice called from the kitchen. "Hello…?"

Raeven looked up. "Joe," she whispered and leaped from her chair and ran into the kitchen.

12

Tgrew, Tgrex, Tgrey, Tgrez "I've been over it ten times," Sparky said. "None of them make any sense."

"Try again," Sweeney said with a stern glance. "Something may strike you."

Pearl sat a banquette in the lounge, her eyes red with tears. Every time she recovered she remembered another name; Tuberculosis, Iron, Emphysema, Asthma; and each one set off a memory that set off a new round of grief. She had worked with the cantankerous old chef her entire adult life. She was the one who'd bought him the *Annie* soundtrack.

Joe told them he had hidden under a banquette all night and went outside at first light to search for his uncle. He knew he was dead: the scream, the roar and the horrific bloodstain proved that, though he found no sign of a body. He didn't know what to do. He knew Sparky was already overwhelmed and he couldn't see the point of an ambulance without a body. He decided to search for them, but the town meeting had ended by the time he arrived.

"I really liked the guy," Pearl said and used a napkin to dab at the black lines of mascara on her cheeks, which only served to further smear them. "We fought all the time and he was an unbelievable asshole sometimes and I don't think I ever understood three words he said, but I really did like him. Poor old Collapsed."

Sweeney tapped his finger on the table to attract Sparky's attention away from Pearl. "The notebook," he said, and Sparky sighed and turned back to the first page. *tgrea, tgreb, tgrec, tgred, tgree*

"Right then," the professor said. "Finished mourning, have we?" Pearl glared at him but he took no notice. "The next thing we must do is find the faerie sword called *An Claiomh Gealach*."

"Faerie sword," Pearl repeated with an expression of disbelief and her eyes still red with tears. "I can't believe we're even talking about this shit. Seriously – faerie swords. I mean in a serious way, I can't believe we're talking about it in a serious way."

"We must," Sweeney said and her tears came again and her voice cracked when she nodded and said, "I know."

"*An Claiomh Gealach,*" Sweeney repeated. "We know from the manuscript that Brendan fashioned her into a cross. Those were the exact words as I remember them – 'fashioned into a cross'. A silver cross. And he carried it here to America to guard the place where they hid the gold, presumably at the entrance to a cavern of some kind, similar to the one back upon the coast of Kerry. We also know, or we have surmised, that the very same silver cross ended up at the church. We know this because Steven went through a good deal of trouble to retrieve it before he dared enter the chamber where the gold lay hidden. We must now discover that chamber and recover that cross. It must be refashioned into a sword. It is the only weapon we have, the only way to kill this thing."

"But that's…" Sparky began, but he sat back, his brow furrowed with doubt. "No, there's something else. Something's not right about that."

Sweeney frowned and said, "The notebook," and Sparky once again returned to his work.

"But even if we do find the cross," Joe said, "and figure out a way to melt it back into a sword, who is going to kill it?"

Sweeney, still holding a fortune cookie, used his little finger to point to Raeven. "She is."

She sat beside Pearl, handing her another Kleenex, and froze with the tissue dangling from her hand. "What?" she asked, her voice rigid.

"As foretold by Moll."

"Wait a minute," Raeven said, crumpling the tissue in her fist. "First you say I'm supposed to be a knight and now I'm supposed to *kill* Raleigh?"

"Not Raleigh."

"Yeah, whatever, the faerie monster thing," she said with a toss of her head. "If Moll was good at telling the future, she must have predicted I would think you're nuts. Because I do. That's what I think."

Sweeney ignored the insult. "She said she was shown a column of wood, though what that means I do not know. And she saw the Three, though again, we do not know who or what she meant by it. Most important, she said that all hope will hinge upon the Knight of the White Bird and I *do* know who she meant by that."

"Forget about knight, okay?" Raeven said. "Have you ever seen anything about me that suggests the word *white*? My car, my clothes, my hair – "

"Your skin," Pearl suggested. "White as a fucking ghost."

Raeven ignored her. "Even my name. If ravens were white, fine, maybe, but they're black like everything else about me, so don't try to make me out to be a hero, okay? I have no interest. It's not me."

"Then why do the stars fall to you?" Sweeney asked and he circled around her, peering over his glasses as he spoke. "Why do the trees come to you? Nature, it seems, is aligning itself to you and around you. Most of all, Raeven, why does *it* come to you – first through Steven, and we can trace it back that far, and then through Raleigh in your apartment. And then last night on the Coachlight Road. Why does it come to you, why is it attracted?"

"Because I was *there!* With the trees and stars; even the thing last night – I happened to be there, that's all. It could have been anyone else."

"Could have, but wasn't. And unlike nearly everyone else – Steven, the Marcottes, Joe's Uncle – you have managed to survive."

"She told it to bugger off and whoosh, off it buggered," Pearl said, which caused Raeven to send an irritated glance her way. "Well it *did,*" Pearl added.

"Because you were there," Sweeney repeated without taking his eyes from Raeven, "which is often the deciding factor in these things."

"Steeple!" Sparky suddenly cried and the others looked at him, puzzled. "Moll saw a column of wood," he explained. "Maybe she meant the church steeple."

"Well done, Constable, but wrong, I'm afraid. I thought the very same thing, but I already checked. There is no cross on top."

"Yes, there is," Pearl said. "Two or three years ago some crows built a nest in the bell tower, right below the roof. I used to watch them with my binoculars. At the very top of the steeple, there's a cross, though you can barely see it."

"Then maybe that's it," Sweeney said, his expression troubled, as though his thoughts had suddenly been corralled into an unexpected direction.

"Can't be," Pearl said. "It's way too small. Looks like it's made of cast iron, and it sure isn't big enough to melt into a sword."

Joe was about to say something when Sparky startled them all again with a sudden shout: "Grey!"

"Geez, Sparkles!" Pearl cried, throwing her hand over her heart.

"Sorry," he said, and held out the notebook. "This talk about the cross made me realize…look, Professor. *t-Grey.*" Sweeney studied it, puzzled. "It's not tee-gree or tiger," Sparky explained. "It's – remember on the floor, the way Father Toomey wrote it? He didn't write a capitol T. He used a small *t* followed by a capitol G."

"And?"

"It wasn't a T at all. I think he drew a cross."

"Ah!" Sweeney exclaimed and pulled the notebook across the table.

"A cross followed by *G r e* and then a letter he didn't finish. If we add a *y* it spells *Grey.*"

"Why would he write that?" Sweeney asked.

"Because that's where Steven's car burned. On the Coachlight Road near the Grey's dairy farm."

"And it's where I saw the trees," Raeven added, and Pearl chimed in with, "And where that thing attacked my car last night."

Sweeney sat back with a satisfied smile. "Well done, Constable," he said and slapped his hands down on his knees. "We shall go tonight!"

Sparky raised his hand. "Sorry, but…you mean, go tonight? To find the cave?"

"I do. This chap appears to be nocturnal. If we go in broad daylight we may find him at home." He scanned their faces, making eye contact with each before passing on to the next. "Are you with me on this?"

Joe and Pearl looked at each other, nervous and unsure. Raeven had no such problem and answered with a firm, "No."

Pearl touched her on the hand. "Maybe he's right. Maybe you have to."

"He's not and I don't," Raeven said and, without thinking, sat down once again in the Seat Perilous.

"I am right and you will go, whether you like it or not," Sweeney countered. Raeven's jaw dropped. "And you may gape and glare all you like but it shall not change a thing."

"Hold on," Sparky interjected. "I don't think we should run up to that cave or whatever it is without a little planning."

"Agreed. And quite naturally, I wouldn't dream of going inside until I had proof the creature was not in there waiting. My interest lies in finding the cross. Nothing more. Now this is what we'll do. You and Raeven and I will take your car."

"Unbelievable," Raeven said and stared at him as though he had gone mad. "How many times do I have to tell you I'm not going?"

"Ten times, a thousand, it's all the same because you're going."

"And I don't care how many times you say it," she said with her teeth clenched and her voice tense, "or what you try to do to get me there," – she leaned over the table – "I am *not* going."

Joe stepped up beside Raeven. "She's not going unless she wants to."

Raeven glanced at him but did not otherwise acknowledge his defense.

Dr. Sweeney pursed his lips and tilted his head back. A long, tense moment passed. "Right then." He shrugged his shoulders. "How easy it is to stay safe in life, to run no risks, the way most do, with no sense of the possible. The knight Donal fell upon Skellig Michael, but not because he was careless or unlucky. Fear killed him, though I don't believe he feared the beast. Certainly he was afraid. He'd be a damn fool otherwise. But Moll warned him not to attempt to kill it until he had slain the beast inside. What was that beast, do you suppose?" Sweeney circled around the table until he stood above Raeven, looking down at her. "It might have been his deep, implacable fear of life." He set his pipe down on the table behind. "In the hospital you told me you hoped you were a strong person. Either you were completely wrong or you are a liar. I choose to think you are neither."

Raeven pushed her chair from the table to get up, but he squatted down before her with one hand on each arm of her chair to block her escape. "What sort of person are you?" he asked. "What sort of person will you be? Will you be someone life happens to? It need not be that way. We do not all require a gallant knight to come to our rescue. You, yourself, can be that knight – and I don't mean the Knight of the White Bird. I mean your own personal knight, waging battle for your own life, your own happiness. The choice is yours. You may leave now if you wish, but if you do, you shall remain as you are."

Raeven looked at the others. "Can you believe this? 'Be your own knight," she said, her voice dripping with sarcasm. "If I don't do this crazy thing I will remain as I am. Good! I *want* to remain as I am, which is alive. This is all 'believe in yourself' bullshit. Get Raeven to believe in herself and become her own knight and she can save the world, as if the world deserves saving by me or anyone else."

"Believe in yourself?" Sweeney said. "Believe in your *self*? No, my dear. Of all the claptrap foolishness of the modern age, I rank that one near the summit, only one step below telling the universe what you supposedly 'deserve'. I tremble at the thought of actually getting what I deserve. No, my dear, no: what I should like above all things is for you to immolate the self, to bend it toward the will of those powers now trying to reach through to you. I am asking you to forsake the self and take up the sword."

"Which sounds fine until I find out the only way to do it is to kill some kind of lizard thing that for God's sake already murdered Uncle Lung and the Marcottes and who knows how many others? You're trying to shame me into joining you, but who would deliberately look for this thing? Would you?"

Sweeney smiled weakly. "I don't have to."

"You would walk up to it armed with nothing but a melted down cross?"

"If necessary."

"No you wouldn't. No one would."

"You will," Sweeney insisted. "Even if you don't want to do it, even if you do everything in your power not to do it, you *will* do it. I don't believe you have a choice in this."

"I am not going with you!" Raeven pounded her fists down on the arms of her chair. "Save the world." She grabbed a fortune cookie and held it out. "If I ever found myself with the world in the palm of my hand…" She closed her hand with a crunch. Pearl looked at Joe, who did not move and did not react at all. Raeven opened her hand and let the shards of broken cookie fall to the table. "The world should consider itself lucky I am not the knight."

The professor returned to his chair and turned his attention back to his pipe. "Maybe so," he said at last. "And yes, I was trying to shame you into it. I admit that, though I also maintain you are mistaken in one respect. I *am* going to confront it. I have to."

"Let someone else do it," she said, calming down. "The police or the army or someone. They can take care of it."

"No," he said, shaking his head. "Only one person can do it, but I am going to try all the same. I must. I am responsible. I helped release it." He turned to Sparky and clamped a hand on his shoulder. "I have kept you from your true work. Go to your sister's house, meet with the state police. I ask only that you tell me where the Greys live and keep the police away until I have done all I can do."

"Yeah, but…" Sparky began after a quick glance at Pearl. "I only wanted to be sure we weren't going to run into that thing. If you're sure the cave will be empty, I'll go with you."

"Me too," Pearl said, and in answer to a disbelieving gasp from

Raeven, said, "That thing killed Asthma. I'm not going into any flipping cave or anything, but if I can help, I will."

"Me too," said Joe. Sweeney smiled at him and said, "Do not give in."

"Don't you see what he's doing?" Raeven said. "He's – look at that smirk – he's manipulating you. You don't have to go."

"I do," Joe said. "I don't know why, but I feel I have to go, even if I can't help. It's like that golden box, remember? The one I told you I dreamed about? It's the same with this."

Raeven lowered her eyes and shook her head.

"Are you with us?" Sweeney asked.

She looked up. Her eyes settled on Joe. She reached up and touched her stitches with her forefinger, took a long deep breath, held it for a moment, and: "No."

13

The old woman, Jin Feng, expected it would be this way – not the lights, not the bustle of yachts and junks in Hong Kong harbor, or the roar of the brilliant city; but she always knew that things would fall before her. An officious bureaucrat, the owner of a small powerboat, security officers on duty at Kai Tak airport: all would fall before the unseen aura that surrounded her to create a field of understanding beyond questions, beyond money and commerce and rules.

She stood in the boat and clutched the golden box and watched the towers of Hong Kong grow increasingly taller, increasingly bright.

Behind her lay mainland China with all its memories of childhood and youth, of marriage and childbirth, her cottage in the pine forest, and the great sweep of her life and years, all behind her now. She longed to turn and look at it one last time but did not, and so she leaned on her cane and held the box close and stared into the brilliance.

14

Daylight faded and winter darkness settled over Burne Notch. Locked and silent houses stood at the end of empty driveways all through town. Streets filled with snow. Nearly everyone had taken Sparky's advice and made their way from town through the narrow notches. Others, mostly small business owners like the Garands at the ski lift, planned to stay the night to secure their shops and then head out in the morning.

Dr. Sweeney glanced at his watch. "Seven o'clock." He wrapped his blue scarf around his neck. "We must be going," he said without looking at Raeven. She had not budged in her refusal to join them, but equally had not left as promised. He wondered why. *It may be that I need not have pushed her so hard. Things truly may have been settled long before.* He had given up trying to change her mind, but had not yet given up hope, even as he doubted they could prevail without her. *But maybe she's right. Maybe she truly is not the Knight of the White Bird. Maybe she is not one of the Three, though I suspect she will become entangled, regardless of how strenuously she tries to avoid it. Even now, her decision to stay long enough to see us off has a touch of fate rather than free will about it.*

"But only until you leave, only until then," she had said six or seven times that day, but when he announced the time had finally come to leave, she said, "For me too."

Joe slumped in his chair, disappointed. She lifted her coat and slipped one arm into a sleeve. "Thank you for staying as long as you did," Sweeney said. She pulled her coat up over her shoulders and, without answering, strode from the table and pushed through the kitchen doors without looking back.

At the sound of the outside door closing, Joe Li sprang from his chair and ran from the dining room.

Outside, he ran around the bloodstain and the chicken wire cage, and called to her.

She stood at her car, with the door open, about to get inside. She stared over the roof and watched him approach. The Golden Panda sign tried to reach him with its steady glow, tried to clarify his form, his face, his eyes, but the snow fell heavy and obscured all but his basic shape and the sound of his voice. "Raeven," He stood in middle of the parking lot, a shadow barely seen. "You don't have to come with us but don't leave."

"Go back inside, it's cold." She started to climb inside the car.

"Please."

With her face down and hair hanging before her eyes, she could feel the cold touch of snowflakes melting through her hair. "Raeven," she heard, "I wish I could – I don't know how to tell you..."

"Tell me what?" she whispered.

"I was hoping..." His words drifted off and she realized he hadn't heard her question. *Tell me what?* she wanted to shout, but couldn't get her voice to repeat the words, couldn't gather her thoughts together to force the question, to force him into the answer she knew he wanted to say and she longed to hear. She brushed an arc of snow off the roof of her car. "Hoping what?"

"Hoping you would stay."

She brushed her gloved hand against her coat. "I can't." With that, she climbed inside and shut the door. She turned on the headlights. The windshield wipers hummed, their motors strained against the gathered snow but finally pushed it up and off. They fell back and attacked it again until they formed two clear arches of glass filled with darkness, empty parking lot, and no Joe.

15

Snow, snow, and more snow, and Sparky fretted, hunched behind the steering wheel. "How is *anyone* gonna get through this? We should have gone to the town garage for the plow."

"We may have to," Dr. Sweeney said in a vacant, half-hearted way. Something was wrong. He felt it as soon as they pulled into the Grey's unplowed driveway and saw the dark farmhouse and darker barn. "They probably left with all the others," Sparky ventured, and when Sweeney pointed to a pickup truck beside the barn, the policeman suggested they might have gone in another car. Sweeney nodded without much conviction. He swiveled around to address Pearl and Joe in the back seat. His blue scarf, so thick and pulled up so high over his mouth, muffled his words. "Constable Grant and I shall take the house. You two inspect the barn."

Sparky turned off the engine and in the sudden breathless silence, Joe asked, "Can't we all go together?"

"It's only a quick look, not that important," Sweeney said. "I should like to ask the Greys the location of the cave, but if they're not here, we shall proceed on our own."

They left Sparky's car and fanned across the dooryard, with Sparky and Sweeney heading for the house, Pearl and Joe for the barn, and all four bending forward to avoid the pin-prick ice crystals swooping down on the wind. "What's going on with this snow?" Pearl cried and grabbed Joe by the arm. "We should have brought a flashlight." They felt their way along the outside wall of the barn, searching for an entrance. "Here it is, over here," she said.

They grabbed the handle and pulled. The bulky door slipped into its track and rumbled open to reveal an entrance large enough to drive a vehicle through. Darkness stared out at them.

Joe called out, "Mr. Grey?" and then to Pearl, "Nothing."

"I don't know why he wanted us to check in here anyway. What's the point? They wouldn't be in here without lights. The house either."

Joe squinted into the darkness. The barn smelled of hay and manure. "I thought he had cows."

"He does."

"I don't hear them."

Sparky opened the unlocked door and brushed the snow from his sleeves before stepping into the kitchen. "Jerrod?"

Sweeney came in behind him. "Lights," he whispered. Sparky felt the wall for a switch and snapped it on. Nothing happened. "Elizabeth?" he called. "Anybody home?" He flicked on his fireman helmet and scanned the kitchen: refrigerator, dishes still in the sink, a needlepoint sampler hung on the wall. Something whined nearby, a high whistling sound. Sparky crouched and lifted the tablecloth. "Oh, my gosh, it's Tred. Hey, how you doing?" The brown mongrel cowered under the table.

"Who are you talking to?" the professor whispered.

Sparky spoke over his shoulder. The light swept around like a lighthouse beacon. "Mr. Parenteau's dog. I heard the Greys took him in. He was the man killed a couple days ago in that lightning storm." He turned back to the table and held out his hand. "Come on, boy."

A scream slit the air. Tred cowered, Sparky turned and caught Dr. Sweeney's eyes at the moment the scream ended in a loud, shrill curse. "Pearl," they said at the same time and ran from the house with Tred slipping through the door behind them a second before it closed.

Sparky's bouncing helmet light illuminated Pearl and Joe staggering away from the opened barn door. He slid to a halt and clapped a hand across the professor's chest: "Stay here!" he ordered, and Sweeney obeyed. He watched the policeman move toward the entrance in silhouette, outlined by the glow of his helmet light. At the door, he stopped with his light shining into the barn, seemingly frozen solid by the icy wind.

He turned away and dropped to his knees in the snow. Dr. Sweeney approached and with a silent gesture, asked for the helmet. Sparky handed it over and Sweeney braced himself before stepping up to the barn door. He turned the helmet around, aimed the light into the barn, and "Dear God," he whispered.

It was a charnel house.

Bodies and limbs of cows lay strewn about, some still in their individual stalls, but most piled in a slick bloody mound. Blood lay thick and red upon the wooden floor, though in some places had gathered in pink puddles – a mixture of blood and milk, Sweeney realized with a shudder. "God almighty," he whispered when the light fell upon the remains of Jerrod and Elizabeth Grey amongst the slaughtered cattle. He searched for a glint of their wedding bands but, as he expected, their left hands were gone, with their arms severed close to the elbow. He tilted the helmet. Snow drifted through a jagged gash in the back wall, nearly as large as the front entrance.

He backed out of the barn and knew at once that he had lost his team. Joe sat in the back of the car with his arms wrapped around Pearl. Sparky stood beside the barn door, his face ashen. Sweeney suspected he had been sick. He handed him the helmet and suggested they start their search from inside the barn. The policeman balked and Sweeney told him about the gash in the back wall. "It got into the barn that way," he theorized, "and with so much blood it was sure to leave tracks."

"Tracks?" Sparky asked, alarmed. "Are we *following* it?"

"Certainly not," Sweeney assured him. Sparky, relieved, said it was probably just as well as the snow would have covered any blood outside.

"Blood or no," Sweeney said, "an animal this size is bound to leave a deep impression. I have no intention of following it, though I do intend to follow its trail back to the place from whence it came. Have you another illuminated helmet?" Sparky told him there was a flashlight in the glove compartment. When Sweeney opened the car door to retrieve it, he said to those inside, "You sit tight, we'll be back in a jiffy."

"You're not going up to that cave, are you?" Pearl asked, her eyes wide with horror. Sweeney said he had every intention of doing so, Sparky did as well, and he asked that they not drive off, no matter how agitated they became.

Pearl looked out the window. Sparky stood at the side of the barn, scanning the surrounding area with his light. She opened the car door, swung her legs around and reached up to the door frame to pull herself out, but didn't: she stayed in the car and watched the policeman move further into the pasture.

Sweeney rejoined him with the flashlight. "I'll go through the barn," he said. "You circle around and meet me at the back." His scarf hid most of his face so he acknowledged the policeman's relief with a wink. "Keep a sharp eye out for tracks."

Back inside the barn, the professor struggled to focus on his goal rather than the blood, the entrails, the torn and mutilated limbs. He studied the floor before the stalls where most of the blood had coagulated into swirls and smears, the signs of a brutal struggle. As he neared the center of the barn, they became clearer, much less altered by conflict, but also more peculiar. He could not make out which track belonged to which creature, cow, man or beast; but then he came upon a single clear mark made by neither hoof nor boot and his blood ran cold.

"My God," he whispered. He tried to swallow, but could not.

Sparky called from the back of the barn. "See anything?" He stood at the gash in the wall, reluctant to enter. He lowered his gaze to avoid a clear view inside: when he did, his helmet light pointed straight down at the floor and he too caught sight of a track. "Holy shit."

It was nearly two and a half feet long. Three gashes in the floor at the front indicated non-retractable talons that had sunk into the wood with each step. Sweeney illuminated another, far enough from the first to indicate a stride of six feet with each step. A thick clear line trailed between the tracks where something heavy had been dragged through the blood.

"What'll we do?" Sparky asked. It was one thing to search for the creature's lair when it was the size of Raleigh Marcotte, but to confront something so much bigger and presumably deadlier put a damper on his already minimal enthusiasm. "Maybe we should wait for the army," he ventured.

"No army is capable of dealing with this."

"Then why are *we*?"

"Because we can."

The policeman's helmet light joined Sweeney's flashlight and the two beams crossed in the dark barn, each focused upon the other. "Back in the car you said only Raeven could do it," Sparky said. "Did you mean it? I mean – did you *really* mean it?"

"I did. And she will be back. I don't know how or when, but I believe it with all my heart." He pointed to the long broad line between the tracks. "What do you make of this?"

"Tail," Sparky said, his voice thick in his throat. "You see it with muskrat tracks. It's dragging its tail. Look. There are more out here."

Sweeney followed the tracks through the torn wall where the policeman stood over a footprint as large as the others, but with fallen snow blurring its outlines. "I didn't realize this was a track at first," Sparky said. "I didn't think it could be. They lead here from somewhere out in the pasture."

"They'll be filled in before long," Sweeney said, gazing at the snow swirling down upon the dark field. "Shall we...?"

Sparky reached out as he passed and grabbed a handful of his coat sleeve. "Do you really believe Raeven will come back?"

The professor nodded and said into his scarf, "I am hopeful."

Back at the car Pearl and Joe saw the two flashlights reappear, this time heading into the pasture with the small form of Tred darting after them. "Let's go," Pearl said. When Joe reminded her that they promised not to drive off, she said: "I meant go with them."

"You sure?"

Pearl watched the lights receding into the pasture. "They might need us," she said and she pulled her scarf over her head and climbed out of the car.

16

Siouxsie and the Banshees blared from the CD player, accompanied by the sharp *crack, crack, crack* of the windshield wipers. Raeven clenched both hands upon the steering wheel and willed the car forward over the unplowed roads, to keep it moving, not to get bogged down. She saw no other cars ahead or behind but only snow rushing into the high beams in an hypnotic pattern of streaking white, and felt only her beating heart, both reflecting the wild careening dash of her thoughts: *I should have stayed, I should have gone with them* and Joe's face, the memory of him standing in the parking lot, *but I can't.*

Dr. Sweeney was right. Yes, the circumstances were extreme and no one in her right mind would willingly accept them, but his underlying message struck home. In spite of her cynical and world-weary persona, she *was* afraid to take chances, she was afraid of life and always had been. It was a caustic, bitter realization intensified by the fact that she had been forced to confront it against her will.

She had pulled her gloves off and jammed them into her coat pocket when she left the parking lot of the Golden Panda. Her lace veil was the next to go. She pulled it off, unmindful of the bobby pins ripping thin strands of hair with it. A sham – all of it! The melancholy air of tragedy, the gloom, the cheap black wardrobe – even the pretentious spelling of her assumed Raeven name was nothing more than an attempt at morbid romance by a wholly unromantic, unattractive little nobody named Cindy: Cindy O'Connor, daughter of a defeated unloving mother and an abusive alcoholic father who walked out on her, abandoned his family without warning or a word of good-bye: Cindy O'Connor, incurably wounded by life: Cindy O'Connor, a common mediocrity who would never accomplish anything of significance, never rise above her deep abiding sadness, never wear truly nice clothes, never be loved.

Even that! How could she possibly think that someone like Joe could have feelings for her? *Why in the world would someone like him care for someone like you? He's well-educated, he's cultured, and you – what are you? A fraud wearing a mask, pretending and –* she shuddered with self-loathing.

Headlights appeared from the side. She slammed on the brakes and the back end of her car swerved and connected with the snow bank. The other car passed by with its horn blaring and she realized she must have run a stop sign.

She breathed deep and closed her eyes. "Okay, okay," she whispered, "okay, pull yourself together." She turned onto the main highway out of town. "Never mind," she said in a voice dull and resigned, and wiped a tear from her chin with the back of her hand. "Just go home, never mind."

Several cars appeared in front of her, all heading out of town with their taillights glaring like demonic red eyes. Bright headlights appeared from behind and sparkled in the droplets hanging upon the lines of the rear window defroster.

More lights appeared behind and she realized she had joined a slow procession along the highway following the curves of the river. A new set of headlights appeared at the side and illuminated a sign beside the road. Clinging ice covered its words but she knew what they said:

LEAVING BURNE NOTCH.

The finality of it sent a fresh spring of tears to her eyes. She failed. It was as simple as that: the adventure that had started small and hopeful had ended, still small, but now without even an illusion of hope. "Just go home," she said again, dull, dark, sad. "Just…whatever."

The headlights at the side came closer with high beams blazing. More appeared opposite and bore down toward her passenger side. She wiped her eyes again, confused by the snow, the unplowed road, the taillights ahead and glaring headlights – *from the side?* She knew of no off-roads along that stretch of highway and no exits at all, yet the lights charged toward her from both sides, brightening as they came, as if the drivers had refused to lower their high beams. She pumped the brakes, squinted in the glare, and realized in a sudden rush of horror that the drivers had no intention of stopping.

A thunderous roar overtook her car and the headlights – *were* they headlights? She glanced from window to window, and saw that no, they weren't headlights at all!

Sparking sheets of blue fire roared down the two hillsides bordering the road, one on each side. The one on the left plunged into the frozen river and plowed the ice up in sheets that exploded into steam: on the right, a grove of spruce trees burst into flame.

The cars in front tried to outrun them. Packed snow spun from their rear tires and they jolted forward.

Raeven knew she couldn't make it. She hit the brakes and turned the wheel. Her car slid sideways and came to a stop at the moment the two walls joined in a maelstrom of sparks and fire to form a single high wall of charges so hot that the snow on her car roof melted into a sudden cascade of water that poured down her windows.

A car passed, horn blaring, sliding on the ice remaining on the road. It slammed into the wall and exploded into a fireball.

Raeven threw the car into reverse. Tires whined and spun. She tried to drive forward but the tires spun again. The car wouldn't move.

She threw open the door and scrambled out, hyperventilating with panic. Looking up and shielding her eyes with her hand, she saw that the fire or electricity or whatever it was had become a thirty-foot high pulsing net of surging voltage that had swept down from the forest on both sides.

Trees burned all along its length. Where it had crossed the frozen river, the water churned and roiled into wide plumes of steam. Noxious black smoke billowed from the burning car. Music continued to pour through her opened door. A car door slammed behind her. A man's frightened voice called out: "What *is* that thing?"

Raeven cried out, terrified the unexpected voice would leave her. She ran toward it, stumbling in the deep snow. "Don't go!" she cried. "Don't leave me!"

Closer, she saw Raleigh Marcotte's friend, Chip Dubee, standing beside the driver's side door of a red pick-up truck. "What is it?" he shouted above the crackling roar.

"Please don't leave me!" she cried and pulled open the passenger door. Chip's face had gone pale and his mouth quivered when he climbed into the truck beside her. "We've got to get out here," she said, trying to catch her breath.

"But *where*? Where should we go?"

"Anywhere," she said without stopping to think. "The other end of town. The North Bridge."

17

Several trails of enormous tracks marred the Grey's pasture. A pattern emerged and before long Dr. Sweeney and Sparky saw the trails converge toward the far end of the field. Tred had already caught up with them (much to Sweeney's chagrin. He worried the dog might give them away if the thing happened to be nearby).

Behind them, Pearl called out but the wind muffled her voice and they did not hear her. She did not realize this and grew increasingly angry at their refusal to wait. A thick patina of fog and melting snow covered Joe's glasses and he could barely see the two wavering flashlights that seemed always to be moving further away.

Something rumbled with a sound like thunder. All four heard it: all four felt it.

Sweeney and Sparky stopped walking. "What was that?" Sparky asked and they turned off their flashlights.

Pearl stared into the darkness. "Where did they go?" Ice pellets whipped over them, scattershot, stinging their faces. The sound came again, a deep quaking tremor, rolling and drawn out. "What *is* that?" She looked back to the house and barn but could no longer see them through the curtains of white. "It's not that thing, is it?"

The flashlights came on again.

"There!" Joe said. "Hurry!"

Sweeney and Sparky followed the converging trails to the far edge of the pasture where they ended in a confusing mass of tracks that wove in and around a series of upright stones. "Graveyard?" Sweeney asked. Sparky said he supposed it was, though he had never seen it before and never knew it existed. "Unless maybe this is the Stonehenge Field."

"Stonehenge," Sweeney repeated.

"Don't know why they call it that. My grandfather used to talk about it but I don't remember ever coming here." They trained their lights upon a small rise that bordered the pasture, topped with snow-covered pines and shivering white birches. Lowering his light, Sweeney squinted. He leaned forward and with a loud gasp sprinted to one of the upright stones where he fell to his knees and brushed the clinging snow away with the end of his scarf.

Sparky joined him and trained his light upon the lines cut into the granite. "What is it?"

"Ogham," Sweeney returned and could barely contain his excitement. He took off his glove to trace the lines with his bare fingers. "The Celtic Tree alphabet, so called because many of these symbols are named for trees; birch, oak, aspen. I don't need the nautical chart from Skellig Michael after all. This will be proof enough. Brendan himself may have carved this." He turned his light on another stone, and another, and beyond them. "There!" he shouted when his flashlight settled on a black pit like an oversized rabbit hole at the base of the low rise.

Sparky laid his gloved hand over the flashlight's beam. "Don't shine it in," he whispered, "and don't be so loud." They cringed when another growling rumble trembled through the air. "I'll check it out. You stay here."

Sweeney crouched beside a tall ogham stone and watched Sparky approach the black hole. He bent low before it with his blond hair buffeted by snow and wind spiraling past him.

From behind, Sweeney heard, "What's that sound?" and he turned to see Pearl and Joe struggling toward him from the pasture.

"Nothing here," Sparky called from the cave entrance. "It's empty. Maybe it's not the right one."

Sweeney called to Pearl and Joe, now standing at the edge of the ogham markers. "You two search for the cross out here," he said and joined Sparky at the entrance. After handing him his flashlight, he slid into the cave.

The policeman followed. "Maybe it's not the right cave," he suggested again but Sweeney drew his attention to a lingering odor of decay and, more telling, to the domed roof of corbelled stone. "The exact same pattern and shape of the *clocháin* back on Skellig Michael, though much larger." He theorized that the hill above must have been man-made too, with earth piled atop the *clochán* to hide the poisoned treasure within. A few roots from the trees above had worked their way through and hung like rat tails. "And what's this?" He had turned his flashlight onto what appeared to be tiny stalactites hanging from the ceiling. He reached up and felt one.

Glass, he thought, or a material very much like glass; hard and brittle, with a glossy blue-grey surface. The same peculiar substance littered the floor. Other than that, the cave was empty: no gold, only broken fragments of smoky blue-grey glass, but then he turned his light toward the back wall and grabbed the policeman by the arm. "Look!"

Startled, Sparky trained his helmet on a heap of rusted metal, nearly disintegrated. "Old tractor parts, most likely," he said. "Jerrod must have used this place to store junk."

"It's armor!" Sweeney said and rushed to the pile. Metal clanged when he pulled an object from the pile and held it up. "Early middle ages, by the looks of it. I shouldn't be at all surprised if this once belonged to the knight Donal." He ran his hand over the ancient breastplate as though it was made of the gold they had expected to find. His hand slipped into a ragged hole in the center. "Where the fatal tooth plunged. If I can date this, I may not need the manuscript after all. This armor, located in this place, will be proof enough for even the most skeptical academic authorities. The same with the ogham script outside. Even if they do not believe Brendan left them, they cannot deny that *someone* from Europe ventured here a very long time ago – certainly long before 1492."

"Yeah?" Sparky said, unable to work up an enthusiasm to equal the professor's. "But where's the gold? I wonder if..." He shook his head and frowned. "I don't know."

"What?"

"This cave isn't very big and, judging by those tracks, it looks like that thing is getting bigger all the time. I wonder if it *was* here but ended up..."

"Moving out," Sweeney said. "Of course. If it continues to grow at the rate it has over the past two days, it wouldn't be able to squeeze through that entrance much longer. It must have taken its treasure elsewhere."

"But where?"

"Somewhere larger than this place," Sweeney said, still staring at the rusting armor. "Another cave, perhaps. Somewhere inaccessible."

18

Maurice and Tim Garand were among the last few stragglers still in Burne Notch. Electrical power flickered and failed, came on again and failed, and a large diesel generator kicked in at the back of the lift house to dimly light the ski slopes and allow them to ride the clattering chair lift a final time to ensure that everything was secured and battened down before abandoning the lodge to join the exodus out of town.

As always, Tim rode two chairs behind his father. He knew

something was wrong with the lift and, seemingly, with the mountain itself as soon as they began the long ascent. His father also noticed and regretted the decision to ride up, but said nothing: once in the air, they could not stop the chairs or reverse their course. *We'll take the toboggans back down as soon as we get up there.* His swaying chair approached the first support. It rattled over the tower and began the ride to the second. *We won't bother to secure the lift house, just get back down as fast as possible.*

He heard Tim call out to him, "Dad, look! What's going on down there?" and he twisted in his seat. A vibrant blue glow filled the southern part of town. Smaller blue lights dotted the forest along the opposite mountain range, as if a series of signal fires had been lit to mark the town's border. He gazed at them, puzzled, until his chair clattered over the last of the tower supports and approached the entrance to the lift house.

Behind him, Tim fiddled with the latch of his chair in preparation for the jump out. His chair passed over the tower. Due to the weakness of the generator, the lights attached to the tower were unusually dim. Even so, they illuminated something moving over the slope below. He thought it was a bear at first, and was about to point it out to his father when he saw another move from the woods at the edge of the slope. It joined the first and they continued on together, ponderous and slow down the hill. Tim squinted and stared at the dark figures, unable to accept what his eyes were seeing for they appeared to be – no, they *were!* – pine trees moving down the slope like hikers descending a glacier.

"Dad?" he said, but couldn't get his voice to rise above a whisper.

Maurice could not have heard him, not over the clank of the cables and the grinding rattle of the turret inside the lift house, but he suddenly turned around in his chair before it disappeared into the darkness. "Tim!" he cried and his expression shocked his son. "Jump, Tim!"

Confused, Tim watched his father's chair slide into the lift house. He reached for the latch, but froze at the sound of a scream cutting through the clack of machinery. A vibrant roar followed that overwhelmed all other sounds. The cable thrashed. His chair rocked from side to side.

Tim grabbed the latch. He couldn't open it.

He pushed at it and tried to slip beneath the bar. His father's empty chair rounded the turret and emerged from the exit, barely hanging from the cable, mangled and slick with blood.

His own chair rumbled toward the entrance and he screamed when the dim light from behind passed through the entrance and shimmered on two reflective eyes, reptilian and glowering, waiting for his slide into the lift house.

19

Sparky's helmet followed the contours of the cave. Its light had noticeably dimmed, as though the batteries were dying, the same with Sweeney's flashlight.

They did not realize the power was going off all through town.

"Here's something," Sparky said and kicked a pile of broken glass away with his foot. He bent down and lifted it into his light. "It's a cross."

Sweeney spun around, his flashlight streaking over the damp walls.

Sparky held it up. A small silver cross dangled from a chain and sparkled in the dying light. "Don't think it's the one we're looking for."

Sweeney took it from him, tilted his glasses up and read the inscription printed in tiny script on the back. "Father Toomey's first name was...?"

"Martin."

"He's still alive. Taken to the new lair with the gold, I should think."

"Still alive," Sparky said, unable to hide his doubt.

"This was his. The inscription reads, 'To Martin. St. John's Seminary. 1983.' But more to the point, it is made of silver. That's why it was abandoned."

"But that doesn't mean anything. Maybe it killed him and – "

"No, no, don't you see? That thing hoards and treasures every fragment of gold, no matter how miniscule. Apparently it does not feel the same about silver. If the creature cared so little about this as to leave it behind, it would never have taken it in the first place. It must have taken Father Toomey here and he dropped it, either by accident or design, that we cannot say."

"Why would it bother taking him here in the first place?" Sparky asked, still confused. "Why wouldn't it kill him like it does everyone else?"

"A valid question," Sweeney said, nodding thoughtfully. "Why, indeed?"

Outside, Pearl and Joe stomped around and dug in the snow with the toes of their boots, searching for the cross. Tred sat shivering beneath a nearby tree in a shallow depression with first one paw and then another held up from the snow. "How big is it supposed to be?" Joe asked.

"I don't know. Cross-size, whatever that is. "It would help if they gave us one of their flashlights. I can't tell if I'm touching a cross or a stick or you."

They paused when the rumbling sound came again, this time from a specific location behind them and closer than before. Tred whined beneath the tree. "What *is* that?" Pearl asked. The falling snow began to ease up, not in intensity but in the size of the snowflakes, and this allowed her to catch a glimpse of the distant lights on the ski slopes. She used them as an anchor back into light and reality and groaned in dismay when they suddenly flickered out. "Strange," she said, and looked around, perplexed, when the sky, the pasture, and the distant barn and house brightened in blue as if illuminated by a sliver of lightning frozen in place...but it wasn't lightning, and it had not come from the sky.

"Hey guys," Pearl said. She crouched at the cave entrance. The two men stood inside studying a bright object in Sweeney's hand. "There's something –" she began, but stopped when, *H-rooom*, another throbbing boom sounded, closer than before.

Joe tapped her on the shoulder and pointed to a shimmering veil of blue light cresting over a distant hill. Brightening, it poured down the slope like a rapid flow of lava smashing and burning through the forest. "That looks like the same fire we saw from the parking lot last night."

"Hey guys, you better get up here," she said. "Something's coming."

Sweeney reached the entrance first. "What the devil?" he whispered and the two men climbed out of the cave. A second, smaller flare of blue rose in the larger one's path and they collided with a *boooom*, followed by a louder, breathy roar – *H-rroooom!* The impact added to its intensity, and on it came, gathering strength by consuming the smaller fires.

By now, it had grown several times larger than when Raeven saw it at the south notch: it towered over the forest as a fifty foot high, twenty foot wide band of raw power that rumbled and seared a wavering course across the landscape. Its forward end writhed and curled through the forest like a ravenous snake fed by massive upheavals of burning trees. Some flared into firebrands where they stood. Others, thrust up by their roots from the onslaught, flew end over end into the air and dropped like enormous flaming arrows trailing smoke behind.

The wall made a rumbling turn toward the pasture. Within seconds, it turned away, which prompted Sparky to suggest they wait to see which direction it took before making a move. "Why is it veering back and forth like that?" Joe asked. It turned again, which forced them to move away from the cave entrance into the pasture to watch its progress. Before long its rampaging forward end disappeared behind the hill, booming and thundering as it went, and left them staring at its humming vibrating bulk towering over the distant trees as a monumental wall of light shimmering in its grandeur.

"Did that lizard thing do this?" Pearl asked.

"I have no idea what this might be," Sweeney returned, increasingly confused and distressed. "No idea at all."

Sparky crouched beside Tred, still cowering under the tree. He pulled him close and stared at the distant wall. The booms echoed in the crisp air like sheets of ice breaking up on a lake.

"Did you find anything?" Sweeney asked. When Joe and Pearl shook their heads, he offered to help them look. Sparky gave the dog a hearty pat on the side and joined them when they moved into the Stonehenge field and rooted in the snow with their boots.

The shimmering wall lit their progress. Ethereal in spite of its size and undeniable power, it had the fearsome beauty of a volcano erupting into the night sky and they found it impossible to ignore its splendor above the distant treetops. Sparky's distractions were compounded by the nagging feeling he'd had since he first heard about the cross back at Father Toomey's house. Something was wrong, something out of place, but he couldn't put his finger on it. Whatever it was, it once again fled from his mind unanswered and unsolved when Joey suddenly ran to an ogham stone and pointed beyond it: "Look!"

Sparky thought he had found the cross, but when he turned, he saw to his horror that the wall's leading edge had veered back their way. Vibrant light poured through the woods above the cave and a shower of white sparks rocketed into the sky. The ground began to tremble and on it came, much faster than expected and with much greater force, as inescapable as a rockslide. They looked around; at each other, at the wall, and "Run!" Sweeney yelled and headed into the pasture.

Sparky grabbed him as he passed. "No time! Into the cave."

The ground trembled. He pulled Sweeney toward the entrance where Pearl and Joe had fallen to their knees and now held each other, as if by doing so they could ward off the sound, the crash of shattering trees, the quaking ground beneath. "Into the cave!" Sparky shouted as he approached. "Hurry!" Fire and ash funneled into the sky behind the hill. Harsh light shot through the forest. It streamed between the branches.

Pearl crawled toward the cave. A burning pine bough landed beside her. "Holy shit!" Charred evergreen needles puffed into a cloud of ash.

Joe helped her climb into the cave and scrambled in behind her. He held back at the entrance to wait for Sparky and Sweeney. Burning pine needles and branches rained around them, and then came a sound of whining within the crackling roars. "Tred!" Joe shouted and he clambered out of the cave at the same time Sweeney and Sparky reached it. He ran past them through a hail of crackling needles. After grabbing Tred by the collar, he dragged him through the swirling sparks, the smoke, the falling snow and ash.

"Hurry!" Sparky cried from the entrance.

The sky lit up in brilliant blue and then orange when a huge pine tree, torn up by its roots and engulfed in flame, screamed through the air like an artillery shell and landed with a fiery crash in the middle of the pasture. A second followed, and a third whistled down from the sky.

Joe staggered to the cave with one hand up to shield his eyes while dragging Tred with the other. Burning branches shot down around them like flaming javelins.

Sparky reached out of the entrance. He caught the dog by the collar and pulled him inside.

Joe started to follow – he looked up – the wall thundered onto the low hill above the cave where it towered over him with its barely harnessed power throbbing and its hum deafening. Blue charges roiled over its surface. It leaned over the Stonehenge field like a monstrous wave but at the moment it should have crested and broke, it began to pull back as though somewhere along its length a ravine or small valley had drawn the bulk of the charges into an altered course.

The wave ebbed, retreated, and surged onto a new path along the edge of the pasture, but not before sending up a last burning maple tree with every branch outlined in blue-white fire.

Joe dropped to the ground and pulled his legs up close to his chest. The tree landed root first between the last two rows of ogham stones, and there it stood, balanced like a blazing phantom of its former self, fully engulfed in crackling flame, wavering, tottering, and finally, toppling forward with a mighty crash. It would have crushed Joe had its upper branches not been stopped by the hill. Fire raged above him. Snow melted around him. Smoke stung his eyes, though he could still see Sparky inside the cave with his face lit up in the glare, urging him on.

A branch broke. The burning tree settled further. Snow hissed and melted.

Sparky leaned out of the cave. Joe reached for him and their hands almost touched when a flash of light beside the entrance caught his eye. Heat washed over him, sparks swirled into the smoke. "Grab my hand!" Sparky cried. Joe squinted at a patch of snow melting from a pile of rocks beside the entrance. He reached out when another flash appeared and the snow melted further to reveal the silver cross taken there by Steven Wilcox, sparkling and blazing with reflected firelight.

20

Chip Dubee raced toward the bridge that marked the northern border of Burne Notch. "What *was* that?" he babbled, on the verge of tears, "that thing, that wall or fence, what was it?"

"I don't know," Raeven said, looking in the side view mirror. "Don't slow down."

"What's going on?"

"I don't know but you have *got* to keep going." She folded her fingers tight together to keep from clenching her hands into fists. They had no time.

The blue walls were following them.

Two lines high and far in the distance tore over the mountains and kept pace with the truck, one on either side. They gathered strength and speed as each one periodically and at different points met smaller points of blue fire and swallowed them whole with a trembling boom.

The more Chip fretted, the more clear-headed Raeven became. Her fear seemed to pour from her into the muscular man behind the wheel. As he began to wilt, terrified of the blue wall and rumors of unknown predators, she now marked the progress of the fire with an icy stare.

They approached the northern boundary of Burne Notch from the top of a low hill. The truck quivered. The rear view mirror rattled.

"Hurry," she whispered.

They rounded a corner. Below, at the foot of the hill, the long low North bridge spanned the frozen river. The rumble intensified. The doors shuddered. She held onto the dashboard so tightly her knuckles turned white. Chip hunched over the wheel and tried to keep the truck steady while he drove down the hill.

A blue glow appeared above the trees.

His breath came fast and heavy when the fire appeared over a rise, racing toward them, churning up everything in its path. A second appeared from the opposite direction, hurtling into the valley with a sound like a locomotive. "Hurry!" Raeven shouted.

He slammed his foot down on the accelerator. The truck barreled down the hill and reached a curve at the bottom. He hauled on the wheel. The truck overshot the road and struck a glancing blow against the snow bank before righting itself and careening onto the bridge.

The two walls thundered down the riverbanks on a collision course. "Go!" Raeven cried. The truck shot forward: Chip instantly gauged their chances and realized they wouldn't make it.

He hit the brakes. The walls roared over the river.

Ice cracked, steam exploded, and the two walls met with a slam so fierce it severed the bridge in half.

Chip hauled on the wheel, desperate to keep the truck from toppling over the side; but on it went, sliding on the ice toward the wall. The bridge tilted. It settled with a metallic moan. Heat washed over them, so intense it melted the ice beneath the tires and allowed the brakes to bring the truck to a screeching halt.

The bridge tilted further. Raeven could now see the water boiling and churning below.

Chip threw the truck into reverse, the bridge shuddered and

lurched further down, and he managed to back onto the road only seconds before it collapsed in a tangle of twisted steel and fire. Steam poured from the river and obscured all but the vibrant wall inside a thick heaving bank of fog. "Now what?" he cried and Raeven stared in shock at the blue walls sparking and hissing and weaving together to seal all of Burne Notch within a surrounding web of blue fire; and she knew — she *knew* they had done for her, to trap her, to hold her inside.

Dr. Sweeney was right.

She could not escape: her stomach lurched and her mind, blood, bones, sinews and soul hemorrhaged into a single liquid realization that she could do nothing to change it. She could not escape. The wall's ferocious hornet hum told her so. *You are the Knight,* it told her with its crackling, vicious hum, and she could not, could not; she *could not* escape.

V.
Damsel

John-Richard Thompson

1

Within thirty minutes of the wall's final joining at the North Bridge, two fighter jets thundered up from Hanscom Air Force Base in Massachusetts. The instant they crossed over the wall, all electronics and computerized mechanisms failed and the sizzling blue light of the wall overwhelmed the resulting fireballs when they fell. Within the hour, National Guard forces within four states mobilized. They could not know it then, but every attempt to break through by force of any kind would fail as surely as the planes.

No one could get in.

No one could get out.

No planes could fly overhead. No radio waves, electrical currents, or armaments of any kind could penetrate the wall.

Burne Notch had become a black hole, dense and inviolable.

To the south, near the seacoast, a Delta Cargo aircraft made its approach into Pease International Airport in Portsmouth. In the hold amongst the battened down crates, Jin Feng listened passively to the rattling turbulence of their approach. The crew had some concept of her presence, but in a muted, recessional way. When she boarded the first of two planes in Hong Kong, no one saw her as form or substance, but as a shadow passing with her coat rustling like bamboo leaves. She carried only her walking stick and the small box now held on her lap and she sat motionless, listening to the icy wind that careened around the plane and prevented its landing in Boston as she knew it would.

The plane began its descent. It would not be long now. All she had trained for would come into play for the first and only time in her life. If she succeeded, centuries of waiting and preparation would come to a satisfactory close and bring honor to her mother, and her mother before her, and all the mothers down through the ages who had been trained and waited and passed the age-old secrets on to their daughters and died without ever putting that training to use.

The landing gear lowered. The plane descended through the snow clouds and she jolted upright, her heart pounding and eyes wide with shock when a wave of airborne malevolence poured through the fuselage. *Him!* The great power from whom all natural and unnatural evils flow, awakened once more, reaching for *It*, urging *It* to strength through his dreadful aura swirling in the frozen wind, felt by no one but her.

So close!

The old wisdom had warned of his power but nothing could have prepared her for the barrage of twisted malice that beamed outward from a point east of the airport like a radio signal pulsing wickedness into the skies. She did not know how far the malignant vibrations traveled, nor could she tell if they reached their destination. She could only sit and bear the assault in silence and clutch the golden box close to her chest with her head bowed over it in prayer.

Fifteen miles offshore, the freighter *Isolde* rode out the storm with the sea pounding her hull and toppling over her decks to wash them clean of blood. The bow sliced into a massive wave and rose upon its back in a slow creaking heave. On the bridge, the radio crackled with static. Several men lay on the floor, their bodies mangled and oozing. Pools of blood rolled with each tilt of the ship, back and forth, each time slower as the blood coagulated.

Beside the radio stood a man, gruesome in his injuries. He kept a tight grip on the wheel and stared through the cracked window at a beacon flashing in the distance. Blood leaked from a constellation of gunshot and knife wounds to saturate his clothing. Bludgeon marks darkened his face and scalp. A single blow of a rifle butt had broken his front teeth into splinters.

He stood at the wheel, unmindful of the radio static and the dead men at his feet, and he stared at the flashing beacon with his single milky eye with the slit pupil and pushed beyond it with driving, pounding waves of thought sent over the sea and lights, reaching deep into the snowy darkness for the Beloved.

2

"Why do we have to drag all this crap back with us?" Pearl asked in the field. "What is it anyway? Looks like junk."

"This 'junk', as you call it," Sweeney said without stopping, "may well be the only known example of early European armor ever discovered in the New World."

"Oh, well then," Pearl said, and clanged two of the rusted pieces together. "Whoop-dee-doo."

The professor hiked the cross higher onto his shoulder. "And please…" The walk through the deep snow had winded him. "…will you please stop banging it about like that?"

They passed through the smoldering trees into the pasture. Tred leaped from footprint to footprint and Joe Li plodded along behind him, astonished the others could carry on a casual conversation so soon after the fiery wall had nearly incinerated them. *But they were inside the cave. They didn't see it hanging over them or the flaming tree falling toward them.* The absence of those moments of terror led them into such casual banter, he assumed, and this led to thoughts of Raeven and her own stubborn, fearful response. The thought of her bore down upon him like a heavy weight upon his chest. He wished she'd had the courage to stay. It made him think less of her that she didn't stay. That thought was intolerable so he tried to push her cowardice into a sensible corner of his mind: she was afraid and with good reason.

When they reached the police car, Sweeney stored the fragile armor and the cross in the trunk while Tred climbed into the back seat and sat between Joe and Pearl.

Sparky turned the key. Nothing happened. He went to check on Jerrod Grey's truck and discovered the key still in the ignition, but when he tried to start it he heard only the same dead-battery click, nothing more.

Inside in the squad car, Joe asked "What's that?" and pointed to the distant mountain.

"Oh, now what?" Pearl asked with an equal measure of annoyance and alarm.

Sweeney wiped the window with his sleeve. The mountaintop glowed with an aura of light sent up by flares of blue fire at the summit. He leaned closer. "It can't be…"

"What can't be?" Pearl asked. "You guys are scaring the hell out of me with all this 'what's that' and 'it can't be' crap. If something shows up will you please just say 'oh look, there's something,' instead of asking what it is or saying it can't be?"

Without answering, Sweeney climbed from the car and stood beside it, staring at the mountain.

Joe did the same from the back. "It looks like that wall cut all the power off. The ski lights, generator, car batteries."

Sparky had left the Grey's truck and now approached them. "Flashlights too."

"An electro-magnetic field," Joe suggested. "What do you think, Professor?" Sweeney continued to stare at the distant form of the rising mountain. "Professor…?"

"The mountain," he whispered, his voice hoarse. "It's

changing."

"Oh, come on," Sparky said but Dr. Sweeney held up his hand. "It is. Look."

Sparky gazed through the snow at the distant peaks, now obviously sharper and higher than before. He thought he could detect a faint grinding rumble carrying over the distance. "Changing into what?"

Dr. Sweeney did not shift his gaze. "Skellig Michael."

"The *island*?" Joe asked, astounded by the thought.

"A replica of it, yes. You see? It's forming two separate peaks with a lower ridge between."

"But why?"

"A signal, I fear. A beacon. One of mind, one of body. This – all of it: the fire wall, the trees, the mountain, everything is preparing for the coming of Lochru. Things are aligning. Rearranging. Summoning. Were that the real Skellig Michael, that fire near the summit would be positioned at the site of the monastery. Is there a building of some kind up there, Constable?"

"The lift house."

"Larger than the cave?"

"Oh, sure, much –" Sparky paused and stared at Dr. Sweeney, who shifted his gaze from the mountain to the policeman and said: "Its new lair, yes." He spun on his heels and climbed back into the car. "We must get this motorcar started."

"Only one way," Sparky said, leaning inside. "We'll have to do a roll start." He thought about the flickering lights in the convenience store and Pearl telling him her car had died completely in the presence of the thing, only to come to life again after it passed. "If we can get it started, the alternator should keep it going as long as that thing doesn't come too close. If it does…well, anyway Pearl, you get behind the wheel, the rest of us will push. Put it in gear and step down on the clutch. When I give the signal, let the clutch out. If we get her moving fast enough, she'll fire up. Ready?"

They succeeded on the first try. "If we stall, we'll have to do this all over again," he warned after Pearl gave up her position behind the wheel and the others climbed back inside.

He pulled out of the driveway onto the Coachlight Road. "Now what?"

Sweeney did not answer. He settled into thought and said nothing until Pearl pointed out the place where Raeven had confronted the creature. The mangled front hood of her car still lay on the snow bank. "This is what we are up against," Sweeney said as they passed.

"It's all theory, of course. Everything must be at this point. I believe the wall is a cocoon of sorts, a protective shield to keep the outside world at bay until the enemy arrives. At the same time, the mountain is changing into a form recognizable to him. It is rising to guide him to his appointed rendezvous."

"What'll we do?" Sparky asked.

"First, we drive to Father Toomey's to retrieve my book of herbals. I couldn't find it earlier, but I know it's in there somewhere. It may contain a clue to Moll's charmed potion. Second – let me think…second we have to melt the cross into a sword, though how we are to do that, I'm sure I don't know. We need a fire strong enough to melt silver. We can try to do it back at the restaurant. Thank heaven for that fireplace. If the power is truly out, we'll be happy to have it."

"Wait a minute," Pearl said. "You think the power is out all over town?"

"Looks that way," Sparky said. "Even the ski slope."

"That means the heat is out too. What about my birds? They can't take too much cold."

"Maybe we should go get them," Sparky suggested, and when Sweeney protested, Pearl said, "If I have time to follow you to a cave, you have time to help me with my birds."

"Very well," Sweeney said and gave in without further argument. "But do hurry, Constable. We don't know how much time we have left."

3

"What is it?" Chip Dubee asked, still frantic as they drove along the unplowed back roads of Burne Notch. "Is it lightning or…what is it?" Raeven breathed deep in an effort to force her pulse back to normal and said she thought it might be electricity. "But where did it come from?" he asked. He had already asked the same questions over and over and seemed not to listen when she offered the only answer possible: "I don't know."

"I think you do!" he said on the verge of tears. "I saw that wall close in front of your car downtown. And later you said it was following us. How could you know that?"

She reached out to touch his arm but didn't dare. "Is there a back road out of town?"

"No!" he yelled and she pulled her hand back. "There's a few logging roads, but those walls are cutting off everything. Even the snowmobile trails. We can't get out."

She looked straight ahead. The truck's headlights barely cut through the newer darkness, the – *unnatural darkness,* she thought. Night and snow had taken on an ominous cast, with snow falling within a thick fog and mounding into sharp drifts stark against the black trees. "We'll be okay," she said in a half-hearted attempt to reassure him.

He startled her by slamming his fist down on the steering wheel. "How? Something's going on and I think it's got something to do with you." Raeven recoiled to hear her own thoughts unexpectedly thrown back at her. "What are we gonna do?" he asked again.

"I don't know."

"Stop saying that!" he exploded. He slammed on the brakes and the truck slid to a stop. "Where do you want to go? And don't tell me you don't know what it is or that you have nothing to do with it. Just tell me where you want to go and I'll take you there, and then I want you out."

Raeven settled against the door, seething over the man's cowardice. "Pearl's trailer," she said, her voice flat and icy.

The drive through what should have been familiar surroundings unnerved them. At the north end where the bridge had collapsed, the boiling river sent its heated water flowing through town where it melted the ice and lifted clouds of vapor that crystallized in the frozen air to give every tree and building and abandoned car a delicate glaze that captured the thin blue glow of the distant wall in hues like that of fitful moonlight. As for the moon itself, it could not pierce the clouds that would not lift no matter how strong the wind. They churned in wild disorder over Burne Notch like a pall from an unseen fire while, below, streams of acrid smoke from real fires roamed the deserted streets like an army of marauding ghosts. Near the river it met and mingled with white steam lifting from the boiling water and the two vapors spiraled in a marble-caked waltz of smoke and fog lit by the unearthly glow of the wall.

Chip pulled into Pearl's driveway and watched Raeven pass through the headlights' glare and approach the wooden vestibule on the front porch. Her shadow spread into the back yard, now empty of trees. When she glanced back at the truck, Chip snorted and whispered, "What a skank."

She pushed through the canvas barriers and opened the front door into darkness and a bone-deep winter chill. "Pearl?"

The headlights seeped through the blinds but not enough to lift the darkness. She saw furniture, but only as dark shapes, undefined and without color. She flicked a light switch. Nothing happened. She stood in the doorway, wondering what to do.

Chip rolled down his window and asked if Pearl was there. Raeven leaned back through the canvas. "Not home," she said, but instead of returning to the truck, she stepped into the trailer. The birds lay huddled around her, she was sure of it, though she couldn't see them and she wondered if the smaller ones could withstand the drop in temperature.

Outside, Chip muttered to his reflection in the rear view mirror, "Now what?" He would have liked to abandon her but didn't dare, not after they had driven through town and found it altered in such menacing ways. He left the engine running when he left the truck to join her in the trailer.

"I don't see them," Raeven said when she heard him climb the stairs.

"What are you doing?"

"Looking for Earl." She knelt down and called his name.

"Come on – let's get out of here."

She heard a low gurgle followed by movement on the floor and she sat back on her heels when a warm bundle of feathers sidled up to her. "Got him," she whispered and lifted him onto her lap.

"Now what?"

"I don't know." She slipped her hands around the turkey's breast and enfolded him in her arms. "The heat is off. Some of them are too delicate for this."

"I don't give a shit. I'm getting out of here. You can come with me or stay, it's up to you."

Raeven listened to the engine purring outside and thought of the heat pouring through the vents. "I thought you wanted me out of your truck."

"I changed my mind."

"What about the birds?"

"Who cares? They can take care of themselves."

As if to prove him wrong another one sidled up to her. "I'm afraid to leave them," she said and reached down to pat it.

Something slick and clammy slid into her palm.

She pulled her hand back as though she had touched a snake and rose to her feet, so shocked she could barely think: though she *did* think, and now realized the shapes in the living room were something other than furniture, something hunched, something jagged. "Go back," she whispered and she stood in the darkness with her heart pounding in her ears. "Go outside." Again – movement from the floor, this time from another direction.

Something curled around her ankle. It slithered up the back of her calf.

She kicked it away and backed into him. "What's the matter?" Chip asked. He pulled a lighter from his pocket and flicked it on. "Don't!" she cried but the flame lit up the darkness and they reeled back before a wall of roots reaching for them, stretching, grasping, slouching across the living room like a tangle of monstrous worms.

Chip gasped in horror. Raeven collapsed against him and the lighter went out. The turkey struggled in her arms.

The door opened behind her and they fell back, stumbling onto the wooden porch and into the glare of the headlights. A root slithered after them like a pale eel out of water.

Raeven recoiled and slammed the door, severing it, and she shuddered at the sound of a thin, piercing wail of pain.

Something slammed against the door from inside. The severed root squirmed at their feet with clear sap pouring like blood from its wound.

They stumbled down the steps and the turkey leaped from Raeven's arms with a panicked squawk and ran under the trailer.

"What *was* that?" Chip cried. Before she could answer, the door whined and bent outward.

A window shattered above them.

The doorframe followed with a clatter of popping rivets and a sound of birds calling and shrieking within. The frame split, a section of the wall screeched outward, and a single hairless root shot through the broken frame and squirmed in the frozen air, coiling, searching for them. Beside it, a window burst from its sash and a brilliant burst of color exploded into the headlights as Pearl's parakeets and finches took to the air. Raeven cried out in despair but Chip pulled her to the truck and forced her inside before leaping behind the wheel.

"What was that?" he asked again, but Raeven did not answer. She rocked back and forth with her hands over her face. "What *was* it!"

"Trees," she said through her hands and he backed out of the driveway with the engine roaring. He pulled one of her hands from her face. "Did you say trees?" he asked, certain he must have misunderstood. "Yes, trees!" she shouted and pulled her hand from his, and the headlights swept over another brilliant spark of feathers darting skyward to their frozen doom.

4

Minutes later Sparky's car pulled up from the opposite direction. "Oh damn," he whispered and a cry rose from the back seat. "Oh, no, no, no!" Pearl leaped from the car and raced to the gaping hole in the side of her trailer.

"Careful!" Sparky called from behind. Shards of broken glass glittered in the snow.

She stepped through the shattered doorframe into the trailer. Icy wind poured through the broken windows. Pine needles carpeted the floor but no trees remained. "Birds?" she called, her voice cracking. "Birds!"

Sparky stepped up beside her and wrapped her in his arms.

Joe was about to get out of the car to join them but Dr. Sweeney turned in his seat to look at him. "What is the golden box?"

Joe's eyes snapped up to his, startled. "How do you know about that?"

"You mentioned it when Raeven was leaving. What is it?"

"I honestly don't know," Joe said, puzzled. "But it isn't real. I saw it in a dream. I dreamt that Raleigh Marcotte was afraid of it, but what it was or where it came from, no."

"No idea why he was afraid of it?"

"None at all. It was a simple box, not very big, made of gold with a Chinese character engraved on the lid."

"Chinese?" Sweeney sat back in his seat and faced the windshield again, perplexed. "Chinese..."

"I couldn't read it," Joe said. "I can't read Chinese. I can't even remember what it looked like, not specifically. Again, it was only a dream."

Dr. Sweeney sat deep in thought, gazing at the trailer but not seeing it.

Do you think it had something to do with all this?" Joe asked.

"I dearly wish it did. We would be in much better shape if that chap on the mountain was of Asian descent. The Chinese dragon is a vastly different animal from his loathsome European counterpart. Great, clanging, boisterous things, they are. Water gods who bring rain and good fortune; a different sort of beast altogether."

"And what is this one?" Joe asked. He rested his arms on the back of the front seat. Tred lay down beside him with a whistling sigh. "I mean, what is it really? And where did it come from?"

Sweeney pulled his scarf up and crossed his arms over his chest. "This one is darkness and it came from darkness, embodied evil spawned of the same, and the only fortune it brings is ill fortune. No rain. No luck. Nothing but wickedness. A grasping, hoarding, miserly force that takes and takes and takes, and that is all it does. As for reality, who among us could have believed such a thing existed outside our darkest fancies? Even I, who have been known to walk the stranger paths of life and who fervently accepts the odder possibilities found there; even I am utterly astonished by its existence."

Pearl and Sparky appeared at the vestibule door, each carrying an armload of small birdcages. Sweeney noted them and quickly asked: "Is Raeven a virgin?"

Joe pulled away from the seatback, surprised. "How would I know?"

"I do not ask out of prurient interest. I have assumed all along that you two are an item." Joe said nothing. "You *are* together, aren't you?" Sweeney asked, still without looking at him.

"No, not at all."

"Oh!" the professor said, genuinely surprised. "I beg your pardon. I would have sworn you two were a couple, or on the verge of being one. My mistake. Come to think of it, I did think it odd that she would so readily leave you."

"So did I," Joe murmured.

The car door opened and Pearl stuck her head inside. "You gonna help with these cages?"

"Certainly not," Sweeny said but a relieved Joe Li leaped from the car to assist. "Stack them inside," Sparky said and pointed to the open trunk. "There's still a few birds loose in the house. She wants to take them to the Panda."

Joe set a cage filled with pigeons against the inside wall of the trunk. Another containing two lovebirds followed. "What about Earl?"

"I can't find him," Pearl said. "He may have tried to follow the parrots."

At that moment, as if answering to his name, a soft gobbling sound came from under the trailer.

After settling Earl in the front seat and the remaining birds in the trunk, Sparky backed out of Pearl's driveway. She wanted to bring them to the restaurant right away but Dr. Sweeney insisted on first going to the parish house to retrieve his book of herbals.

The drive through the center of Burne Notch appalled them.

Every house stood desolate and every window stared blank and black. No cars patrolled the street (though Sparky pointed out a set of fairly fresh tire tracks, an indication that at least one car had recently passed their way). Thick abysmal fog hovered in the leafless trees and mingled with the smoke that prowled the vacant streets.

The church came into view, burned and gutted, with the white clapboards above every window tainted by smoke and the steeple rising like a ghostly tower and disappearing in the fog.

"We should probably consider stocking up on petrol," the professor said when they pulled into the driveway of the parish house.

"How long do you think it will take to find your book?" Sparky asked.

"It could take five minutes, could take an hour."

"Okay, do what you need to do. I'll fill up the tank with gas from the town garage; maybe get a couple of extra jerry cans. Want to come with me Pearl?" She looked at Dr. Sweeney, though she had already made up her mind.

"Do," he said with a sharp nod. "We should none of us be alone from here on out."

5

"Where now?" Chip asked. As before, Raeven shook her head and said she didn't know. Before he could flare with anger, she added, "I know I keep saying that, but you keep asking, and I truly *don't* know. We've tried all my ideas and now I don't know what to tell you."

They sat idling in the parking lot of the Golden Panda. Raeven had circled around the bloodstain and went in through the kitchen but found the place empty. "They may still be up at the Grey's farm. Maybe we should go up there."

Chip drove down the steep driveway. "How come you know so much about all this?"

"I've been around it a little more."

"But around *what?*" His voice rose upon a new updraft of fear. "First that wall, then whatever those tree things were in Pearl's trailer, and now I don't know where we're going or what we're looking for."

His pendulum moods from reasonable calm into sudden anger had begun to wear on her. In a quiet tone designed to avoid antagonizing him, she told him they were looking for Sparky, Pearl and Joe Li, along with a professor named Dr. Sweeney. "He knows more about this than any of us."

Chip turned onto a small, unplowed side road. She asked where he was going and he told her it was the Melbourne Hill Road, the back way to the Grey's farm. "It's faster. You want me to take it or not?"

"Yes, fine, go any way you want."

They drove up a low incline. When they reached the top, the headlights guttered and began to fail. Chip snapped the switch on and off. Nothing happened. The engine skipped. "What the hell? I just had this looked at. Something's wrong." The truck reinforced the point when the engine, lights, and heater clicked off, shut down and died, and they rolled to a long, slow halt.

Darkness overwhelmed everything. Their eyes soon adjusted and diffused it into the dim glow of the distant fire wall and they saw they had stopped beside a field bordered by dark forest on three sides and a high stone wall running parallel to the road.

Raeven glanced at Chip, afraid to speak for fear of setting him off again. She took a chance: "What's the matter with it?"

"I don't know." He tried the key again. Nothing – a tiny click.

Raeven studied the rows of standing stones within the field, each one wearing a beret of snow. "What is this place?"

"How should I know?"

"You're not making this easier."

"I'm not trying to make it easier. I want to get out of here."

Raeven folded her arms and heaved a weary sigh. "We're in a tough situation. You think you could possibly focus on ways to help instead of sniping at me?"

"Wait a minute," he said, leaning against his door. "Who picked you up? Who's taken you everywhere you wanted to go?" With one swift jab, he punched the roof of the truck, which startled her even as she half-expected such a reaction. "I *am* trying to help," he yelled. "I could have left you where I found you." He slammed the heel of his palm against the steering wheel and turned the ignition but again, nothing happened. "Wonder what's wrong with this thing," he said, and for Raeven, this sudden swerve back into rational calm proved his latest outburst came not from understandable fear or anxiety, but as a natural eruption, as much a part of him as normal speech. He felt perfectly at ease and within his rights to talk to her as he did and she thought she understood why: in all likelihood, no woman had ever fought back. They had all submitted meekly, fearful of losing his favor. This was his default strategy. He lashed out and stung with verbal abuse and kept them off guard and pliable by quickly applying the soothing balm. *But not with me*, she thought, and with no further word, she opened the door and stepped onto the road.

"What are you doing?" he asked, his voice tinged with alarm. This was not at all what he expected.

Raeven did not answer. She calmly closed the door and began to walk along the stone wall, slipping on the ice until she reached a gate in the center. The words *St. Bernadette* arched over the entrance in wrought-iron letters black against the blue-lit sky.

"Cemetery," she whispered and remembered it as the place where Steven Wilcox was to be buried. Unexpected tears rose to her eyes and she gripped the bars of the gate. They were not tears for Steven: she knew that. They were for her, for all the confusion and terror, the bravery not shown, her apparent inability to escape the driving whips of fate, and she found herself longing for those few short blissful hours when she could comfortably hide within a fog of mourning over a man she did not know.

She pushed against the gate. Its hinges squealed. Behind her, the truck door opened. "Oh, leave me alone," she whispered and strode into the cemetery.

"Come back!" Chip called. "I didn't mean it."

"I did," she said under her breath. Her black coat billowed out behind as she searched along the neat rows for Steven's grave. There had to be a mound, a freshly dug plot. *There*. She saw it, black against the pale snow. She walked toward it, but slowed down, distracted by the sight of another beside the first, and another behind that, and she stopped, perplexed by what appeared to be mounds of dirt piled throughout the cemetery.

Toppled headstones lay here and there, some leaning against others as though weakened by grief, others lying senseless in the snow. She approached one, trying to understand the presence of so many new graves, and when she reached it, she froze – it wasn't a new grave at all. It was a very old grave and what she first took to be mounded earth was a shattered coffin. A body desiccated into mummification lay halfway out of it. Its left forearm was missing.

Another body lay behind it, sprawled beside its casket and a pyramid of dirt.

She held her hand over her mouth, barely able to breathe as she approached the second corpse. It, too, was missing its left hand.

Chip called to her from the gate. She heard him, but did not answer. Her sudden realization left no room for further thought; *left hands – wedding bands*; and she shuddered at the memory of her class ring on Raleigh's tongue. She looked at a woman's corpse. Large chunks of flesh and skull had been torn from each side of her head. "Earrings," she whispered and, turning, saw that she stood within a field of corpses. A thin dusting of snow gave it the appearance of a winter battlefield, but with fallen soldiers in varying states of decay and mutilation and most wearing formal clothes, the men in dark suits and women in dresses with white hair neat and permed.

It had been there. It had vandalized the cemetery. It had dug up all the bodies and stripped them of their gold. But when? How long ago?

She began to turn toward the gate and stopped again, her gaze riveted to the ground. A corpse lay in the snow beside his opened coffin with the oil stains still spattered upon the silk-screened pine tree inside. His eyes were closed and his mouth open, the same as the last time she saw him. He wore a brown suit now torn and soiled. His broken glasses lay in the snow beside him. "Poor man," she whispered. "Poor, poor man."

Chip called again.

She turned to answer when she heard a sharp hollow crack from the back of the cemetery. She peered at the black line of the forest with its sharp triangular treetops silhouetted against the pale light.

"What are you doing?" Chip asked from inside the gate.

A treetop shivered and tilted with a low crunch of branches. A second jerked to the side, this time closer. It swished back into place.

Chip approached her from behind. "What's going on?"

"Quiet," she whispered. "Don't move."

The trees shuddered. One cracked and fell. The sound of its rushing collapse washed over the cemetery. "What is it?" Chip asked, sidling up close behind her.

"Don't *move*," she whispered, insistent.

"What is it?" he asked again, but before she could answer, he grabbed her by the shoulder. She reached up and laid her hand on his and there they stood, paralyzed by the sight of a massive head lifting between two treetops like a snake rising from a field of grass. Faint currents of blue light played about its snout to illuminate its scalloped black scales. It snorted and the force of its breath bent the tops of the nearby spruce. A long narrow tongue whipped out and it lifted its head higher, sniffing, tasting the air.

Chip tightened his grip. "Raeven," he whispered and the thing turned, its head snapping to. It focused in upon them with eyes that reflected the dim light like cauldrons of dark red fire. "Oh my God,"

Chip whispered so softly Raeven could barely hear him.

But the thing heard.

It cocked its head and lifted it further until it hovered above the highest treetop. Raeven's heart leaped when its long, swan-like neck expanded with a sharp *whoosh* into the wide flat hood of a cobra.

The creature threw its head back and roared. The sound thundered and reverberated through the graveyard. Full-grown trees bent before the rush and the cemetery lit up in brilliant blue when a crackling stream of electricity sizzled from its mouth. The charges played about its face and swirled like blue smoke before dissipating, and it growled and cocked its head again, staring.

"Oh, my God," Chip stammered again and the hood retracted at the sound, the neck dropped, and the head disappeared behind the tree line.

Branches whined and snapped. Trees fell.

It was coming.

6

While Joe and Dr. Sweeney began the search for his missing book of herbals within the ruined parish house, Pearl and Sparky drove to the town garage. It was a cavernous building made of corrugated sheet metal over a steel frame, built at the foot of the mountain to house municipal equipment. Sparky unlocked the enormous metal doors and pulled them open. Each one whined on its hinges before banging against the outside walls. "Drive in," he said and directed her toward two steel drums near the massive snowplow that took up most of the space inside. "A little closer. Good."

"Okay?" Pearl asked, sticking her head out the window. An unlit cigarette dangled from her lips. "Better not light that in here," he said and opened one of the barrels. Air hissed out. An odor of gasoline filled the garage. Pearl pushed Earl off her lap and went outside while Sparky siphoned gas into the car. She tapped on the trunk as she passed. "You kids okay in there?" A low squawk. "Glad to hear it."

Outside, she leaned against the garage and stared at the mountain looming jagged against the sky. Cobalt blue fire swirled in silent violence near the summit and plumes of smoke issued from fissures along its flanks. Spires of stone had cracked up from the earth and defiled the ski slope where the Garand's lift had collapsed in a snarl of towers, chairs and cables. She was amazed the garage could remain so close yet sustain no damage at all.

She finished her cigarette and threw it down. Its orange coal illuminated a small plant sticking up through the snow before hissing out. "What in the world?" She crouched beside it. A dark green stem ended in a spike covered with tiny greenish-yellow flowers and two large purple-brown leaves curling over the spike like a hood. "Hey, Sparkles, look at this." She brushed the snow from the leaves. Sparky appeared at the garage door: "Look at what?" he asked. She tapped a leaf with her forefinger. "This plant, it's not supposed to be here. It *can't* be here. It's a jack-in-the-pulpit."

"Yeah? So?"

"So it can't grow in the winter, not with this snow. It's impossible. I've seen them in the bog below the Panda, but only in spring."

He shrugged, unable to summon the same enthusiasm. "I'd like to stop at my sister's on the way back to the church, see if she got out all right." He backed the car out of the garage and got out again to lock the garage doors. "Wish we could take the snow plow, but no way to start it. Too bad."

Pearl slipped into the passenger's side. "That's really weird," she said, still musing over the unexpected plant. She said it again, "*really weird*," when he pulled away from the garage and the headlights glistened upon two more jack-in-the-pulpits poking up through the snow, as fresh and green as the first day of May.

7

Raeven jammed her fingers through the openings in a chain link fence. Beyond, she saw another field filled with oddly shaped mounds of snow. "What is this place?" Before Chip could answer, another sonorous rumble came from behind and they looked back in time to see a swath of electrical currents surge over the cemetery wall and engulf Chip's stalled truck. Everything came on at once: alarm system, engine, windshield wipers; the chassis rocked back and forth and the headlights snapped on and blazed down the road to illuminate them cowering against the fence.

The chain links began to quiver and jangle. Thin electrical charges appeared at the far end. Their darting lines crawled along its length, outlining the individual links in a blue sizzle as they came.

"The gate," Chip said and led her to a wide chain link gate at the far end. He pushed it open as another jolt of electricity lit up the sky and a filthy white sign: *Tipsy Tom's Salvage Yard*.

Inside, lay hundreds of crushed and battered cars piled two deep in long rows with each row separated by a wide snowy aisle. The junkyard contained other items too: washing machines and refrigerators (without doors as legally required to prevent the accidental suffocation of curious children), air-conditioners, washing machines and fans; all in segregated mounds along the fence. A long, low mountain of cast-off tires bordered the back of the lot.

Chip led her down one of the wide aisles. At its end he slid to a stop and slapped his hand against the side of a dark red van, its front end crumpled in a long ago accident. "Used to be mine." He reached for the handle on the back door, but spun around when an explosion beyond the trees sent an orange fireball curling into the sky. "My truck!"

Raeven opened the back door of the van and the fireball illuminated the interior. All but the two seats in front had been removed and replaced by a rubber mat now stiff with age and an old quilt torn to shreds by squirrels and mice. Faded paneling lined the sides. A water-stained Metallica poster hung from one, its edges curled and yellow. Up front, the windshield had been cracked into a thousand fractures and the front seats tilted into a jumble of twisted metal.

She climbed inside without hesitation. "Hurry," she said and he followed and shut the door. Darkness closed over them and they sat side by side, listening. The echoes of the creature's calls warped all sense of distance and they couldn't tell if the thing had followed them into the salvage yard or had remained behind in the cemetery. Before long the calls began to diminish: it had either given up or had lowered the intensity while continuing its search. Raeven chose to believe the latter, even after its growls had faded into thick silence.

She closed her eyes and concentrated, listening for movement outside, and was startled by the sound of a choking sob beside her. Chip rolled to the side and lay down upon the quilt. Raeven listened to the soft hitch of his breath. She wanted to do the same, but the sound of his fearful sobs choked off her own tears. "Shhh, its okay," she said and lay down beside him. Chip turned away from her, struggling to hold back the sound. She laid her hand upon his arm but he shrugged it away. "My truck," he said, high and boyish, and he began to sob openly, no longer caring if she heard him or not. "What *was* that thing?"

Raeven laid her head on his arm – unexpected thing to do, but he did not shrug her away this time. She felt the swell of his bicep through his coat sleeve. "It comes from far away," she whispered. He did not respond but lay beside her, weeping like a frightened child. "It comes from a place where…" She rolled onto her back. He turned to her and rested his head upon her shoulder, and he draped his arm around her and lay there with silent tears flowing hot against her neck. She froze – not daring to move, but wanting to move.

"From where?" he whispered.

"It came from…."

"Where?"

"It comes from a place where a knight once lived who was gallant and bold and he…" She stopped again and stared at the dark ceiling, now fighting back tears of her own. "He was brave but deep in his heart he held a secret that he alone knew."

"What secret?"

"That he wasn't real."

"Wasn't real…"

"He was a real person, but he wasn't true. He wasn't what the world thought he was. His bravery, his armor, his image of himself as a chivalrous knight was all a fake. He thought if he played the part long enough, he would become the part, and he almost made it. He had it all together: the armor, the look, the attitude. He had changed and conquered everything except the terrible thing inside, the terrible thing that made him afraid."

"Afraid of what?"

"Afraid of everything. Afraid of people. Afraid of life. Even afraid of the things he had already conquered. And he almost made it. He would have gone through life without ever facing the terrible thing inside and he almost made it." Chip pulled her closer, and she tilted her head, resting hers against his. "Almost, " she said and a tear rolled down her temple and fell. "But along came a dragon."

8

She opened her eyes, confused, and disoriented, and shocked to discover she had fallen asleep, but then: *how long since I last slept?*

Chip lay beside her with his breath warm against her neck and his head heavy on her arm. She shifted. He moaned and moved his head closer. His breath came in steady waves.

She listened beyond him to the outside night.

No growls. No branches cracking. No sound at all.

"I think it's gone," she whispered. She touched his hair. "Chip?" He shifted again and she closed her eyes, shocked by the touch of his lips caressing her neck with light kisses.

She tried to say "Chip, don't," but could only form the words with no sound. He moaned, deep and gravelly, and shifted again. His breath rushed into her ear and she shivered when his lips closed around her ear lobe. "Don't..."

"Don't talk," he whispered. His cheek scraped against hers with a rasp of stubble and she caught her breath when he lifted his head and rubbed his rough chin over the side of her nose and kissed her closed eyelid.

She dropped her arms flat against the tattered quilt, palms up, and he rolled onto her with his right leg across her thighs. His hair hung down as a single black wave about to surge and crest, and his eyes, pale blue even in the dim light, stared and slipped into hers, overwhelming her sight and narrowing it into his eyes alone, his gaze alone.

He bent down but she pulled away and turned her head: "Wait," she whispered.

"What do you want me to do?" he returned, and she gasped when his hand slipped under her coat and began to pull up her dress. "No, wait..."

He unbuckled his belt. "This what you want?" The full weight of his hips pressed down upon her, and he kissed her again, open and full, covering her mouth, but she pulled back again. "No..."

He caught her hair in his hand and gently pulled her head down to the quilt. "Be quiet," he said and punctuated it by giving her hair a sharp tug.

She squeezed her hand between them and pressed against his chest, tried to push him away. "I've never done it."

He lifted his head, looked down at her. "A virgin? You're kidding."

"No."

"That's okay."

"But no...but why...?"

"Why you?" That wasn't what she was going to ask, but before she could say a word, he smirked and answered his own question: "Because you're here. And I don't care."

He dropped but she squirmed away. "Oh, no, no, no," he said, pulling her toward him. "You're not going to leave me like this."

"Don't," she cried and tried to push him away again. "*Don't!*"

He exploded as he had back in the truck. "Shut up!" He slammed his palm down on her forehead and drove her head back against the rubber mat. "You're not going to pull this on me now."

He forced her hands over her head and pinned them down.

"No!" she cried but he rolled onto her. She struggled beneath him, fighting to keep him off. She pulled one hand free, she reached out, reached for anything; she grabbed his ear and twisted as hard as she could while driving her nails into the side of his head. Chip cried out and rolled off her with his hand to his ear. "I can't believe you did that!"

"I told you not – "

He struck out with his fist and she fell back with a cry, stunned by the force of the blow and the pain that exploded from her wounded lip. "Don't say anything, don't say a word!" He kicked the back door open and slid outside where he brushed his hair out of his eyes and turned to her, his chest heaving and breath coming in angry blasts. "And don't fucking follow me no more!"

Raeven stared, open-mouthed, unable to think, move or say anything. A hot trickle of blood rolled down her chin. "You..." she said, "you're..."

He sneered at her, his eyes cold as ice. "I'm what?"

She couldn't finish. She fell back onto the quilt. He slammed the back door of the van with a curse and turned around and nearly bumped up against what he first thought was a black car.

But it wasn't a car.

9

It lay before him, crouched in the aisle between the cars with its head close to the snow, facing the back door of the van like a monstrous cat waiting outside a mouse hole.

It did not move. It did not blink. It stared and Chip stood paralyzed before it. A breathy snarl wafted over the short distance between them and his belt buckle jingled like a tiny wind chime in a light breeze.

Inside the van, Raeven heard the snarl and knew at once what had happened. Chip reached behind, fumbling for the door handle. "Raeven," he said in a husky whisper. "Open the door..."

Another growl and it slid toward him. Its eyes shimmered with a burnished glow from the tiny hairline traces of electricity that squirmed over its scales. Its putrid breath buffeted his hair and jacket, and its tongue slithered out forked and black and reeking of rot to brush against his legs. It scraped up under his jacket, tasting him. He couldn't move. He couldn't run. A trail of dark gray slime dripped down the front of his jeans. It nudged him. His belt buckle jangled.

Inside, Raeven reached for the door handle. Before she could open it, Chip panicked. He staggered sideways and ran into the wide pathway between two rows of cars where he stumbled and fell to his knees.

Behind him, the head rose from the ground. Its cobra hood rustled and expanded. When Chip spun around at the sound, two fangs sprang down from the roof of its mouth with a watery snap, and it dropped. He did not cry out. He did not have time to react. The right fang pierced his chest and drove down through his intestines to emerge again, slick and bloody from his anus. He flailed and tried to scream but couldn't. It lifted him into the air, impaled upon the fang. Blood gushed from his mouth, his nose, his chest, it spread over his jeans, and he gurgled, twitching until his spine separated and it cut him in half with a quick snap of its jaws.

Raeven recoiled at the thump of something heavy falling onto a nearby pile of rusted cars. A smacking, chewing sound came, followed by silence.

She crouched in the dark, listening. Her pulse throbbed in her ears.

A tremor passed through the van, the paneling, the metal flooring.

It pushed against the side. A snort of rancid breath followed, and a slap of its tongue at the back door.

Raeven huddled behind the mangled front seat. The dome light snapped on, dim at first, but quickly wavering into full strength. She rose to her knees to turn it off but dropped with a scream when two fangs punched through the top of the van like those of a viper being milked for venom. Thick gray liquid poured from each and sizzled down upon the rubber mat on each side of her.

They swung up toward the roof and pulled and the top of the van crinkled with a metallic shriek and rolled back like the cover from a tin of sardines.

She scrambled into the front. Behind her, venom pumped and hissed. Bitter smoke filled the van. She pushed at the driver's door but the original crash had sealed it shut, the same with the passenger side.

It withdrew its fangs with a screech of metal. Broken headlights snapped on. Taillights and dashboard lights flashed. Bent windshield wipers clattered over the fractured glass.

It struck again, this time through the front roof. The left fang impaled the top of the driver's seat while the right pumped a jet of poison over the dashboard. She crawled to the rear door over the smoking quilt.

The van lurched and lifted off the ground, front end first.

She slid against the rear door and managed to twist the handle. The doors fell open and she rode the quilt and rubber mat into the snow when the van swung creaking into the air. Diamonds of shattered glass rained over her. The Metallica poster drifted down, swinging gently in the air until a chunk of metal caught it and tore it streaming down upon the snow.

She leaped to her feet and ran across the aisle where she hid between two cars and caught her first clear view of the thing: immense, with a lean muscular body covered with scales as shiny and slick as those of a water snake and a row of ridges that flowed over its back to the scorpion-stinger tip of its tail. Far more nimble than its size suggested, it rose onto its hind legs, supported by its powerful tail, and its neck rounded in an elegant arc while it reached up with its forelegs to pull the van from its fangs.

It peered into the vehicle and licked it with its tongue. *Looking for me,* she realized. It grunted and casually tossed the vehicle end over end to crash upon a row of cars.

Raeven turned to run but fell back with a strangled cry when she saw Chip staring at her from the roof of the car beside her. His eyes were open. His black hair blew gently in the wind. His shirt and coat had been sliced away and what once had been a slim, muscular waist was now a jumble of pale, fractured ribs poking from his steaming flesh.

And – *there!* Mouth open, fangs lowered, it slammed into the narrow space between the cars with the sides of its jaws lifting them outward in cresting waves of twisted metal. On it came, snapping and snarling, with cars upending and rolling away and Raeven riding an upwelling of snow with Chip's upper body tumbling along beside her.

She landed on her back between two piles of flattened cars.

It reared back and shook its head. Thick, viscous drops of venom spumed over the cars. Paint blistered wherever they landed.

It dove in for another strike.

Cars tumbled with shrieks of metal on metal. Its tongue lashed out, searching, slapping against the cars. It touched Chip's lifeless arm and coiled around it with the lightning speed of a python, and Raeven stared in horror when it dragged the severed corpse between the cars.

She crawled into another clear aisle.

Behind her again, cracking, chewing sounds and then a pulse of static electrical charges following her, seeking her out, crackling around her and setting her hair on end. She scrambled to her feet and ran across the aisle toward a mountain of discarded refrigerators lying atop one another beneath a thick mantle of snow and she climbed the pile until she found one that stood like an upright coffin with its back facing the salvage yard and its open, door-less front facing the chain link fence.

She slipped into it and listened to the screeches and clatter as on it went, searching, scraping, rooting, and she huddled in the refrigerator, mouthing a prayer it would not find her.

The sounds began to fade. A bumper dropped and fell with a clank. A car scraped against another, and then she heard no sound at all. No quivering footstep. No growl. Nothing.

But it was there. She knew it was there.

She sat back, startled when a sudden red glow lit the air. Terrified to move or even breathe, she huddled inside the refrigerator. Its tall rectangular shadow fell upon the chain link fence and the trees beyond, cast there from an unwavering scarlet glow from behind. She stared at it and tried to remain as still as possible, but before long had to shift position to keep her leg from going to sleep. She wondered if the glow came from fire. But no: it was too red, too steady and constant. It did not flicker like firelight.

She peeped around the side of the refrigerator.

Hundreds of taillights blazed throughout the salvage yard. No headlights diluted their demonic glow and no blinking hazard lights leavened it with yellow; only hundreds of red lights glowering from hundreds of long-dead cars.

A low hum rose around her, followed by the whir of a motor chugging to life. Raeven looked around, puzzled. *From where?* A vibration passed through the refrigerator. A white glow appeared below and grew brighter as the refrigerator lights snapped on, one by one, to illuminate rusty racks and vegetable drawers and freezers, some still containing ice cube trays corroded with rust. *Impossible – they aren't plugged in.*

She then felt the vibration of the motor within her own refrigerator clanking to life.

Its light snapped on behind her and filled the refrigerator's dark rectangular shadow upon the fence with her own shadow enlarged and defined and her every move now delineated across the fence and trees.

Without thinking, she left her now-useless hiding place and descended the mountain of refrigerators. Some lay on their backs and sent their lights straight up to illuminate her passage from below. Others, upright and tilted, marked her progress with angled shafts that lit her path like searchlights following an escaping convict. Sheet metal boomed with every step. One refrigerator, precariously balanced, toppled over and crashed down the side of the hill to dash all hope of a quiet escape, but on she went, sliding and climbing down the refrigerator mountain.

Jagged metal tore her dress and coat, her hand bled from a small cut, and her lip still bled from Chip's fist. When she reached the ground, she ran from the refrigerators into a wide aisle where the taillights blazed like red eyes surrounding her and –

Eyes!

The thought nailed her in her tracks.

She stood in the snowy aisle with her heart pounding, not knowing what to do or where to go; and she looked around, and around again, knowing that somewhere hidden in the glare of a thousand red lights lay two real ones, smoldering, waiting, and watching.

10

The squad car rounded a corner and Sparky's heart jolted at the sight of a state police car upended in front of his sister Judy's house.

"Wait, wait," Pearl said, pre-empting his panic. "Her car is gone. She got out."

He slammed on the brakes and they slid to a stop beside the battered car. "Stay here, don't let the engine stall." After he ran from the car into the house, Pearl pulled Earl onto her lap. "Hey turkey," she whispered and passed her hand over his feathers. "How'd we ever get into this mess?"

She heard a sound like steam escaping from a radiator. She turned, puzzled, listening over the steady purr of the engine. Tred heard it too: she saw him sit up on the back seat with his ears tilted forward. A light chirping sound came from the trunk. "Poor things," she said and the steamy hiss came again. This time she knew for sure it had come from outside the car. She peered through the windows but saw only the silent street lined with empty houses receding into darkness.

She thought about the possibility of fumes from the jerry cans in the trunk.

"Stay here, Earl," she said and released the trunk latch. "You too, Tred." Outside, she opened the trunk and lifted the quilt she had placed over the cages. Their occupants stared up at her with beady eyes reflecting the same taillight glare that lit her in brilliant red. "Everybody alive? Everybody warm?"

She was about to fold the quilt back down when it came again, a low breathy hiss. Whatever it was, it was right behind her. She froze with one hand on the trunk.

A voice spoke from the front of the car: "Don't move."

"Sparkles..."

"Shh, don't say anything. Don't move."

She swallowed hard. "What is it?" A shadow fell upon the snow beside her. "Sparky," she said, fighting down a scream.

"Don't talk, don't move" he said. "It's going away."

She stood with her heart pounding and her hand on the trunk for what seemed an eternity before the sound began to fade. Sparky circled around to meet her. "You all right?" he asked and she fell into his arms. "Look," he said and she turned.

A lone hunched figure like a monk dressed in a black robe with a pointed cowl shuffled away from them alongside the road with its roots undulating around its trunk like seaweed in a current. Other roots coiled into the snow banks and contracted to drag the tree forward in halting jerks, hissing over the ice.

"They're coming up from behind the house too," Sparky said. He closed the trunk. "You drive," he said and circled around to the passenger side. Inside, he held up his pistol, checked to see if it was loaded, then snapped it shut and jammed it into his holster.

"Judy?" she asked.

"Gone, thank God. She left a note for me. One of the troopers didn't make it."

"In the house?"

"Most of him." Pearl turned away with a grimace. "Drive slow," he said. "Don't get too close to those things." Pearl shuddered as they pulled away from the house and passed another with its roots squirming and hovering. "Look at that," she said and pointed at the path made by the tree. A single jack-in-the-pulpit stood rooted beside it.

11

"I'm certain I brought it here with all my other books," Dr. Sweeney said in the darkened parish house. "Light a fire, will you Joseph? I can't see a bloody thing."

Joe Li felt his way through the living room to the fireplace and a box of matches on the mantle. He lit one and, "Oh, wow," he said, astonished by the destruction illuminated by the tiny flame. Curtains hung in ribbons and wafted in the cold draught pouring through broken windows. He set another match to the end of a rolled up newspaper.

"Where *is* it?" Dr. Sweeney sputtered.

Joe saw a candle on a nearby table and lit it with the newspaper. A small shadow crossed the wall and a light high cry sounded beneath a toppled chair. "Hey, look," Joe said and tossed the flaming newspaper into the fireplace. He scooped the little cat up with one hand and held it close to his chest where it purred the loudest purr he had ever heard.

"Her name is Soot," Sweeney said.

"What'll we do with her?"

"Take her, I suppose," Sweeney said with an exasperated sigh. "Why not? We've already a cur and an assortment of fowl, might's well have a puss too." He suddenly threw his hand up, the cat leaped from Joe's arms, and they stood where they were, motionless, stung by the sound of a distant roar trembling through the air like rolling thunder reverberating, echoing, quivering in the walls. "Holy suffering Christ," Sweeney whispered. "Quickly. Help me look for it. It's a large volume, leather bound, gilt edged."

Joe lifted the candle. "Ah-ha!" the professor cried and retrieved *The Book of Medicinals and Herbals* from beneath an overturned desk. "Come," he said and rushed to the front door.

Joe lifted Soot back into his arms, blew out the candle, and nearly ran into Sweeney when he stopped short with a gasp.

Joe looked beyond him and stared, amazed to see a line of hunched figures slouching down the road in single file. "Trees?" he asked in a tentative whisper. "Those are *trees*?"

"They are." Sweeney stepped back from the door. "Pine trees. Let's wait for the Constable inside, shall we?"

Joe set a toppled chair onto its feet and sat on it, numbed. "I don't understand," he murmured. "Why trees?"

"I've wondered that ever since I saw them at Pearl's house." Sweeney sat on a radiator before a window and peered through the torn curtains at the gathering pines. "Good heavens, look at them. Appalling."

"But what are they? I mean, I know they're trees, but what *are* they?"

"We seem always to be asking that, don't we? My guess is they are part of the alignment now taking place."

"You said that back at the Greys too. What alignment?"

Shadows hid Sweeney's face. His wild hair and high collar stood silhouetted against the window. "The druid-witch Moll called it snowfire. Nature aligning unnaturally in ways we cannot fully understand. The spirit of Lochru, possibly that of Moll, or perhaps a force emanating from the creature itself – who can say which it is, but *something* is aligning and re-aligning nature to each side. The wall belongs to the enemy. So do the trees. The shooting stars belong to us."

"But the wall isn't natural."

"Ah, but it is. It embodies nature in its purest, most devastating form, as powerful as lightning; a gathering of electrical forces from the earth, the sky, power lines, batteries, from every source imaginable and all conspiring to build a barrier around Burne Notch."

"Back at the Greys you said the creature built it as protection. But from what?"

Sweeney turned to the window again and saw Sparky's headlights beyond the slouching pines. "Here they come," he said. "Let's meet them outside. Mind the trees. Don't get too close."

"What in the world would that thing need protection from?"

"The one thing in the world it truly fears," the professor said on his way through the rubble to the door.

"Which is?"

Sweeney stopped at the door but did not turn back: "A knight, strange and fearful."

"Her?"

"Her. Yes."

12

The refrigerator lights went out. Their motors rattled into stillness. She stood in the wide aisle with her pulse racing, crimsoned by hundreds of red tail lights and staggered by the sudden understanding of its game.

It had forced her into the open by design. Not daring to move forward or back, she turned in a slow circle and scanned each bank of glowering taillights for a sign of the creature, all the while terrified of finding one.

Somewhere in the junkyard a piece of metal fell with a light ping. Behind her, a refrigerator settled against another with a hollow clank.

Tension crackled in her mind. Something that large could not hide for long. She could *feel* its presence like a knife blade lightly scraped against her skin.

Tears blurred her vision. "Come on, come on," she whispered at the rows of lights and her heart leaped when – *there!*

Two taillight eyes blinked at the far end of the junkyard.

She studied them, memorizing their location, fearful of losing them in the scores of surrounding lights. Her pulse quickened when she saw a dark mound hunched behind.

The creature had miscalculated: its position at the far end of the junkyard left a clear path to the front gate. If she could make it through, she could cross the road into the woods where no lights could snap on or motors whir to life. She turned to face a high pile of junk and, beyond it, the open gate.

She stepped toward it and chanced a look back. The eyes blinked again in the same place with the dark shape huddled behind.

She swallowed hard and began a slow steady walk to the gate. Closer, she saw that the pile of junk beside it was a mountain of old air conditioners and fans.

She passed a derelict Winnebago with its long-dead taillights blazing vibrant red. More taillights burned in the shadows behind.

She glanced back again. The same pair of lights blinked in the distance, and then – "oh, no," she whispered, "oh *no!*" and her knees went weak at the sight of a second pair of taillights blinking beside the first. A third pair flashed, and then several pairs at once, and finally, "Oh, no, no, no," she whispered when lights throughout the junkyard began to blink, all red but for those few bare bulbs that pulsed through broken or cracked coverings. The flashing glow illuminated the hulking shape behind the cars at the far end.

It was the mound of tires.

A deep hiss washed over her from the darkness beside the Winnebago. There, a single pair of lights burned steady while all around her and all through the junkyard the others twinkled and flashed.

And then they moved.

It slid from the darkness with its head upon the snow and its eyes riveted upon her, dimming from bright taillight red to glossy black.

Raeven stood before it, hypnotized by the shimmer of its eyes beneath the thick bony ridges of its brows. She didn't move – she *couldn't* move, even when it slid up to her, plowing a small furrow of snow with its lower jaw. It stopped so close she could have touched it. It breathed in and her hair lifted in the cold air pulled into the creature's lungs.

It nudged her – a small move, but enough to send her down on her back in the snow. She sat up, supported by her elbows. It lifted its head. Ridge upon ridge of the dark gray underside of its neck rose up to support it. From behind the Winnebago came a sound of cars shifting and falling as it rose to its feet.

It towered with its head poised above her, staring down. It

snorted. Fetid air rushed over her, so hot that the snow around her melted in an instant and she sank into a circular pool of warm water six inches deep.

It opened its jaws. Rows of serrated teeth dripped with milky gray saliva. Tiny lines of electricity zapping back and forth from row to row.

She sat up in the puddle. "Bugger off," she whispered, barely able to get the words out. It responded, not by running away as before, but by throwing its head back with the thunderous, reverberating roar heard miles away by Joe Li and Dr. Sweeney. Its fangs swung from the roof of its mouth with a snap and it dropped, sweeping up a wave of snow that lifted Raeven from the puddle in a groundswell of water, mud, and ice. She came down with a crash amongst the fans and air conditioners, though so much snow had been thrown with her that it broke her fall. A blade from a broken desk fan had cut through her dress and grazed her leg, but she did not notice.

The creature strode toward her. With a mighty swing of its tail, it toppled the Winnebago onto a pile of cars.

It lunged. She rolled to the side and it missed. Its snout crashed into the fans, crushing some, scattering others. It pulled back again and shook its head and made a thick grunting sound. A pulse of electricity throbbed over the pile and it began to stir, the same as the refrigerators before.

Motors hummed to life around her. Blades began to move. Raeven sat up, breathless, her heart pounding so hard she felt it banging against her ribs.

Desk fans, vent fans, large fans in wire cages and propeller-like ceiling fans began to revolve, slow at first, but quickening. Air swirled. Snow lifted. The creature lunged again and they crackled into a higher speed to whir and slice at the air.

Raeven pulled up close to an air-conditioner's surge of frigid air; desperate to avoid the chopping blades now blurring around her. Motors overheated. A pall of blue smoke lifted.

The creature darted in again, but caught the rush of wind and hesitated. It pulled back and cocked its head, confused. It couldn't see the blades; it couldn't understand where the wind was coming from.

It hissed and moved to the side of the pile, still focusing on her.

Metal began to vibrate. Raeven gasped when a ceiling fan lifted into the air. Once out of range of the electrical field it died again and fell with a crash into the refrigerators. Two more followed, both small rusty desk fans: the blades separated from the motor and whirred up over the junkyard and fell again.

The creature glanced at them, distracted by their flight, and shifted its attention back to its prey.

Another blast shot over the fans and Raeven fell back with a scream. It plunged in. The fans whirred into a high-pitched shriek and lifted, buoyed on a storm of self-made wind. They flew at its face with slicing blades revolving so quickly it could not see them. Ceiling fans lifted like helicopters. Fans inside wire cages rose more slowly, held down by their own weight, until they too lifted from the pile, trailing their electrical cords like kite tails.

A small fan hit the creature on the side of its face. The blades cracked against its hide but could not cut through. Another flew into its right foreleg and splintered against the steely scales. It growled in fury, electricity surged and sent up a new squadron of fans. Some left a trail of white sparks as they flew and these the creature snapped at like a dog snapping at flies. Others diverted its attention by exploding at their greatest height and falling like blazing comets when they passed from the electrical field.

She made her move. She picked her way through the remaining fans. The greatest danger lay in those too heavy to fully rise. Some of these moved sideways across the pile in short, deadly hops. Others hovered at eye level with their cords caught in the debris below and either hung stationary in place or whirred around in wide circles, tethered by their cords, unable to break free.

Raeven wove through them. Sparks fell around her. A ceiling fan crashed into the snow.

The creature stood before her with its tail swinging back and forth like a wrecking ball, with a host of fans whirring and sparking through the air and the creature's massive head darting this way and that, trying to catch them.

It snarled with frustration and fury and more tormenting fans took to the air. Raeven lifted the hem of her heavy wet dress and ran past its claws through the front gate. Fans fell around her, one by one, deadly missiles clanging in the road, in the trees, on the derelict cars, while behind another surge of crackling blue tore skyward into the clouds.

13

"Stop, stop!" Sweeney said and leaned over the front seat to tap Sparky on the arm. "What the devil is that?"

Sparky stopped the car a little past the intersection with the Melbourne Hill Road on the way to the Golden Panda. Pearl sat beside him with Earl huddled on her lap. Joe sat in back with Dr. Sweeney, the cat Soot, and Tred the dog. "Up there," Sweeney said, pointing. "Over those trees."

Missiles rose and sparked and fell again in flaming trails. The echoing roars they had heard for some time accompanied them, but louder now. "Back up," Sweeney said.

"We're not going *up* there, are we?" Pearl asked.

"Certainly not. Only far enough to see what it is."

Sparky backed up to the intersection and pointed to a single set of tire tracks veering onto Melbourne Hill. "Someone drove up there not long ago. Maybe they're in trouble."

Pearl shifted the turkey from her lap to the seat. "Got news for you, Spark – we're *all* in trouble."

"Okay, look...I'm going to drive just a little ways up the road, enough to see what's going on." He did not have to go far. When they rounded the first corner, the red glow of taillights and shuddering white light of falling sparks filtered through the distant trees and spilled into the road before the cemetery. A surge of brilliant blue followed and lit up the smoking hulk of a pickup truck.

A figure appeared on the road, at the edge of the headlight's glow, running toward the car. Joe leaned forward and peered over Sparky's shoulder. "That looks like Raeven," he said and Dr. Sweeney snapped to attention. "It *is*!" Joe cried.

She ran toward their headlights with her dress held up from the snow with one hand and waving them away with the other. "Go back!" she yelled with breath heaving and lungs burning, trying to force her voice across the distance. "Go away! Go!"

Before anyone in the car could react, a monstrous figure tore through the chain link fence beyond the cemetery and careened into the trees across the road. Snow exploded into clouds of white smoke from the boughs.

"Good *God!*" Sweeney cried when it rose to its feet with a shattering roar.

Joe pushed Soot off his lap and opened his door. "Hurry, Raeven!" he cried and left the car to meet her.

The creature rumbled toward them on all fours. When it reached Chip's burned truck it didn't stop but plowed straight into it, knocking it end over end into the forest.

Joe ran up the snowy hill. Raven ran down it toward him,

closer, closer, her hand outstretched. When she reached him, she collapsed against him, sobbing. He tried to pull her to the car but a tremor passed along the road and knocked them both to the ground.

A blue streak surged toward them. It passed overhead and slammed against a maple tree beside the police car, outlining every branch and twig in vibrant, crackling charges.

"Get up!" Joe cried. His glasses slipped. He caught them as they fell and stuffed them into his pocket. "Hurry!"

He grabbed her by the arm, but it was too much. If she had been forced to run all the way to the car she might have made it, but safety had come too soon. She could not run again. She could barely force another tortured breath into her lungs.

"Get *up*!" Joe yelled and grabbed her by the arm. The creature rumbled toward them. Its tail slammed into the roadside trees, cutting the smaller saplings like a scythe and sending up plumes of snow from the larger pines.

"Hurry!" Sparky called from his open door. Joe hauled her to her feet.

"I can't," she said.

"You *can*!" he shouted, and dragged her half-walking, half-sliding to the car. Sparky caught her around the waist and pulled her in on top of him. Joe reached for the back door.

The creature leaped and landed with a crash. The car lurched back, forcing Raeven further inside, but ripping the door handle from Joe's hand.

He slipped in the snow.

His arm hit the door.

It closed with a bang.

The creature slammed the front of the car with its snout and it slid backward down the icy road, leaving Joe behind. Pearl threw her hands over her mouth when it lifted him into the air with a single swipe of a claw.

Raeven sat up. "No!" she cried and the creature rose onto its hind legs and lumbered away from the car, "No! No! No!" and when it came to the wall of St. Bernadette's, it leaped – a single talon on its rear foot struck the top of the wall with a sharp crack – and over it went and disappeared into the cemetery.

The electrified tree dimmed beside them. Its crackling fires trailed off into smoke. Embers of the smallest twigs drifted like springtime petals of flame.

Raeven laid her head against Pearl's shoulder and sobbed; "He's dead, he's dead, he's dead," and Pearl stroked her hair, too shocked to utter a word. Sparky stared at the road ahead.

Dr. Sweeney sat back, as stunned the others, and he whispered three words so softly no one heard him: "No, he's not." A thought that had been forming for some time now crystallized into brilliant focus and he knew she was wrong. *He is not dead.* His heart began to beat wildly. *And Raeven is not its chosen target. She is not the damsel in distress. She is not the virgin I thought it desired. She never was. It was Joe the creature wanted. And Father Toomey.* He sat up in his seat. *It's female,* he realized with a shock, *and the virgins it covets are men!*

John-Richard Thompson

VI.

Knight

John-Richard Thompson

1

Chinese lanterns and candles burned throughout the Golden Panda. Their flames cast trembling shadows over the red walls and glistened on the thin bronze wires of the birdcages where Pearl's flock lay huddled in sleep. Tred and Soot lay curled up on opposite sides of the crackling fireplace where Sparky sat beside Dr. Sweeney with his elbows on his knees and hands curled into fists beneath his chin, staring at the fire, lost in thought.

Raeven sat on a banquette behind them, staring at the tabletop. Pearl sat beside her: now and then she tried to touch her hand to comfort her, but Raeven would have none of it and pulled it away each time. These small movements stopped at widely spaced intervals when a distant, tremulous roar stabbed through the silence.

Bottles rattled behind the bar. Candle flames shivered. Glasses tapped against one another other like crystal chimes.

Dr. Sweeney shivered too, as if the sound had been carried on a frigid wind that crawled beneath the door to wrap its icy fingers around his spine. "Do you think this is working?" he asked.

Sparky touched the silver cross with a poker. Its edges glowed in the fireplace flames but it had not softened. "Not at all. We could try the stove, but I don't imagine it's all that much stronger." He lifted his arms above his head, stretching, and tried to stifle a yawn.

"You should get some sleep," Sweeney said, disheartened. "All of you. Pearl, Raeven, we've none of us had a wink of sleep since heaven knows when."

Sparky made four beds out of cushions from the lounge banquettes, with tablecloths for blankets and rolled up coats for pillows. Exhaustion was total and within minutes Pearl and Raeven (who had hardly said a word since her rescue) had fallen asleep. "You coming?" Sparky asked, sitting up on one elbow. "In a while," Sweeney said without moving from his chair. "You rest now, you need it." He needed it too, desperately, but unruly thoughts scrabbled through his mind to keep sleep at bay. He turned from the cross upon the fire to study the prostrate form of Raeven – the Knight – and he snorted a quiet, bitter laugh.

Sparky opened his eyes. "You say something?"

"No. Go to sleep."

"I can't," the policeman said and kicked his tablecloth blanket off. "I'm wicked tired but I can't sleep."

"Well then, why not pour us a brandy and join me?"

Sparky found a dusty unopened bottle of Hennessy, poured a shot for each into two snifters, and took his seat by the fire. A log popped and settled under the cross. "What are you thinking about?"

"Do you remember my assertion that the wall was built to protect the creature from any and all outside forces?"

Sparky nodded and the professor took another sip of brandy. With the snifter still at his lips, he said, "I was mistaken," and lowered it again to cradle it in both hands. "I believed the creature or its allies had somehow created a defensive wall, but consider this: no outside force can harm it, so why on earth does it need to defend itself? And from what? There is only one single thing in all the world from which it needs protection."

"And that is?"

Sweeney indicated Raeven with a tip of his head.

"Are you *sure*?" Sparky asked, once again appalled by the notion.

"I wish to God and Patrick and all the saints I was not."

Raeven lifted her head and pulled her coat closer, trying to get comfortable, but she never opened her eyes, never rose out of sleep.

"Which means what?" Sparky asked, lowering his voice to a whisper.

Dr. Sweeney set the snifter on the floor and slumped in his chair with his hands in front of his mouth, fingers entwined and forefingers steepled against his chin. "Which means the electrical wall was never intended to keep anything out, but to keep something in. It is not the barrier I believed. It is a corral, a giant blue cage built for only one reason – to keep Raeven inside."

"Which means…" Sparky began, and the professor picked up on his dawning realization: "Which means the wall is *ours*," he said with a sparkle in his eyes. "The power behind the beast would not use it to wall her in. Why would it intentionally contain the vehicle of its doom within the same enclosure as itself? Therefore, it *must* be ours; mine, yours, Pearl's – and Raeven's, of course, though not by choice. She tried to escape all this but cannot. I am convinced, now more than ever, that sides are being drawn up in preparation for a great battle. Nature herself is splitting apart and realigning, snow and fire, shooting stars and electricity."

"Moll and Lochru."

"Two that personify the forces at the heart of this, yes, though heaven only knows how many other, unseen mysteries are involved and what they may control."

"Is that why the trees are moving?"

"It is, though I do not believe they are with us. Indeed, I hope they are not, for I find them most unsettling. The enemy has the trees and the clouds – I include the clouds for it appears that the sky is his, the way it remains in that abysmal darkness. And the creature, of course."

"What do we have?"

"The wall. The Northern Lights and shooting stars. This cross." He touched the end of it with his sneaker. It shifted on the burning logs and sent a spiral of sparks into the flue.

"I don't know about that."

Sweeney glanced at him, puzzled.

"There's something about it I can't quite…" He shook his head in frustration and rubbed his hand across his brow. "You know how you get those feelings in your gut that something's not right? I get it whenever I think about the cross."

"You think this is not the cross we want?"

"I didn't say that. Only that I've felt this way since I first heard about it." He pounded his fist on his knee. "Oh, man, I can't find the right words."

"Are there other crosses at the church? What about that one on the steeple?"

"You heard Pearl, it's too small. And really, Professor, I'm not saying this isn't the one. I'm saying I would feel this about *any* cross. I can't quite put my finger on why that is."

"Maybe when it's melted," Sweeney suggested.

"Maybe." One of Pearl's birds chirped. The fire crackled. "You think that thing can breathe fire? Or fly?"

"I shouldn't put anything past it now," Sweeney said. "The one in Brendan's time never flew, but neither did it spew out electricity. I *saw* that electrical charge streak out from the creature and destroy that tree beside the car. It was generated from within. It may be the ancient ones created and used fire due to its role as the primary form of energy in those days, but now, surrounded by a web of man-made electrical impulses, this new one has access to power sources more potent than anything used by the older devils. The power outages, the flickering lights, failed electronics of every type: the creature has drained all the electricity in town for its own use."

"Then why is that electrical wall ours?"

Sweeney shrugged his shoulders. "Indiscriminate nature. Fickle. Thoughtlessly switching loyalties, or dividing them. We may both have electricity."

"And the trees, are you sure about them?"

"I have given up firm pronouncements, but between Raeven and the creature, I vote that the trees belong to her."

"Raeven?"

"No."

"You said 'her'."

"Yes."

Sparky stared with widening eyes as the new revelation visibly dawned on him. "Oh wow," he whispered. "I didn't expect that."

"Nor did I, but it makes sense it would be female when I think back to Moll's declaration that the union of the Beast and Lochru will result in more very like itself."

Sparky dropped his head in his hands. "Oh, man, one thing after another. We don't have too much going for us, do we?" He pointed to Raeven. "But why her? Why couldn't it be you? You know about these things. We'd stand a chance."

"I have wondered that myself. Who or what has chosen her I do not know, for there seems to be very little logic in it and no wisdom at all." Raeven shifted, restless, as though responding to their whispers. She mumbled something and rolled over. "Everything, Constable," Dr. Sweeney continued, lowering his voice. "Do you understand? *Everything* hinges on her."

Sparky responded with a hopeless shake of his head. He finished his brandy and sat back to stare at the cross in the flames, its edges barely reddened. A long moment passed before, "Hey," he whispered, "Hey, wait. This fire might not get hot enough, but I know something that will. There's a welding torch at the hardware store, an industrial one from Howie Taylor's old welding shop. We can get it first thing in the morning. If that doesn't melt it, nothing will."

Sweeney relaxed into his chair. "Excellent," he said, drawing the word out like a cat's satisfied purr. As he did, Raeven sat up behind him, still immersed in a foggy dream world, and pushed down at her coat, trying to flatten out a bulky, uncomfortable spot.

2

Morning arrived, occasioned by nothing. The sun did not shine. The sky did not clear. No winter birds sang outside. Pearl's birds did not sing in their cages and their owner might not have awakened for several more hours had the cold not pulled her from sleep. The fire had burned down to a few glowing coals and most of the candles into puddles of wax. She lit new ones inside three tasseled lanterns, set two more into empty Tsing Tao bottles, and shuffled through the kitchen to the outside door to check the weather. Streaks of gray light tempered the horizon in the east and tried to reach through the clouds. She might have been able to fool herself into viewing it as overcast day or the beginnings of a storm but a glance down at the wide circular bloodstain dashed all thoughts of normalcy.

A flock of chickadees flew over the parking lot into the trees. Pearl pulled her satin red jacket close and watched them dart among the branches. "He didn't do it," she said aloud, and then, "What?" perplexed by her own statement. She shook her head, confused, and stepped back inside to put a pot of water on the stove to boil

She thought of Joey and Raeven's final embrace in front of the car before the thing carried him off. They had strong feelings for each other – much stronger than Pearl had realized, *though I knew she liked him, the way she looked at him when she knew he wasn't looking. Why didn't she go for it? Maybe she didn't know he felt the same. Oh, bullshit – she had to know.*

After the water came to a boil, she opened the door again and poured it over the bloody ice. "There," she said to the rising clouds of steam. "No one'll step on you now, you crazy old coot." She looked at the bushes where the chickadees still flitted from branch to branch in a confusion of flight. One hung upside down and swung back and forth like a tiny trapeze artist. "He didn't do it," Pearl said again, and once again shook her head, bewildered by her own words.

Behind her, the dining room door whined on its hinges and Raeven stepped into the kitchen.

"Boys still asleep?" Pearl whispered. Raeven nodded and sat down on a stool beside the warming trays. Pearl closed the back door and set the empty pot on the stove. "Thought I'd make us some omelets. Want one?" Raeven didn't answer. "Ah, kid, I know how you must feel." Raeven turned away, her face contorted by a suppressed sob. Pearl approached to embrace her but Raeven recoiled and said, "What?"

"It's okay to let it out," Pearl said and dropped her arms. She tried to run her hand over her hair, but again, Raeven drew back from her touch and asked, "Let what out?" in a cold, flat voice.

"Well, you know...what you feel. You must feel something."

"No. Guilty, I suppose, that I couldn't..." she pushed her hair from her face, "with Chip, I couldn't stop it." Pearl stared, certain she misunderstood. "I couldn't help him," Raeven said in a monotone while looking at the floor. "If I'd let him do what he wanted, he wouldn't have gotten out of the van. I should have let him."

"Let him do what?" Pearl asked, bewildered.

"Make..." She hesitated, unable to say the word.

"Make what? Make...oh no, you can't mean make love, that can't be what you mean." One of her eyebrows lifted. "Is it?"

"Yes," Raeven said. "If I hadn't stopped him, he might still be alive."

"Joey? You and Joey?"

"Chip."

"Chip?" Pearl repeated, still mystified. "Wait, wait, wait – you mean, Chip Dubee?" Raeven nodded and Pearl leaned back against the warming counter. "You and *Chip*?"

"He tried to make love to me," Raeven stammered, unnerved by Pearl's incredulity. "That's what it's called though I wouldn't call it that. I don't really know what I'd call it. I refused and he got out of the van and was killed by the...the thing that..."

"By the thing that killed Joey?" Raeven looked up sharply. "Oh, sorry, you didn't like hearing it that way?" Pearl asked with a smirk. "Even though it's true, unlike your fake little story?"

"My story is true. It happened in the junk yard."

"Good place for it."

Raeven heaved the same mournful sigh she displayed at Steven's memorial service and said in the same resigned tones: "Absurd. It's all absurd."

"Oh please. It's all bullshit. It is!" Pearl insisted before she could protest. "Just like all the rest is bullshit: the veils, the gloves, the black...*everything*. The mourning for people you don't know. Steven Wilcox, who you only met once–"

"Twice."

"Fine, twice. First time he tries to strangle you, the second time he blows his head off. Oh, but he kissed you first, which was nice of him. And now this. Screwing around with Chip Dubee of all people. I've never heard you mention him, except to call him a prick, which he is, and now you say he almost 'made love' to you. Oh my God, as if that's not the most completely unreal thing I've ever heard."

"I don't have to listen to this."

"Yes you do!" Pearl shouted, startling her. "Want to know why? Because I might be killed by a monster Godzilla thing and you're the only person who can do anything about it. What a freaking nightmare. Here we are, hoping you'll face a giant lizard and you can't even face the fact that you loved Joey."

Raeven stared, her mouth open as though about to say something, but she shook her head and headed for the dining room door. "Oh no you don't," Pearl said. She picked up the empty water pot and threw it over Raeven's head. It hit the door with a sharp bang and fell clanging to the floor.

Inside the dining room, Sweeney and Sparky bolted upright in their beds. The doors swung open – Raeven appeared briefly but a hand on her shoulder pulled her back into the kitchen. "I'm not finished!" they heard, followed by a sound like a silverware drawer crashing to the floor.

Sparky began to get out of bed but Sweeney stopped him. "No, no, let them have at it."

Back inside the kitchen, Raeven ran around the counter. "Are you crazy?" she cried at Pearl circling around the other side, holding an empty rice tray. Raeven stopped at the sink and picked up a wok, brandished it by the handle. "Stay away!"

"First Steven," Pearl said, approaching with the tray. "You made a big presentation over that. Mysterious, tragic, shoving it into Joey's face, even when you knew he loved you far more than Steven ever could, or would."

"I don't know what you're talking about," Raeven said and once again averted her eyes.

"Oh, don't play this – *don't!* You knew he had feelings for you, but that didn't stop you from making a big show at Steven's funeral. What was that for? To make Joe jealous? To hurt him?"

"I would never hurt him, not deliberately."

"Yes, deliberately," Pearl said with a vigorous nod. "You loved him but you *deliberately* hurt him. Why?"

"Because he didn't love me." She backed away as Pearl came closer with the rice tray.

"For God's sake, what is the matter with you? Why is it so hard for you to believe someone could love you?"

"Because they don't. They can't."

"You believe that? You really...how *can* you believe it? What, are you one of those messed-up, scarred people because – I don't know, did some neighbor molest you when you were a kid or something like that?"

"No."

"Then why can't you believe Joey loved you?"

"Because he doesn't!" Raeven cried and banged the wok down on the counter. "Because he can't. No one can. And even if I wanted to…" She paused, threw back her head. "Even if I felt something, and even if wanted to tell him, I couldn't."

"Why not?"

"God, Pearl, leave me alone."

"Why *not*?" Pearl insisted and Raeven closed her eyes as if disgusted with herself. To confront and acknowledge such longstanding insecurities and weaknesses made them seem so trivial and small, even as she felt bound by them, as rigid and unyielding as iron chains. "Because I was afraid."

"Afraid of what?"

"Of what, of what," Raeven said, as if the answer should have been obvious. "Afraid he would turn out like the others, that's what."

"What others?"

"You can't show too much, Pearl. That's the way it is. You can't say too much – you can't *feel* too much because it all goes wrong. Look at me. I mean really – look at me." She pointed at herself with both hands. "Who could love…*this*? They leave, Pearl. They go. They don't see who I am, what I am, what I really am. They don't look at me; not me, not the *me* inside. They only look at the outside."

"Oh please. What are you, twelve? What is the 'you' they're expected to see? Do you even know yourself?"

"I thought I did…"

"So you put all your feelings into a stranger like Steven and a low-life jerk like Chip, and even when Joey is safely dead, you don't have the guts to love him. You're pathetic. You really are." Pearl tossed the rice tray into the sink. "You have *got* to get over this. This is all made-up shit in your head. 'They only look at the outside.' Whatever the hell that means. And even if they do, so what? It's not like you dress in ways to hide it. I'd like to find someone who *didn't* look at you, the way you walk around looking like you just crawled out of a tomb. Dress like a weirdo with Cleopatra raccoon eyes and then complain when someone notices, because they're – oh who knows? And who cares? We don't have time for this. We can't afford it. It's all so selfish. You do everything you can to alienate the world and when the world responds exactly as it should, you say 'Oh, what a cruel and horrible world'. You're supposed to be some kind of knight, and that's fitting. You already wear so many layers of armor no one can get through to you. Walls built a mile thick all around, stronger than steel, nothing able to penetrate from either direction, inside or out. The clothes, the attitude, even your miserable, self-centered cynicism – all a suit of armor built to protect some 'real you' who you don't even know and probably wouldn't recognize if you met her. But you gotta take off the armor, Raeven. You gotta strip it off. All of it. Down to nothing. You have to face up to this or you'll never face up to – my God, can't you do it even now? Can't you admit you loved him? He's gone, just like Steven and Chip and all these mysterious 'others' you say go all the time. You said you expected it, so you should be used to it. Gone. He's dead, Raeven, which should make things easier for you."

Raeven's fingers slowly uncurled. The wok fell and hit the floor with a sound like a gong. "You..." she whispered and the two women stared at each other. Raeven broke first: she lowered her eyes. Pearl clicked her tongue and shook her head. On her way to the dining room, she stopped before opening the door: "He loved you," she said, and as she left the kitchen, she added, "Christ knows why, but he really did love you."

3

"He's still alive," Dr. Sweeney said in reference to nothing said before. Everyone at the table looked up from their omelets; Sparky and Pearl with their forks suspended and Raeven staring with a gaze so intense he had to turn away. "Or so I believe," he added.

"We saw that thing take him," Pearl said.

"It took Father Toomey and he's alive as well."

They looked at each other and back at him, hesitant, afraid to believe him. "Are you sure?" Pearl finally asked. "You gotta be sure. We've been through too much to be let down."

"Joe is a virgin," Sweeney said. Pearl glanced at Raeven who quickly shook her hair over her eyes. "As a virgin, he was of supreme interest to the creature. The same with Father Toomey."

"It's female," Sparky explained.

"And yes," Sweeney said in answer to Pearl's questioning gaze, "some priests truly are both celibate and virgins. He is still alive, I'm certain. That is why I believe Joe is alive." He reached into his pocket and withdrew the small cross hanging from its chain. "Father Toomey's.

We found it in the cave. I know he was brought there because the creature would never intentionally take a silver cross. Therefore, I believe they are both alive." He turned to Raeven. "And you believe it too."

A long moment passed: "Yes."

"How do you know?" Pearl asked. "Did the real you inside tell you?"

"Knock it off, Pearl," Raeven said with a toss of her head. "Remember that night at your house, the night of the Marcotte fire? Joe said something about a gold box and how Raleigh was afraid of it."

Pearl rolled her eyes. "Oh, great, the gold box again."

"But he also said he saw a blue cage. Remember? I saw it too. A few hours ago."

"Where?"

"In a dream."

Pearl rolled her eyes again and muttered, "Think I'm having one now."

"There's a bright blue cage," Raeven said. "That's all I see and then it fades away."

"What's it got to do with Joe?" Sweeney asked.

She turned to face him. "He's in it."

"Remember, I only said I *think* they're alive."

"They are." Raeven looked around the dining room. "Where are the fortune cookies?"

"Kitchen," Pearl said. After Raeven rushed through the doors to retrieve them, she leaned over the table. "I think she's crazy. Seriously. She's always been a weirdo. I mean, that tattoo on her wrist. Doom. Who *does* that? But it's more than that. I think she was molested or something when she was a kid and it's made her nuts."

"Let this go," Sweeney whispered. "I don't know what's happening, but let her go with it."

Raeven returned carrying a large clear plastic bag filled with fortune cookies. "I know it's here." She dropped the bag on her chair. "Do not give in, the blue cage, column of wood," she said and began to push the plates aside.

"Hey, what are you doing?" Pearl said. "I'm not finished."

"Yes, you are," Sweeney said and dragged the tablecloth along with all the plates and glasses onto the floor. Raeven dropped the bag in the center of the table and upended it. Fortune cookies spread over the wooden surface. Some fell to the floor, others into Sparky's lap.

"Oh, fine, look at this," Pearl sputtered. "We couldn't have used another table?"

"Shut up," Raeven said without looking at her and Pearl immediately gaped at Sparky with her lips pursed and eyebrows raised in feigned shock. Sparky turned away, afraid he might laugh.

"It's here," Raeven whispered and pawed through the fortune cookies. "I know it's here."

Sweeney moved closer to the edge of his seat. "What's there?"

"The blue cage, the....don't give in, the blue cage..." She stopped with her hand hovering above a cookie. Sparky and Pearl stared, fascinated. Raeven picked it up, snapped it in two, and withdrew the fortune.

"What's it say?" Pearl asked. Raeven looked at her. Their eyes locked. "You are good with animals."

Everyone stared, breathless, until – Pearl: "What the fuck does that mean?"

Raeven dropped the fortune on the table and sank into her chair, bewildered. Sweeney picked up the fortune and studied it.

YOU ARE GOOD WITH ANIMALS

"Open another one," he said. Raeven sighed and picked up the closest cookie. She broke it and pulled out the fortune.

WHAT IS LOST WILL BE FOUND

She looked up at the others, her eyes bright with tears.

"Open another," Sweeney said, his voice gentle but insistent.

"It doesn't matter."

His hand shot across the table and grabbed her by the wrist. "Why do you give up so easily? You know he's alive. These cookies, why did you get them?"

"I thought something would be in them. I was wrong."

"God's sake, woman, I felt it myself. There is something within you. It's the catalyst, the motivator – the *attractor*. You felt it too. No, no, don't say you didn't, I know you did. Something overtook you, but you're stopping it now. Why?"

"Leave me alone!" Raeven leaped up from the table. "First Pearl, now you – I know the thing is attracted to me but I–"

"Not only the thing, not only the creature," Sweeney said, circling around the table. "Other things too. Stars. Trees." He grabbed a fortune cookie and pushed it into her upraised hands. "Open it."

Raeven dropped it and backed away from him. "No."

Sweeney stepped up to her and pulled her hands from behind her back. "Open the blasted cookie."

"Hey, hey," Sparky said, stepping up to them, but the professor ignored him. He caught Raeven by the arm and dragged her to the table where he forced her back into her chair. He grabbed a fistful of cookies and shoved them into her hands. "Open them!"

"I can't!"

She tried to get up. Sweeney pushed her down again and leaned over her, his face nearly touching hers. "I am sick to death of your '*I can't*'. I know you can't. We all know you can't. We all understand with crystal-bloody-clarity that you don't have a molecule of nobility or bravery within you, but for the love'a God, will you for once in your miserable life say '*I can*'?" Raeven lashed out; her hand swung out in a wide open-palmed arc and hit Sweeney so hard that his glasses flew into the air. "Jesus, Mary and Joseph," he exclaimed, shaking his head and blinking.

Raeven picked up a cookie and broke it in half. "This what you want?" she cried, and threw the pieces at the professor.

"My glasses." He dropped to his knees to search on the floor.

"Can't see it? Here – let me read it for you." She slammed her fist down on a cookie and extracted the fortune. "'A new business is coming your way.' Good for me." She broke another. "Oh! 'Your smile brings happiness to everyone you meet.' Yeah, that sounds like me. But what I really need," – she broke another – "what I really need is a fortune that tells me how to get away from you and this place and everything that – " She stopped dead, her hand in front of her eyes with the tiny slip of paper held between her thumb and forefinger.

Dr. Sweeney looked up, sharply. "Pearl," he whispered. "My glasses, find my glasses."

He did not take his eyes off Raeven. She stood over him, staring at the fortune. She handed it to him and sat down.

"I can't see it," the professor whispered. He crawled toward her on his knees. "What does it say?"

Pearl called to him from the fireplace. "Here they are, Prof." She rushed to him and handed him his glasses. He put them on and studied the fortune.

BLUE CAGE DREAM NOT

"Not a dream," he whispered. "The dream is not a dream?

Open another."

Raeven broke open another cookie. She handed the fortune to Sweeney.

MOUNTAIN ON THERE IS BLUE CAGE LOVE

"Another," he whispered.

CAGE LOVE COLUMN BLUE LOVE COLUMN WOOD

"Raeven, please." Dr. Sweeney came closer, still on his knees, and he clasped her hands in his. "Use this. Ask it something." She stared at him, her eyes red and puffy. "We can't understand it, none of us," he said. "Not me, not you, not a single one of us, but *please* go with this."

"I…"

Dr. Sweeney tightened his grip on her hands. "You *can*," he whispered.

Raeven nodded a slow, nearly imperceptible nod.

"There's a good lass." He rose from the floor and sat in the chair beside her. Raeven held her hand over the scattered cookies. Pearl and Sparky moved closer to the table and stood behind her. "Is Joey alive?" she asked and dropped her hand. She closed it around a cookie and looked at Dr. Sweeney.

He nodded. She broke it open and read the fortune. Her eyes filled again and she dropped the paper.

"No, no," Sweeney whispered. "I won't read it this time. Tell me what it says."

Trying to control her tears, she read aloud:

BLUE JOEL CAGE IN ALIVE LOVE

"Where is he?" Sweeney asked.

"Where is he?" Raeven repeated in a quaking voice. She broke open another cookie.

MOUNTAINTOP BLUE CAGE MONK

"Monk," Sweeney whispered. "Does it mean Brendan?"

Raeven looked up to the ceiling and spoke, focusing on nothing specific but trying to encompass the room in her mind, the surrounding air, the shadows. "Is it Brendan?"

TOOM MOUNTAIN KENLI BLUE TOOM CAGE

"Father Toomey," she said. "You're right, he's alive. They're together."

Pearl and Sparky sat down and she reached into the center of the table, lifted another cookie, broke it open.

WHITE BIRD

"White bird," she said, and added, "which I'm not."

Dr. Sweeney ignored the assertion. "Pearl, what could 'white bird' mean?"

"Snowy owl, maybe. But I can't imagine a snowy owl getting involved in all this shit. They're kind of smart. Cockatoos. Doves. And of course there's Earl, but I'm sure it can't mean him. Not because he's smart like an owl, but because, you know…who'd want him? Oh, and seagulls."

"Gannets and gulls." Sweeney sat back, puzzled, and looked at the turkey nestled on Pearl's bed on the other side of the room. "White bird. Knight of the White Bird."

Pearl also looked at Earl and beyond him at the cages where her finches whirred back and forth, fluttering with color. She shook her head and turned away. "I don't get it."

"Don't get what?" Sparky asked.

"A thought keeps coming into my head but it doesn't make any sense. He didn't do it."

"Who didn't?"

"That's just it, I don't have a clue. I don't even know why I brought it up."

Raeven picked up another cookie.

ARMOR SHIELD ANOINTED ONCE MORE

"What does that mean?" she asked and handed it to Dr. Sweeney.

"A part of the prophecy, the same as the column of wood. Donal's armor anointed once more."

"Anointed with what?"

"I have poured through my herbal book in the hope of finding an answer, but no luck."

Raeven pointed to the last fortune opened. "So what does this mean?"

"Ask."

She looked up at the ceiling, and then from side to side, as though fearful of seeing something. "Who is answering?"

"We don't know. Ask the air, ask the table, the cookies. Ask."

Raeven stared straight ahead at nothing. "Anointed with what?" she asked and opened another.

YOU ARE GOOD WITH ANIMALS.

"No, no. Armor and shield anointed once more. Anointed with what?" She broke open another cookie.

WHAT IS LOST IS FOUND

"No, that's not – Dr. Sweeney, it's not working."
"Try another."

WHAT IS LOST IS FOUND. BIRDS.

"Again," the professor said.

WHAT IS LOST IS FOUND. BIRDS.

Raeven tried again and again with the same result, while far to the south, Jin Feng stood on a deserted beach and with failing strength tried to send another thought into the night. Her mind struggled against the power emanating from the sea in waves far more forceful than her own, and she concentrated and willed her mind over the distance – Raeven broke open another fortune cookie –

DO NOT GIVE IN

– and Jin Feng stopped, overpowered by the malignant thoughts that surged like a tidal wave to sweep all before it and drown her own. As they did, Raeven felt her newfound determination and courage melt away like breath upon a mirror while new feelings poured in and replaced them with ice cold fear.

"Again," Dr. Sweeney said and she looked at him with eyes

filling with panic. Terror swelled and clutched at her heart. "I can't," she whispered.

"What is it?" The professor grabbed her by the hand. "Something happened, what happened?"

Without answering, she rushed from the table to the fireplace and dropped upon her cushion bed. She lifted Soot from her rolled-up coat and held her in her lap. Sweeney followed and studied her while she stared at the fire, her eyes grim and blank, devoid of emotion, as though she had constructed a wall inside as dense and impenetrable as the one surrounding Burne Notch. Things suddenly became clearer now and he wondered why he hadn't understood it before. Her own personal Beast, the Beast within called *I can't* had revealed itself as something far more potent than vague fears and insecurities: it was a form of nature as substantial as the trees, the wall and the shooting stars, and he understood Raeven as 'The Knight' for the first time. She, herself, her deepest core of emotion, feeling, and subconscious dreaming had become a field of battle. Snowfire burned within her and raged in opposing forces. When and how this happened, he did not know. Nor did he know if these forces built upon foundations of weaknesses and strengths already there or if they had been imposed upon her wholly from the outside, with Lochru's fear-filled version of *I can't* gaining the upper hand...*Against whom? Who or what is the other force, the one who opposes him and guides the stars and alters the fortunes in the cookies? And is this other force connected to the golden box?*

He sat beside her on the cushions while Pearl and Sparky began to clean up the plates and cups he'd thrown to the floor. He scratched Soot beneath the chin and joined Raeven in her hypnotic stare at the flames. She leaned on her coat with one arm. Soot purred in her lap. "You *are* good with animals," he said and Raeven ran her hand over Soot's fur.

"I like cats. Especially black ones. I was a cat once." In answer to Sweeney's puzzled gaze, she said, "In a past life. And not some distant past life either – my last life. That's what I was told. I was in a Wicca shop in Portsmouth and a lady working there told me. She said I was a black cat in my last life. She said I had an owner who I loved very much and he loved me. But he died and I didn't understand. As far as I could tell, one day he just disappeared. He abandoned me. His family didn't care about me and threw me out to fend for myself, and I never found another owner to take me in. I spent the last of my days wandering the snowy streets, alone, abandoned, never understanding what had happened. And when I died, I became...me. Me as I am now. We have to find Joey."

The last was said so quickly and so out of context, it took the professor by surprise. He reeled from the brief exchange and wondered where this tiny display of courage had come from. Before he could contemplate it further, Pearl called from the table. "Is this your glove, Raeven? It was on the floor."

"How did it get over there?"

Pearl tossed the long black glove across the room. "I don't see the other one."

"Probably still in my pocket." Raeven unrolled her coat and reached inside. "Yes, here it is, it's–" She stopped, remembering something...*almost* remembering.

"What's the matter?" Pearl asked, unsettled by her expression.

Raeven withdrew her hand from her pocket. A rolled up ball of stiff paper lay in her palm. "I kept laying on this last night. I thought it was my glove."

"What is it?"

"I can't believe it," she said, touching her chin with the fingers of her free hand. "All this time, I forgot about it."

"What?" Pearl asked. "That paper?"

"He put it in my pocket. Everything was so confused I never thought to look. I forgot about it until now. He put his hand in my pocket. It was the last thing he did before he shot himself."

Dr. Sweeney spun around. His gaze shot to Raeven's palm. "Yes!" he shouted and he snatched the wadded-up ball from her hand. "Oh, Notable Scholar, I *knew* you wouldn't leave us with nothing!" He ran to the fortune cookie table. "Candles, candles!" he shouted and swept a wide swath of cookies over the side.

"Oh, for the love'a Mike, I just cleaned the floor."

Sweeney ignored her. "Hurry, Constable." Sparky carried two candles to the table and set them on the table. Raeven lifted Soot into her arms and stood while Dr. Sweeney sat down and carefully unfolded the paper, transfixed by the task. Pearl and Sparky joined him at the table, one on each side, while Raeven stood behind him with the purring cat held close to her neck.

"Old Gaelic," Sweeney whispered when a line of writing appeared, nearly faded upon the ancient vellum.

"Can you read it?" Sparky asked. He moved his chair in closer.

"I can." He dropped his glasses down to the end of his nose, pulled one of the candles closer and, tilting his head back, unfolded the paper further and translated the first sentence at the top of the page.

"From the battle raven, Badb Catha, her sacred herb inspires bravery. Even this shalt thou wear, for by its charm shall courage cleave to thee."' He sat back and stared straight ahead, stunned. "Clever lad," he whispered. "Clever, clever lad to leave us this, the only page he saved."

"What is it?" Sparky asked.

"An incantation," he said, barely able to conceal the tremor in his voice. "In truth, it's more of a recipe."

"For what?"

"Donal's armor."

Raeven looked over his shoulder. "Anointed once more," she whispered and held the cat close.

Dr. Sweeney unfolded the paper further and tilted it, letting in the candle-light. "Raeven..." She looked down at him but he didn't turn around, didn't wait for a response. "Has this been in your coat since you met Steven?"

"Since the night he killed himself, yes. I forgot about it."

"And you've been wearing it ever since? Or had it with you somewhere nearby?"

"Yes. Always. It's the only winter coat I have."

Sweeney nodded. "Sit down, please." She pulled out the chair beside him and sat down with Soot on her lap. "Tell me again what happened that night," he said without taking his eyes off the paper. "I want you to think very hard." Raeven told him everything, as she had already so many times before. Steven had been hiding in the shadows behind the yew trees. She got out of her car and he came to her and said 'beautiful'.

Dr. Sweeney leaned closer, holding the folded paper. "You stopped your car and got out and he approached you and said beautiful. That's the sequence, is it?"

Raeven told him yes, and that was when he kissed her. He had blood smeared on his face and lips. She didn't know where it came from, though she assumed the wound on his leg. He kissed her and said 'beautiful' and then he said – it had all happened so fast – and then he said she was the Knight, and "wait, now I remember," she said. "That's right. He stuck his hand in my pocket. I was confused; I didn't know why he did it. That's when he lifted the gun and pulled the trigger."

"You didn't tell me about your pocket."

"I forgot about it. It didn't seem important."

"It was. Vitally important."

"Why?" Raeven asked.

"It is because of that small, quickly forgotten act that you are the

Knight." She gazed at him, perplexed. Dr. Sweeney gently laid his hand upon her wrist. "My dear Raeven. You are the Knight, not because he said it, but because of this, the thing he put in your pocket."

"But that would mean..." she began, her face going pale. "Are you saying that Steven *made* me the Knight?"

"I am. And he did. It explains why Raleigh came to you, and the trees, and later the Evil One. It may explain the stars. You have been carrying it around with you all this time."

Raeven stared, confused, unable to respond. He beckoned her forward into the candlelight and tilted the folded page. When he did, a single link of golden chain so small and delicate they could barely see it fell onto the table.

4

There had been a grave miscalculation.

The pale-eyed man had seen a flashing beacon and maneuvered the freighter *Isolde* toward it. Howling gusts lifted spray from every wave and threw it over the deck and against the bridge, obscuring his vision. He guided the ship as best he could toward the beacon, all the while shooting into the night divergent thoughts aimed at his Beloved but veering off at regular intervals with newer, crueler thoughts aimed like a poisoned dagger at the heart of the White Bird.

That heart *had* to fail. That heart had to be consumed with fear and indecision. It was already weak and full of doubt and more than susceptible to his influence, but he could not ignore it. He had to destroy that heart for it contained the seed of his doom. Nothing could be left to chance. Mastery was his. "Closer, Beloved," he intoned in ancient words not heard for a thousand years. "Closer I am and shall be, and we shall feast upon one another."

He turned the wheel. The bow swung toward the flashing beacon. The freighter lifted upon a cresting wave. He gripped the wheel, and – *something wrong!* – the bow dropped with a gut-wrenching crash.

The pale-eyed man slammed against the wheel. Charts, coffee mugs, the radio receiver; everything loose fell to the floor when the ship plowed with an immense grinding roar into the sea-swept rocks of a low island, one of several that made up a barrier called the Isles of Shoals.

The beacon stopped flashing: its harsh white light took on a steady golden glow and it hovered above the rocks like a will-o-the-wisp before floating away from the ship, ethereal, transient, and he realized it wasn't a lighthouse at all. The pale-eyed man howled with fury and ran from the bridge to look over the side. The bow lay crushed and torn upon the rocks. Seawater poured into the hull. He looked beyond the golden light and the falling snow and saw a string of lights in the far distance. He had run aground six miles from the mainland.

The light that lured him there flickered and went out and he slammed his fists down on the deck rail, aware for the first time that he had been joined in battle.

Six miles away, standing on the snowy beach with wind blowing through her thin grey hair, Jin Feng listened to the distant roar of the freighter piling up on the rocks and allowed herself a small, grim smile.

5

Joe Li woke in blue, floating inside a circular web of interlocking humming charges of raw electricity. His side and chest throbbed from two broken ribs. A smell of rot hung thick in the air and the air itself quivered with deep sighing growls. Wood snapped and groaned. Stone grated. He didn't dare make a sound, though he wanted to scream. Nor did he dare touch the web, though he wanted desperately to claw through it. He did nothing but float, weightless and slowly spinning, with no notion of up or down, or side to side. As time passed – an hour, maybe more, he began to make out indistinct shapes beyond the blue cage and assumed his eyes were growing accustomed to the intense light but no…the charges were subsiding. Their blue fires gradually weakened and he floated down as slow and gentle as snow settling in a snow globe.

His knee touched the web. A mild electrical shock tingled up through his hair but quickly fled. The charges congealed into a darker substance with the blue fire dimming within until it vanished and he settled on what he now realized was the bottom of a round ball-like cage made of thick strands of smoky grey material as translucent and hard as glass. He kicked at one but it didn't move and didn't crack. He could squeeze his hand through the spaces between the strands but found none wide enough to allow him to slip through.

The electrical hum faded into rumbles punctuated by sharp cracks and a low hiss, as if a colony of snakes had taken up residence somewhere nearby. He peered through the gloom, unable to make out anything until he remembered his glasses. He pulled them from his pocket and put them on, and regretted it at once for he now saw his true peril.

He was in the lift house, but he did not realize this at first. His teardrop-shaped cage hung suspended eight feet above the floor of a dank, cavernous room. Its walls had tilted and shattered, but did not collapse. Electrical charges had rushed in each time to fill every tear and break. There, they dimmed and hardened into webs made of the same translucent grey-blue glass, and in this way the lift house expanded, tore, and healed itself over and over again, with its gashes filling and spreading outward to form a far larger structure than before.

Stalactites surrounded him like a forest canopy made of dangling spears. Through them, he saw what appeared to be another web cage about thirty feet away, and beyond that, in the distance, the chamber's glassy walls pierced by open spaces shaped like the arched windows of a ruined Gothic cathedral.

Enormous granite boulders lay strewn throughout as if tossed together in a cataclysmic upheaval, each with one flat side with a deep, round hole the size of a dinner plate carved into the center. Interspersed among them lay an array of reminders that this reeking cavern had once been the Garand's lift house: an upended table with a red and white checked tablecloth; cans of Diet 7-Up and Budweiser littering the floor; a toboggan leaning against a granite block; a mangled lift chair stained with dried blood; and among these a glittering of golden chalices, necklaces, shields, crowns and coins.

He rose to his knees. Pain shot through his side as though he'd been stabbed. "Oh wow," he said, and lay back down again.

A soft, low voice whispered, "Don't speak."

Startled, he sat up in spite of the pain and looked around in the darkness.

"Over here."

Joe couldn't see anyone, could make out no sign of movement. "Where?"

"Not so loud. It'll hear you."

He squinted through a space between two stalactites and gasped at the sight of a pale, moon-like face peering at him from the other cage. "Father Toomey!" he whispered. "We thought you were dead."

"Almost," the priest whispered. He was pale and drawn, with his eyes surrounded by dark circles and his lips cracked and bloody. "I'm so thirsty."

"I don't have anything," Joe returned, overwhelmed with pity. The priest smiled sadly. "I know." He looked to the side: his eyes widened with alarm and he fell back against the far side of his cage. Joe followed the direction of his panicked gaze and his heart leaped, stung by the sight of a massive wall of scalloped black scales moving past and filling a thirty foot high gap in the chamber wall. It *couldn't* have grown so large in so short a time! A rumble followed, so deep and quivering it shook the cavern like the rock-shifting tremors of an earthquake. A stalactite fell and shattered and his cage vibrated in the intensifying sound.

"What's happening?" he whispered as loud as he dared.

Two granite boulders toppled over onto their flat sides.

"No need to worry yet," Father Toomey said in his frail voice. "It's only turning around."

6

*"From the battle- raven…*What the heck?" Pearl asked. "How do you say that?"

"*Badb Catha,*" Sweeney said. "First word pronounced *Bave.*"

"*From the battle-raven, Badb Catha, her sacred herb inspires bravery. Even this shalt thou wear, for by its charm shall courage cleave to thee. Wild marjoram then, and with it sage, envenomed bite shall they assuage. Thyme, this too, for invigoration and sweet rosemary to bind this incantation. Infuse them all, in thickness brew, a plant far greater than the rest. Anoint thy shield with Dragonroot, and by its charm, be valor blessed.*" Pearl set the notebook down. "Battle-Raven…" Dr. Sweeney had translated the manuscript page into English and asked Pearl to read it back to him.

"One of the Morrigan."

"That's my last name," Pearl said, surprised. "Morgan."

"No, no, *Morri*-gan, spelled with two *R*s and an *I*. The dreaded Morrigan, the triple war goddess of death and battle and destruction, formed of three separate Celtic deities. A kind of trinity, if you will. Badb Catha is one of the Three."

"The Three the witch talked about?"

Sweeney raised his eyebrows in surprise: the thought had not occurred to him. "I dearly wish that were so for they were formidable women. Nemain, which means Frenzy, and Macha, meaning Crow. And Badb, our battle-raven."

"Which is what?"

"The shape taken by the Morrigan. As a raven she used her powers to alter the course of battle, swooping low over the battlefield and screaming prophecies of victory and death while Nemain whipped the soldiers into a frenzy. The Celts dearly loved crows and ravens. They kept them as sacred birds. Fed them the impaled heads of their enemies."

"Ah, nice."

"How did you become such a bird enthusiast?"

"Runs in my blood. My mother was the same. Grandmother too. I even have a bird book that belonged to my great-great-grandmother. It's a book about birds in stories and myth. Really old. Pages all yellow. I loved that book when I was a kid, read it over and over. One story said the crows and ravens are black because they were the sacred birds of the pagans, like you said, and the priests got all mad about it so they turned them black."

"Not surprising," Sweeney said. "The early Christians used many images to symbolize their triumph over paganism, ravens being only one of them." He pointed to the notebook. "Let's get back to this, shall we?" Pearl looked down at it, but before she could utter a word Sweeney stopped her: "In that book of yours, what color was the raven before the priests turned it black?"

Pearl opened her mouth to speak, but looked up sharply, the unspoken word echoing in her thoughts with new complexity. "White."

Sweeney gazed at her. "It all folds in upon itself, doesn't it?" he said after a thoughtful pause. "Meanings and symbols and messages. Possibly all coincidence, though it does make one's head reel."

"Yeah, well, it makes mine reel anyway. White raven, white bird. And..." She bit her lower lip. "And if I said something like...you know, if I said, 'he didn't do it,' would that mean anything to you?"

"Who?"

"I don't know. He. That's all. He didn't do it."

Sweeney thought for a moment. "He didn't do it," he repeated and shrugged. "Afraid not." He lifted the *Book of Herbals and Medicinals* onto his lap. "Shall we?"

"Right." Pearl held up Sweeney's notebook and read his translation again. *"From the battle raven, Badb Catha, her sacred herb inspires bravery. Even this shalt thou wear, for by its charm shall courage cleave to thee.* What does that mean?"

"I'm not sure." The professor leafed through dusty pages of the herbal and turned to the index at the back. "Let me see now. Badb. B. Nothing here. But have no fear, we shall make a simple transference. War gods and goddesses are often interchangeable and have many of the same attributes, mostly unpleasant ones: blood, death, joyous slaughter. We'll look to one who was really into that sort of thing." He scanned the index and softly read aloud while tracing his finger down to the middle, "Mahogany Birch, Maiden Fern, Mallow, Mandrake, Marjoram –

ah, here he is. Mars, Herbs devoted to. Page 232."

"The planet?"

"The Roman war god." He adjusted his glasses. "232. 232. Here we are. With a delightful engraving of a soldier disemboweling an unarmed peasant." He pulled his glasses down to the end of his nose. "How peculiar."

"What is it?" Pearl asked, prepared to hear the name of a plant she had never heard of.

"Garlic. Should be simple enough to find."

"Oh, sure, we have plenty in the kitchen. Asthma used it all the time." She held the notebook close to the candle and read the next part of Sweeney's translation. "*Wild marjoram then, and with it sage, envenomed bite shall they...*what's that next word?"

"Assuage. It means to relieve."

"*Envenomed bite they shall assuage.* Wild marjoram. We have regular marjoram, I think, but just in case – I think you passed it already. Near mandrake."

"Ah, yes. Marjoram, wild. Perennial plant that grows wild in Mediterranean and so forth...creeping rootstock...purplish stem with opposite ovate leaves. Common names. Wild marjoram, oregano, mountain mint."

"We've got oregano out back, I'm sure we do. I bought a bunch of new spices a while back, got sick of Asthma's duck sauce and black bean paste junk. Probably some marjoram there too, but I don't know how wild it is."

"What about sage?"

"Only powdered."

"That'll do. What's next?"

"*Thyme, this too, for invigoration.* We've got thyme." She leaned closer to the notebook. "*And sweet rosemary to repel evil and bind this incantation.* We have that too."

"What's next?"

"*Infuse them all, in thickness brew, a plant far greater than the rest. Anoint thy shield with Dragonroot, and by its charm, be valor blessed.* Geez. Sounds strong. What is it?" Sweeney shrugged his shoulders and Pearl said, "Probably another name for that weird crap in the spice rack no one ever uses. Fenugreek, whatever the fuck that is. Look under D."

"Dragonroot," he said, and ran his finger over the page. "Rootstock is turnip shaped, and so on...leaves are ternately divided, leaflets ovate or oblong-ovate."

"Do we have it in the kitchen?"

"I'm coming to that. Let me see. Official name *Arisaema triphyllum*, also called Indian Turnip and Bog Onion and so on. I don't see a common name. It doesn't appear to be a household herb like the others."

"But it's the most important one. We've got to have it. Keep reading."

He scanned the page. "Green and purple bract known as a spathe....flowering takes place April through June."

Pearl stared, obviously trying to come up with another idea. "There's got to be something more. It's got to be in the kitchen."

"Not necessarily," Sweeney said. He closed the book but kept his middle finger between the pages to keep his place. "Remember, Moll did not write her spell based upon the assumption that fifteen hundred years later two people in a Chinese restaurant would try to follow it in the dead of winter. Look at this book. There are hundreds of herbs and plants listed, the vast majority of which are weeds found in inaccessible places and only in spring and summer. We should consider ourselves fortunate beyond all expectation that we already have most of the ingredients."

"But we don't have the most important one," Pearl protested.

"Maybe it's not that important."

"It's called Dragonroot. If it was called, you know, Cocker Spanielroot, then okay, yeah – not important. But Dragonroot. It must be something we can find. Moll wouldn't leave us high and dry."

"It may not be important," Dr. Sweeney said, touching her wrist. "This charm is to anoint the armor. Armor will not kill it. Only the sword Gealach can do that. And armor means someone has to wear it."

Pearl stared, deflated. She gazed across the room at Raeven, now sitting beside Sparky in front of the fire. The silver cross lay at their feet, cooling on the bricks. "So now what?" she asked. "This doesn't make sense to me. Steven stuffing it in her pocket and us finding it again; and already having most of these herbs in the kitchen…we couldn't have been brought all this way only to get hung up on one plant. Come on, open that book again. Read the whole thing."

"I did."

"No, you didn't. You said so forth and so on. Read it all this time."

Dr. Sweeney sighed and opened the book to the place held by his finger. "Dragonroot. The rootstock is a turnip-shaped acrid corm from which grows…"

"Not that. The common names part. Start there."

"Official name *Arisaema triphyllum*, also called Indian Turnip, Bog Onion, Wild Turnip, Bog Onion, Wild turnip, Jack-in-the-Pulpit, Wakerobin."

Pearl sat up straight.

Dr. Sweeney noticed: "What is it? Wakerobin?"

"I should have known," she said, and called over her shoulder. "Hey Sparkles, listen to this. Read it again."

Dr. Sweeney read the list of names again.

"Well, what do you know," Sparky said and Sweeney asked him to explain. "Jack-in-the-pulpit," he said. "We found some last night at the town garage."

"And...?" Dr. Sweeney asked, bewildered.

Pearl pulled the book from his hands onto her lap, swiveled it around and ran her forefinger over the page. "Here," she said, and slapped her hand down on Dr. Sweeney's knee. "What month is it?"

"February."

"Right. And this is what you read: 'Flowering takes place from April through June.'"

Sweeney's expression changed from confusion to enthusiasm in a split-second. "You saw one last night?"

"In the snow, and we saw more than one. I can only imagine what the bog looks like."

"Where is the bog?"

"Down the road from here. It's the only place I've ever seen Jack-in-the-pulpits, and only in late spring, early summer. Until last night."

"Incredible," Sweeney said and Pearl closed the book with a triumphant snap. "Raeven, are you listening?"

She wasn't, and hadn't been: her mind was consumed with thoughts of betrayal. The revelation of what Steven Wilcox had done cast her foolish mooning over his death in a harsh new light and she shuddered with disgust at the memory of herself at the wake, wearing her funeral veil and carrying a white rose, publicly mourning a man who had separated her out, targeted her, made her The Knight. *What an idiot I am, thinking it's all so tragic and romantic and all the while unaware that he set me up. He did this to me. He's killed me!"*

As if to confirm her conclusion, another harrowing roar passed through the restaurant and each of them, at different times, glanced with foreboding at the re-folded piece of vellum on the table. The tiny link of gold, once part of an ancient chain, lay nestled inside. Sweeney had theorized that it sent out some form of primitive beacon that called forth the Beast. It would stalk them as long as they had it. He now spoke as though he'd read their minds. "You must know it will do us no good to abandon it."

Pearl and Sparky nodded but Raeven stood at the fireplace. "Why not? We could throw it in the river. It won't know where we are then."

"It would find us sooner or later regardless. We have few places to hide these days."

"But that gold is like a signal," Raeven said. Her dress rustled as she strode to the table. "If we get rid of it we'll gain some time."

"No, Raeven. We will not get rid of it. We will use it to our advantage. While it is true it has been attracted to the gold link, and therefore, to you; it is also true it has not killed you."

"It tried."

"Yes. But in the road with Pearl, you frightened it away. On Melbourne Hill, it made a valiant effort but still failed. You have a form of protection none of us yet understand. Part of it may be inner fear."

"Here we go again," Raeven said and clenched her fists in frustration. "I'm full of self-doubt, I'm full of inner fear."

"I didn't mean *your* inner fear," Sweeney said with a wry smile and tilted his head in the direction of the still-quivering roar. "I meant hers, though I should imagine it's more akin to caution than fear. I'm not certain of this, of course."

"Of course," Pearl repeated, and when he looked at her, enquiring, she added: "Well, you *have* been wrong now and then."

"I'm learning as I go along," he admitted. "We all are. Various bits and pieces of this great puzzle have been revealed to us, most recently the jack-in-the-pulpit. Taken together, they begin to form a picture. The first thing we must do – and truly, this is vitally important though difficult in the extreme – we must first understand and accept that everything is now under the control of things unseen, and from both sides, ours and the enemy's."

"Us and them," Sparky said. "Stars and trees."

"Correct. But deeper than that. When I say everything, I do mean *everything*. If you've noticed, even our most casual statements can turn into keys to unlock particular pieces of the puzzle. We have become a part of the snowfire web, our thoughts, our dreams, our deepest fears, even our knowledge – Pearl's knowledge of the white raven and jack-in-the-pulpit, for instance. We could dismiss it as coincidence, but why did she go over the herbal recipe with me? What if it had been you,

Constable? Or you, Raeven? Would either of you have recognized a jack-in-the-pulpit, much less understood it had been seen in a place and time considered impossible?"

"I wouldn't," Raeven admitted.

"Pearl was shown the impossible plant, and came to me, and together we arrived at this conclusion."

"Which is?" Pearl asked.

"Which is that we must re-anoint the armor. I suggest a trip to that bog you mentioned. You said we can walk to it from here. If you saw dragonroot in the road and at the town garage, think how much more you'll find if you go to a place where you expect it. And Constable, your excellent suggestion of the welding torch is one we shall follow. As for you Raeven, you are simply brimming with these opposing powers. The Beast is attracted and repelled by you, afraid and unafraid. It would like to kill you but it is not certain it *can* kill you – not yet anyway. I assure you, however, when the coupling takes place between it and its master, all such uncertainty shall vanish."

"When will that happen?" Raeven asked in a breathless voice.

"Soon, I should think. This is my plan. Pearl and Raeven will go to the bog." The two women glanced at each other, apprehensive. "I shouldn't worry too much," he said. "You're after dragonroot. The enemy shan't go near it. Gather as much as you can. In the meantime, you and I, Constable, shall retrieve the welding torch. We'll all meet back here, melt the cross back into a sword, re-anoint the armor, and then…" He hesitated, glanced at Raeven, "And yes, so yes," he said and smiled in an attempt to sound an optimistic note. "We'll see what happens then."

7

The pale-eyed man stared with unbound fury at the far off string of lights. In his reaching strands of thought, he saw the old woman climb into a small white machine that moved along a flat gray lane, heading north.

He paced back and forth on the tilted deck, raging and howling at the skies. He had to find a way to the mainland. He had already inspected each corpse aboard the freighter for a spark of life he could slip into, but found none. He had been too thorough. The battered, broken body he now inhabited could not swim the distance; it could not row a boat.

Why had he killed them all? He should have kept one strong

young one alive and unhurt, someone capable of taking him away from the snow-swept island, someone to carry him northward!

He roamed the ship like a mad thing, shrieking and mangling his present form; purposely breaking glass and lacerating his arms, his face and legs; banging his temporary body's arms against the railing and his head against the walls until the bones cracked and blood mingled with the salt spray to streak the decks with watery red. Ancient words and powerful incantations filled the air until, with a shriek of rage, he threw himself over the bow rail.

Down he fell past the painted white letters of *Isolde* to land with a bone-crunching smash upon the rocks. His neck snapped, one arm broke, the jagged edges of a cracked femur cut up through his thigh, and the right side of his skull crushed inward, obliterating his scarred-over eye socket.

Waves thundered upon the rocks to pour over him before hissing back to the sea with a wash of blood.

He opened his remaining eye and rolled onto his side. Bones did not move as they should. Joints had dislocated. His face dropped into a tidal pool. Stinging salt water poured into his lungs until he rolled over with his head lolling onto the rocks and used his unbroken arm to drag himself from the pool.

Something moved nearby. Snow and blood nearly blinded him, but he pulled closer to a crevice in the rock and peered inside.

A seagull.

Frightened and trapped inside the crevice, it tried to back away but couldn't. The broken man smiled a ghastly, broken-toothed smile. Watery blood seeped from the sides of his mouth. The gull huddled against the rock and, with a hand dangling lifeless from a broken wrist, the pale-eyed man reached inside the crevice and touched its feathers

Seconds later, the white bird opened its one remaining eye, pale blue now, with the other scarred over. It pushed the dead hand away with its beak and waddled up close to the man now truly and thoroughly dead. It tore at the bloodied flesh around the battered eye socket, eager to build a reserve of strength before the flight to the thin strand of light along the distant shoreline, and it choked down its fill in great bloody gobs, and moved beyond the dead man to the craggy rocks where it hissed and lifted into the air with a triumphal scream to begin its flight to the mainland.

8

Raeven and Pearl stood behind the police car. "Now," Sparky called from inside and they leaned against the trunk and pushed. "With gusto!" Sweeney added, calling through the window.

"I'd like to gusto you," Pearl muttered.

The car began a slow roll down the steep driveway. Sparky popped the clutch near the bottom and it roared to life, with the headlights and taillights the only lights visible in all directions.

The two women watched until they disappeared. "And off to the bog we go," Pearl said and picked up an empty bushel basket.

Raeven lifted two plastic Chinese lanterns, one in each hand. Candles burned inside, undisturbed by the wind that sent the red tassels leaping against her hands as she followed Pearl down the driveway, toward the low, swampy area known as Bracket's Bog.

Once on the road she could not shake the feeling they were being followed. She stopped every few feet to look around and ask if Pearl had heard anything. As they approached the bog she stopped again and peered into a stand of bare maples at the side of the road. "What was that?" she whispered in response to a small crackle within the few dead leaves still clinging to the branches.

Pearl stopped in the road, the basket hanging against her leg. "You know that really loud sound we hear off and on?"

"That roar?"

"Right. Where is it coming from?"

"The mountain."

"Right. And where is the mountain?"

Raeven pointed at the dark hulk of the Golden Panda on the hill behind them.

"The restaurant?" Pearl asked.

"Beyond it."

"Far beyond?"

"Yes. Why are you asking me this?"

"I have a reason. The roaring sound is coming from the mountain, which means we know the thing is up there, right?"

"Right."

"Which means we know it can't be down here beside the road."

"Right."

"Then do me a favor."

"What?"

"Stop asking me what's in the fucking bushes every two

minutes."

Pearl plodded ahead with her basket and Raeven followed until she heard another sound. She stopped and lifted her lantern. Something…bare limbs, dead twigs, something wintery and dormant shifted and moved at the side of the road. A prickly vine slipped up the side of a sapling.

Pearl stopped and turned in the middle of the road. "Now what?"

"Nothing," Raeven said and rushed to her side.

Tred sat between the two men in the front seat and leaned against the professor. "Oh, come, come," he said but the dog refused to budge. After they passed out of sight of the restaurant, Sparky said, "Okay, I need something from you. You gotta tell me everything."

"I have."

"You haven't. You let things slip a little at a time, but I need to know everything. I'm serious. Don't keep things to yourself. You mentioned something a while back. We've been concentrating on The Knight, but remember? You also talked about The Three. I don't know about you, but I'm starting to believe I'm one of them."

"The Three," the Professor said. "I'd nearly forgotten about them."

"I haven't, though I wish I could."

"Why?"

Sparky turned on the heater. "There are four of us."

When they reached the center of town, he slowed down and came to a stop. "Geez, look at them." An orderly procession of pine trees moved in single file down the street, each one stretching its roots in front to catch the snow and drag its trunk forward. A second line of trees moved down an adjoining street and melded with regimented precision into the first, as if marching to orders only they could sense and understand.

"Ghastly," Sweeney said and pulled his scarf up around his neck. He pointed in the direction the trees were heading. "What's at the end of that street?"

"The church. And behind that, the river. There's a big open field between the church and the river, but not much else."

"Ghastly," Sweeney said again.

Sparky drove past the trees to the abandoned hardware store and left the car running while they climbed the three wide concrete steps to the front door. He broke the glass with the butt of his pistol and reached through to unlock it.

Inside, the floor creaked with every step. The headlights streaming through the front window cast wide dusty beams of light over the ceiling. "I saw some small hurricane lanterns at the end of that first aisle," Sparky said. "Grab a few to take with us. Lamp oil too."

Sweeney wandered down the aisle to a basket of silver lanterns. He filled two with oil, lit them, and bought them to the policeman, now squatting on the floor to inspect an enormous propane tank. "This thing is wicked old, but still in good shape," he said. "Heavy as hell though. We can roll it to the door but I'm worried about those outside stairs. Let's look around a bit first. I need some welding goggles and gloves. Grab as many of those lanterns as you can. Candles too."

"What else?"

"A hammer to bang that cross into shape. Axes, too, in case those trees get frisky."

The two men wandered through the hardware store, each carrying a lantern. Sparky pulled four new axes out of a rack and carried them to the front door. Sweeney met him there with an armload of additional lanterns. "I don't dare drop these," he said, clutching them close. "I'll bring them to the car now."

"Put them in the trunk," Sparky said. "We'll lay the welding tank across the back seat. I'll look for the goggles and hammers"

Sweeney stomped down the stairs, opened the car door, and leaned inside to pop the trunk. "Now be a good cur, won't you?" Tred answered with a single lick of his cheek. "Many thanks," he said, and to his surprise, the dog began to growl – he did not realize that Tred was looking past him toward the front of the car. The drone of the engine hid the light hiss of movement over snow. "Now, now, we'll be right back," he said and shut the door. He placed the lanterns in the trunk and climbed back up the stairs without noticing the shadow moving toward him from the side of the steps.

"Ready?" Sparky said after they'd lifted the propane tank. He carried the heaviest end and, though he strained and heaved, he had much more confidence in his strength than the professor.

"Holy Mother of God," Sweeney said through clenched teeth as they carried it to the door. "And we have to go down *stairs*?"

"Only three," Sparky returned, and then, at the front door – "Whoa, whoa, whoa," he whispered and set his end down on the floor. Sweeney laid his end down too, though not so gently. He stepped over the tank and looked over Sparky's shoulder.

A single pine tree, about eight feet tall, stood between the hardware store and the car. Pale white roots wafted around its base.

"You think it's trying to scare us?" Sparky whispered.

"If so, it's doing a masterful job."

"Okay, look, this is what we'll do. We'll carry the tank down the steps and around to the passenger side. From what I've seen, they can't move very fast." He lifted his end of the tank. "Ready?"

Dr. Sweeney nodded, hiked his jeans up and lifted his end of the tank.

The tree stood in the snow, motionless but for its roots.

Sparky descended backward, with both feet meeting on each step before lowering to the next. The tank tilted down, which gave him the majority of the weight but gave the professor a precarious hold on his end. "You okay?" Sparky asked. Dr. Sweeney nodded, red-faced and white knuckled.

Sparky reached the ground. Sweeney took another step and the tree lurched. A long root shot out. It wrapped around the professor's wrist like a clammy bullwhip and he recoiled in horror.

"The tank!" Sparky yelled, but too late. Neither could later say if Sweeney dropped it or the root pulled his hand away, but his hands slipped and the tank fell.

The brass valve landed on his right foot with a sickening crunch unheard by Sparky who leaped out of the way and watched the tank roll into the snow. "Man!" he cried. "That was close."

After Sweeney collapsed on the top step, the root released him and withdrew and the tree began to move, hissing across the snow toward the distant procession of pines. Sparky watched it go and, turning back, was shocked to see the professor's agonized expression. "You okay?" He ran up the steps. "Did that root get you?"

"My foot." Dr. Sweeney clenched his fists and lay back on the top steps, fighting a wave of pain. Sparky inspected his high-top sneakers, searching for a sign of injury. "Which one?" he asked, but rocked back on his heels when a dark stain soaked through his right sneaker and began to seep into the laces.

9

Pearl lifted her lantern high. "Would you look at that." They had left the road and followed a narrow winding path through a stand of white birches to the edge of a wide snow-covered bog where thousands of glistening jack-in-the-pulpit plants poked up through the icy crust, each one green and fresh and adorned with a small crown of snow.

Raeven, too, held her lantern high, but could not concentrate on the plants. Something was following them, she was sure of it, though she couldn't say what: a low rustle and a shadowy movement in the trees, thin and clandestine, but nothing obvious. She stepped up close to Pearl but did not take her eyes off the woods behind.

"Let's gather as many as we can," Pearl said and she brushed the snow off the nearest dragonroot. "Gosh, I hate to do this," she said and gently lifted the hooded leaves. Raeven had no such qualms. She yanked one up by its bulbous root. Pearl sighed and did the same, and together they moved, dusting the snow from the plants, pulling them up and dropping them into the basket. The lanterns flickered and their boots cracked through the icy glaze and sank into the softer snow below.

Raeven straightened and pressed her hands against the small of her back. "How can I kill that thing?" Pearl bent down for another plant and did not answer. Raeven sighed and pushed up her sleeve to scratch her wrist. "These things aren't poisonous, are they?"

"Probably not a good idea to eat them. Why?"

"Just wondering." She dropped another plant in the basket and once again stopped to scratch her wrist. "But I have to do it, right?" she asked. "Kill it. I don't see how I can. I really don't."

Pearl straightened again and asked if she remembered Dr. Sweeney mentioning the Three. When Raeven said she didn't, Pearl said: "That's because you're the Knight. I wouldn't remember anything else either. He said the Knight is separate but part of the Three."

"Which means what?"

Pearl shrugged. "I think it means I'm one of them." She smiled and punched her lightly on the shoulder. "Come on, kid. Let's move a little faster. I'm getting cold."

Minutes later, Pearl tossed a last dragonroot plant onto the basket, now filled above the brim. "Think this is enough?"

Raeven stood behind her, scratching her wrist and gazing at the surrounding trees. "Not much room for more."

"That's what I say. Besides, how much anointing are we going to do?" She held her lantern high over the carpet of dragonroot. "Take a good look. You'll never see this again, not in winter." Pearl swung her lantern toward an opening between two spruce trees. "This way." Carrying the basket between them, they passed around the stand of birches and came to a stop before a tangled stand of brambles. "Blackberries," Pearl said, lifting her lantern higher.

"Where's the path?"

"It's here somewhere. Look on your side."

Raeven held her lantern low. "No. Nothing."

"It has to be," Pearl said, puzzled. "Look. Our tracks lead into the bog from here."

The two women glanced at each other, their expressions laced with anxiety. The lanterns held them in a circle of dim comforting light while around them the icy bog and surrounding woods seemed to close in. "This *has* to be the path," Pearl said. She waved her lantern over the disordered snarl, bare of all leaves and berries. "It's the one I always use to come here."

Raeven took off a glove and touched the tiny thorns. Beside her, Pearl stared deep into the brambles. She suddenly straightened and stepped back.

"What happened?" Raeven asked, startled.

"We need to find another way out. Through the woods, across the bog, it doesn't matter. This is the path we came in on."

"It can't be. We would have remembered these briars."

"No." She lifted Raeven's arm and the two lanterns cast their light into the twisted interior where it fell upon two sets of footprints beneath the thorny vines.

"Are those ours?" Raeven asked, and when Pearl nodded, she said she didn't remember climbing through the vines.

"We didn't," Pearl said. "They weren't here."

Raeven stepped back from the brambles as if suddenly realizing they were draped with poison ivy. Pearl threw her arm across her shoulders. "Okay, so there are a few blackberry vines in the way," she said. "So what? We'll be fine. We go around them. We cross the bog and go through the woods on the other side. We'll be fine." They lifted the basket of dragonroot and began their trek across the frozen bog, with Pearl assuring Raeven every few yards they would be fine and Raeven saying nothing at all.

10

"Bollixed things up this time, did I?" Dr. Sweeney flinched when Pearl slipped the knife under the last stubborn bit of bloody shoelace.

"We don't know that yet." She cut the lace, pulled his sneaker off and stared at his foot. "Now we do." Blood saturated his white sock. "Oh, Lord," she said with a grimace and pulled it off. "Look at this, Spark." He lifted a candle and leaned over her shoulder.

"Yowser," he said and whistled softly.

Swollen and purple with a jagged tear along the top, clearly a bone or two had been broken. "Okay, Prof," Pearl said. "This is the story. It's not infected, but we need to sterilize it, the way you did with Raeven's lip. God only knows what's living in those sneakers of yours."

Sweeney agreed and moaned in agony when she poured a hefty shot of whiskey over the ripped flesh. "Wicked creature," he said in a hoarse whisper.

"Shh, boy," she returned, patting his hand. "It'll pass."

Sparky nodded at Raeven and she followed him into the kitchen, now lit with a warm glow of hurricane lanterns. He leaned against the warming counter and looked at her; and the doors continued to swing behind Raeven, in and out, diminishing in their movement until they settled and she stood before him, dark against the wooden doors, wearing black, standing in shadow.

"So what should we do?" he asked.

She gasped, horrified by the question. "Why are you asking *me*?"

"He's not one of us anymore. He's not one of the Three, that's obvious now. He can't move with that injury. Not far anyway."

"So what does that mean? You, me and Pearl are the Three?"

"Looks that way."

"No, Sparky, no." She dropped heavily onto a wooden chair. "We can't do this without him. Look at us. What do we know about this kind of thing?"

"Nothing. That's why I wanted to talk to you." He sat on the counter and drummed his fingers on his knees. "You're the Knight of the White Bird. I didn't see how that could be possible, but when Pearl told us about that white raven…"

She dropped her head on her hand and ran her fingers through her hair.

"You are," he said again and she lifted her eyes to his: "I know," she said and she heaved a despairing sigh. "Want to hear something funny? Not too long ago, I used to think of myself the way Dr. Sweeney talked about the Knight. Someone who didn't fit in and didn't belong anywhere, thinking no one truly understood me. And now that I've been singled out and truly set apart, I see how truly ordinary I am. The joke is on me. I'm just another ordinary, common person, the same as every other ordinary, common person, and it's taken this uncommon situation to show it to me." She shook her head. "I feel like…I don't know if I can explain it. I feel like there's a river…"

"A river?"

"An unseen river that flows under everything, under all living things, under everyone, and through everyone. It's always been flowing. It always will. Somehow, my thinking I was so different and so unique cut me off from the river. But no..." She closed her eyes and shook her head again. "It's hard to describe what I mean. I wasn't cut off because you *can't* be cut off. But I didn't know it was there. I didn't know I was part of it. I didn't know I was being carried along, carried on the current of the river, the same as everyone else. And now..."

"And now?"

"Pearl said I needed to strip off my armor. I've finally managed to do that, only to find I have to take it up again. And now I wish I really was as special as I once believed. I wish I truly did have something different and unique that set me apart. I wish I still didn't sense what I feel about the river, the...everything carried along. But I don't have anything different or unique about me. I can't do this, Sparky. I can't. I don't have what it takes. There are a million others who could have been chosen."

"But they weren't."

She rolled up her sleeve and held out her wrist. "Look at this." Her *doom* tattoo had blurred at the edges, as if someone had spilled water on fresh ink, with one line beginning to trail up her arm like blood-poisoning darkening a vein. "I thought I'd gotten into something like poison ivy. But look. Tattoos don't run like this. I have no idea why it's happening or what is going on, and so..." On the edge of tears, she held out her hand as though begging for an answer. "So why?"

"So why you?" She nodded and he said, "I don't know." She rolled her sleeve back down and dropped her hand into her lap. "But the reason why doesn't matter now," he said. "You *are*. That's all. And because you are, I wanted to ask you what we should do."

"But I don't know anything! Why are you asking me?"

"Because no one has before." She sat back and stared at him, open-mouthed, incredulous. She couldn't see his eyes. His face lay in shadow, lit from behind, topped with an aura of golden hair. "Ever since this all began everybody's been telling you how you should feel, how you should react, what you should do. But maybe we shouldn't be telling you those things. Maybe we should be asking you." He bumped his heels against the counter and studied her for a long moment. "So what should we do?"

Raeven gazed at the floor, silent, motionless. He nearly gave up when she looked up and said, softly: "Shields."

"Shields?"

"I'm supposed to wear all that rusty armor, but in the charm, Moll didn't mention armor at all. Remember? She said anoint the *shield* with dragonroot. Besides, I don't know how I can wear all that armor anyway. How am I supposed to move?"

"I thought maybe if we anointed it..."

"No. The shield."

"But we don't have one. We didn't find one in the cave."

"So...do you think...?" Raeven began, unsure of her thoughts. "If we get one, does it have to be strong? Or does the anointing make it strong?"

"I think the stuff makes it strong. So what do we do?"

"I thought...no, it's stupid..."

"No, no, please," he said, and slipped off the counter. "It's not stupid, not if you say it." He crouched beside her. "Tell me. What is it?"

"Garbage cans. Out back. The lids."

Sparky sat back against the counter, still crouched on the floor. She thought he might laugh but no. "Why not?" he said and she relaxed. "Sure, why not?" he repeated. "If they're anointed, that'll make them stronger, right? And the cross. Once we melt that into a sword, will that be all we need?"

"I'm not sure. But the garbage can lids will work. I think they will anyway. I'm not really sure."

11

The Golden Panda hummed with activity. Pearl stood at the stove and grimaced while stirring a pot. The smell of the boiling dragonroot was appalling, like forest detritus and decay, but so overpowering that it snuffed out any pleasant earthy associations. "No wonder this works," she offered. "Who wouldn't run?"

Sweeney sat beside her with his bandaged foot on a chair, studying the ancient sheet of vellum and comparing it to his *Book of Herbals and Medicinals*. "How much garlic did you put in?"

"Not enough."

Outside, Sparky and Raeven, both wearing protective goggles, worked on the crooked cross with the welding torch; first hammering it out of shape and then trying to reconfigure it into a sword. Raeven couldn't understand the procedure, couldn't envision the sword within the twisting metal, and the flying sparks made her nervous.

"Oh, look at that," Sparky finally said and pulled the torch away from the cross. "That doesn't look like a sword at all!"

He sat back on his heels and took off his goggles.

Raeven did the same, though with her face lowered in an attempt to hide her dismay. It looked like someone had tried and failed to straighten an oversized corkscrew. She put her goggles back on. "Let's try again."

Sparky sighed, disheartened. "Hope we have better luck with the armor."

12

"Young man, are you hurt?" Father Toomey's voice echoed in low reverberations throughout the cavern.

Joe Li turned in his cage, wincing as he did. "A little. Broken ribs I think."

"What about an open wound? It didn't claw you, did it?"

"No."

"Be thankful for that. Is anyone coming to look for us?" Joe hesitated. "I see," the priest said, and a long moment passed, filled with hollow booms and creaking walls.

Joe straightened his legs as best he could, all the while grimacing from the pain in his chest. "Are we going to die?"

"I am."

Joe tried to see the priest's cage but could barely make out the circular web in the gloom. "Is it going to kill us?"

"Possibly," Father Toomey whispered. "It hasn't touched me since it caged me. To tell the truth, I don't think it much cares what happens to us now. I've quite a deep gash on my leg." He shifted in his cage. "That thing's claws are septic. Infection. Gangrene. Blood poisoning."

"It's possible someone will come, it's possible they'll find us." Joe's voice sounded small and plaintive in the cavernous gloom. "I think they will, if they can get by that thing."

The priest shifted in his cage. "Who will come?"

"Dr. Sweeney. And maybe Raeven."

"Ah," Father Toomey said, disappointed, and dropped his head back against the glass web. "I don't think I shall count on them. How will they know where to look?"

"They already do. We saw this place from the Grey farm. We knew the thing had moved up here to the lift house."

"Even so," the priest said, "it will take more than courage to—" He sat up and gripped the strands of glass. "Why were you at the Greys?"

"To look for the cross."

"But why there?" A note of urgency had slipped into his voice.

"We followed your directions, the ones you wrote on the floor."

"But I didn't finish," the priest said with rising panic. "It dragged me away before I could finish."

"We figured out what you meant." Joe glanced at the entrance, fearful the priest's frantic voice might rouse their captor. "We found the cross Steven Wilcox took from the church, as you hoped we would."

"But I didn't finish!"

Something shuffled at the front of the cavern, a rumbling, papery growl. The prisoners slumped in their cages and listened until the sound died. "I didn't mean for —" Father Toomey stopped again when a deep hiss washed through the gloomy chamber. He lowered his voice but could not contain his alarm. "I didn't mean for you to go there." He reached into his jacket pocket and withdrew the packet of folded parchment he'd found in the cellar. "The cross came from the Greys."

"We know. And Steven brought it back there."

"No, he didn't."

"He did," Joe insisted. "The one from the church, we found it at the cave."

"For God's sake, listen!" the priest said and clutched the glass bars of his cage. "You found *a* cross. You didn't find *the* cross!"

Another hiss. Joe glanced at the front of the cavern.

"It won't work," Father Toomey said and rose to his knees. The packet slipped from his lap. He tried to grab it but it fell through the glass net and dropped to the cavern floor.

"It has to work," Joe said. "They're melting it back into a sword."

"It's not the silver cross," the feverish priest said, and the cold hiss exploded into a thunderous roar that severed the stillness and swallowed his voice; but not before Joe heard him cry, "It's not the silver sword!"

13

Jin Feng had found the car in the parking lot at Pease Airport, white and small, and now travelling northward through the snow. She lifted the golden box onto her lap and held it tight and turned to the empty driver's seat. The accelerator lowered and the car picked up speed. She had not felt his presence in some time and assumed he had not yet found a way off the rocky island. Unless he found something seaworthy, maybe a lifeboat from the freighter, he could be trapped there for days.

She focused on the windshield for signs upon the unseen horizon and before long a glow appeared upon the low clouds like the glare thrown up by a distant city lit in blue.

That was it. That was the place.

Snow flew at the windshield. The engine raced. She willed it into greater speed.

Something caught her attention – she couldn't say what…a growing awareness of something outside the car, moving beside it in the darkness. She cleared a circle in the fogged-over glass with her fingers.

Nothing.

She turned her attention back to the distant blue glow, but again…something. She passed her sleeve across the window and cupped her hands around her eyes to peer through the glass.

There *was* something there.

A large white bird flew beside the car, keeping pace with strong, steady thrusts of its wings. Snow lashed it but it did not veer from its path.

Jin Feng stared at it, puzzled, and nearly screamed when it turned and looked at her with a single eye like a distant planet seen upon the horizon, pale, cold and dead, but shining all the same – *Him!*

A shocking wave of hate-thought spilled into the car. The white bird moved closer, beating its wings against the snowy air and bobbing its head like a mother bird regurgitating food for its young. Jin Feng threw her hands up in horror when a gob of partially digested flesh spattered against the window. Blood spread over the glass in tiny rivulets buffeted by the wind.

The gull screamed and the trembling old woman watched it dart forward and fly above the hood, keeping pace with the car. It bent its neck and peered back at her with its head upside down and its cold eye glaring with contempt. Seconds later, it pulled away. The headlights caught it moving ahead into the snow with its white wings pounding against the wind as on it went, moving away from the car toward the distant blue glow until it passed beyond the reach of her lights and disappeared into the gloom.

14

Sparky and Pearl stood silent and pensive beside the police car. The engine idled. Blue-grey exhaust billowed over them in weak imitation of the shuddering clouds above.

"How did we ever get into this, Sparkles?"

He tried to smile, but couldn't. He shrugged his shoulders.

Dr. Sweeney appeared from behind the restaurant using an upended broom as a crutch, with the straw spread beneath his arm and the end of the broomstick clacking on the ice. He held the newly fashioned sword in his free hand. "Remember now, we must instill confidence," he said as he limped toward the car. "Have we everything we need?"

"In the trunk," Sparky said. "Lanterns, axes, extra garbage can shields."

"And I've got the gold link in my pocket."

"That sword," Sparky said and pointed at the twisted weapon in Sweeney's hand. He had saved some time by cutting off the arms of the cross and the overall effect was that of a young boy's wooden sword, all bulky angles and dull tips. "Does she really have to use it?"

"She does. Regardless of its appearance, it is her only protection and our only hope." He glanced back at the restaurant. "See if she's all right, will you Pearl?"

Pearl started toward the restaurant, but stopped when she reached the chicken wire cage and turned back with an uneasy glance. "Here she is," she said and began to walk back toward the car. The small flock of chickadees she'd seen earlier passed over the parking lot. She watched them spiral into the trees behind Dr. Sweeney. "He didn't do it," she whispered, and began to laugh. "I still have no idea what that's supposed to –" A flash of red stopped her in her tracks.

A cardinal had flown up from the bog to join the darting chickadees in the trees.

"Oh my God," Pearl said and stared over Sweeney's shoulder.

Alarmed by her expression, he spun around but saw only a few small white and black birds and a vibrant red one. "Oh, I see," he said and relaxed his shoulders. "From the look on your face I thought you'd seen something."

Pearl turned to Sparky. "Can you...Spark, just for a second, can you...?" She was too flustered to finish, but Sparky knew what she meant. As soon as he moved to the other side of the car to give them some privacy, she leaned in close to Dr. Sweeney and said, "He didn't do it."

"Who didn't?"

"The knight Donal. He didn't do it."

"Didn't do what?"

"He didn't kill the Evil One."

"Oh, really now," Sweeney said, drawing back from her intense gaze. "And how on earth would you know that?"

She grabbed him by the sleeve. "I don't know how, but I *know* he didn't do it."

Sweeney pulled his arm away and leaned on his broomstick crutch. "I read it in the manuscript, I remember it clearly."

"Do you?" Pearl asked, moving in closer. "Think."

Sweeney looked at the ground, his brow furrowed. "Yes, I'm certain. Brother Aodhan wrote that the smoke was thick and he couldn't…Wait, yes. Now that I think of it, he didn't actually *see* it happen. I was a bit disappointed to read so little of the actual slaying."

"What did he see?" Pearl asked. From behind, she heard a scrape of metal, a grind of rust upon rust. "Try to remember."

"Donal lying upon the rocks, dying from his wounds."

"Where was the sword?"

Dr. Sweeney's eyes widened, his mouth dropped open. "Brendan," he whispered. "Brother Aodhan saw Donal lying on the rocks and through the smoke he saw Brendan carrying the sword, which means…"

"Brendan killed it."

Sweeney nodded and swallowed hard.

"Brendan who didn't have a thing, whereas Donal had it all," Pearl said. "The silver sword, the anointed armor and shields – if the knight couldn't do it back then, can Raeven do it now?"

Dr. Sweeney looked into her eyes and tilted his head down so she could see his own above his glasses. "She must," he whispered.

"Hey guys," Sparky said and tapped on the hood of the car. The distant blue light fell upon a figure appearing around the corner.

Donal's ancient armor hung upon her as a collection of disintegrating rust. Nothing fit, nothing matched, nothing appeared remotely capable of protecting the wearer against a determined hornet, much less a colossal creature many times her size. She peered at them from beneath a visor Sparky cut from a stew pot and welded to the fragile helmet found in the cave. He had welded a flattened pie tin over the hole in the breastplate and fitted her arms with what appeared to be stovepipe.

Some of the original armor had so decayed that Sparky rejected it and substituted pieces of metal found in the kitchen: a large tin can that had once held pineapple wedges, a non-stick cookie sheet, another can covered with Chinese characters; and they hung in clanking sheets over her coat and long black dress like caparison armor draped over a war-horse.

In her left hand, she held a garbage can lid smeared with putrid green mud.

A deep low rumble shuddered through the air. The mountain continued to rise, pushing and grinding up into new jagged heights. They listened in tense silence until it subsided. She took a clanking step toward them. No one said a word until Pearl whispered, "You don't have to do this."

Raeven's voice came back small and muffled from inside the helmet. "I think I do."

Sweeney approached her with halting painful steps. He held his hands out with the bent sword lying across his forearms. "Here is…" He had planned a ceremonious transfer of the beast-slayer *An Claiomh Gealach*, but now that the time had come, he could only manage a second, weak, unfinished, "Here is…"

The Knight of the White Bird lifted her visor and took it from his hands. Dragonroot dripped from her shield. Flecks of rust fell from her squealing armor. The fire from the mountain sparkled in her eyes, dark with uncertainty and fear.

She looked at the others – the Three – and with a nod, she dropped her visor, swung the misshapen sword over her shoulder, and said: "Let's go."

VII.

Dragon

John-Richard Thompson

1

They stopped on a hill on the Coachlight Road, engine idling, headlights off, while Dr. Sweeney scanned the mountain with Sparky's binoculars. Pearl sat squeezed between the two men in the front seat. "Do you see it?" she asked.

"Oh, I hope not," Raeven said from her horizontal position across the back seat. Metal jabbed into her each time she tried to sit up.

"I see its new lair," Sweeney said. Several massive domed structures clustered on the summit in grotesque imitation of the monastery ruins of Skellig Michael. Behind them, a jumble of crumbling walls pierced by gothic windows towered into the gloom. "Its calls have remained steady over the last hours. It hasn't left since it abducted Joe, which means it hasn't eaten in quite some time. It will leave its lair sooner rather than later. Good news for us."

"Good news?" Pearl asked. "Really? Personally, I'd rather that thing stayed up there."

"If it does, we haven't a prayer of saving your friends." Sweeney lowered the binoculars. "You do realize that's your destination, don't you?"

Sparky leaned forward to stare at him. Pearl's mouth dropped open. "What if that thing comes back?"

"We'll have to take a chance that it will be so busy chasing me it won't bother with you."

"Chasing you?" Sparky asked and the professor said he would explain later. "No, no," Sparky protested. "Remember what I told you before. No secrets."

"Very well," Sweeney said with a quick glance into the back seat. "I'm not going with you." In response to their shocked silence, he added: "I can't climb with this injury. It's better this way. Trust me."

"*Trust* you?" Pearl said. "You're the one who got us into all this crap in the first place. Can't climb with your injury – I'd like to give you an injury that would stop you from coming up new ideas. This is kind'a like suicide, isn't it? We have no proof that Joey is alive, but here we are, on our way up to that thing's nest. I go from serving dinner to *being* dinner in…what? Three days? None of this would have happened if you hadn't showed up."

"You don't have to go," Raeven said. "I can make it on my own."

"Oh please, listen to Frodo in the back seat."

"I'm only saying–"

"What, that you're going up there alone? You can't even sit up for God's sake." She jabbed her forefinger at Sweeney: "You're not going to weasel out of this. You're the one who went looking for the manuscript, as if anyone gives a shit if Brendan or Columbus or some Pilgrim got here first, like the Indians weren't already here before all of them, and now you're the only one who's *not* going up the mountain? Bull. You're coming."

Sweeney adjusted his scarf and shifted in his seat. "One of the reasons I hesitate to explain everything. Reactions based in emotion, not in fact. Drive on, Constable."

"Where to?"

"The town garage."

Sparky's headlights swept across a field of vibrant green jack-in-the-pulpit that now surrounded the garage on all sides. The sight was enough to drag Pearl from her resentful silence: "This is where we saw the first one," she said, "but look at them now. Looks like the bog."

Behind them, Raeven dropped a piece of armor on the floor. Dr. Sweeney spun around in his seat. "It keeps jabbing me," she explained. "Besides, I only took off a pineapple can."

He scowled and asked Sparky if the massive front door was the only way inside. "No, there's a smaller door out back." He drove along the right side of the garage to the rear parking lot, all the while grimacing at the crunch of jack-in-the-pulpit beneath the tires.

At the far edge of the parking lot, the land rose to form the lowest slope of the mountain, though its familiar lines had cracked and warped into unfamiliar shape. Dull, ghostly light from the summit fell upon a low hovering fog. Within this, they saw the collapsed lift towers lying at the foot of what used to be the ski slope and a dark line trailing up its center, as if a fault line had opened to slowly split the mountain in half.

Dr. Sweeney suddenly gripped the dashboard and Pearl sat back, panicked by the move. "Now what?"

"An error," he said. "A small one, but an error nonetheless – and, for once, not one of ours. You see that dark line leading up to the summit? Recall that the mountain is transforming into a replica of

Skellig Michael. This is one detail it should have left out, but it hasn't, and it shall make things a good deal easier." He smacked his knee with his fist in satisfaction and answered the question before anyone asked. "It's a staircase."

2

The white car pulled to the side of the road near the electrical wall. Jin Feng could go no further. Mayhem and confusion reigned, with tanks and armored personnel carriers criss-crossing the streets, and trucks and vans clogging every road leading toward Burne Notch.

She fought unnoticed through the crowds, all the while scanning the surrounding trees and rooftops for a sign of the white bird. He was somewhere nearby. She felt his presence. He had won the race to the wall but had yet not crossed beyond it. She focused on the glittering voltage towering before her and its low hum and she shuddered when a sudden malicious vibration oozed through the air from behind. She spun around and scanned the trees, the sky, the rooftops – and *there*.

A tiny bright pinpoint of reflected blue light stared from the shadows of a chimney.

A thunderclap of thought broke upon her. MINE KILL MINE FIRE DEADKILL. The bird stepped hissing from the shadows. She staggered toward the wall. FIRE ALL WORLDMINE SNOWFIRE KILL. He tried to grind her down with a barrage of malice, but she fought back. She raised her arms. She lifted the golden box.

The assault of hateful images and words came to a dead halt.

The bird scuttled down the snowy roof with its wings outspread and beak open in a silent scream, and a new wave passed over her: *fear*, she realized. The seagull shrieked and rose above the sirens and flashing lights. Jin Feng didn't hesitate: she tucked the box under her arm, leaned upon her walking stick, and hobbled to the wall.

A soldier saw her. "Hey!" he yelled and motioned to others nearby. "Stop her!"

She touched the wall. White sparks sizzled around her hand. The soldiers ran toward her, but she calmly stepped into an explosion of consuming fire without looking back. After passing through a hissing mass of electrical currents, violent, swarming, she emerged from the blue wall on the opposite side, unharmed.

She took her first step into Burne Notch and tried to get her bearings when a screaming missile tore through the searing charges behind. It glanced off her shoulder and up it went, trailing smoke like a stricken fighter jet. It wheeled with an insane shriek and dropped again.

The old woman lifted her cane. The bird flapped its singed wings and hovered before her, beating the air. With shocking speed, Jin Feng swung her cane in tight whirring circles that ended in a snap and lethal thrust that would have broken its neck had the enemy come in human form, but the bird swerved and the stick only grazed its wing.

The gull darted in before she could lift it again. It battered her with its wings and dove in with its beak, snapping for her eyes. Jin Feng dropped to her knees, clutching the golden box with one hand while staving off the bird with the other. She rolled to the side and, rising in a single swift motion, swung her staff in an undercut – this time it connected and the seagull tumbled shrieking into the snow.

Jin Feng dropped to her knees again, breathless, and there they remained for some moments; the old woman kneeling in the snow and the bird lying before her, wings outstretched and beak open, panting. She rose to her feet, using her staff for support, and approached the bird. Its single pale eye shimmered with hate.

She lifted the stick to finish it off.

Hate-thought poured forth – *KILL!* – and the bird sprang from the ground – *uninjured*, she now realized. It drove in with its beak and, with one swift jab, it tore out her right eye.

The old woman screamed and threw the snapping bird into the snow and once again fell to her knees.

She bent over the golden box, moaning, with her hands over her ravaged eye. Blood streamed through her fingers and pain sliced through her, yet through it all she felt a light tap upon her hand. She opened her undamaged left eye and peered through her bloody fingers. The gull stood before her. Smoke rose from it like steam. It tapped the back of her hand again with its blood-spattered beak. Hate-thought followed and a stream of ancient wickedness flowed into her mind: *COME NEXT NEAR ME* – it stared, murderous, steady, its single thin black pupil glistening with malice – *I KILL YOU*

It spread its wings. A puff of smoke spiraled and it lifted, staring at the old woman and the golden box with its demonic pale blue eye, and there it hung, flapping heavily three feet above the ground, before turning and flying off into darkness.

3

"Our new headquarters," Sweeney said upon entering the cavernous garage. The massive snowplow took up the bulk of the space, with snow-shovels, tire chains, a snow blower, and bags of rock salt lining the walls. "Come. We've some planning to do and haven't much time."

"What about my birds?" Pearl protested.

"These are temporary headquarters until this ordeal is over. We shall not abandon the menagerie. Now, this is what I propose." Before he could continue, the roaring call sounded for the first time since they arrived. With no forest or hills to muffle the sound, it rolled down the mountain and trembled like an earthquake through the corrugated walls and roof. "Sounds like its right outside," Sparky whispered.

"Go stand by the back door, will you Pearl?" Sweeney asked. "Keep an eye out for it."

"Why me?"

"Oh, honestly. Could you possibly, for once could you *possibly* do something I ask without a preliminary interrogation?"

"Fine, I need a smoke anyway," she said with a dismissive wave. She passed behind a pallet stacked high with bags of rock salt and stood at the opened back door while the others sat on folding chairs behind the snowplow. Sparky finished lighting the hurricane lanterns. The four axes leaned against a back tire of the truck.

The silver sword lay across Raeven's lap. In spite of Sweeney's objections, she had already taken off two more pieces of armor in order to sit comfortably. She still wore the breastplate, helmet and two rusted chainmail gauntlets, but had discarded all the ludicrous hanging pieces. Her long black skirt, torn from her ordeal in the salvage yard, draped over her combat boots and onto the floor.

"This is my strategy," Sweeney said.

"Speak up," Pearl called from the door. "The car engine is still running, I can't hear you." Her lighter flame briefly illuminated her profile.

"This is what I propose," he said, louder. "The three of you will climb the mountain."

"Four," Pearl said.

"*Three*," Sweeney repeated. "I realize it's a frightening prospect, but a necessary one if we expect to rescue your friends."

"We do," Raeven said, her voice muffled by the visor. She had tried to keep it up but it closed each time with a startling clang and she soon gave up.

"I have climbed Skellig Michael many times – not with armor, though carrying heavy packs and in all forms of inclement weather. It will be an arduous climb, but not overly so. There are, however, a few treacherous places you should know about." He opened his notebook and showed them a likeness of Skellig Michael, hastily drawn. He drew a crooked line up the side of the mountain to indicate the staircase and pointed to a spot near the top. "It becomes quite narrow here, with a cliff on one side and a deep gully on the other. This version of it may be a good deal worse. We don't know that yet. Once you pass, the way is clear to the ruins. The trick is to refrain from looking down. Trust me on this."

He tore the page from the notebook and handed it to Raeven. She opened her visor to study it while he drew another diagram, this time a bird's eye view of the summit with a map of the *clocháin* and the oratory. "The large round circles here are the monks' cells," he explained. "This larger structure behind...I'm not entirely sure what it is. It appears to be a massive and profane replica of the tiny chapel upon Skellig Michael, built in later centuries in honor of the Archangel Michael, though I daresay Michael is nowhere to be found in this particular version. This one is large enough to be Romanesque in design. If so, it will be shaped like a cross, with this central part, the nave, as a Great Hall, which we may also assume is the main lair."

Raeven's visor slipped down with a sharp clang that made everyone jump, even Pearl, twenty feet away at the door. "Will you *please* stop doing that?" she said with her hand over her heart.

"I can't help it."

"Then take it off."

Raeven complied in spite of Dr. Sweeney's disapproving scowl. "Be certain you put it back on before you start," he said and returned to his map while Pearl returned to her vigil.

Something moved.

She threw down her cigarette and squinted, and she gasped, her heart stung by the sight of two fiery points of lights staring down from the top of the mountain. "Hey guys," she whispered, but couldn't make herself heard.

"As for me," Sweeney continued, tearing another page from his notebook, "I'll be down here, trying to keep it from following you."

"It's out there," Pearl said, stumbling toward them. Sweeney blanched and snapped his notebook shut. They followed her to the door and saw the two smoldering lights moving along the summit. "That's it," Raeven said in a sudden panic. "That's what I saw in the junk yard. Those are its eyes."

"Now what?" Sparky asked in a strained whisper. Sweeney looked around and wiped his mouth with the back of his hand.

"Better tell us fast," Pearl said. "It's coming down." She brought her hand to her lips, nearly covering her mouth when she said, "It's *sliding* down."

"Help me to the car," Sweeney said.

Sparky didn't hesitate. He grabbed the professor around the chest, pulled him to the car and dropped him into the front seat. Sweeney felt his pockets. "My coat! The gold link is in the pocket."

Pearl ran back into the garage to retrieve it.

"I'll drive through town," Sweeney said, fighting down his alarm. "I'll try to lure it away while you attempt to rescue Joe and Father Toomey."

"But what about–?"

"No time to explain, Constable. Do your best. We'll meet back here after you've found them."

Pearl emerged from the garage and handed Sweeney his coat and broom crutch.

"Here it comes," Raeven said and they lifted their gaze to the summit. Its eyes burned as before, but now they could make out the shadowy bulk behind, moving steadily down the slope.

Dr. Sweeney rolled down the car window. "Stay inside until it has passed. Do not make a sound. We want it to follow me." He reached through and grabbed Raeven by the arm. "Be valor blessed, my dear." After rolling up the window, he drove in a wide circle around the driveway. The headlights snapped on and swept across the jack-in-the-pulpit to give him a last glimpse of Sparky, Raeven and Pearl – the Three – heading back to the garage to search for places to hide. "Be valor blessed, all of you."

4

"Blow out the lanterns," Sparky whispered. "Is the back door locked?"

"Yes," Pearl said, terrified but trying to remain calm. "What about the front?"

"Locked."

Raeven stripped off more armor. "I can't move in it," she said in answer to Sparky's frown.

"Okay, whatever, fine. Blow out that lantern beside you. Pearl, get the one on the tailgate." Two puffs: the garage dimmed. Sparky stepped up to the last remaining lamp but froze at the sound of the corrugated metal walls and roof shivering as though caught in a sudden, chill wind.

It was right outside.

Nobody moved.

The lamp still burned on the chair beside Sparky. They looked at each other, not daring to move, not daring to breathe.

With a low rumbling snarl, it pressed against the building and clattered over the corrugated wall, bending each sheet of metal inward as it passed.

Pearl closed her eyes and swallowed hard. Her knees were so weak she feared she might collapse.

Sparky blew out the lantern. Darkness dropped over them, and seconds of blind tension that felt like long minutes.

It grated against the outside wall again, this time with a throaty growl.

The three stood motionless and stared at nothing while it lumbered to the front of the building. The rhythmic tremor of its footsteps vibrated in the concrete floor.

It pushed against the front doors. They bent inward. The steel hinges whined.

Sparky prayed the locks and latches would hold and nearly sighed with relief when the doors moved back again. It seemed to be testing the building's strength, though he couldn't understand why something so large and powerful would bother when it could smash through the flimsy walls with a single swipe of its claws.

He jumped, startled, when the entire garage lit up in blue. Raeven waved her hand to get their attention: she put her finger to her lips and pointed at the ceiling.

The metal roof squirmed with electrical charges. They chased each other in silent frenzy through the corrugated valleys and along the connecting steel beams and rafters.

Sparky moved up close beside her. "What's it doing?"

Raeven gasped and clapped a hand over his mouth. Too late.

The electricity went out.

A few lingering traces flickered across the ceiling. Raeven's eyes widened and she looked around in a sudden panic. Her gaze settled on the snowplow. She rushed to it and dropped to the floor and the others followed her under the truck as the last of the charges sputtered out.

Darkness once again swept over them, and silence but for the sound of their breathing, tight with fear.

A sudden harsh shriek of metal followed as wide panels and twisted aluminum girders crashed in and around the truck and another charge of blue light surged through the garage, this time with a deadly sizzle.

Pearl covered her ears. Raeven grabbed her by the wrist and shook her head, once again warning them not to make a sound.

They huddled on the cold cement floor and listened to the assault on the roof. Back-shivering screeches of metal echoed around them. A thick, gelatinous drop of venom landed on the floor with a splat. It bubbled like acid eating into the concrete and sent acrid yellow smoke drifting under the truck. Raeven recognized the smell from the junkyard van. She imagined it had torn a hole in the roof and that its head now hovered above them, peering straight down.

She knew this was so when its tongue, the thing she most dreaded, dropped into sight and began to wander through the garage, flicking objects out of its path. Each of the forked pointed tips moved independently and at times gave it an appearance of walking, as if two tiny legs carried the bulk of the black stinking mass over the oily floor. Every fifteen seconds or so, it pulled back with a hollow slurp, only to reappear steaming and glistening with a fresh coat of venom.

It wandered over the bags of rock salt and brushed against the chairs where they had been sitting only moments before. A hurricane lantern fell from one and rolled with a clatter beneath the truck. Raeven's heart stopped when the tongue followed, slithering in a path leading straight to Pearl, who now looked at her, her face a distorted mask of horror.

The creature snorted. Dust lifted from the floor and rolled over them.

The tongue moved closer. One of the forked tips stretched toward Pearl's foot.

Raeven knew that one touch would send it coiling like a python around her leg as it had with Chip's arm. With as much calm as she could muster, she picked up the overturned lantern and rolled it away from the truck. The tongue followed, leaving a blistering trail of slime behind.

Pearl slumped and her eyes rolled back. Sparky caught her before her head hit the floor.

The tongue touched the lantern and passed over it, once again inspecting the chairs. Raeven touched Sparky's ankle and pointed at the floor beneath her chair. The armor.

The tongue circled around it, lazily investigating the surroundings. Terrified it would recognize it as Donal's and realize for certain they were inside the garage, Raeven tried to mentally will it from the helmet and breastplate, *Move away, move away,* but the circling continued, tightening inward toward the helmet.

They touched.

The tongue froze.

It touched the breastplate and froze again before drifting up out of their sight without a sound.

The light dimmed.

Nothing happened. A full minute passed in silence.

A footstep – and another – and then came a series of footsteps quivering away from the garage. Pearl took them as a sign to move. The rancid smell of venom and saliva repulsed her. "I've got to get out of here," she whispered and Raeven nearly fainted at the sound. She knew the monster's stealth, knew its cunning, and she waved her hands in the dimming light and shook her head.

"I don't care," Pearl whispered. "I can't stand it."

Raeven took a chance. "It's still out there."

A horn sounded, thin and distant, as insistent as a car alarm. They realized Dr. Sweeney had seen or heard the attack and was trying to lure the creature away from the garage.

A low grunt came from outside. Pearl's jaw dropped. Raeven was right – it *hadn't* gone. It was still there, waiting for them to emerge, but after the grunt came heavy plodding footsteps with no effort toward concealment and before long even Raeven felt certain it had been lured away to follow what it believed to be the Knight and its lost golden link.

"Now," she said and they scrambled out of their hiding place. Sparky lit a lantern while Pearl retrieved the sword. Raeven removed the last few pieces of armor. "It's useless and we don't have time." She paused, startled to see more lines had twined from her *doom* tattoo with the same midnight blue of a broken blood vessel. "All we really need is the sword and the shields," she said and hid her wrist from the others. "Maybe the helmet too."

"Should we take the lanterns?" Pearl asked.

"One each." Raeven cradled her helmet in the crook of her arm. "And maybe we should take–" She stopped speaking and looked down at the floor and behind her chair.

"What's the matter?" Sparky asked. Before she could answer, he came to the same realization and slapped his open palm against his forehead. "Oh man! I left them in the trunk!"

"What?" Pearl asked.

"The shields," Raeven said, and dropped her helmet against her leg. The visor clanged. "Doesn't matter," she said with a shrug. "If that thing catches us up on that mountain, it won't matter how many shields we have."

Sparky pulled the back door open a crack. "All clear," he whispered. Raeven followed him to the side of the garage, staying as close to the wall as possible. He peered around the corner but saw nothing. Pearl appeared in the doorway behind them, silhouetted by lantern-light.

"I see why it didn't tear down the garage," Raeven said. She pointed to a wide band of jack-in-the-pulpit around the garage. "No tracks." Beyond the dragonroot patch the snow had been trampled into slush. "It didn't touch any of the plants around the garage. It must have been standing in the woods and used its head to push against the walls. That's why it went for the roof. It could reach down through without touching the dragonroot."

"Maybe we should take some with us," Pearl said, awed by the power of the lowly plants. "I'll find something to put it in."

"Use this," Raeven said and held out her helmet. "I don't want to wear it anyway."

5

They left the garage and passed through the field of jack-in-the-pulpit to the edge of the parking lot. "Here we go," Raeven said and stepped onto the first of the low granite steps. She had tucked the hem of her dress into her belt to free her legs, exposing her torn black tights and combat boots. Sparky held the lantern high and peered at the garage and beyond it toward the empty town. Nothing moved. Nothing made a sound. He turned to follow Pearl and Raeven and tripped, nearly dropping his lantern on the granite steps.

"Be careful," Raeven called from the front. "There's ice all over these stairs."

"Vines, too," he said.

The two women looked at each other. "Vines," Pearl repeated with a nervous smile and Raeven began to climb.

The fog-bound stairs were interrupted every thirty steps by a short narrow landing that served as a natural resting place. As soon as they passed above the tree line, Sparky suggested they extinguish the lanterns so they wouldn't be seen from a distance. They left them on the next landing to be picked up on the way back down, and they continued on with the ghostly flares at the summit lighting their way through a thickening fog that crested over the landings in billowing waves.

"You okay up there?" Sparky asked after passing over a rough spot where some of the stones had loosened and threatened to break away.

"Fine," Pearl said, "but I'm afraid to look down. And these stairs are as icy as - ow!"

"What happened?" Sparky asked from below.

"Got caught on some thorns."

"Me too," he said. "They're all over the place."

Puzzled, Raeven took off her glove and felt the step above, clear and cold with a thin veneer of ice. "Pearl, you see this step?" She slapped it with her open palm. "Tell me when you get to it." She put her glove back on. "There's another landing up ahead."

Once there, she chanced a quick look down. Burne Notch sprawled out below as a lightless realm of shadow surrounded by the brilliant fire wall that lay over the land like an illuminated snake. Beyond it, tiny flashing red and white lights moved to and fro, and further, small constellations of light glittered from the neighboring lake towns where the snow lay upon the hilltops and pastures in swaths of royal blue splendor. She tucked the hem of her dress back into her belt and sat down. "You reach that step yet?"

"I'm here now. What about it?" Raeven asked her if she felt anything. Pearl took her glove off and patted the surface. "Only vines, the same as the others."

Raeven stood again. "I don't think we should take a break."

"I do," Pearl said and climbed the last two stairs to the landing. "Need to catch my breath." She inhaled deeply and let it out again. "Freakin' cigarettes," she said and reached into her pocket for another.

Raeven eyed the stairs above. "We need to keep moving."

Sparky reached the landing and stood at its edge, gazing over the valley. "Those flashing lights outside the wall must be fire trucks, or maybe military."

"Please, let's go," Raeven said. "Something's going on."

Sparky studied the tilted ski slope that ran alongside the landing. "There's a clear trail of ice over here. That's what it slid down, that's why it came so fast."

Pearl wasn't listening: she had noted the anxiety in Raeven's voice and now watched her move further up the stairs. "Hey, Raev, you all right?"

"That step you touched, the one with the vines…it was clear when I passed."

Pearl flicked on her lighter. "Oh, wow," she whispered at the sight of a thin tangle of blackberry vines emerging from under the snow like baby snakes. They wriggled and snarled into a loose flat web upon the stairs separating her from Raeven. "Come on," Pearl said and pulled Sparky forward by his sleeve.

The climb became more grueling, with vines impeding their progress, sometimes requiring all three to help untangle a trouser leg or coat sleeve. Each time, Raeven urged them on.

"I can't," Sparky said. "I'm still stuck here. What *are* these things?"

"Blackberry vines," Pearl said. "We saw them in the bog."

Sparky studied the steps below, now writhing with vines, and the clear ones above Raeven. He felt a thin strangling rush about his feet and a vine twined around his leg. Pearl cried out and he knew the same had happened to her. "Grab my hand," Raeven said, but when Pearl reached for it, a whip-like vine snaked around her wrist. Pearl untangled it but another twined around her elbow. Briars snagged her glove. "I can't break loose."

The blackberry vines did not touch Raeven. They snarled around Sparky and Pearl and knotted their ankles with prickly shoots. They rose further to their knees, and now it became more than clear these were no ordinary vines, this was no ordinary entanglement. Pearl looked at Raeven, her eyes filled with silent alarm. She handed her the helmet filled with dragonroot. "Wait, Pearl," Raeven cried in a panic. "Don't!"

"They're dropping away," Sparky cried and the two women gasped with relief, though it faded when the vines released Sparky and spread over Pearl. "Oh, no, no," she said when they spread up to her waist and higher, encircling her in a squirming net. She tried to push them away, but each movement of her arm brought additional brambles to twine around her elbow. Every twist of her leg attracted two more to wind about her ankle.

Sparky pulled at the briars from behind, Raeven pulled from the front, but it was no use. They twisted over Pearl's head. She stared at Raeven from inside the snarl, her eyes wide with terror. "Don't leave me!" Raeven shouted but Pearl dropped away and disappeared in the enclosing briars. "Don't go!" She lifted the sword and brought it down with a strangled cry. The thick blade glanced off without cutting through a single vine and clanged on the granite step at her feet.

Pearl heard her cries but could do little more than fight the twisting snarl. The thorns did not harm her, did not give her even a superficial scratch: they seemed to retract whenever they touched bare skin but came out in force to tear into her clothing and in this way pulled her away from Raeven and transferred her down a step, and another, buoyed within their bulk until she felt a strong hand close around her arm from behind. "Oh, my God, Sparky," she cried and the vines eased her further down. Sparky threw his arms around her and pulled. When he did, the vines relaxed into a jumble of coiling shoots and released her before advancing another step higher.

"How could that happen?" she exclaimed, undone by the ordeal. "Where's Raeven?"

Sparky's grip tightened at her question.

She swiveled within his embrace and stared at the briars, now thick on the stairs, utterly still, and risen to a height of over fifteen feet. "Oh no," she whispered. The same realization had come to Raeven on the other side.

She had ended her struggle when she heard Pearl emerge into Sparky's arms and she stared at the thorny lattice, impenetrable, with no weak place to climb through. They couldn't go around at the sides. The tangle occurred at the very spot Sweeney warned them was most perilous, with sheer cliffs on both sides.

"Can you cut through it?" Pearl called. Raeven told them the sword wasn't sharp enough. Sparky suggested the axes but they had left them in the garage and would have to climb back down to get them.

Raeven looked up at the summit with its crooked walls and domed rooftops grim against the murky sky. "You guys, I think..." She ran her glove over her cheek. "I think I should keep going." Pearl and Sparky exchanged glances. "And that was a good idea, Sparky," Raeven continued. "Go back down for the axes. I'll need to get back through this on the way down."

"Wait a minute, we can't just leave you here," Pearl said. "We're in this together. We're the Three!"

"I'll be fine." Raeven tried to mask the tremble in her voice. "I've got the sword and the dragonroot. You two go. I'll look for Joey and Father Toomey. We'll be back down to meet you here in no time, right?" She heard no answer from the other side. "Right?"

"Right," Pearl whispered.

"Right," Raeven repeated and she lifted the helmet and once again looked at the summit. She took her first step toward it but stopped again with dread falling thick upon her heart when Pearl said: "Good luck, kid," and left her to follow Sparky down the stairs.

6

The car stalled.

Dr. Sweeney had tried to rescue it: he shifted gears, he groaned when he slammed his injured foot down on the clutch, but it was no use. He turned the headlights off and sat back and listened, first to the click of the cooling engine and then to a low distant growl worming its way into the car.

Soon after leaving the garage, he came to the same realization that had struck Sparky: all three shields were still in the trunk. His earlier regret about this now turned to relief. They might be his only hope.

He hobbled to the trunk, hyperventilating. A slow pulse of footsteps quivered around him. Light flashed over his shoulder and fell upon the shields. He turned and was stung into near paralysis at the sight of the creature looming out of the darkness at the far end of the deserted residential street.

Lights flickering at the roadside played over its body and defined its muscle structure with shadows and light and imparted an ephemeral quality overall, as if the monster was materializing and disappearing in sections. It moved its head from side to side and periodically thrust it forward. Each time it did, a new light flashed and it cocked its head and listened for a moment before continuing on.

Coming closer, it once again made the peculiar thrusting movement. Windows brightened, an outside streetlight flashed, and Sweeney realized it was pushing power into houses in its search. Porch lights flickered until it moved on, satisfied the house was empty. Lights snapped on at the next house in its path, this time illuminating strings of Christmas bulbs still there from the previous December. It peered into a car parked beside the road and nudged it with its snout. The car rocked. The headlights snapped on. Its tongue snaked out to taste the air and it snorted. The lights went out.

The stalled police car would be useless as a hiding place. He pulled one of the shields from the trunk and hobbled to the front. On his right lay a field with its far edge bordered by a band of trees stretching toward a solitary farmhouse in the distance. On the left, a steep snowy hill rose up from the roadside, impossible to climb with his injury.

Not much of a choice.

He clutched the shield close and used his broomstick crutch to limp into the field where he faced a new decision: band of trees or house? If he made it to the house he could hide in the cellar. The trees were closer, but he did not know if he would find shelter in their depths or a thicket of sinister pines.

He headed toward the house. As he did, all movement stopped behind, and all sound.

He took another step. His breath rose in a cloud.

He felt it then, eyes staring at him, boring into his back. He froze with his injured foot off the ground and the crutch under his arm. He held the shield tight against his chest.

He tried to swallow but couldn't. He glanced over his shoulder.

It was there.

It was looking at him.

It had emerged from between the rows of houses and now stood motionless in the road, a colossal figure of darkness, black against the surrounding shadows. A broad expanse of field lay between them, but the creature could cross it in no time. Sweeney could not make it to the house, could not make it to the forest. He had nowhere to go and didn't know what to do. He stood without moving, praying it would think he was something else, a tree or stump, and move on.

But no, he realized. The gold link lay within in his pocket. He might as well have held up a flare.

He scanned the field, hoping to find a place to hide. Nothing, nothing…until a black circle below the road caught his eye. It looked like the entrance to a tunnel. *It better be*, he thought when a rush of movement stirred behind.

He didn't wait. He didn't look. He used his crutch for the first two steps but a loud snort persuaded him to throw it down and run toward the black circle, injury be damned. Pain tore up from his foot but he couldn't stop. He focused on the black circle looming before him and tried to block out the huffing breath and throb of footsteps, closer now, crushing ice and snow.

Electricity squirmed in a thousand hissing tendrils to illuminate the field, the black circle, and he saw that – yes! It *was* a tunnel, a drainage culvert built beneath the road to divert the spring run-off from the hill on the other side.

He raced toward it and dove and the massive jaws closed behind him with a blistering *crack*!

He tumbled in a heap before the entrance. It lunged again. He rolled onto his back and lifted the shield.

It stopped short and pulled back, shaking its head. Venom spumed and hissed, and in that brief pause, Dr. Sweeney dropped the shield and scrambled into the culvert, unaware it had once sheltered a tortured Raleigh Marcotte transforming into the atrocity that now clambered onto the roadway above.

He cowered inside and prayed it would lose interest and go away – a futile prayer, he realized, when he lay against the cold steel surrounded by the broken phones left behind by Raleigh and listened to a violent rasp of claws tearing into the asphalt above.

Seconds later, a great talon ripped through the steel. He scrambled back toward the entrance when it pulled back and tore a long gash that sent soil and lumps of asphalt pouring down like sand in an hourglass.

It leaned in close, its nostrils over the gash. A snort of malodorous breath filled the culvert.

It snorted again and moved away. The gravel stopped clattering. Dr. Sweeney imagined it crouched upon the road, glancing from side to side like a cat waiting for a mouse to emerge from a cardboard tube. He worried it might have created a large enough hole to reach through and he moved further from the center, closer toward the field – as soon as he did, a claw dove in at the side, clattering on the steel, grasping.

The curved tip of a talon caught his coat and dragged him toward the entrance but he struggled and slipped out of it.

The claw withdrew with the empty coat and Sweeney pounded his fist on the corrugated wall at the growl of frustration above. "Ha! Missed me," he whispered, even as he knew it hadn't missed at all. It had his coat, and with it, the gold link. It had what it wanted without confronting the person it thought was the Knight. He began to relax a bit, believing he was safe. It would not continue its excavation.

A vein of electricity appeared beyond the end of the culvert where the hill rose up beside the road. It flitted and traced a jagged steaming line in the snow. A second current joined it and a thin stream of run-off water from the melting snow lifted over the bottom lip of the culvert and glistened with reflected light. "Now what are you up to?" he whispered, perplexed by the twining charges.

A third charge braided into the first two and they began to hum. Dr. Sweeney moved closer to the center, cautious but fascinated. The first trickle of warm water passed through the low piles of dirt, asphalt and broken telephones.

A thought struck him, but he banished it as too complex for a reptilian brain, too analytical. Still…a fourth charge of electricity joined the others to melt more snow and the water rose higher. Steam began to lift and fill the culvert.

"Ah, you're a bold one," Sweeney whispered as yet another of his theories began to collapse and he realized that the creature was, indeed, using guile instead of brute force to extract him from the culvert. A sudden great flash finalized his fear.

A blanket of voltage spread over the hill. Heated water poured from the top and melted more snow. Within seconds the hill ran dark with rivulets of hot water that met in a larger flowing stream with nowhere to go but the culvert.

The water rose from six inches to eight. Loose sticks floated inside and gathered at the pile of dirt and asphalt until the piles softened into mud and gave way. Thick, steamy fog surrounded him.

Sweeney dug his fingers into the corrugated sides of the culvert valleys, but each time he caught hold, a new surge of snow-water poured through to loosen his grip and push him closer to the field-side entrance.

A last sizzling blast melted the remaining snow into a flash flood that overwhelmed the capacity of the culvert. He could no longer endure it – not for lack of strength, but lack of air. The water rose higher, he took a final choking breath, it roiled over him and, *this is it,* he thought and let go.

He shot through the culvert and emerged in a gush of steaming water into the field where he slid on the melting ice, turning this way and that until he plowed straight into a monstrous foreleg.

He lay on his back before it.

It stared without moving. A series of thin scaly folds at the sides of its neck began to expand, one by one, until its hood stood out, taut and full.

It snapped at the air, but did not attack. *It thinks I'm the Knight.* Remembering Raeven's confrontation on the Coachlight Road, he sat up and mustered enough strength to say in a weak, hoarse voice: "Bugger off."

It jerked back and tilted its head.

Sweeney tried again. "Bugger…" he began, but his voice trailed off.

A claw shot out and closed around him. It sat on its haunches and lifted him close, staring. It glanced at the coat tangled in its left claw and back at Sweeney. It jerked its head. Tiny veins of electricity appeared as if thrust from its pores. They played about its snout and the bony ridge above its eyes, and cast enough light to illuminate the professor's face. It leaned closer, studying him – its eyes suddenly widened and it reared back in something close to shock.

Its hood retracted with a whooshing *crack*, its neck twisted sharply, and it cast its eyes upon the distant mountaintop.

It threw its head back with a howl of rage and strode onto the road on its two hind legs. It held Dr. Sweeney close, but careless now, and when it stormed past the stalled police car it dropped him…a mindless action, the casual discarding of a forgotten object, but to terrible effect. The back of his head struck the car with a blow nearly as strong as the one dealt him by Steven Wilcox on Skellig Michael. He fell rolling onto the road and by the time he stopped, coatless, wet and unconscious, the great monstrosity was already on its way to the mountaintop to catch a trespasser.

7

Pearl and Sparky collected the lanterns they'd left on the landing and lit them before reaching the bottom of the staircase. Once down, they ran to the garage through a field of jack-in-the-pulpit that had rippled out to cover the entire parking lot up to the edges of the woods.

Inside, Sparky lifted his lantern and studied the hole in the roof and the torn strands of sheet metal littering the floor. Pearl, still distraught over their separation from Raeven, brushed past him to gather up the axes to cut through the briar wall. "I don't know how she's supposed to do this. I don't know how anyone thinks she can do it alone."

"No one thinks that. Be careful of that metal, those edges are sharp."

"Someone does, or some *thing*. Whoever or whatever is doing all that aligning crap. Where are they?"

Sparky held his lantern higher. "There against the tire."

"I don't think she can do it, Spark. Not with wilted jack-in-the-pulpit and that sword, which I think is a piece of junk."

Sparky nodded in sheepish agreement. "Yeah, I'm not too good at blacksmithing."

"I didn't mean that." She shouldered two axes and picked her way back through the torn metal to the door. "I mean the sword itself, and the cross it's made from. It doesn't seem right to me. It never did."

Sparky stepped in front of her. "What's wrong with it?"

"I don't know, I can't explain it." She hesitated. "I know – I don't know *how* I know, but somehow I know that Donal didn't kill the thing on Skellig Michael. Brendan did. And there's something about the sword, something wrong with it. We better go."

"Wait, wait, we need to figure this out."

"I don't know what it is," Pearl said and left the garage. "I don't know."

They had decided to risk keeping the lanterns lit on the climb back up as the icy stairs and briars were far too treacherous now. Sparky continued to pester her until, finally: "Now, Pearl. I'm not moving another step until you tell me what you think is wrong with the sword."

They had reached a landing a little more than halfway between the bottom of the mountain and the briar fence. Sparky coaxed her to sit on a step and held his lantern up to illuminate her face.

She dropped her head into her hands. "It's not the sword, it's the cross."

Sparky knelt beside her. He pulled one of her hands from her face and held it in his. "I'm pushing you on this because I feel the same thing."

"I felt it back at the cave," she said. "Steven Wilcox supposedly brought it there."

"Right, yes."

"He found it at the church."

"Right."

Pearl looked at him, her eyes dark and questioning. "So who told him it was there?"

Sparky sat back on balls of his feet. Pearl could tell by his expression that a dam had given way to release a flood of thought. "That's it," he whispered and let go of her hand. "That's *it!* That's what's been bugging me all along. The cross was supposed to protect him. Steven was guided to it, the same way he was guided to the cave. And we assume Lochru – the *mind* of Lochru was the guide."

"Right. So?"

"So why would Lochru guide him to the one thing that could protect him?" He looked at Pearl: she looked at him. "It's not the right cross," she whispered.

Sparky nodded. "Which means it's not the right sword. He must have known Steven wouldn't go for the gold unless he thought he was protected. He tricked him. Pearl…"

She had turned to look beyond the briar fence at the summit. A distant roll of thunder rumbled in the sky. "We can't leave her."

"We have to find the right cross."

"How?" she asked, her voice strained. The thunder rumbled again, louder.

"I don't know, but we have to try. It's the only way to kill this thing. If we don't find it, it won't matter if we help Raeven or not. It'll be over for all of – "

Pearl grabbed him by the arm, her stricken gaze fixed upon the road far below.

Sparky spun around on the landing.

As soon as their minds registered it by sight, their hearing transformed what had sounded like rumbling thunder into the full throbbing reality of its footsteps storming down the deserted road. Snow exploded from the roadside trees like smoke trailing behind a fearsome missile.

When it reached the garage, it came to a sliding stop at the edge of the parking lot and snarled in fury. "Dragonroot," Pearl whispered.

It circled around the hated weed and crashed into the forest beside the parking lot, heading for the stairs.

"Lanterns," Pearl said. She reached for the latch to extinguish it.

"No time!" He grabbed them by their handles and threw them as far as he could down the icy path the creature had used on its earlier descent. Flames filled their glass chimneys and they exploded in a wash of burning oil.

Pearl searched for a way off the stairs. "Over there!" She pointed to a stand of maple and birch saplings about ten feet away from the staircase. The upward thrust of the mountain had been so extreme that their trunks lay nearly horizontal and appeared more like the rungs of a ladder than trees. "Can we get to them?"

Sparky crawled to the edge of the landing. A nearly vertical drop straight down to a pile of jagged rocks separated the trees and staircase. "This is what we'll do," he said. A pine tree whined below. It boomed down upon the garage. "I'll go first. Let me get a good grip on those birch trees and then you follow. Leave the axes here. Think you can do it?"

A second tree snapped and fell below. "I'll try." She looked down the staircase. Trees moved beside the garage, whining, cracking, falling. "Go," she said, and he took two running steps and leaped.

He landed in a clatter and swish of branches. The smaller birch saplings bent beneath his weight but he managed to wrap his legs around a sturdier maple and haul himself into a sitting position. "Okay, now you. Get a running start like I did. Hurry."

Another tree fell, and another, and then there were no more trees.

Pearl looked down again. "Oh man," she whispered, stung by

the sight of it heading for the staircase.

"Hurry," Sparky said. The creature began to climb. Its claws gouged into the stairs. "Now!"

Pearl ran and leaped, but not far enough. Sparky leaned out and caught her coat sleeve and she gasped, afraid to scream even when she plowed into the trees below his feet. She reached up through her sleeve and caught him by the wrist with one hand and pawed at the saplings with the other. She kicked at the slippery birches, trying to find a solid footing.

"Don't struggle," he said and he leaned from his tree with his legs wrapped around the maple trunk. He slipped his free hand around her forearm and whispered, low and intense: *"Don't. Move."*

The great beast raced up the staircase like a locomotive out of control. Granite stairs tumbled beneath the violence of its claws. Pearl closed her eyes, shocked by intensity of sound and the torrent of cracking stone and ice as its head passed with a flash of red from a luminous eye, the colossal body, and finally the ridged tail swinging back and forth. It swept over Sparky and uprooted three of the maples into a tumbling fall to the rocks far below.

He hauled on Pearl's arm and she slid closer to his tree. "Now," he said through gritted teeth and pulled her up into its branches.

A dark shape hurtled down the broken staircase and plummeted off the landing. They looked up – the creature tore at the stone steps beneath the briars to dislodge them while thrashing at the vines with its teeth, and the granite blocks now came tumbling down, end over end.

"Raeven," Pearl said in a choked whisper and Sparky threw his arms around her: "Nothing we can do now."

They began to half-slide, half-climb down the trees to escape the falling stairs. "There *is* something," Pearl said. "Dr. Sweeney said the monks 'fashioned' a cross from the sword; I'm sure that's what he said. I wouldn't use that word to mean 'melting'." He looked at her, puzzled. "Oh, Spark, it's all so close, it's right here in my mind, but I can't–"

A single, unexpected, drawn-out *caaaaw* interrupted her. They looked down and saw three ravens wheeling through the air above the garage. One soared up toward them and passed through the horizontal trees before dropping again to join the others. Pearl watched their elegant flight, the graceful wings and intricate spirals, and she gasped as if struck by a sudden thought. "I know where it is," she whispered. "Can we climb all the way down on these trees?"

"I think so. Where to?"

"The church," Pearl said and she slipped down through the

branches to the next tree. "It's what we thought before. It's on the steeple."

"But wait, you said the cross up on top was too small, you said it was black."

"It is."

Sparky ran his hand through his hair, trying not to betray his frustration. "The one we need is silver."

"I know that," Pearl said, climbing down to another tree. "And if you ever worked in a restaurant – a really nice one, I mean – you'd know what I meant."

"I don't understand," Sparky said climbing down beside her. "If it's silver how can it be black?"

She touched his mouth with her fingers and whispered one word: "Tarnish."

8

After leaving the briar wall, Raeven tried to follow Dr. Sweeney's instructions. *Don't look down. Keep a steady even pace.* She climbed the last of the treacherous staircase and passed into the shadow of the abbey with weakened legs and knees trembling from the exertion, and she sat on a large flat rock with her chest heaving. The hem of her dress had fallen out of her belt again but she didn't bother to fix it. She rolled her head back and winced at the burn of frigid air entering her lungs. She looked at the flat rock and saw that a hole had been cut into its center the size of a dinner plate. She reached into it, felt its smooth sides. *Wonder what that was for?*

She turned to the abbey and saw a Seven-Up sign swinging back and forth against the wall. She began to notice more reminders that this had once been the lift house: an overturned lift-chair, a wet cardboard box filled with snow-covered packets of Swiss Miss hot chocolate, a set of deer antlers set jauntily upon a boulder, as if the rock had sprouted them; a soft drink dispenser leaning against a large circular building she took to be one of the *clochán* Dr. Sweeney spoke about.

Broken bottles littered the ground. She used one to cut her dress into a more manageable length below her knee and approached the first dark cell. "Joe?" Her voice sounded dank and resonant, as if she had whispered into a slimy well. "Joey? Are you in here?"

No answer. "Joey?" She slid one foot over the stone floor. The word echoed in the stillness. He wasn't there. She sensed it. No one was there. She backed out of the first *clochán* and headed for the next when a gust of icy wind moaned over the summit. She turned to shield her face from the blast and saw a shift in the dull blue glow that filtered through the arched windows of the monstrous abbey.

After setting the helmet filled with dragonroot in the crook of her arm and laying the sword over her shoulder, she straightened–"okay then," she said, "okay,"–and walked toward the high ruin.

She entered the main hall through a gaping hole in the wall and gazed upon a ceiling forested with stalactites. Most pulsated with an inner fire, blue, silent, and shimmering. Those closest to the tilting walls hung like illuminated daggers. Moving inward, they grew dimmer by degrees until those in the center hung dark and glassy, emitting no light of their own but reflecting the more brilliant spikes in their grey-blue depths.

The same flat-sided stones littered the floor, with the same hole cut into each and a host of bright objects scattered among them. Raeven made her way to one of these, a crown of gold that sparkled in the blue light. A medallion hung beside it, draped over the side of a rock. Beyond it, lay a sky-blue princess phone. Other objects lay nearby: broken chairs, golden necklaces studded with jewels, upended tables with plastic tablecloths, shimmering chalices, and telephones everywhere.

Her class ring was there somewhere. She shuddered at the thought that Uncle Lung's teeth were probably there too, still embedded in his mutilated jaw. She tried to push the gruesome notion from her mind but a glimpse of a withered arm stolen from St. Bernadette's Cemetery with its fingers bejeweled with rings reinforced the nightmare. She wandered through the gloom like a sleep-walker, using the silver sword as a walking stick to keep her balance and holding the dragonroot helmet close each time she stumbled. The sword struck something soft. She peered down into the shadows and saw a leg. It had been severed above the knee. A gold ankle bracelet shimmered above a fuzzy orange slipper.

9

"Please don't be dead," Joe whispered to the cage in the gloomy distance. The priest had not spoken in some time and did not respond when Joe called. "I can't be here alone. Please wake up, please." Grief and fear of isolation collided and he slammed his fists against the glass cage. It didn't budge. It didn't crack. Tears of frustration rose to his eyes. If only he could get out, if only he could warn Raeven about the false sword, but now a new thought intruded, laced with despair: *it doesn't matter, nothing can stop that thing.* It was futile, hopeless, and he now faced a long, painful slide from life by dehydration or starvation like the long ago lost maidens of *Baile na Sceilge*. Father Toomey was already dead or close to it. He called to him again, but again heard no response.

And then a voice called from the shadows, a single word echoing through the cavern.

"Joey?"

He sat up but didn't dare breathe for fear the figure standing in the gap in the wall might be an hallucination that would evaporate at the sound of his voice – but it called again. "Joey...?"

"Raeven!" He collapsed with relief when she cried out and shouted his name again and again while scrambling over the granite blocks of the abbey floor. "I can't see you!" she cried. "Where are you?"

"Here!" His cage hung within a side chamber, smaller and much darker than the cavernous Great Hall. "Up here!" Joe slapped the glass webbing and Raeven looked up and gasped, shocked to see him inside the circular teardrop, the same as in her dreams. She stumbled over the stones with her eyes never leaving his until she stood beneath the cage.

He thrust his arm through an opening. She tried to touch his hand but couldn't reach it.

He shifted, his broken ribs flared, he inched down further, reaching.

She stood on her toes.

The tip of her middle finger barely grazed the tip of his but this fleeting connection ignited a flare of warmth and emotion that threatened to overwhelm them. Raeven dropped back on her heels. "Sit back." Joe pulled his hand into the cage. She set the helmet down and lifted the sword above her head with both hands.

"That's not it," Joe whispered but she didn't hear him. She tilted the blade back and swung it humming over her head to slam against the cage. Dark glass rained down upon her. She had broken through one of the webs.

Light flashed beyond the windows. Joe noticed it with a quick glance before it disappeared. "Try again. If you hit it in the same place, I think I can slip through."

The sword struck again with a thick metallic clang and the entire bottom let go. He dropped with a startled cry but grabbed one of the strands and hung swinging within a hail of tinkling glass shards. He released it and dropped to his feet and sank to the floor.

Wincing with pain, he grabbed her hand and rose to his knees. She fell to hers. The sword clattered beside them and they embraced. Pain coursed through his chest but she whispered "tighter," and he pulled her closer, and the pain swept through and told him he was alive, alive, he was still *alive*, and he covered her face in kisses, her cheeks, her eyes, her nose, the sutures with their tied off ends prickly against his lips; and she threw her head back and he kissed her throat and felt the vibration of her voice in his lips when she said, "I didn't know if I'd find you, I didn't know if I'd ever see you again."

Another light flashed beyond the window, this time with enough intensity to draw Joe's attention away from her. "Something's…"

She looked at the arched window in time to see a streak of light shoot past the window. She had seen them before, of course, but no longer viewed them as accidental meteors shooting out of a vast indifferent sky: she saw them now as messengers.

A pit opened in the center of her stomach – *but what is their message?*

She clambered over the stones and nearly tripped over a broken lift cable before reaching the arched window where she studied the radiant display of diagonal lines cutting through a cloth of darkness. The sky lit up with a sudden splash of green light, iridescent, pulsing, dancing and flitting. Another meteor shot through it: she traced its path to the slope now illuminated by the Northern Lights and – "Oh, my God," she said and stepped back from the window. "We've got to get out. Now."

"What is it?" Joe asked, and the answer came when a deep shivering growl filtered up from below.

"The briar wall might hold it back, but not for long." She looked past him and caught sight of the second cage hanging in the gloom. "Is that…?"

Joe followed her gaze. "We've got to get him down. Hurry!" They rushed over the stones and stood beneath the priest's cage.

Another furious growl swept through the cavern, followed by the clash of stairs torn asunder.

"Give me the sword," Joe said. He lifted it, but winced and dropped it again and clutched his side. "Something's broken," he said and handed it to her.

She shrugged to stretch her neck muscles and swung the blade. Again, the first blow broke off a piece. Before she could swing it again, a white bundle fell from the cage and landed on the rocks.

Joe crouched beside it. "What in the world...?"

"What is it?"

"A seagull!" He touched it with his forefinger. "It's dead."

Beside it lay the packet of folded parchment Father Toomey had earlier dropped from the cage. Joe slipped it into his coat pocket and moved away from the dead gull. "Try again." Outside, the growl sounded again, closer, louder; and Raeven swung the sword. The floor of the cage broke free and the priest's body dropped heavy upon the rocks.

He didn't react at all. "Father Toomey, are you all right?" Joe whispered. They could not see his face. He lay with his back to them, as inert and lifeless as the white bird. Joe reached out and poked him on the shoulder and the priest opened his eyes, one sightless and scarred and the other shimmering, pale, and exultant.

10

Dr. Sweeney groaned and "Oh, no, no," he whispered and shut his eyes against what he thought was an extension of a nightmare. A fragile cracked voice echoed his "no, no, no," and he opened them again to gaze upon a wizened toothless crone with a face deeply latticed with wrinkles, kneeling beside him and cradling his head in her lap. A blood-soaked rag tied around her head covered one eye. The other stared darkly.

He shivered and heard a crunch of frost. He had fallen in the road, wet and unconscious. His tweed jacket had frozen stiff. The ancient woman touched his cheek and pointed to the stalled police car.

"No good," he whispered but she pointed again and pulled at his arm. He sat up with a moan. "I told you, it's..." He fell silent when the lights snapped on, dim at first, and brightening when the engine turned over with a grinding effort and purred to life. The old woman stared down at him with her one visible eye and the headlights sparkled in its depths with such vitality that Sweeney could not help but marvel at its clarity in one so ancient.

She hobbled to the car and opened the back door.

Without protest, he climbed into the soft depths of the back seat and relished the feel of upholstery beneath his frigid hands and, more, the first breath of heat spilling over the front seat.

The front passenger door opened. He heard her slide inside, heard the gear shift move. He felt the first lurch forward and the deep vibration of the car moving down the road. He heard and felt everything except a driver.

They drove through town, past the shattered windows of Cumberland Farms and the hardware store, and there they came across a procession of trees. The car turned onto a side road to avoid them but they immediately came to a snowy intersection and another silent march of pines. This time a shudder passed through the car. "Heaven help us," Sweeney whispered at the sight of several massive, fully-grown pine trees moving with ponderous gait along the road. Unlike their smaller brethren, these did not drag themselves but walked upright upon thick roots that moved like the legs of a monstrous tarantula. They passed in front of the car, unmindful of their presence. Torn power cables and phone lines hung from their branches. A child's tire swing hung from one. On another, a collection of bird feeders clacked and swung, illuminated in the headlights.

Dr. Sweeney wished the ancient stranger would turn them off, but she sat motionless in the front seat and stared through the windshield while the car inched through the protesting slather of roots across the windows. "What are they?" he asked, clutching the back of the front seat. She pointed out the window and said, "Mu."

"I don't understand."

"Mu. Xian." She rapped upon her walking stick with her bony knuckles. "Mu."

"Stick? Cane?"

"Mu." She rapped the walking stick again.

"Wood? You mean wood?"

The old woman turned and nodded. He cringed at the sight of the bloody rag. "Xian."

He heard the word as *Sann*. She pointed at the trees and moved her finger straight across in the air. "Xian."

Sweeney still didn't understand. "Left to right. Line, maybe?" She straightened, as if she had sensed when he had hit upon the right answer, even though she could not understand the language. "Wood. Line. Woodline." Sweeney furrowed his brow, concentrating. "Wood in a line, a…" He wiped his sleeve across the window to clear away the steam. "A column of wood," he whispered toward the trees shuffling toward the church and the river in single file.

11

Father Toomey sat up and spoke ancient words in a dialect long forgotten, but with an overlay of English that made them intelligible. "Shall I be affronted?" he asked with a leering smile and one eye ablaze with pale malignant fire. "Shall I spit and lash out, and rend my flesh?" The voice speaking two languages at once sounded hollow, as if spoken from the depths of an abandoned mine. "What does one do when such a pathetic insect reveals itself as weak and useless as…" He lifted the dead seagull. Its limp neck drooped over his hand. He sniffed it with disdain.

Raeven and Joe stared, bewildered by the sudden burst to life and the twist in his demeanor. "Father," Joe whispered, and the priest turned on him. "Father!" he spat out. "This form, this shell, this faithless *thing* I inhabit is nothing and was nothing!" He closed his fist around the dead bird's head. "I tire of it," he said and they shuddered when he used the seagull's beak to slash his cheek over and over with quick lacerating jabs until it ran thick with blood. "But you, virgin-man," he said, eyeing Joe, and making a soft gurgling sound deep in his throat. "Beloved of the one who calls herself the Knight, *you* I shall not tire of." He wiped the blood from his face with the bird's body and dropped it on the rocks. "You, I shall pour into, and together shall we come unto the Beloved and then, father, yes! Father to more, father to all!"

Father Toomey tried to stand but couldn't. The priest's gangrenous legs had broken in the fall and forced the being inside to adjust to the deformity. "Come to me, dark-eyed virgin man," he commanded. Joe resisted and the priest's eye flared with anger. "I could have taken you when you touched me, I could have invaded you then!" Using his hands, he crawled toward them over the slabs of granite, dragging his useless legs behind. "I could have flown to you instead of this…this *thing*!"

Joe backed up against Raeven, terrified of the maniacal being creeping toward him.

"You dare defy me!" His voice rose into an insane shriek. "*I* who ruled the court of Tara, I who was the glory-fire, who was and shall remain the snowfire!"

Raeven held out the sword and in a weak, quivering voice stammered: "And I…and I am the Knight of the White Bird."

The sorcerer threw back his head with a shriek of laughter and said in sharp, single words, dripping with scorn: "I – think – *not!*" He lunged. Father Toomey's body tore over the rocks like a lizard scrambling over pebbles. He spat at them and raced in, dragging his fractured legs behind, with his tongue darting in and out lasciviously.

Raeven threw her arm across Joe's chest – he doubled over with pain. Hearing his cry, she turned and noticed the helmet at her feet. Without stopping, she snatched it up and they continued their retreat until Joe's back settled against a wall.

Raeven pressed against him. They could go no further.

"Don't let him touch you," Joe said.

The priest clambered over the last of the rocks and sidled up to them. Raeven held the sword down with the blade pointed at his glowering face. "I'll do it, I swear," she said. Her voice quivered like the heart of a trapped bird.

Father Toomey stared with his mouth open and eye shimmering. "With that!?" He reared up with another wild, demented laugh, and said again: "I think *not*!"

"*An Claiomh Gealach*," Raeven said, losing her nerve even as she brandished the misshapen weapon.

The priest squirmed in mock horror. "Ooh, a faerie weapon, I tremble with fear!" He fixed her with a deadly gaze. "Loathsome mortals. So eager to believe in things you long to believe, and therein lies your doom. How pleasing it would be," he growled, "if all Tuatha swords were thus o'erthrown." The priest touched the tip of the blade with his forefinger and it drooped and began to melt. Drops of silvery metal fell to the rocks and rolled like liquid mercury into crevices.

Raeven stiffened. She leaned back against Joe.

"It's not the sword," he whispered.

The pale-eyed priest shrieked and lurched. He caught Raeven by the wrist and pulled her to her knees. The helmet clattered to the rocks. His slashed cheek oozed with the coagulating blood of a man already dead. Raeven struggled but he howled, "I am the Beloved," and pulled her closer, "as hereafter shalt thou become."

A surge of power passed from his hand and began to crawl up her arm – *Him!* she realized, *the spirit of the sorcerer Lochru!* – pouring from the damaged body of the priest into hers.

Her skin began to ripple. The lines radiating from her tattoo squirmed upon her forearm like snakes defending a nest.

"And unto you I come," he intoned. "To fill you. To inhabit you."

With her free hand, she reached into the helmet. Her fingers closed around the wilted weeds.

"To own you," the false priest chanted, "and to *be* you, and together as One shall we stand before the Beloved and gather unto to us All!"

Raeven struck. A slimy shred of dragonroot dropped upon the sorcerer's hand. A larger piece slapped over his face and lay sizzling upon his mangled cheek. He released her with a shriek and rolled on the rocks, yowling, grasping, clawing.

"Run!" Joe cried and they stumbled away as, "Kill you!" the sorcerer screamed over and over, "Kill you! Kill you – *Kill* you!"

His howls echoed through the abbey and surrounded them with resounding hatred that lasted until they reached the gap in the wall where they came to an abrupt stop – stifled, choked, blinded by a plume of rancid breath when *It* came from the darkness, slithering forth with blazing eyes fixed upon them, staring in ravening fury.

12

Raeven dropped the helmet. It hit the rocks and sent a single sharp echo through the chamber. Joe stepped in front of her in a hopeless attempt to shield her from the Beast. Its hulking body lay out of sight within the larger Great Hall, which gave its head and long sinuous neck the appearance of a monstrous horned snake.

Something black hung from the side of its mouth. It slithered closer and Raeven recognized it as Dr. Sweeney's coat. It flicked its head and flung it onto the rocks and scattered coins, and the gold link that had caused so much ruin was at last reunited with the rest of its treasure.

On it came, snorting and glowering, until a small cry from behind brought all movement to a halt– the lowering fangs, the forward thrust of its head, even the rancid current of breath faded as it focused its gaze beyond its prey.

Raeven glanced back. Father Toomey lay upon the rocks, reaching up with one outstretched hand still seared and steaming from the dragonroot and his blistered face twisted into an expression of rapturous desire.

The great reptile stared at the man and her expression changed too, though instead of mirroring the sorcerer's radiating lust, she appeared to withdraw. Her eyes cooled into subdued darkness. The aggressive electrical currents dimmed upon her scales. Rage and fury dissipated. Soft blue phosphorescence as pale and dim as moonlight spread over her facial armor and flowed in meandering currents along the curve of her neck. All traces of assertive power had turned to submission; but submission *as* power, as primal female strength, a fatal lure, a black-widow's murderous patience, and a drawing together of all things; light, darkness, cold, heat, ice and fire drawn irresistibly unto *her*.

She slid past Raeven and Joe, no longer interested.

Joe squeezed Raeven's hand and gestured toward the gap in the wall. Before passing through, Raeven turned, and what she saw next became seared into her mind as if burned there in acid.

The possessed, ensorcelled body of Father Toomey sat before the monster with his arms outstretched, chanting in the ancient tongue. The Beloved hovered above him, staring. Like a cobra with a rat, she struck with lightning speed. Venom throbbed into him. Her jaws snapped around his legs and he fell back with his arms above his head and she began to pull him in.

Her jaw unhinged. Her throat muscles rippled. The sorcerer's spirit continued its ancient incantations while the mortal remains of Father Toomey slid further into her ecstatic maw, with his body hissing and steaming in those places where the venom burned through his clothes and dissolved his skin.

He moaned with pleasure when her teeth shattered his pelvis with a sharp crack and he ran his hands over her snout, caressing her scales and poisoned fangs as she pulled him in further, swallowing him whole.

Joe threw his arms around Raeven and together they passed along the curve of the massive neck through the wide doorway into the cavernous Great Hall. There, the full bulk of the monster lay with muscles rippling and blackberry vines still entangled in its talons.

Joe urged her on and they ran alongside the creature's ridged tail now quivering in ecstasy. They followed it out of the Great Hall into a sunken courtyard where they saw a sharp black scimitar-like appendage at its end, curved like a scorpion's stinger and lengthening before their eyes. A luminous drop of venom seeped from the tip: it hung like a poisoned pearl and gleamed with sudden brilliance when a shooting star passed over the ruined walls.

"This way," Raeven said and led him to the top landing of the stairs. Another star fell, closer this time, and now a wavering green light came flashing across the sky and she stopped before taking her first step down. "What's the matter?" Joe asked, and the Northern Lights blazed and shimmered and illuminated the ski slope in radiant silence. "We can't," she whispered. "Look."

It had torn out the staircase in its furious climb to the summit. An impassable gorge of jagged stone and ice remained.

"Now what?" Joe asked, and Raeven turned to him, her eyes filled with her answer: "That was the only way down."

Joe studied the ruined stairs. "Maybe in the back." They circled around the abbey, only to gain a new, enlarged view of the hopelessness of their search. The back side of the mountain dropped as a sheer cliff without even the ruins of a staircase to soften the vertical drop to the rocks below. Icy wind screamed up the side of the cliff to tear at their hair and clothing.

Joe turned to the abbey, struck by a thought. "Back inside." He grabbed her hand and led her through a gash beneath one of the arched windows and back into the Great Hall. Red charges now surged with the electrical blue sizzling amongst the stalactites and together they created a violet glow that illuminated the colossal body of the Beast. Its stinger had grown to nearly five feet long. Venom pumped from it freely and lifted a noxious cloud of fumes. The tail, too, appeared longer, thicker, with larger scales. Its head was still hidden from view in the side chamber and its neck no longer lay as a single expanse of slender muscle but had swollen with a bulge midway – *Father Toomey*, Raeven realized with a shock, his body swallowed whole and moved along by constricting spasms of peristalsis rippling along its throat.

Joe urged her deeper into the abbey. At one point they came within ten feet of the creature. Raeven pointed to a tear opening up along its side. Thick skin, now translucent but still bearing the outlines of each individual scale, peeled away from its body. Shimmering black scales replaced the older gray ones. The creature was metamorphosing before their eyes; expanding, molting, shedding her former self while her consumed beloved continued his long, spasmodic slide toward her black heart. A newly-formed hump upon the creature's back split with a rending crack and a shining black object emerged and began to unfold. Scalding liquid streamed off it as fold after fold of wrinkled skin stretched and opened like an enormous black moth emerging from its cocoon.

Joe pressed on with his insistent journey, back into the side room where he had been caged and where the creature's head now lolled upon the rocks with her skin splitting and falling away and new scales breaking through and glistening in the violet light. They passed along the wall, careful to prevent any sudden noise that might alert her, but it was a useless hope.

She knew they were there.

She lay motionless and reveled in her transformation. She would kill them, of course, but she had plenty of time for that. They could not escape the mountaintop: she knew that too. They believed they could find a way down and would continue to search, for that is what mortal things do, so eagerly believe in things they want to believe, *and therein lies your doom.*

Sloughed-off skin dropped from her snout. One eye had withered and scabbed over beneath her glowering brow, but the other, pallid and milky blue with a slit pupil, opened wide enough to watch the pathetic, helpless Knight follow the stolen virgin through the dark room. *In time, in time,* she thought in rumbling waves of hate. The Knight would be the first to die, and the virgin man with her, *in time, in time.*

She closed her eye and gave in to her ecstasy with a deep snorting sigh that stopped Joe and Raeven in their tracks – not from the sound, but from the sight of their shadows upon the far wall, outlined by a searing glow of firelight.

They looked at each other, each expressing the horrifying realization without words. The creature sighed and another exhalation of fire ripped from its nostrils. Joe tried to comfort Raeven with a look. When he saw he could not, he nodded past the flaming breath. She followed his gaze to the object of his search and saw that he was right after all: there *was* a way off the mountain. The creature sighed. Another curl of flame burned through the air and sent its harsh light streaming over the lovers scrambling toward the abbey wall where the Garand's toboggan leaned against the rocks.

13

Dr. Sweeney nearly shouted with frustration and horror. Each time the police car emerged from a tangle of pine trees, the old woman guided it toward another. Boughs hissed. Branches broken off into sharpened stakes scraped and stabbed over the windows. A root curled around a windshield wiper and snapped it off.

He draped his arms over the front seat. "For the love'a God, whoever you are, these ghastly things are…" He paused, struck by the sight of a small box in her lap. "The golden box," he whispered and flinched when another root slapped the window beside him. "That's it, isn't it?"

Without taking her eyes from the windshield, the old woman grasped his hand. Clutching his forefinger in her fist, she traced his fingertip over a single Chinese character engraved upon the lid.

"What is it?" he asked. "What does it mean?"

She traced the character with his finger again. "Shui."

"I don't understand."

"Shui."

Something more frantic and violent than the steady thump of tree trunks struck the front of the car. Dr. Sweeney gazed through the windshield and cried out when a curtain of boughs parted to reveal someone clawing at a root around her neck with one hand and pounding on the hood with the other.

"Pearl!" he shouted, horrified. He reached for the door handle. The old woman spun around and indicated with a sharp nod that he was to move to the middle of his seat.

She opened her door: a root shot in and squirmed toward Sweeney. The old woman touched it and it withdrew as if stung. She stepped outside, closed the door, and moved through the trees, now rustling and parting and swinging their boughs in violent agitation, though none would touch her. When she reached the front of the car, the strangling root released Pearl and slithered away like a panicked snake and she collapsed over the hood, gasping.

Sweeney sat up when the pines parted further to reveal Sparky Grant in the glare of the headlights, kneeling upon the icy road with his coat open and his hands slick with blood. A tree stood beside him with one branch sharpened, dripping, glistening red in the light.

The old woman held up her walking stick and approached him. The trees hissed. Hot drops of sap spattered over her, but on she came, brandishing her weapon, and the trees fell back with a dark whisper of boughs.

Pearl staggered toward Sparky, gasping for air, but the old woman pointed to the car and she obeyed. When she opened the door and saw the professor, she collapsed over him in tears.

"There, there, you're safe now," he cooed, "you're safe."

The stranger helped Sparky to the back seat where he sat down heavily beside Pearl and winced with pain.

"Let me see," she said, wiping her tears. The old woman climbed into the front seat while Pearl pulled back Sparky's coat and lifted his shirt to reveal a gash so deep it looked like he'd been struck in the abdomen with an axe.

"Suffering Christopher," Sweeney whispered. "Why were you out here? Why aren't you on the mountain?"

"We were on the road, heading to the church," Pearl said. "They swarmed over us from the woods. We tried to fight them off with the axes but we couldn't, too many of them, we couldn't do it. They made noises when we hit them with the axes, like screaming…and…" She shuddered and closed her eyes, took a deep breath and opened them again. "Will he be all right?"

Sparky stared at the professor with an intense gaze that communicated across the small space between them. *Don't tell*, his eyes pleaded, *go against what I said before, keep it a secret, don't tell her.*

"Oh yes," Sweeney stammered. "A fine strapping boy-o like him, he'll be fine."

The old woman gestured and the car moved forward. The trees brandished their branch daggers. "Shui," the old woman said and Pearl looked at Sweeney, her eyes swollen with tears. "Why would she say that?"

"You understand her?" he asked.

"It's Chinese. It means 'water'."

The old woman looked at her and nodded, her bandage now fully soaked with blood. "Shui," she said again and lifted the golden box.

14

The curved front of the toboggan jutted over the edge of the mountain like a car tottering at the brink of a cliff. Joe sat in front and gripped the rope handle. "Ready?"

Raeven whispered a quick, "yes," even as she felt weakened by the same gut-churning fear she felt at the top of a roller coaster.

A crack and rumble lifted behind, the ground trembled, and Joe pushed off as a great scorching volley of fireballs roared through the arched windows like a broadside from a man-of-war. The toboggan tilted, the fireballs mushroomed over them, and Raeven gasped when the world opened below: her heart and breath and thoughts hung there, it seemed, momentarily suspended – and *down!*

Wind howled, gravity pulled, her thoughts caught up, and the toboggan plummeted straight down through the air like a diving falcon before it touched and shot along the ice path taken by the Beast on its descent. Down they went, tearing over ice and snow. Joe tried to control it but they were going too fast. They approached a curve as if barreling down a bobsled run and they both cried out, certain they would shoot over the lip and crash into the trees, but they swept around it and started down again; down, down, racing down with the wind screaming and the jagged snowfire realm rushing by in a blur of white ice and black trees.

They hit a mound at the bottom and sailed into the air. The toboggan tilted, but Joe leaned to the side, and the sled tilted back again before landing with a jolt for its final rush to the end.

Dragonroot plowed up before them. It caught beneath to act as a drag on the wooden sled and brought them to a stop less than ten feet from the back door of the garage. There they sat for a stunned, disbelieving moment, with their chests heaving and pulses racing.

Joe turned to face her. The wind had forced his hair straight up. He took his glasses from his pocket and put them on. Raeven's hair hung about her face in thick waves. Blood flushed her cheeks and she stared at him, her mouth open with shock and surprise. Filled with a surge of exhilaration and unaccustomed triumph, they shouted and threw their arms around each other. "We...!" she cried, unable to finish. She tried again. "We..."

"I knew we could do it," he returned, and he pulled her close and rested his forehead against hers. "I don't mean *we*," he said, suddenly quiet. "I knew *you* could."

"Not only me," she returned and she smiled as she had never smiled before.

Her eyes met his. The gate that had always come crashing down to keep her aloof and protected did not fall this time. Her smile faded into a smaller, more satisfied expression and she leaned forward and kissed him.

It was a small moment of genuine happiness, the first she had ever known.

It did not last.

A single deadly tremor shuddered from the mountain.

It jolted the toboggan and passed through the garage and on it went, a single ripple passing through woods and fields in an ever widening circle.

In its wake came an immense brooding stillness that settled over Burne Notch like a shroud.

Nothing moved.

Nothing made a sound.

Every living thing remaining within the borders of the fire wall stopped and listened, unnerved by the paralyzing aura of menace that draped over the barren branches and fallen snow.

And quietly, without warning, the power came back on.

Tred, Soot, Earl and Pearl's caged birds sat up, startled when the lights snapped on throughout the Golden Panda. Pearl's escaped birds, kept alive all this time by huddling in the steamy branches overhanging the warm river, now ruffled their feathers at the sight of houses brightening one by one in a spreading ripple that followed the path of the tremor, radiating from the central point of the mountain until it reached the blue fire wall. Sweeney and the others in the police car saw them too, lights brightening everywhere while beyond the borders of Burne Notch, military personnel roused themselves into new rounds of frantic confusion as the wall began to waver and dim and slowly congeal into hardened glass.

Back at the town garage, Joe and Raeven sat on the toboggan, unsettled by the surrounding calm. Light poured from the broken garage roof in a wide beam that shot straight up to the churning clouds.

Light changed upon the mountain too. The blue glow turned to blue fire. Red flames clawed through it until their demonic hues swallowed the cooler ones and they spiraled skyward with the sudden violence of a volcanic eruption. A crescendo of fractured rock rent the air and up billowed an immense cloud of ash and pulverized stone. Beneath it, cloud upon cloud of roiling fire melted the remaining snow into steaming torrents that reflected its light as if molten lava and not water flowed down the mountainside to destroy all in its path.

The summit began to heave. "Look at that," Joe said. "The mountain is lifting!"

The earth shuddered. The sky rumbled. Raeven grabbed him by the arm, her eyes pinned to the summit. "That's not the mountain."

Lighting shot down from a swirling cloudbank. It twisted and crackled and struck the rising figure again and again, strengthening into fuller vibrant life the melding together of the Sorcerer and Beloved into One.

Shooting stars slashed through the clouds in a vain attempt to stop it. They struck in pitiful blasts wholly unnoticed by the monstrous vision glistening in the firestorm. The Northern Lights appeared and attacked it in clustering waves, futile and impotent, a silent scream of light.

Its great head rose into the lightning-wracked clouds. Talons slashed at the sky. Two gargantuan wings snapped out and spun the surrounding fires into cyclones of flame.

It scanned the mountainside with a pitiless gaze that swept over the trees and down the slope until it settled upon Raeven.

Its glare paralyzed her: it seemed to chain her there, bound in cords of iron. From behind came a low rumble of engines turning over and humming to life in the garage.

A sudden high-pitched wail dropped into a shattering roar and Raeven fell back against Joey as the dragon-sorcerer clawed through the collapsing abbey walls and began to descend.

15

"Can't she say anything else?" Pearl cried, exasperated.

"Shui," the old woman said again without turning her eyes from the windshield.

"We have to get him to a hospital, we have to bring him somewhere."

"We have to make do with what we find," Sweeney said as gently as he could, and Pearl slumped in her seat beside Sparky and held his hand.

The steeple came into view. Pine trees surrounded the church with the majority gathered in a large open field behind it where they formed row upon row of unyielding guardians with sharpened stakes exposed and roots coiled to spring. The full-sized pines Sweeney saw earlier stood like generals at the periphery of a battleground, propped up by their thick woody roots and armed with branches sharpened into massive lances.

"What lies beyond those larger trees?" Dr. Sweeney asked.

"The river," Pearl said and he wondered aloud why they appeared to be guarding it. "They're not." Sparky moaned and she held him tight. "It's okay, Sparkles, you'll be okay." Turning again to Sweeney, she said: "They're guarding the church. They don't want us to reach the steeple, the column of wood."

"No, no, these rows of trees are the columns, I'm certain of it."

"You've been certain of a lot of things, Prof. Doesn't matter anyway. We've got to get to the steeple, whether it's a column or not. *Gealach* is up there."

"That's not possible," Sweeney stammered. "Raeven has it."

"We were wrong about that too," Sparky whispered and Sweeney sat back, aghast. "But if that's not..." He ran his fingers nervously over his chin. "Then she's unprotected." He gazed through the window at the trees. The engine idled. The headlights lit the first row of lethal boughs in bright white. "We've *got* to find that sword or we're doomed, all of us. Unless..." He reached over the seat and touched the old woman on the arm. "Can you help us?"

She did not look at him. "Shui," she said without turning around and Sweeney sat back again with a heavy exhale of frustration.

"I know where it is," Pearl said and looked beyond the trees at the church, still bearing the marks of the fire several days before. Soot fanned up from each broken window pane, most with missing or cracked stained glass panels. The high column of the steeple had remained untouched and glowed in the headlights like a tower of white marble. Above the bell tower, the four-sided roof rose into a sharp point. A raven wheeled around the roof. Another approached from behind and joined the first in black spirals of flight. "That's it," Pearl said with even more certainty. "It's up there, I *know* it is."

16

Raeven and Joey stood in the garage, staring from the back door in mesmerized horror at their approaching doom.

It had retracted its wings and now came crashing down the side of the mountain. The fires left no ice to slide down as before, but on it came with a thunderous call, digging its talons into the granite. Flames raced over its scales and a host of brilliant firebats wheeled in patterns traced in sparks. Smoke billowed from its nostrils but surged away in tatters, scattered by another roar aimed at the garage below.

"What'll we do?" Joe cried.

Raeven looked around the garage. The huge snow plow idled quietly. The walls began to shake beneath the onslaught of sound from the mountain.

"Come on!" Raeven cried. She ran to the truck and climbed inside. Joey climbed in behind her.

She looked through the windshield at the enormous front doors, still locked as Sparky had left them. The engine purred. The walls rattled. A loose sheet of metal fell from the roof and clattered into the truck bed. Joe looked at the controls and then at Raeven. He saluted his glasses up his nose. "Stick shift," he said. "I haven't driven one in years."

"I have," Raeven said and slid behind the giant steering wheel. "Okay," she whispered and stepped on the clutch – she had to grip the wheel to force the pedal down. She pulled on the shift. "Whoa, wrong one." The truck bed began to rumble and rise behind them. Leftover sand and debris from the shattered roof clattered onto the concrete floor.

"Try another," Joe said. She did and the huge yellow plow tilted up below the headlights. "That's good," he said. "We need it to get through that door."

Outside, the creature approached the bottom of the mountain with a lumbering gait. It stopped at the field of dragonroot and studied at the garage, so flimsy now in comparison to its gargantuan bulk. Its thoughts centered on the prize inside. It could easily destroy the building with one incinerating blast, but its new guile made it reluctant to end the chase all at once. Prophesy had determined the Knight as its only serious threat, and as such, would provide the most pleasurable slaughter, seconded only by the death of the old priestess with that thing – *that golden box*, it remembered with a twinge of unease.

It shoved the thought from its mind and moved in, leaning over the dragonroot field with its mouth open, smoking, gaping toward the roof.

Inside, Joe shouted, "Now!"

Raeven dropped her foot on the accelerator.

The truck shot forward. The plow connected and ripped the padlocks from their latches and the metal doors flew open and slammed against the sides of the garage with a hollow *boom*.

The creature reared back, startled. The truck rumbled from the garage onto the road. Joe glanced at the side rear-view mirror. Behind them, its neck swept down into an S-curve. A spout of fire ripped from its mouth and slammed into the garage. Sheets of corrugated metal exploded into the air like a startled flock of magic carpets.

The building collapsed. The creature reared up for another blast.

"The back of the truck," Joe said. "How did you do that?"

Flustered, Raeven did not dare take her eyes off the road. "It's that…I think it's the yellow lever."

The sorcerer-dragon stepped off the mountain. As soon as it did, a legion of jack-in-the-pulpit sprang up through the slush and crusted snow and unfurled into full bloom. One of the creature's talons touched a tiny leaf and it lifted its foreleg, stung by the plant's poison. With its fury now compounded, it rose onto its haunches and focused on the retreating vehicle.

Joe pulled the lever. Hydraulic cylinders strained to lift the heavy steel truck bed from the chassis.

The sorcerer-dragon lurched. A wild, curling wash of fire tore down the length of the road. The flames struck the truck bed and glanced upward and outward, deflected in all directions by the angle of steel.

"My *God!*" Joe cried when the diverted flames swept around the sides. Heat filled the cab but no flames penetrated the shield. "Go, go!" he yelled and Raeven clamped her foot down on the clutch and changed gears. The transmission clattered and the engine churned into higher gear while around them the fire receded into thick smoke.

"Where should we go?" Raeven asked.

He reached into his pocket and withdrew the folded papers that had fallen from the priest's cage. "Father Toomey had it, he must have found it in the church." He spread the pages over the seat. "Something about the Grey farm, something about a cross." He held a page under the dashboard light and shoved his glasses up his nose.

"Look out!" Raeven cried and they cowered when another veil of fire surrounded the cab. It dissipated as before – she tried to see the creature but the mirror had been torn away in the blast. She looked through the back window at the truck bed, now smoking. The sides drooped in rounded folds like melted wax. "I don't think we can take another hit."

"Here's something," Joe said, and he read aloud. "*'27th day of March, year 1821, Patrick Grey wed Mary McGuire, daughter of John and...* No, that's not it." A thick growl rumbled through the air. "It's gotta be here."

Raeven lifted one of the papers and flattened it against the steering wheel. She alternated quick glances from the road to the page. "This – here, this! *'Found in the back field, a most marvelous object...'*"

Joe pulled the paper from her hand. A blast of fire raced into the trees beside the road. Their branches disappeared, pulverized into ash, though the trunks remained standing as roaring pillars of fire. He held the paper closer to the light and read aloud: "*...a most marvelous object of intricate design and this being a sword, Celtic in design and wrought of finest silver. This we did take unto us, for this great weapon, found buried among the Stonehenge rocks*"

"That's where it came from," Raeven said. "But where it is now?"

He squinted and leaned closer to the dashboard. "*How came such an object to be found so far from our homeland, but as a sign of Divine favour? Thus, the parish of Burne Notch resolves to set the great sword into the highest place of reverence...*"

Joe looked up at her. "The church?"

Raeven nodded. "The steeple."

Behind them, the dragonroot sprouted and prevented their pursuer from giving chase.

So be it, thought the sorcerer-dragon. It threw back its head and sent forth a coil of flame into the upper heights where it spread beneath a pall of soot and smoke. Dragonroot would not stop it now – nothing *could* stop it now. It roared in joyous exultation, flexing its muscles and relishing its newfound power. A spiral of fire swept around it like a demon of the underworld, screeching as it tore through the air and circled the colossus several times, gaining speed each time before dropping to scorch the trees and melt the snow and incinerate the entire loathsome field of jack-in-the-pulpit with one searing blast.

The great wings unfurled to sweep the burning pillars of trees aside until they hung fully expanded, enormous, bat-like and glistening. They lifted and pushed down. Fire churned and poured into the ruined forest on both sides, and the wings lifted again, sucking up a stream of smoke and ash. Its claws scraped up from the troubled earth and up it went to fill the blackened sky with fiery jubilation.

17

"I don't know if I can do it."

"Buck up, Sparkles, of course you can." He looked up at her and smiled. She brushed his sweaty hair from his forehead.

"We've got to get inside the church," said Dr. Sweeney, though another glance at the surrounding trees showed a slim chance of success. He leaned against the front seat. "I don't know who you are but somehow you are able to withstand these wretched things. Please help us." The old woman stared at the trees, serene and impassive. Blood dripped from her bandage. "Shui" she said and Dr. Sweeney slammed his fist down on the seat. "Listen, sister. We are in desperate straits and shui – water – has nothing to do with it. Trees, in point of fact, are our primary preoccupation. We *must* get inside that church?"

She did not move. She stared at the trees.

Sparky lurched, assaulted by a new wave of pain. He reached for Pearl's hand and clenched his teeth. "What'll we do?" Pearl asked and Dr. Sweeney slumped in his seat, defeated. He laid his head back on the seat and stared through the refracted glass at the top of the rear window. The sky above swirled with red and black clouds. "This is all my fault."

"Oh, my God," Pearl said. "That's like the last thing I want to hear right now."

"It was not an attempt to garner pity or forgiveness, simply a statement of fact. All my theories have fallen by the wayside. I have been wrong nearly every step of the way. And now it's come to this, and – " He froze, still staring at the sky.

A figure passed before the clouds, large, powerful and silent. Fire rolled and encircled it and tore along its wings before dissipating into trails of smoke. A stark, harsh light blazed through the branches of the surrounding pines. Alarmed by his expression, Pearl asked what had happened. Sweeney looked at her, his mouth working soundlessly until – "He's *here!*" he croaked in hoarse whisper. The glare brightened. Pearl squinted and lifted her hand over her eyes, and the monstrous light swept in upon them.

It left no time to react: Pearl threw her arm up, unable even to scream. White glaring light and a crackling rumble filled the car and Sparky whispered at her shoulder. "My truck..."

Pearl lowered her arm. Headlights blazed above a smoke-streaked yellow plow. A voice called: "Everybody all right?" Pearl tried to sit up but Sparky leaned heavy against her. "Raeven," she whispered, and rolled down her window to call out, "Raeven!"

"I'm here!" the voice returned. "I'm with Joey. Is everyone okay?"

Pearl began to sob: she couldn't help it. Tears rose so suddenly she couldn't respond. Sweeney had no such problem. He threw open his door and, balancing on his uninjured foot, emerged from the car. Trees approached but held back as if fearful of the lights. He threw his scarf over his shoulder, pointed at them, and bellowed: "Plow those sons of bitches into the ground!"

"My pleasure," Raeven said and she slid back into the truck. The motor raced, the tip of the plow caught the end of the police car's bumper and, dragging it forward, plunged into the grove of pines and scattered them into a shrieking horde.

Some fell beneath the plow and were crushed by the tires. Others lashed out and wrapped their snaky roots around the car's bumper and the truck's plow, but the vehicle tore them away and moved on, splintering and gouging them into a tumbling wave of trunks and boughs. A wall of white clapboards appeared. Raeven couldn't stop in time. The plow slammed into the church and cracked through the clapboards beneath the steeple. A protesting *caw* rose over the shrieking trees. The police car's trunk swung open.

Joe climbed from the cab and yelled for everybody to get into the church.

"I can't," Sparky whispered but Pearl urged him into a new round of strength. "Oh please, you're starting to sound like Raeven with all this 'I can't' bull." She helped him to the edge of the seat. "Come on, Sparkles. You can do it."

"Yeah, sure," he said and he clenched his teeth and slid from the car.

Air quivered. Night closed in. Tremors shuddered through the ground.

Pearl climbed the front steps and pushed the door open. "Hurry, hurry," she shouted to the others.

Beyond the snow plow, a phalanx of the largest pine trees advanced with huge boughs slashing at the air. They all stopped at the same moment as if by command and their trunks leaned back with the creaking whine of a hundred wooden ships rolling at anchor. "Look out!" Pearl cried when they snapped back to release a volley of branches sharpened into lethal points. Nearly all came in too high and struck the side of the church. Some penetrated straight through.

Fiery light flashed from a tumbling airborne conflagration, now descending, and a cry as sharp as a dagger slit the air.

"Hurry!" Pearl called again. She helped Raeven pull Sparky into the church where they laid him on an unburned pew near the door. Headlights streamed through the broken stained glass windows and bathed the charred walls in wide bands of white light bordered by fragmented color.

Still on the steps and stunned by the rending cry, Joe and Dr. Sweeney cowered when a curtain of fire touched down. Ghastly wails filled the air and the host of trees fell before the inferno. Branches and pine needles burst into flame. The larger ones fled to the edges of the field trailing sparks and fire and howling at the betrayal by their master. A second blast swept over the screaming mass of smaller trees and reduced them to ash in the blink of an eye.

Joe ran into the church and called to Raeven. "The steeple!"

Dr. Sweeney remained behind with Sparky while Joe led Pearl and Raeven up the stairs to the choir loft. At its far end he threw open a door and began to climb a narrow spiral staircase into the bell tower with Pearl at his heels and Raeven close behind. Before passing through, she chanced a look through one of the broken stained glass windows.

A storm of ash and skeletal tree-trunks circled the churchyard, whipped up by the descending wings. In their midst hobbled an old woman – but the wrong way, heading away from the church. Raeven had never seen her before. *She must have been turned around in the confusion, she must have lost her way.* The stranger dropped her walking stick and held something close to her chest. "Dr. Sweeney!" Raeven called over the choir loft rail. "The old woman who was with you!"

The professor blanched, stung by her words. "Where is she?" he cried, scanning the interior of the church. "We need her. She's got the golden box!"

Raeven froze with one foot on the lowest step. *The Golden Box.* Something rose within her, a feeling, a certain knowledge, something she could neither explain nor understand but knew was deeply connected to the realignment, the truth underlying all the events of the last dreadful days. She looked through the window again. The old woman stood in a maelstrom of sparks and smoke and wind, with one eye hidden behind a bloody rag and the other staring up at the window, staring at *her,* and –

WATER!

The word slammed into her and filled her with crystal-clear understanding. Water: the source of life, the bane of fire, the cool, clear bloodstream of the world and the primal baptismal mother in whom all things polluted, foul and pestilential are diluted and purified and washed clean. Reeling with terror, she called to Joe and Pearl to go on without her. Before they could respond, she raced to the stairs leading back down from the choir loft. Hot wind poured through the broken windows and carried a hail of sparks to spiral around her. Dr. Sweeney met her at the bottom. "The box, I know what it is," she said and rushed past him.

A blast of heat stopped her at the foot of the front stairs. Flames engulfed the snowplow and licked at the side of the church – it wouldn't be long before the walls began to burn. Sparky's police car had not been touched yet, but fire surrounded it on three sides.

A burning brand landed on her sleeve. Raeven slipped out of her coat. Embers landed on her sweater and she pulled it off. Noxious blankets of smoke from the burning tires billowed over her. Sparks slashed the air. A rippling wall of iridescent scales appeared and she caught a glimpse of its long neck curving upward and its head looming high in the blinding pall.

The neck began to drop. "Down!" she yelled, but the old woman stared at her, stricken, helpless, yet defiant. She held out the golden box. "Shui!" she called and Raeven gasped when she realized the thing tearing down from the smoke was *not* the creature's neck.

The scorpion stinger hummed out of the smoke. It streaked toward the old woman and the golden box tumbled from her hands when it drove through her chest and lifted her twitching into the smoky air.

The tail did not stop. It swept over Raeven's head and slammed the impaled woman into the side of the steeple. *Bong!* The church bell swung with the impact. White clapboards popped with a sound like gunfire. The steeple cracked and began to pull away from the church.

The tail pulled back and Raeven recoiled from the sight of the limp bloody mass hanging from the stinger. It swung and slammed against the steeple again. Wood whined and splintered. The church bell rang, *Bong!* and again the tail crashed in, pulverizing the mangled body. *Bong! Bong!*

Pearl and Joe appeared at the windows of the bell tower high above, their faces twisted with alarm. The bell tolled continuously – *Bong! Bong! Bong!* – deep and sonorous with each assault by the monstrous tail. Timbers cracked. Nails shrieked from wood. The steeple leaned further and Raeven turned and fled when it began a slow cracking fall to earth.

Inside, Joe and Pearl dropped to the floor. The wooden frame splintered and groaned around them. The stairs collapsed. The bell stopped ringing, but its weight now became the guiding force in bringing the steeple down. "Here we go," Joey said through clenched teeth, and they held on as the final timbers separated and the steeple landed with a crash. The bell broke free and smashed through the roof, carrying all of the boards and shingles on one side with it. It tumbled across the churchyard, clanking and hurtling past Raeven and over the burning clearing until it landed in the river with a mighty splash.

18

"Are you all right?" Joey asked. Behind him, Pearl coughed within a cloud of dust. The steeple wall had torn open beside them. "Fine," she said, rising to her knees. Joe clutched her arm. He pointed through the broken wall. "Look!"

Raeven stood in the charred clearing between the church and the river.

The sorcerer-dragon stood before her with its wings retracting and its head ten feet above hers, its neck arched up behind and single baleful eye riveted upon her.

She stood before it, transfixed, wearing only her tattered sleeveless dress and combat boots.

No helmet. No dragonroot.
No sword.
No shield.
No armor.

Pearl held onto Joe, not daring to breathe. Inside the church, Dr. Sweeney stared through the open door at what seemed a nightmare suspended, with no movement apart from the billowing smoke and no sound but the fire crackling along the walls of the church.

The sorcerer-dragon snorted. A puff of ash spread in a wide ripple with Raeven at its center. She pulled her gaze from the pale eye and lowered it to the scales on the underside of its neck, its powerful chest; and lower, beyond its muscular forelegs to Sparky's police car beside the church. Smoke spiraled from the opened doors and trunk.

The retracted leathery wings rustled, its tongue whipped the air, and Pearl screamed from the broken steeple when it arched its neck and struck.

Raeven ducked and sprang toward the car.

The sorcerer-dragon overshot its mark. Its jaws snapped behind her with a murderous crack. She circled the grasping talons and ran to the open trunk. Hissing and spitting, it swept its massive head to the side and hurtled toward her with jaws opening again.

Raeven spun around and lifted a garbage can shield caked with dried dragonroot. The monster slammed into the car and sent it rolling. Its chin struck the shield with a glancing blow that ripped it from her hand to sail into the air, and it reeled back with a shocked cry.

Pearl saw her chance: she crawled from the wreckage and dashed to the church. When she reached the top of the stairs, Dr. Sweeney appeared in the smoke with his arms around Sparky. "Go back inside!" she cried, but they couldn't. The fire had spread too far and burned too fast and hot.

Joe called to Raeven from the steeple. She ran toward him, her eyes filled with panic. He pushed at the broken wood and crawled out to meet her.

A shadow descended. A claw slammed down. It sank into the seared earth and tore out a gash between them, separating them. It scattered the dirt in a frenzy of rage and came down again.

Joe escaped the blow by scrambling back through the hole made by the renegade bell while Raeven tried to run around the tear in the earth. A second slash of claws blocked her way and she fell onto her back, unable to withstand the tremor. The monster's claw pulled back for the final strike. Raeven rose onto her elbows. Something scrabbled over her neck and arm, but she dared not look. She dared not move.

Behind her, Joey climbed deeper into the steeple. He pulled at a board. A shaft of firelight streamed over his shoulder into the interior of the pointed roof, up to the top where it settled upon a long black sliver of metal pointing straight at him, covered with dust and cobwebs. His mind instantly translated what he saw beneath the roof to what he now knew stood on top. *It isn't a cross up there at all. It's the handle of a sword. This is the blade!*

He scrambled out of the bell tower and ran to the pinnacle of the fallen steeple where the hilt of the sword, shaped like a small black cross, protruded from the top of the roof. He grabbed it with both hands and pulled but it didn't budge. He wiped his hands on his coat and pulled again. This time the sword began to slide out, but not with the shrieking groan of a rusted spike withdrawn from a board, but with a rush and a low breathy hum, as if gathering air and wind and light unto itself. "Raeven!" he called and the blade ripped free. She chanced a look over her shoulder – a blast of fire curled into the air above her – and he threw the sword.

Up it went, tumbling end over end. It passed though the stream of dragon fire and emerged with its tarnish burned away and the silver weapon, *An Claiomh Gealach*, the Sword of the Moon, sailed through the air, radiant with an incandescent silver glow and faultless in its hurtling arc through smoke and flame.

The blade tilted and dropped as if guided by unseen hands to plunge into the ground beside her. She rose to her knees and grabbed it by the handle: when she did, she saw the source of the scrabbling movement over her skin. Her *doom* tattoo had spread and now coiled like indigo blue vines into masses of intricate tattooed Celtic knots and spirals that surged up her right arm and shoulder, down her side to spread over her right leg and up the right side of her neck and face into her hairline; and she knelt in the firelight, brandishing her sword like one of the Morrigan, the triple warrior queen bearing the blue marks of battle, with a host of battle-ravens and crows calling in a frenzy from the edges of the battlefield.

The dragon snorted and the fight was on.

The blast of rancid breath threw Raeven to the ground once again. The claw lifted for a crushing blow. Its shadow fell over her. She rolled and lifted the sword straight up. The claw crushed down so heavy that the blade slipped between its pads like a knife into a ripe plum before emerging through the top, glistening with blood.

The dragon lurched and, slowly, as if stunned that such a thing could happen, it lifted its wounded claw into the air.

Raeven did not let go of the hilt. The rising claw lifted her to her knees, to her feet, and into the air where she hung suspended with her grip tight upon the sword.

The dragon lowered its head. The mass of scar tissue over its blinded eye prevented it from seeing her dangling from the sword. It swung its head and there, only inches away, appeared the massive single eye, milky blue and pale, rimmed with fiery red and widening into an expression of furious disbelief, with Raeven's reflection shimmering along the length of its slit pupil.

Pulled by her weight, the sword eased down from the paw and slid free with a rush of following blood. She dropped and landed in a crouch, but did not hesitate. The dragon lifted its head, and with a mighty cry, Raeven drew back the sword and with as much strength as she could muster, sprang up again and slashed the blade across its throat.

It reared back in shock. Blood throbbed from the gash and with a gurgling scream of fury it struck.

A fang tore into her upper thigh, deep into the muscle. The blow forced her down again onto her back. As she fell, the sword lifted – not through effort or design, but through momentum. Sweeping up, it clanged against the fang and hurtled into the roof of the monster's mouth.

The dragon could not stop. It had come down too fast. The blade sank in at the same time the venomous tooth ripped through Raeven's leg and sank into the ground, pinning her there even as the sword drove in deeper, burrowing into the core of the sorcerer's black mind.

Unable to fully comprehend the fatal sting, the dragon pulled back with a gurgling roar. The fang tore from Raeven's leg and the sword withdrew from its deadly sheath. Blood pumped from the dragon's mouth and throat. It poured over *Gealach* and spattered over Raeven and sprayed the air with bloody smoke.

It snapped its mouth closed and Raeven, with a last burst of effort, stood and grabbed the sword with both hands. Swinging it, she sliced the dragon's neck in a deep vertical stroke upward past the previous horizontal slash to the underside of its chin, forming a bloody cross in its flesh. Again, in shock – how *could* this have happened? – it looked down to see its attacker, but the downward motion gave Raeven the chance for a final thrust. She shoved the sword straight up. The blade plunged through the fleshy part beneath its lower jaw to pin its mouth shut.

This time it reared in panic, clawing at the blade, trying to tear it from under its chin while trying to open its mouth.

Raeven fell to the ground beneath the slashing, frantic monster. The venom's icy pain had already begun to take hold, but she sat up and searched through the smoke and fire, hoping to see a small reflective shard of light. *There!*

"Water," she whispered and crawled toward the golden box.

Behind her, Sweeney and Pearl knelt beside Sparky, terrified of the dragon's death throes. It reeled out of control and shook its head with its mouth pinned shut and its eyes wild with rage and panic. Its head passed over them and slammed against the church, pushing the sword in further, deeper. The creature shuddered, its forelimbs straightened, and it craned its neck, bending its head back to furthest limit. Blood spattered from its slashed throat; a savage muffled scream tore the air; and in the pause that followed, the scream echoed and faded into a raucous call of ravens wheeling.

Another shudder. Its legs collapsed. Its body slumped heavy to the ground. The wings crashed and the neck began to drift down, one ridge at a time.

A quiver passed along its length and it glared at Raeven as she lifted the golden box, its single eye shimmering with malignancy and…*something else, something more*, Joe thought, for he could see the monster's hateful gaze more clearly than anyone else.

Satisfaction.

Death was on the scene, but not only for itself. It, too, had struck its mark and now watched the Knight struggle to her feet with bitter satisfaction. It knew her final minutes would be filled with agony and ruin beyond endurance, followed by nothing. Oblivion.

A last weak puff of flame billowed from the crossed gashes in its throat. It tried to stand, but could not. Smoke seeped from the sides of its pinned mouth and it rumbled a final raging growl before it quivered and fell. Its lower jaw slammed upon the ground, which drove the sword in so deep that its tip cracked up through the top of its snout to shimmer between its eyes while the fires below darkened and faded and with a last trembling flicker went out.

Pearl and Sweeney stared. "She killed it," Pearl said, her voice hushed with awe. She leaped to her feet and threw her arms around the professor. "She *killed* it!" She broke away and yelled to Sparky. "Did you see that, Sparkles?" Smoke poured from the church door behind. "Sparky…?" Pearl asked, her smile fading.

Joe ran up to them. "Look!" he cried, and Sweeney turned around, startled. Steam rose from the monster's body. Its muscles began to quiver and undulate – at first he thought it might still be alive but its scales rattled as if all the moisture had been withdrawn and began to fall one by one, dropping like brittle autumn leaves. The wings collapsed. Their webbing burned away to reveal the thin skeletal structures beneath. With a series of hissing, snapping sounds, the neck began to retract and drag the head toward the shrinking body, leaving a trail of steaming blood.

They could see beyond it now to Raeven standing in the distance with her back to them, facing the river, a solitary figure on the charred field, marked with the Celtic battle signs, her torn black dress fluttering around her in ribbons. A raucous *caw-caw-caw* sounded all around; at the sides of the field, among the burnt branches and flying in tight black circles in the air above her; *caw-caw-caw*, a wild barbaric chorus above the battlefield where she staggered along a path of ashes to the river.

She did not see the black birds. She did not hear them. She did not see the dragon's demise. Venom clawed through her body and filled her veins with smoldering ice and gave her only enough sight for one thing, only enough thought and energy for one thing. Self-will guided her now and urged her past the pain. "I can," she whispered through gritted teeth while dragging her leg, and she focused on the river and said it again and again. "I can. I can." Smoke poured in with every breath and ashes stung her eyes, but she continued on with the box close to her chest. "I can. I can." Behind her, a small thin vine crawled over the scorched earth like a thread of her tattoo, slithering toward her and joined by another, and another; rising from the ashes and squirming into the firelight, but she did not see them. She saw only the river and the tendrils of mist wafting over the dark water and, "I can," she whispered again and again, "I can do it. I can. I can."

19

Back at the church, the transformation had nearly ended. *An Claiomh Gealach* lay on the ground beside an undulating mass of black slime. Joey circled around it, desperate to run to Raeven, but something stopped him each time, first the craters left by the dragon's claws, then fire, and now a mat of vines that appeared from nowhere and began to weave into a high tangled wall.

The dragon mass rumbled. Steam poured and hissed and the slime disintegrated further, drawing in upon itself, molding into a pattern, a small frame with stretching limbs. A face formed and resolved into flesh and the steam cleared to reveal an ancient man, toothless and frail, wearing a wretched gray cloak so tattered and worn, it barely covered his naked flesh. Blood seeped from the sides of his mouth. It flowed freely from a cross of gashes on his throat. A long-healed scar trailed down the back of his bald head and where his right eye should have been, an empty black socket gazed sightless upon the world while his left eye glowered pale and menacing. A freshly bloodied spot oozed between them.

Dr. Sweeney's own eyes widened and his mouth dropped open. "Lochru…" He could barely form the word.

Before he could say another, the sorcerer sprang up on his bony legs and grabbed the silver sword. He choked out a scream from his slashed throat and in strangled guttural tones, he cursed in a language none of them had ever heard, even Sweeney. Bright red foam bubbled at his lips and spattered from his throat with every word.

"Look out!" Sweeney cried and Joe ducked. The sorcerer shot past him, gurgling wildly and brandishing the sword. He reached the briar wall and severed the vines with a single easy slash of *An Claiomh Gealach*. They began to weave together again, but Joe followed and leaped through in a tumbling roll before they could bar his way.

The sorcerer hobbled over the charred clearing, dragging the sword, with his bare feet lifting puffs of soot and ash with every step. Crows and ravens clamored and cawed in the trees. Some lifted from the branches and dove in to snap at the old man but he fended them off with wild swings of the sword.

Raeven stood on the riverbank. She looked over her shoulder, her eyes dull, her expression listless. She lifted the box.

The sorcerer stopped in his tracks. He stared at her, stared at the box. He dropped the sword and strode toward her with his hands out, pleading. Blood poured from his left palm and marked the place where the blade had pierced the dragon's paw. "Give it here," he said in a rasping voice, the same as the priest's within the dragon's lair, an ancient tongue overlaid by words she could understand, hollow and now gurgling with blood. "Give it to me."

Raeven wiped her mouth with the back of her hand. Dragon's blood spread into her mouth and she tasted it, hot and sweet. She lifted the box.

"No, no, you must give it to me!"

"Must I?" Summoning the last of her failing energy, she lifted the golden box above her head and smiled a grim, triumphant smile. "I think not," she said and threw it.

The box tumbled through the air and landed in the river. Water closed over it with a single clap and the sorcerer Lochru fell howling to his knees.

Behind him, Joey picked up the discarded sword.

A sudden gust of wind passed over the clearing, warm and ripe and devoid of winter. Thunder rumbled. The sorcerer turned his pale eye to the skies where the roiling black clouds began to shift and move. He threw a handful of ash into the air and slammed his fists on the ground and cursed until his voice strangled into a bloody growl.

Raeven did not hear him for the icy venom had continued its spread.

Lightning crackled through the sky. Rain began to fall with each heavy drop marked by a small puff of ash. The sorcerer whispered dark incantations and crawled toward her on his hands and knees, with red foaming and dripping from his lips.

Raeven lifted her hand again and licked the dragon's blood from her wrist: a smell of humus, of rotting leaves and vegetation overpowered her and she saw and felt and understood many things: she felt the rain; she saw it through a cloudy veil of pain and weakness, saw it patter on the still waters and spread in a thousand rippling circles; and she saw the shooting stars and *aurora borealis* too, and the wall of fire and the jack-in-the-pulpit, and she now understood that things she believed had opposed her were for her all along, supporting her, guiding her. The stars were hers, as were the vines upon the stairs. They had formed a wall to separate her from her friends, but only to bring her closer to herself; for they were a part of her; the briars *were* her and she was the briars – she knew that now, and the total course of her life, the falling star, northern light, blackberry, snowfire essence of *her* came rising up through the venom and tried to hold it back. "You are *not* alone," was its tale, "and you never were. You are not separate. You are connected to many, many things, and have been always." She saw that now and knew it to be true and a cry lifted from her soul and heart, *if only there was time!*

But there wasn't.

She collapsed upon the riverbank and sat in the ashes with her legs straight out before her. The hot dragon's blood in her mouth countered the venom and spread forth a blanket of heat to battle the ice, and the rain fell and spattered on the fires to extinguish them one by one, and it fell upon Raeven slipping further down the sooty riverbank.

A sound came from the river: low and deep and watery.

Bong.

The river began to churn like water slowly coming to a boil.

Bong.

A column of steam appeared, and another, twining and braiding as they rose from the surface. Water bubbled. Light appeared beneath it, and again, *Bong* from the submerged steeple bell, solemn and austere.

Bong. Bong. Bong.

A flare of green and white fire lifted from the water and fizzed upon the surface. A blue one appeared beside it and shot from the river to whistle and gyrate in the darkness and explode with a boom. A host of gold and red sparks whistled and banged within a plume of silver and soon the river blazed with a conflagration of missiles tearing from the water into the air. They thundered overhead and the sky roared with color while the rain fell and fell. Joe Li ran through it, holding the sword, but another wall of vines rose up before him to tangle him in their web.

"Raeven!" he called. She turned to him, tried to reach out to him, but she couldn't lift her hand. He cut through the vines with the sword, his coat became entangled, but he slipped out of it and cut through a new coil of rising vines.

Lochru had no such obstacle. No longer able to form words, he crawled toward her through the rain, hissing like a serpent. Raeven stared at him, indifferent, unable to summon a breath of fear. The venom's ice had paralyzed her limbs and now began a slow, inexorable advance toward her heart.

The shriveled little man reached for her with his claw-like hand and bloody palm.

Raeven, no longer able to sit up, slumped to the side: when she did, the sorcerer's gaze fell unobstructed upon the river and he froze with his pale eye widening at the sight of the water churning and parting to reveal an enormous shape heaving to the surface.

It came in a blaze of light and watery bells and gongs, with rain falling through the sparks with a sputter of tiny crackling explosions. It was light, it was gold; a throbbing force rising; a reptile shimmering and clanging with blazing eyes and golden scales; and up it came in an explosion of light and smoke and color to roar as the thunder rolled and the rain lashed down and snow began to melt along the edges of the churchyard and riverbank.

Raeven could not move at all now. Her eyes were open but glazed over, unblinking. She saw the glory of the golden dragon rise and clang, but she could not move and could not react, even when the sorcerer grabbed a fistful of her hair. He leaned in close, his breath foul and toothless gums bared. "You have *killed* me," he hissed with a steamy spray of blood, and his hands closed around her neck.

Joe Li raced toward them. Vines grabbed at his legs, tangled around his feet, reached for his arms.

Two golden wings spread from the sides of the beast with a thunderclap of sound. A claw shot from the river. It grabbed the sorcerer around the middle and tore him from the Knight to lift him high and squealing, clutched in its glittering talons. The great beast sprang skyward from the water and the wailing scream of the sorcerer trailed away as up it went; and the colored fires whistled and banged and illuminated the ground below, the melting snow, the new buds on the trees, the sudden stir of plants beneath the pine needles; and Raeven stared unseeing into the sky.

Behind her, Joey fought through the briars, desperate to reach her. Rain drove down around him, soaking him to the skin.

Her hand fell. Her head dropped to the side. She closed her eyes. And she saw him.

She saw Joe cutting through the vines with the Sword of the Moon and she saw herself lying on the ground, pale and still, her black dress torn, and half her face tattooed with indigo blue knots and spirals. Up she drifted, separated from herself, rising above Joey. She looked down and saw the burning church, its fires dimming beneath the onslaught of rain. Dr. Sweeney sat on the steps. She saw him, saw his detached, stunned expression, and Sparky lying on the charred ground with Pearl beside him.

Higher she went into blazing fires surrounding her with red, blue and green, and past them to where the clouds parted and swirled and receded into what appeared to be blue sky and daylight. She saw the golden dragon's shadow spread over the scorched land to heal it from darkness and winter, from cold and heat, from snow and fire; and she saw the dragon itself, clutching the limp figure of the sorcerer, spiraling higher toward a bright blue sky with barely seen sparks trailing behind until it disappeared – not in a rush of fire, not with an explosion, but in a grand, hissing tendril of white smoke that faded into the clouds, and the clouds closed around her and held her in their foggy grip and she was lost, cloud-bound, with only the barest glimmer of stars and endless night beyond, and she called out when the clouds closed in to form a continuous wall around her. "Joey?" she called, but heard no answer.

She drifted and stepped on something firm. Looking down, she saw only swirling white. She took a deep breath and pressed her hands against the small of her back but stopped, realizing the numbness and pain had gone from her leg. She reached down, felt through the tear in her dress. No blood, no pain, though she felt a deep furrow in her flesh. She reached up and touched her lip. The stitches had disappeared, the soreness gone – everything had healed, leaving only scars behind.

She looked around in the mist. She sensed something in there with her...a vague shadow in the vapor, though she could not tell who or what it was. "Joe?" A rush of wings answered from behind. She turned and saw a hazy, indistinct figure. "Joey?" The mist spiraled in lazy circles, the figure resolved, and Raeven stepped back with a startled gasp.

A wooden stake had been set down in the fog. A severed head clung to the top, impaled straight through. Not fully human, nor fully reptile, it appeared to be a hybrid of the two, decayed and torn, eyeless and bloody. Even so, she recognized it as the sorcerer Lochru.

Another flap of wings sounded behind her, and then came a voice, low and cracked. "Well done, Knight." Raeven turned and nearly screamed at the sight of a decrepit old crone shuffling through the fog wearing a robe streaked with white and a dazzling white seagull upon her shoulder.

Raeven didn't know what to do, didn't know if she should move, or speak, or even breathe. She took a faltering step forward. "I don't know where I am."

"You are with us," said the crone, and the mists cleared behind to reveal a heavy wooden door, partially open and flanked by torches in iron sconces.

A raspy *caw* rent the air, the mist parted further, and Raeven now saw that she had been standing between two long rows of severed heads, all on posts evenly spaced until they faded into the distant fog. A large white bird perched on each one. Some stared at her with brooding eyes but most ignored her and continued to tear at the bloody flesh. Raeven gazed at the gruesome heads. "Who were they?"

"Enemies," the old woman said. "Fears. Strong and willful once, but conquered nonetheless."

"Mine?"

"Some. Most belonged to them."

"Who?" Raeven asked and, turning back, saw that the woman had changed – no longer old and bent, she now stood youthful and tall before her, a fierce warrior with the same blue tattooed spirals and knots upon the same right arm, leg and right side of her face as Raeven. Upon her shoulder stood a large bird – not a seagull, Raeven now realized, but a pure white raven, staring at her as the raven in the snow had so long ago when it gave her its name. All the white birds feasting upon the severed fears were battle-ravens. The warrior woman turned to the wooden door and held out her hand, beckoning Raeven to enter.

She did and found herself at the end of a long wooden chamber, gloomy and dank, lit by more torches in sconces.

There, facing each other on two long rows of wooden benches, sat fifty or so of the most burly, muscular men Raeven had ever seen, most with long matted hair hanging below their shoulders. They wore armor: some elaborate, some as dented and frail as the armor she once wore, and each sported horrific scars; some on their faces, some on their bare tattooed arms, and some that trailed through their chest hair like paths through a wicked forest.

They stared at her, not warmly, not coldly: they simply stared. Some looked at her leg and at her lip, and though they said nothing, she thought she detected cool approval in their gaze.

A man with sleek black hair and gray eyes and wearing a homespun robe rose to meet her. He smiled as he approached and held out his hand. "I am Brother Brendan." Before she could react, before she could speak, he gestured toward the others. "And these are the dragon slayers."

Armor clanked and squealed as the men stood.

"Gawain," said Brendan, pointing to one of the knights. "And beside him, Lancelot du Lac." Another stepped forward, and another. "Parsifal. Galahad. Perseus." He nodded toward the man closest to Raeven, whose pattern of Celtic tattoos on his arm and one side of his face mirrored her own. "Donal O Ruain of the Glens."

"Donal," Raeven whispered and the knight nodded. He wore a bright red garment, torn and caked with dried blood.

"And him," Brendan said and pointed to the end of the long line of burly knights.

He sat on the wooden bench, dazed and confused.

Raeven stared at him. She stepped toward him. "Sparky..."

Brendan moved up beside her. "The first of the Three to join us," he said, and Raeven took another step toward her friend. "But...no, but Sparky..."

Brendan stopped her, held her by the arm. "A later time," he whispered. "You may not stay."

"But why? Am I not a dragon slayer?"

"You are. One of the greatest of all. But your time has not yet come. It almost did...but not quite yet. You are needed still."

"But Sparky – I can't leave him."

"Your time has not yet come," Brendan repeated. He glanced down the long hall at the dazed policeman. "His has."

"But I can't leave him!"

The warrior-woman approached from behind. "Your time has not yet come, Knight," she said, repeating Brendan's words. "Return. We shall be here. We be shall be waiting for you. Return."

Raeven reached out, tried to touch the warrior-woman's arm, but her fingers closed around a vision and she slipped away. "Sparky!" she cried and the mists began to close.

"I'm fine, Raeven," she heard, and she saw him waving at the far end of the long hall, his hair shining in the torchlight. "Tell Pearl," he called. "Tell her I'm okay."

"Sparky!" she cried, choking on her words.

"I'm okay!"

Mist swirled around him and Raeven slipped down and fell as she would into a deep sleep, but where darkness and unconscious dreaming normally reigned, she emerged into a brightening world of blue sky and parting clouds as down she drifted into a shimmering silver rain.

From above, she saw Burne Notch surrounded by the charred hulk of the wall, now black and smoking. Beyond the wall, in all directions, the earth lay white with winter: barren trees, frozen fields, and white ice; while inside – Spring!

Rain fell from clouds isolated over the town and where the golden dragon's shadow had fallen, there emerged the colors of new leaves and blossoms bulging from branches. Lilacs sprouted over the hillsides. Wisteria vines and honeysuckle coiled through trellises. Iris sprang up in amethyst waves along the river bank where Pearl's escaped birds darted and chattered, and the ski slope glittered with daffodils trailing from the summit like a flow of golden lava.

Clouds swept across the sky, shredding light and shadow, and Raeven drifted down, buoyed upon an unseen wind, down toward a column of smoke rising from the smoldering walls of the church. Before it, she saw her friends: Dr. Sweeney standing, his head bowed, and Pearl lying over Sparky with her head on his chest and her arms embracing him, and the churchyard around them carpeted glossy green with unfurling dragonroot.

Raeven swept by, unable to tell them it was too late, that they couldn't do anything, and that it was all right, that it was okay.

She moved beyond them and hovered above herself and felt herself drawn down to where Joey continued to fight through the briars. His coat was gone. His shirt was torn. The vines intertwined with an explosion of green leaves and glistening blackberries that met her as down she went, streaming toward her own body, motionless, pale, no longer alone.

    Joey tore through the briars. "Raeven!" he cried, and she called to him as she slipped past. She could not make him hear her. She could not reach him. But she knew what she could do: she knew she could reach herself, and she knew she would be there for him by the time he broke through the blackberries, aware, alive and unarmed.

Acknowledgements

For their inspiration and support, I send my thanks to my own flock of Battle-Ravens who have helped in some way with this novel: Vitali Aukhimovich, Jude Bascom, Lilly Cataldi-Simmers, Susan Cohen, Tatsumi Fukunaga, Kristopher Imperati, Dr. John Loomis, Kevin O'Connor, Kerry O'Malley, Diego Miranda, Bobby Peaco, Father Joseph Uhen, the Condylis and Thompson Clan, and, most especially, Anne Ford.

December, 2017
John-Richard Thompson

John-Richard Thompson

John-Richard Thompson
www.j-rt.com

Made in the USA
Middletown, DE
18 December 2017